THE KARAJAN DOSSIER

Herbert von Karajan: the Philharmonic autocrat. Photograph taken on 7 December 1980 on the twenty-fifth anniversary of Karajan's appointment as artistic director of the BPO

The Karajan Dossier

Klaus Lang

TRANSLATED BY
STEWART SPENCER

faber and faber
LONDON · BOSTON

First published in 1992
by Faber and Faber Limited
3 Queen Square London WC1N 3AU

Photoset by Wilmaset Ltd, Wirral
Printed in England by
Clays Ltd, St Ives plc

A CIP record for this book
is available from the British Library

ISBN 0-571-16408-0

2 4 6 8 10 9 7 5 3 1

Contents

Contents

Illustrations

Illustrations

Chronology

1908 5 April: Karajan born in Salzburg, the younger son of Dr Ernst von Karajan and Martha, *née* Kosmac (his brother Wolfgang b. 27 January 1906).

1912 First piano lessons with Franz Ledwinka.

1913 First public appearance as a pianist.

1916 (to 1926) Studies at Salzburg Mozarteum, where his teachers include Bernhard Paumgartner, who advises him to train as a conductor.

1917 27 January: first piano recital at the Mozarteum.

1926 K leaves Salzburg's Humanistisches Gymnasium; writes essay on thermodynamics and internal combustion engines for his school-leaving examination. Studies engineering at the Technische Hochschule in Vienna.
(to 1929) Studies at the Vienna Academy and completes a course in conducting.

1928 17 December: K conducts in public for the first time at a student concert in Vienna.

1929 22 January: conducts first full-length concert with the Mozarteum Orchestra in Salzburg.
(to 1934) Principal conductor in Ulm.

1933 30 January: Hitler seizes power.
8 April: K joins the NSDAP (Nazi party) in Austria.
1 May: K joins the Württemberg NSDAP.

1934 (to 1941) General music director in Aachen.

1937 1 June: début at Vienna State Opera (*Tristan und Isolde*).

1938 8 April: first concert with Berlin Philharmonic Orchestra (BPO) in the Alte Philharmonie.

26 July: K marries Elmy Holgerloef (d. April 1983).
30 September: début at Berlin State Opera (*Fidelio*).
21 October: *Tristan und Isolde* at the Berlin State Opera.

1939 (to 1945) State conductor at the Berlin State Opera and chief conductor of the symphony concerts given by the Staatskapelle.
1941 9/10 April: State Opera destroyed in air raid.

1942 22 October: second marriage, to Anita Gutermann (divorced in 1958).
7 December: State Opera reopened.

1944 29/30 January: Alte Philharmonie razed to the ground.
27 June: first experimental stereo recording by the Reich Radio Company at Broadcasting House: K conducts the Berlin State Opera Orchestra in a performance of Bruckner's Eighth.

1945 3 February: Berlin State Opera destroyed.
8 May: unconditional surrender; K banned from conducting.

1946 Initial concerts with the record producer and founder of the Philharmonia Orchestra, Walter Legge.

1947 K conducts at the International Music Festival in Lucerne.
27 October: ban on K's conducting activities officially lifted.

1948 K works closely with the Philharmonia, the Vienna Symphony Orchestra and the Salzburg Festival; appointed artistic director of the Vienna Gesellschaft der Musikfreunde (appointed for life in 1949); conducts at La Scala, Milan.

1951 (and 1952) K conducts at the Bayreuth Festival.

1952 28 May: first post-war concert in Berlin (with Philharmonia).

1953 8 September: first post-war concert with the BPO in the city's Titania Palace.

1954 30 November: Wilhelm Furtwängler dies.
13 December: BPO votes unanimously to appoint K as Furtwängler's successor.

1955 27 February–1 April: first concert tour of America and Canada with BPO under K's direction.

5 April: appointed chief conductor of the BPO, with contract for life valid from 26 April 1956.

1956 1 September: artistic director of the Vienna State Opera.

1957 (to 1960) overall artistic director of the Salzburg Festival.
November: BPO's first tour of Japan under K.

1958 Third marriage, to Eliette Mouret (daughter Isabel b. 25 June 1960; second daughter Arabel b. 2 January 1964).

1959 1 October: Wolfgang Stresemann appointed intendant of BPO.

1960 26 July: inauguration of Grosses Festspielhaus in Salzburg; K resigns Salzburg directorship.
19 September: foundation stone of Berlin Philharmonie laid.

1961 13 August: Berlin Wall built.

1963 15 October: inauguration of Berlin Philharmonie.

1964 31 August: K resigns as artistic director of Vienna State Opera; becomes member of Salzburg Festival board of directors.

1967 19 March: K launches first Salzburg Easter Festival.
21 November: début at Metropolitan Opera, New York.

1968 5 April: K made freeman of Salzburg on sixtieth birthday.
25 September: K announces establishment of Herbert von Karajan Foundation in Salzburg and Berlin.

1969 (and 1970) artistic adviser of Orchestre de Paris.
Foundation opens Research Institute for Experimental Music Psychology at the Psychological Institute of Salzburg University.
September: first international conducting competition organized by the Herbert von Karajan Foundation in Berlin.

1970 September: first international meeting of youth orchestras run by the Herbert von Karajan Foundation in Berlin.

1972 Orchestral Academy of BPO (run by the Herbert von Karajan Foundation in Berlin).

1973 K founds Salzburg Whitsun Festival.
24 November: K made freeman of Berlin.

1975 22 December: first operation on intervertebral discs.

1977 8 May: K returns to Vienna State Opera.

1978 31 August–1 September: Wolfgang Stresemann steps down as intendant of the BPO and is succeeded by Peter Girth.
21 September: K suffers stroke and falls from platform.
25 September: fifth and last meeting of youth orchestras run by the Herbert von Karajan Foundation.

1979 27 January: concert to mark fiftieth anniversary of K's conducting début.
29 October–1 November: BPO's first concerts in China, conducted by K.

1980 7 December: K celebrates twenty-five years as conductor of BPO.

1981 14 August: Karl Böhm dies in Salzburg.

1982 30 April–1 May: K conducts two concerts to mark the BPO's hundredth anniversary.
16 November: BPO refuses to give its consent to a one-year probationary contract for the clarinettist Sabine Meyer and to extend Peter Girth's contract as intendant.
3 December: K cancels all tours and audiovisual productions with the orchestra.

1983 16 January: Girth signs a one-year probationary contract with Sabine Meyer against the orchestra's wishes.
17 January: BPO demands Girth's immediate removal from office.
7 June: K's second operation on his vertebral column.
1 September: the violinist Madeleine Carruzzo becomes the BPO's first woman member; Sabine Meyer begins her probationary year.

1984 2 May: foundation stone of Philharmonie's Chamber-Music Room laid in K's absence.
12 May: Sabine Meyer resigns from the BPO.
11 June: K invites the Vienna Philharmonic Orchestra to replace the BPO at his Whitsun concert in Salzburg.
13 June: BPO revokes its recording contract with K.
20 June: Peter Girth is relieved of his duties; the former intendant Wolfgang Stresemann takes over as temporary intendant.
20 July: Stresemann celebrates his eightieth birthday.

25 July: BPO's concerts in Salzburg and Lucerne are called off by the Berlin Senate.
29 September: K conducts Bach's B minor Mass in the Philharmonie with the BPO: the two sides are reconciled.
12 December: K celebrates thirty years working with the BPO.

1985 15 May: death of Herbert Ahlendorf, co-ordinator of the Karajan competitions in Berlin.
26 September: eighth and last conducting competition.

1986 22 February: Hans Georg Schäfer appointed intendant of BPO; Wolfgang Stresemann's definitive departure.

1987 1 January: K conducts the Vienna New Year concert.
1 May: K conducts BPO to open celebrations marking 750 years of Berlin's existence as a city.
28 October: Chamber-Music Room inaugurated; K conducts the BPO with Anne-Sophie Mutter as soloist in Vivaldi's *Four Seasons*.
4 November: death of brother Wolfgang von Karajan.

1988 28 March: *Der Spiegel* cover story: 'The Financial Wizard: Herbert von Karajan at 80'.
5 April: K celebrates his eightieth birthday.
19 April: K cancels his appearance at a concert due to be held on 24 April to celebrate Berlin's status as Cultural Capital of Europe.
22 April: Berlin Senate cancels the BPO's autumn tour of America with K.
1 September: K steps down as member of the board of directors of the Salzburg Festival.
31 December: K's last concert with the BPO in Berlin (Prokofiev's First Symphony and Tchaikovsky's B flat minor Piano Concerto with Evgeni Kissin as soloist).

1989 27 March: K's last concert with the BPO in Salzburg (Verdi Requiem).
23 April: K's last concert with the VPO in Vienna (Bruckner's Seventh).
24 April: K resigns as artistic director of BPO.
16 July: K dies of heart failure at Anif at the age of eighty-one.
8 October: the BPO elects Claudio Abbado as K's successor.

Foreword

'A man like that can't be pumped completely dry, he needs to be kept topped up.' I remember Herbert von Karajan telling me this in the course of a conversation on 17 February 1977. He was talking about the abilities of a young conductor. It always needed weeks of inner preparation, he went on, to master any new score. There was nothing worse than dashing from one place to the next. 'Do very little,' he advised the conductors who won his competitions.

It is the sort of advice which could be given only by someone who, over the years, had himself done far too much, a workaholic who, wherever he went, attempted to stage the musical counterpart of the gladiatorial games of ancient Rome: Herbert von Karajan, a charioteer in charge of high-performance players, a conductor to whom the notion of circus races can effortlessly be applied – 8.5 kilometres round the course, seven circuits completed in the fastest possible time, his quadriga filled initially with slaves, later with freemen and, finally, with emperors.

Karajan – the 'inimitable emperor', as his first violinist, Michel Schwalbé, affectionately called him; Karajan – the conductor of superlatives, the head of the Vienna and Berlin Philharmonic Orchestras, a man with a keen artistic sensitivity and an instinctive feel for the worldwide draw of the technological media; Karajan – the founder of international festivals, of competitions for youth orchestras and conductors, the pedagogue *par excellence*, about whom so many books have already been published that the reader is bound to ask: why write yet another book for – or against – him? But then again, why not? Why should someone not do so who, like myself, has for the last twenty years kept a close eye on the Berlin Philharmonic, its home – the Philharmonie – and its former conductor, Herbert von Karajan? Should I allow the huge pile of newspaper cuttings, the reviews and reminiscences, to say nothing of the conversations with Karajan and his intendants, with guest conductors, soloists and members of the orchestra simply to go to waste?

What has emerged is certainly no paean in praise of the maestro. What interested me, from my critical observation post, was not only the time

Karajan spent in Berlin but also his years in Vienna, his youth in Salzburg, his brother Wolfgang, and his illnesses. How did the orchestra judge its conductor? How could the mutual admiration of the early Karajan years take the turn that it did and come to an almost tragic conclusion? Karajan was not the only charioteer in Berlin: so, too, was Wolfgang Stresemann, his intendant of many years' standing. Stresemann was a diplomat, a man of considerable stature who, as far as I am aware, has not received the sort of attention which is his rightful due. It was Stresemann's perspicacity and behind-the-scenes activity which allowed the players to work together with their chief conductor for almost thirty-five years, a period in musical history which will always be worth recalling.

Such were the manifest failings in Herbert von Karajan's character that I could never have offered him here the victor's garland. Rather, it was my concern to shed some light on the orchestra's fascinating inner life and conflicts and to do so from the varying standpoints of the members of the orchestra, their intendants and guest conductors. If I have succeeded in this aim, it is thanks to all those who have not been averse to replying to my questions.

Klaus Lang
Berlin, May 1990

I

'How quickly life goes on'

From Karajan to Abbado

The scene is the Philharmonie in Berlin, the date 16 December 1989 at 8 o'clock in the evening. Extra lighting has been brought in for the television cameras to record a very special event. The audience sits in anticipation, awaiting the arrival of the fifty-six-year-old Italian maestro Claudio Abbado, who is about to conduct his very first concert as chief conductor-elect of the Berlin Philharmonic Orchestra, and as Karajan's successor. Just as they did for Karajan, the members of the orchestra have fielded their most impressive players: on the front desks to the left are the two leaders, Leon Spierer and Daniel Stabrawa; in the middle the solo cellists Ottomar Borwitzky and Georg Faust; while the group of solo strings is rounded off to the right by the two solo violas, Neithard Resa and Wolfram Christ. This élite band of leaders is here to celebrate Abbado's appointment and is joined by Rainer Zepperitz (double bass), Andreas Blau (flute), Hansjörg Schellenberger (oboe) and Gerd Seifert (horn). The programme is made up of Schubert, Wolfgang Rihm and Mahler. A hush descends on the hall. Abbado's entrance is greeted by loud applause all round, a clear demonstration of the delight felt not only by the orchestra, which, in a free and secret ballot on 8 October, had appointed him their new chief conductor, but also by the audience.

The Schubert is symbolic. At the memorial concert for their late chief conductor, the orchestra, led by the first violin, had played the second movement of the 'Unfinished' on a platform bordered by white begonias. It was a moving occasion, though one which encouraged certain listeners to ask the age-old question: why have a conductor at all? But the players know the answer better than anyone else: with Karajan, as with other conductors before and since, they have learned the art of listening to each other. In such situations – which few other orchestras in the world are better able to overcome – they have sharpened their music sensors to a pitch of extreme perfection, turning themselves into independent interpreters, conductor and player in one and the selfsame person.

In Abbado, however, they now acknowledge their newly appointed chief conductor, gladly leaving him, of course, the task of interpreting the 'Unfinished' for them. The supporting railing round the conductor's podium is noticeably missing, for a young conductor like Abbado is not afraid of falling. Wilhelm Furtwängler was thirty-seven when he took over the Philharmonic, while Karajan was forty-seven. Abbado will be fifty-seven. On each occasion, ten years were added – a symbol of security and reliability, but also a waning readiness to take any risks?

Abbado marks the initial downbeat and the strings blossom into life. Here is a man who, unconcerned with outward show, radiates youth, flexibility, sympathy and humanity – a conductor who, unlike Karajan, you sense you could reach out and touch. And, unlike Sergiu Celibidache or Georg Solti, he does not force his players into the straitjacket of an over-rigid interpretation. He gives them the freedom they need to breathe and play, a freedom to which they had grown accustomed under Karajan; they are famous, after all, for their very real autonomy and refusal to be spoonfed. Abbado's humanity gives him the licence to err: the timpani invariably come in too soon and a certain emptiness makes itself felt in the second movement. But then there are glorious transitions for clarinet and oboe; the Philharmonic sound grows denser and develops an inner tension.

For at least the first half-hour it is Karajan's spirit that hovers over the scene: as yet, there is nothing specifically new. Abbado, too, likes a 'beautiful sound', the hallmark of his predecessor. The Andante con moto sounds almost too perfect. There is loud applause, though – in keeping with the closing bars – it could not be described as euphoric. No doubt that will change at the end of the Mahler symphony. At least Abbado's appointment has ensured the most seamless succession.

It was an appointment which had surprised not only the music-loving public but also a number of members of the Berlin Philharmonic itself. A press conference naturally followed and so it was that we journalists found ourselves in the foyer of the Philharmonie's chamber-music room on 7 December 1989, to be met by the somewhat surprising sight of no fewer than ten television cameras to welcome a single musician, together with a table almost collapsing beneath the weight of the microphones. Thanks to Abbado's linguistic skills there was information in German, English and French, but of substance there was little sign: illuminating insights into the intellectual background of Karajan's successor would have to wait for another occasion.

It is worth recalling that invitations to attend the conference had been made in the name of the Berlin Philharmonic Orchestra and its interim intendant, Ulrich Eckhardt. The previous incumbent, Hans Georg Schäfer, had taken up office on 1 March 1986 and had initially been not unpopular. The son of the famous producer, Walter Erich Schäfer, he had studied with the conductor Hans Swarowsky, which, as far as his new employers were concerned, was the best possible *carte de visite*. Conducting engagements in Ulm and Heidelberg, together with a ten-year appointment at the theatre in Bremen, had proved him to be a solid practitioner. He had also been active (albeit of necessity) as concert manager for the Jahrhunderthalle in Höchst and for the Ansbach Bach Festival, so that he was cordially welcomed to Berlin as the ideal successor to Wolfgang Stresemann. But from that moment onwards the organization of Philharmonic concerts broke down almost completely. An additional difficulty was the opening of the Philharmonie's new chamber-music room in 1987, which required further detailed planning. Disagreements with the chief conductor and various other hitches began to occur with increasing frequency, quickly turning the helpless Schäfer into a liability.

When Karajan stepped down as artistic director of the BPO in April 1989, the difficulty of finding a successor was made even worse by Schäfer's lack of resourcefulness. Schäfer himself did the decent thing and opened the way to future decisions by announcing, two days before Abbado's election, that he would leave his post prematurely on 31 October 1989. The orchestra and the Berlin Senate suddenly remembered Ulrich Eckhardt, whose name had already been mentioned as Schäfer's potential successor, and who for many years had been successfully running the Berlin Festival. Eckhardt was duly appointed as the BPO's new intendant and, at the press conference on 7 December (to which we must now return), was hailed by Abbado as the intendant of his dreams.

What did the newly ensconced chief conductor have to say to the microphones and cameras? He had, he insisted, always had great respect for Karajan, but now there was much more modern music than there had been before. The number of concerts given in any one season needed rethinking, in order to allow more time for rehearsals. Final rehearsals could certainly be open to the public. When asked if he might consider moving to Berlin, his reply was: 'I have my inner dwelling-place.' Of course, the maestro wanted to retain his post as music director in Vienna, though with a reduction in the number of his performances. He was not thinking of appearing at the Deutsche Oper in Berlin ('No, thank you!'), where the principal conductor at that time was Giuseppe Sinopoli. (There was a moment when it looked as though all of West Berlin's key musical posts would fall into Italian hands, with Abbado at the Philharmonie, Sinopoli at the Deutsche Oper and Riccardo Chailly with the city's Radio Symphony Orchestra. In the event, Chailly had the foresight to move to Amsterdam to take over the Royal Concertgebouw Orchestra, while Sinopoli succumbed to the lure of the Dresden Staatskapelle.)

In the presence of the assembled press, Abbado was unstinting in his praise, which helped to loosen the tongues of those responsible for the event. The Philharmonie's two concert halls were the best new concert venues in the world, he insisted. He had never had any problems with the Philharmonic and was delighted to be able to conduct the two greatest orchestras in the world. In answer to the insistent question about how things stood with his contract, he replied that a contract was not so important: after all, he had worked with the Vienna Philharmonic for twenty-five years without such a piece of paper.

Two sensitive points concerned the past and his predecessor's innovations. No, he himself was not interested in a competition for conductors, Abbado maintained. It was impossible to say after only twenty minutes whether or not a young musician was capable of conducting: 'I'll certainly never sit on a jury.' Finally Abbado spoke enthusiastically about his own youth orchestras, for he was once the guiding spirit behind the European Community Youth Orchestra (ECYO) and the Gustav Mahler Youth Orchestra in Austria and Eastern Europe, while his current position as chief conductor of the European Chamber Orchestra (COE) entitled him to call its members his 'children'.

He was, he went on, in favour of small instrumental groupings and could well imagine a chamber orchestra made up from the ranks of the BPO. Since this very subject had caused an unforgettable row during the Karajan era, those members of the orchestra who were present craned their necks and noted a look of deep embarrassment on the face of the double-bass player, Rainer Zepperitz.

To Abbado's right sat Ulrich Eckhardt, while the seat to his left was taken by Dr Anke Martiny, a relative newcomer to the post of Minister of Education and the Arts in Berlin's coalition Senate. With her usual refreshing insouciance, she used this occasion to deride the Schauspielhaus in East Berlin and, far from praising its facilities, found fault with its acoustics as a concert hall. Everyone knew that the Philharmonie in West Berlin would have to be closed for the whole of 1991 while its roof was repaired and all traces of blue asbestos removed. From that point of view the breach in the Berlin Wall had come like a gift from the gods, for only in this way was it possible to ask the eastern half of the city to provide accommodation for the Philharmonic's urgently needed subscription concerts. A supplicant in senatorial robes ought to show a little more diplomacy instead of seeking to humiliate the opposition.

2

'That's wonderful'

From Furtwängler to Karajan

Abbado had first appeared with the BPO in 1966 but since that date had rarely conducted them. Indeed, his only regular appearances had been at the previous Berliner Festwochen. It was as an outsider, therefore, that he won the race to be Karajan's successor: 'For two minutes I couldn't breathe when the committee asked me,' Abbado remarked. Had the same been true of Herbert von Karajan?

Karajan's first invitation to conduct the BPO had been extended by its then intendant, Hans von Benda, in 1938, and the programme, performed in the Alte Philharmonie in Bernburger Strasse on 8 April 1938, had comprised Mozart's Symphony No. 33 in B flat major, Ravel's Suite No. 2 from *Daphnis et Chloé* and Brahms's Symphony No. 4 in E minor.

Further concerts followed. On 27 September 1938 he conducted a 'Master Concert' for *Kraft durch Freude* (Strength through Joy) and the Berlin Concert Society, when the programme consisted of Sibelius's Symphony No. 6 in D minor, Haydn's Cello Concerto in D major, with Arthur Troester as soloist, and Beethoven's Symphony No. 5 in C minor. On 14 April 1939 a special concert featured Haydn's Symphony No. 103 in E flat major ('Drumroll'), Debussy's *La mer* and Tchaikovsky's Symphony No. 6 in B minor ('Pathétique'). A charity concert was given on 27 December 1942, a works concert at Borsigwalde on the 28th and, on the 29th, a concert of works by Johann Strauss with Irma Beilke as soprano soloist. And that was it. Between 1938 and 1942 Herbert von Karajan conducted the BPO in no more than half a dozen concerts, involving only four different programmes. The reasons, of course, were not hard to find, for they lay in Karajan's poor relationship with the then chief conductor of the orchestra, Wilhelm Furtwängler, who would cheerfully have banned his rival from setting foot inside the Philharmonie. (Karajan, it will be recalled, was at this time conducting symphony concerts with the Berlin Staatskapelle.)

Even after the end of the war, the younger conductor – already hailed as the 'Karajan wonder' and clearly anxious to climb the musical ladder – was still denied access to the orchestra. The Alte Philharmonie had been razed to the ground in a bombing raid on the night of 29/30 January 1944, so that the handful of concerts conducted by Karajan during these years were given in the Titania Palace and the newly built concert hall at the city's College of Music. Their programmes were as follows:

8 September 1953, Festwochen concert in the Titania Palace

Concerto for Orchestra	Bartók
Symphony No. 3 in E flat major op. 55 ('Eroica')	Beethoven

23 September 1954, Festwochen concert in the Titania Palace

Symphony No. 39 in E flat major K543	Mozart
Piano Concerto No. 3 (soloist Géza Anda)	Bartók
Symphony No. 1 in C minor op. 68	Brahms

21 and 22 November 1954, concert hall at the College of Music

Fantasia on a Theme by Thomas Tallis	Vaughan Williams
Symphony No. 9 in D minor	Bruckner

Between the end of the war and Furtwängler's death on 30 November 1954 Karajan conducted the BPO in a total of only four concerts involving three different programmes. In other words, he conducted only ten concerts during the whole of the sixteen years from 1938 to 1954 and these ten concerts involved a mere seven different programmes with twenty-six different works. It could scarcely be described as a particularly close relationship – more as a nodding acquaintance.

If I have itemized Karajan's early concerts in Berlin in such great detail, it is because I should like to take a brief look at the press reports of the time in order to show the sort of reaction that he encountered. His name, after all, was already well known. But was he, from the outset, the 'messiah' for whom the musical world was waiting?

Writing in the *Tagesspiegel* of 10 September 1953, Werner Oehlmann opined that

Every encounter with Herbert von Karajan has a new, incalculable charm about it ... Beethoven's 'Eroica' is a known quantity, a work in which every note is imbued and weighed down by a century's inspiration and awe. It was interpreted with a naturalness and simplicity that were innocent of portentousness and significance, devoid of titanic pride and hero-worship, offering only a symphonic experience in abstract form: the noblest, richest and most artistic of musical forms, the marriage of sensual beauty and sense of structure on the level of pure, dispassionate playing ... In much the same way, Bartók's Concerto for Orchestra, which introduced the evening, acquired a new aspect under Karajan ... It was particularly clear from a piece as yet untouched by tradition's iron grip in what his manner of making music consists – the combination of a highly lucid, all-controlling consciousness and a magical spontaneity from which the musical image emerges with all the clarity of a mysterious dream. The orchestra took to this unusual style of making music with an admirable understanding, though the same could not be said of the audience, whose applause was somewhat reserved.

A year later, the Berlin *Telegraf* headed its review of Karajan's Festwochen concert: 'Great Evening under Karajan'.

The concert in the Titania Palace was notable for the lively and lasting impression it made. Karajan's interpretation was at all times gripping and utterly convincing, a quality which is due to the fact that he grasped the essential nature of each of the works he conducted by working from the centre outwards, from the point of intersection of consciously planned formal structure and irrational receptivity . . . The orchestra played with complete commitment, carrying out their conductor's wishes in the most subtle manner. The audience expressed its appreciation with lengthy ovations.

When Karajan raised his baton two months later, on 21 November, to conduct Vaughan Williams's Fantasia on a Theme by Thomas Tallis in the concert hall of the city's College of Music, Wilhelm Furtwängler already lay gravely ill in a private clinic in Ebersteinburg near Baden-Baden. He had only a few days left to live. Meanwhile, the Romanian conductor Sergiu Celibidache continued to see himself as Furtwängler's legitimate successor. During the difficult post-war years he had helped the Berlin Philharmonic to regain its former high artistic standards and, as Furtwängler's locum and friend, had contributed more than anyone else to the city's musical life. Since the end of the war he had given no fewer than 414 concerts with the orchestra, as against Furtwängler's 222 and Karajan's four. But the crown was not destined to pass to Celibidache, who had long since fallen out with the players. A high-performance machine, along American lines, was what he had in mind, hence his threats to dismiss those older members of the orchestra who were no longer as efficient as they had been in the past. Karajan, by contrast, showed no signs of wear and tear, at least in the players' eyes. Thanks to the international interest aroused by his work in Vienna and London, Milan, Lucerne and Bayreuth, his star was currently in the ascendant, eclipsing that of all his rivals. The Berlin press was committed, therefore, to Karajan, and one of its leading spokesmen, Hans Heinz Stuckenschmidt, offered his own contribution in the *Neue Zeitung* of 24 November 1954.

Only a highly refined sense of sound can divine the ultimate secrets of the Tallis Fantasia's impressionistically ecstatic score. It is precisely this, however, which is Herbert von Karajan's forte. His whole interpretation of music takes tonal quality as its starting-point, setting out from the perfection of a sound picture for which he has special sensibilities.

Of Bruckner's Ninth, Stuckenschmidt had this to say:

Nowadays Karajan has what might be termed great breath control. He knows how to pace a work, how to locate its moments of tension and release so that the need for large-scale forms becomes clear and so the Adagio's Alpine massifs can be taken in with a single sweeping glance ... The house was sold out, the reception ecstatic.

Six days later, Furtwängler was dead.

On 25 and 26 November Celibidache had conducted Brahms's *German Requiem*, scoring a major success with both critics and public alike. But behind the scenes there were violent disagreements between orchestra and conductor, as Celibidache – the meticulousness of whose rehearsals bordered on the fanatical – accused the players of incompetence and total lack of discipline. The orchestra finally saw the danger that was threatening.

Wilhelm Furtwängler lay close to death. On 27 November he lost consciousness and on the 28th and 29th Celibidache gave his last concerts with the Berlin Philharmonic, bidding his final and – to this day – definitive farewell with Bartók's Concerto for Orchestra. The then Minister of Education and the Arts, Joachim Tiburtius, presented him with the German equivalent of the OBE, after which he settled back to wait for the call to come.

But these final moments proved to be painful for Celibidache. Karajan, meanwhile, was receiving the reward for his long and patient wait in the form of a telegram with an anonymous message: 'Le roi est mort, vive le roi.' Barely two weeks had passed since Furtwängler's death and the Berlin Philharmonic had already drawn up a resolution dated 13 December 1954 in which it was stated:

The full members of the orchestra believe ... that in Herbert von Karajan they see the artistic personality capable of carrying on ... the tradition. They therefore ask their intendant, Dr von Westerman, to begin negotiations with the aim of inviting Herbert von Karajan to conduct the major Philharmonic concerts and tours for a period of time as yet to be specified. This resolution was taken unanimously.

Karajan now held all the aces but the security that he so dearly coveted was still as far away as ever. He began by accepting the Senate's invitation to conduct the American concert tour which, planned for many months, should have been led by Furtwängler. An enormous programme had to be mastered within a matter of weeks, and Karajan wanted to be sure that the fruits of such a committed gesture should not be reaped by anyone else. Since his declared aim – a contract for life – was something that could not be rushed, he sought to gain the attention of the whole international scene in order to have as many witnesses as possible for a game of question and answer that was clearly put up from the outset.

In playing this trick, Karajan found an ally in the economist Joachim Tiburtius. An opportunity presented itself on the eve of the orchestra's departure for America. It was 22 February 1955 and Karajan had just conducted the BPO at a concert held at the College of Music, the programme of which had comprised Haydn's Symphony No. 104, Wagner's Prelude to *Tristan und Isolde* and Beethoven's Fifth. In later years we grew used to the sight of Karajan throwing a coat round his shoulders and fleeing the building as soon as the last note was sounded. On this occasion, however, the maestro stayed and, delivering himself of a pragmatic speech, nailed his colours firmly to the mast.

TIBURTIUS: This tour has the backing of the Federal Chancellor, who has personally emphasized once again how keen he is that it should go ahead and how much he is looking forward to it. Thanks to its great willingness to help and its immense and active understanding, the High Commission has done much to facilitate this tour for us. Everything has been done to ensure that this positive co-operation is felt over there as well. And on Wednesday evening the best wishes and thoughts of all Berliners will be with you, my dear Herr von Karajan, and with the members of the Philharmonic, as your plane lifts off for America. It falls to me now to direct your thoughts to the future, and, as I see you sitting here all agog, ladies and gentlemen, pencils at the ready, all eyes and ears, I who have a certain training in reading people's minds have little difficulty in telling the question that is on your lips. It is, as you know, the Senate in Berlin and the committee of the House of Representatives which have to decide such matters: so that I can propose the name that I have it in my heart to propose – in short, so that my wishes and thoughts have the necessary backing – I would like to ask you, dear Herr von Karajan, whether you would be prepared to be Wilhelm Furtwängler's successor at the head of this Philharmonic Orchestra, and under what conditions and in what form can you give us your opinion on the matter?

KARAJAN: Senator, it would give me infinite pleasure. What more can I say?

TIBURTIUS: That's wonderful.

KARAJAN: If you'd heard the solidarity with which we made music today! For two weeks we've been making music for six or seven hours a day in a spirit of indescribable harmony, and I can say to you in all honesty that I am not in the least bit tired by it all. I left the rehearsals fresher than when I went in. You know, when you've felt something like that, there's nothing more to think about.

TIBURTIUS: Then let's not do so, but let us, rather, make it as easy as we can for the Senate and the House of Representatives and thank you from the bottom of our hearts. But perhaps you would like Herr von Karajan to say a few more words, from an artistic point of view, about his plans for this tour? It may be that not all of you are familiar with them.

KARAJAN: The tour itself involves twenty-six concerts. I took over the programme quite consciously – with only very few changes – just as Dr Furtwängler had arranged it. Primarily, of course, it consists of the basic works of the Classical and Romantic repertory, Beethoven's Fifth and Seventh Symphonies, Brahms's First and Second, then a Tchaikovsky symphony, a few works by Wagner – the *Tristan* Prelude, which you heard today, the Prelude to *Meistersinger* and the *Tannhaüser* Overture – then a Haydn symphony and the 'Haffner' Symphony. One of the very minor changes I made was to include Handel's Concerto Grosso No. 12, rather than No. 6. Contemporary music is represented by Herr Blacher's *Concertante Musik* [applause], American music by Samuel Barber's Adagio for Strings. An American pianist, Jorge Bolet, will play Beethoven's G major Concerto in Chicago, and in Syracuse we'll have a female soloist in Gustav Mahler's *Lieder eines fahrenden Gesellen.* That, in very general terms, is the programme. The orchestra, as you know, will be taking 104 players on the tour. We've got replacements for all the individual sections, including the strings, at least to the extent that they've not already been doubled, so that, in case of illness, we'll still be able to field a full orchestra.

It's usual to talk of the 'Philharmonic spirit'. Indeed, it has almost become something of a catch-phrase. But it really is true: you can tell from every note the orchestra plays that it is conscious of the responsibility and obligation which it has taken upon itself. But what I also like about them is that you can make music for half an hour in the most concentrated manner and then fool around for the next three minutes. They have a wonderful sense of humour, which relaxes the atmosphere marvellously. Someone makes a joke and, within three minutes, we're all feeling fresh again, and the rehearsal continues.

It's a value judgement, of course, but I firmly believe that this orchestra plays first and foremost from the heart, there's nothing ice-cold or crystalline about them – it all comes from feeling. It's this that makes it so good, because you feel an immediate sense of contact when you stand there in front of them and feel that contact being taken up. Basically, many of them had already been associated with me since, as you know, I conducted the Philharmonic before, and many of them have come over from the Staatskapelle. I've also been associated with many of them in Bayreuth. So it's already really a family, a family that has grown up over many years. It's always good to come back here and to know that, right from the outset, I'll find exactly what I was wanting to hear. At some point – when I have more time – I'll explain all this in a book which I'm planning to write about the conductors who were my great heroes. And there will have to be a very special chapter on Dr Furtwängler because, I believe, none of the existing biographies has really said the essential thing about him and explained in what way he was so unique, and how he created a completely new expressive language in music, a language that was not imposed on the orchestra by the conductor but created in collaboration with them. Sometimes he even left this decision to them – as all of you here will know – these transitions, when the old is played out and the new has not yet begun, these almost magical transitions, where the listener did not know whether that point had yet been reached or not. The result was a language of music and expression on the part of the orchestra, of a kind that had not existed before him.

Things have often, falsely, been said about us which, I think, are simply not true. I see now, when I stand in front of the orchestra, that I really speak the same language, or at least that I was brought up to speak the same language. I may add that I spent fourteen years following every one of Furtwängler's concerts, both in the provinces, when I would travel from Aachen to Cologne for the Philharmonic's concerts there, and in Vienna and at the Salzburg Festival. They were bound to leave a mark. You take away whatever impressions you can. And when you come back and see the sort of response you get from a body of musicians which is second to none in its ability to express its personality and its way of thinking in music, well, it's a wonderful feeling – which is really why it would give me such great pleasure to accept this appointment, because I know how precious this special kind of tradition is. It's a tradition which exists in virtually no other orchestra and which needs to be carefully tended, because only in this way will we have the essential, expressive language needed to interpret the great works of the Classical and Romantic repertory. That is one of my main reasons for accepting, and I believe it is something I should like to pass on, above all, to a younger generation.

May I say in this context that it was very much the impression left by Dr Furtwängler's death which persuaded me to agree to give a course in conducting in Lucerne which will be run under completely different conditions from those that have obtained until now. I myself studied in Vienna for two years and during that time conducted for perhaps fifteen or twenty minutes. On this course, because I myself shall be available for six or seven hours every day, all the participants will have a certain amount of time with the orchestra. In other words, each of them in turn will rehearse for about twenty minutes, so that it will be possible to observe their progress on a daily basis. I am expecting – and I know from the names of those already enrolled on the course – that a number of professional conductors will be taking part. An orchestra will be formed from composite elements; it doesn't need to be particularly good. What I should like to teach these young conductors is this: how to realize certain things in a score – I'm almost inclined to say, an assorted complex of sounds – which can't be interpreted in terms of musical language and which don't even have to be discussed, but without which the piece cannot begin to sound inherently right. I mean the length of a note and the rhythm. Everything else – forgive me for saying so – is probably unteachable. It would be wrong to impose one's own interpretation on someone else. The conductor should be capable only of making his hand do what he feels, it is that which the orchestra then has to play. To show people how to do that is the challenge I've set myself. I should add that the course is divided up in such a way that, at the end of each day's rehearsal – and we'll be starting very early – everyone taking part will have the opportunity to spend an hour or an hour and a half attending a rehearsal taken by one of the Festival conductors. They'll then have a standard of comparison and can see how others do it. I am very optimistic, and if there is anyone here who would like to take part, it would give me infinite pleasure to talk about it . . .

TIBURTIUS: I hope the course will not only be held in Lucerne . . .

KARAJAN: I was just about to say that, whenever I am here, there is nothing I would rather do than organize classes. After all, the orchestra would be there and I could always see the sort of progress that people were making. I made a start last year in Japan and it gave me an immense feeling of satisfaction. I received two letters from people who had difficulties with their right arm. One of them was slow to bring down his arm, and I was able to rid him of his inhibition. I saw then that I'd not yet grown too remote from these problems. By the time you're sixty-five, you've probably already forgotten what it used to be like, so you can no longer remember anything about it. Today I can still remember that I struggled for ten years to find a conducting technique. And it is here, I believe, that you can help someone, if you really want to.

3

'You'll become a conductor'

Bernhard Paumgartner on Karajan

I have consciously refrained from saying anything about Karajan's youth, not least because this is Bernhard Paumgartner's province. Paumgartner was a man who saw a great deal in his long life and held a number of positions of influence. Born in Vienna, he was twenty years older than Karajan and had studied conducting under Bruno Walter. In 1920 he helped found the Salzburg Festival and in 1960 became its president. He was always one of the leading figures in Salzburg's musical life, conducting both the Mozarteum Orchestra and the Camerata Academica; and although, as an orchestral trainer, he never achieved the qualities of his successor Sándor Végh, he was altogether unique in his ability to discover unperformed and unknown works by Mozart. With the exception of the war years, he was director of the Salzburg Mozarteum from 1917 to 1959 and, as a result, his path was bound to cross that of the town's most gifted son (apart, that is, from Mozart). He had the following to say about his erstwhile pupil and later colleague on the occasion of the latter's sixtieth birthday:

On some of the smaller committees of the Salzburg Festival board of directors I was immediately struck by a man who, well versed and deeply interested in music, was also to be found, much to my astonishment, among the players in the Mozarteum Orchestra, where he played the clarinet with considerable expertise. This elegant and educated man was the chief doctor and leading surgeon at St John's Hospital, Dr Ernst von Karajan. Our Mozarteum Orchestra at that time was certainly not the professional orchestra that it is today, but was made up of teachers at the Mozarteum Conservatory, members of the tiny theatre orchestra – which at that time had twenty-seven players in it, I believe – and a number of quite distinguished amateurs, including Dr von Karajan himself.

The Karajan family is believed to have come to Vienna from Macedonia as early as the sixteenth or seventeenth century and by the first half of the nineteenth century was already playing a leading role in Austrian intellectual life. Karajan, as you know, is a name made up of a Turkish element, 'kara', and a Christian, Greek element, 'jan', Johannes. Theodor von Karajan was an outstanding linguistic historian who was ennobled for his services to the subject. A friend of Grillparzer's, he worked under the Austrian dramatist in the Ministry of Finance and in 1841 was appointed to the Vienna Court Library. By 1850 he was Ordinary Professor of German Language and Literature at Vienna University and in 1866 was elected

President of the Academy of Science. He wrote a whole series of authoritative scholarly works, chief among which were numerous new editions of Middle High German poems. He had a link with Salzburg in the form of an exemplary edition of the Friendship Book of the St Peterstift, a famous literary work dating from the Carolingian Age. A more recent member of the family, Emanuel von Karajan, was rather closer to the world of the performing arts. An engineer and former member of the Austrian Navy, he later became technical director at the Vienna Court Opera and ultimately director of the Vienna Hofburg. Throughout their history the Karajans seem to have been lively people, open-minded, gifted and versatile, to say nothing of their fondness for the fine arts.

Dr Ernst von Karajan, too, was in charge of a well-respected musical household in Salzburg, where, much more versatile in my musical activities than I am now, I always found a friendly welcome. At musical soirées within the Karajan circle, many worthy chamber works were played, including pieces that were little known. The good doctor himself would always play the clarinet, whenever possible. I myself was a former pupil of the famous Viennese horn player, Karl Stiegler, but I could also play the viola well enough for my own purposes and was a keen pianist, so that I could always switch from one to the other and help them out in a variety of different ways.

The most attentive listeners on these occasions were, without doubt, the two sons Wolfgang and Herbert, both of them good at school and, in spite of their youth, no less good and well respected at our musical school. Most of all they enjoyed their piano lessons with that excellent teacher, Professor Franz Ledwinka. But, as I recall, they also studied the violin in addition to the requisite theory.

It was not only my artistic association with their parents but, more especially, the boys' multiple gifts, their lively open-mindedness and love of sport which particularly held my attention at a time when I was still very young myself. In neither of them was there a trace of that dreamy far-away look that is often found in young and highly musical people. Although music was an important element in their active, carefree lives, there were also countless other things – science, technology and sport – which kept their interests engaged. They were entirely typical of their time – two exceptionally bright young people from a good Austrian family background. It is scarcely surprising, therefore, that we had other points in common apart from music, most notably motor sport, which, during those early years, was only slowly gaining in popularity. I had a whole series of excellent motor bikes, ending up with a powerful Norton 600, on which I used to race round Salzburg and the surrounding area, without a silencer, of course. I also took part in a number of primitive competitions of a kind that only slowly became fashionable after the First World War.

The two Karajan boys were my faithful companions on these various trips and expeditions, and I am just as proud of the musical knowledge, the insights and experience that I was able to offer them as I am of the fact that I taught them how to drive. Herbert's musical talent very soon became clear, whereas Wolfgang, the elder of the two, turned more and more to technical matters, without, of course, giving up music altogether.

Herbert was nine when he first appeared in public on the platform of our concert hall at the Mozarteum, and he was still only eleven when he played the D major Rondo at a Mozart celebration, holding his listeners spellbound with his playing. But his performances of Liszt, Brahms – whom he particularly loved – and a number of modern composers all revealed astonishing sensitivity.

I must, however, confess to feeling proud that it was I who, in spite of all these successes, recognized where his real talent lay. I remember saying to him, quite emphatically, on the occasion of one of his piano recitals: 'My dear Herbert, you'll never be a pianist, you'll become a conductor instead.'

4
'Brown clouds'
The unpolitical opportunist

Even before the two Super Six Clippers of Pan American Airways had taken off from Berlin's Tempelhof airport, the orchestra was already prepared for a discordant note on the other side of the great divide. A press agency report from New York had announced:

Members of the New York Musicians' Union affiliated to the American Federation of Trade Unions have agreed to send a petition to the union leadership, asking them to put a stop to the advertised concerts of the Berlin Philharmonic Orchestra in Carnegie Hall. It is said in the protest that the conductor of the orchestra, Herbert von Karajan, and his intendant, Gerhart von Westerman, are politically compromised by their support of the National Socialist regime. The union further objects to the fact that the Berlin orchestra is receiving financial support from the government of the United States.

An item in the *Depesche* of 22 February 1955 was able to offer some reassurance:

When questioned on the subject, the American concert agency which signed the deal with the Berlin Philharmonic for its American tour announced that, in spite of the protest by 750 American musicians in the USA, there are no grounds for fearing any serious disruptions to the tour.

Of course, Karajan himself can scarcely have felt reassured at being reproached for his Nazi past at this of all times. Was he in fact a Nazi?

Technically speaking, he certainly was, since the twenty-five-year-old conductor had twice used the National Socialists' seizure of power to work his way up to high office. On 8 April 1933 he joined the Salzburg branch of the National Socialist Workers' Party, and on 1 May 1933 he registered with the Ulm branch in Württemberg. For a man with talent and the right party membership number, there were no longer any obstacles in the way of his appointment as general music director in Aachen. 'He didn't like Hitler,' his brother Wolfgang once said, 'no doubt because two dictators never get on with one another.' But Hitler, in turn, had no great love for the single-minded conductor and ensured that, if Karajan pursued his career in the Third Reich, it was along strictly limited lines.

*

Karajan's name was already well known in Berlin long before 1938, since the municipal concerts that he gave in Aachen had the whole of Europe talking. Works performed with the Aachen Choir included Haydn's *The Seasons* and Bach's B minor Mass and *St Matthew Passion* – the latter was even announced as being given 'with authentic forces (chamber orchestra and chamber choir)'. Famous soloists such as Lubka Kolessa, Elly Ney, Enrico Mainardi, Wilhelm Kempff and Antonio Janigro descended on the town, and the maestro himself could be admired performing chamber music at the piano.

Sentimentality and devotion were always two of Karajan's more endearing characteristics. And so it was only natural that, in 1975, he should return to the scene of his early exploits and deliver himself of the following words of encouragement:

It gives me very great pleasure to have this opportunity to congratulate the Aachen Stadttheater on its 150th anniversary. During the seven years that I worked there the house gave me so much that it will always remain in my thoughts. I came here, as a young conductor, from Ulm, where there were relatively limited opportunities. Here, for the first time, I found a body of players of the kind I'd been hoping to find. There was also the famous Aachen Choral Society, with which we enjoyed a number of great successes over the years, not only in Germany but in other countries too.

My work in the choral field was a source of particular satisfaction, because it was a type of work that involved no intermediaries, and the warmth that develops between a choir and its conductor is one of the most wonderful things that a conductor can ever experience.

I learned a great deal at the Aachen Stadttheater, above all how an organizational enterprise has to be run. This is something that was of particular help to me in the long years that followed, when I was artistic director at the Vienna State Opera, when I planned the Easter Festival, and then the Whitsun Festival, in Salzburg, and during the twenty-eight years that I have been on the committee of the summer Festival. This was something I picked up and learned from my earliest youth.

My debt of gratitude to this town is especially great, and I wish you every success for an equally splendid future. From a personal point of view, I would like to express the hope that one day you may finally have a proper concert hall. I promise the town that I would be ready to take part in the opening ceremony together with the Berlin Philharmonic. I wish you many long years of wonderful artistic work.

Karajan's appointment in Aachen lasted from 1934 until 1941. It was in March 1941 that the following revealing report appeared in the then *Zeitschrift für Musik*:

Among recent events, the highlight was undoubtedly the first performance of Carl Orff's choral masterpiece, *Carmina burana*. Splendidly prepared by the chorus master, Wilhelm Pitz, it received three performances under Herbert von Karajan's rousing direction, each of which met with an increasingly enthusiastic response. The composer, who was present, placed the achievements of the Aachen choir above those of any other that he had heard – which says enough. In Irma Beilke we heard a coloratura soprano of bell-like purity, in Josef Daus a tenor astonishingly equal to his task and in Karl Schmitt-Walter a vocally beautiful and versatile bass. In short, everything had been done to ensure that the *Carmina burana*, with all its attendant risks, was a brilliant success. Let us hope that this success will finally persuade Herr von Karajan to give us more contemporary works: Aachen's concert-going public is literally thirsting for them. Bach's B minor Mass also received another fine performance; with their three performances of the work in Paris, the Aachen forces won special acclaim from both the German *Wehrmacht* and also from the Parisians themselves.

In other words, Karajan won special acclaim in occupied France. In contrast to Furtwängler, he personally insisted that his concerts be prefaced by a performance of the *Horst Wessel Lied*, but he was certainly never seriously interested in politics. No written remarks of his have ever been found either in support of the Nazis or against the Jews. Could he, as a thirty-year-old conductor, know how long the Thousand-Year Reich would last? There is little doubt that all he ever thought about was how to advance his own career: even at that date he was being described in Berlin – with visionary insight – as having 'all the gifts of a true-born conqueror'.

While the triumphant success of his first concert with the BPO at the Alte Philharmonie in 1938 was still ringing in his ears, Karajan was already being courted by the State Opera in Berlin: its general intendant Heinz Tietjen and his superior, Hermann Goering, had been wondering how to fill an appreciable gap at their venerable institution, a vacancy that had arisen as long ago as 1934, following the almighty row that had broken out when Wilhelm Furtwängler threw his whole weight behind the music of Hindemith and thus fell into disfavour with the Nazi government. Furtwängler resigned all his appointments, including those as director of the Berlin State Opera, chief conductor of the Berlin Philharmonic and Vice-President of the Reichsmusikkammer.

It was decided to put the younger conductor – he was twenty-two years Furtwängler's junior – through his operatic paces. Even by the end of his performance of *Fidelio* on 30 September 1938 it was clear from the tumultuous applause that Karajan was something special, while his performance of *Tristan* three weeks later ensured that the 'Karajan wonder' was born, at least as far as the press was concerned.

On Tietjen, too, these appearances left a lasting impression. On 21 May 1963, at a ceremony held to mark the sesquicentennial of Wagner's birth the following day, he had the following to say:

Now comes the real sensation. After Clemens Krauss had suddenly been recalled to Munich and another of our conductors, Leo Blech, had left the company, I summoned Karajan from Aachen. I intended him to be Leo Blech's successor, since Blech had left an enormous gap at the State Opera. Blech was our great Wagner conductor; his *Ring* was fantastic.

Well, one can say a great deal or nothing at all about Karajan: with people who are vastly talented, it is usually better to say nothing at all. Initially, this young man was something of a tearaway, towards the orchestra too. But things calmed down and – I have to say – he was an exceptional person. Richard Strauss was sitting with me in my box and suddenly nudged me. They were giving *Elektra*, with Karajan conducting: 'Look, look, the rascal!' At first I had no idea what he meant. Well, the rascal was conducting by heart. OK, that's easy enough to say. But anyone who knows the score of *Elektra* – I couldn't do it myself, I can tell you that now, even though I've also conducted in my time. To conduct *Elektra* by heart is sheer impertinence as much as anything else. It's a work that's so insanely difficult that it is the easiest thing in the world to go wrong, which would be a catastrophe for the orchestra. They'd never get back into it again. And the boy – that's what I called him then, today I call him 'Herr Karajan' – also conducted *Die Meistersinger* by heart, at least until I told him not to, because the score, ultimately, is a form of visual help. It takes some of the burden away from your brain, and it's important not to have constantly to rummage around in your memory but to be able to concentrate entirely on the work.

But I gave Karajan something and it bore fruit for us here in Berlin, as well as being important for his subsequent development, as he himself would have to admit. I was able to give him the State Opera's subscription concerts. Another reason why I mention him especially is because he was the only person who – more's the pity indeed – came close to embodying the sort of person that Richard Wagner was; I'm talking now about his works. It is something that passed to his son and from his son to me, in other words, when I acted as both conductor and producer of the Bayreuth canon. Such a conductor-cum-producer should be able to do both and should have a profound knowledge of both, though he would not need to do them both at once. Siegfried Wagner and I always staged the works first, so that the works could at least stand on their own two feet. We'd then conduct the revivals.

Another contemporary witness whom I found was the composer, arranger, conductor and legendary colleague, Werner Eisbrenner. Although he devoted his life to light music, he always wanted to be acknowledged as a passionate supporter and connoisseur of classical music. In June 1981 he was admitted to the Westend Clinic in Berlin suffering from a potentially fatal illness. I hesitated for a long time before finally taking my tape recorder along with me to what was to prove to be one of our last encounters. Born, like Karajan, in 1908, Eisbrenner spoke ardently and passionately about pre-war Berlin and Furtwängler's polar opposite:

I believe Karajan conducted *Tod und Verklärung* at the State Opera, and I can remember exactly – I had a regular seat in one of the boxes on the right. The actor Gustav Knuth was sitting on about the same level. When Karajan took a certain passage in a particular way – no one had ever taken it like this before [*singing aloud*] – he paused briefly at the climax. My eyes moved to the left, and Gustav Knuth's eyes moved to the right to look at mine. We were simply speechless. That was Karajan. There was something completely different about him – an uncanny youthful energy which he radiated.

If I describe these two men as polar opposites – or whatever term you like to use – what I mean is that, with Furtwängler, it was a question of the whole. I do not believe he would ever, consciously, have produced an effect like that; with Furtwängler it was the incredibly glorious, self-evident transitions which he always managed to bring off, the tempi which were self-evidently right, the illumination of the individual instruments. And the same was true whether they were works by classical or modern composers. As you know, he also did the odd modern work. In fact he almost came a cropper with a piece by Theodor Berger, which resulted in a wonderful chorus of booing at the Philharmonie. I was among those who were there [*laughing*].

Of course, Karajan numbered himself among those who regularly observed Furtwängler's activities and the latter insisted, in turn, on comparing his rival's appearances at the State Opera with the enthusiastic reports in the press. In drawing this comparison, Furtwängler came to totally different, negative, conclusions: almost certainly it was the incompatibility between the two men, on a personal and artistic level, rather than pure envy at the other's success, which gave rise to his lifelong antipathy.

Furtwängler found Karajan's vanity highly amusing: after all, it spoke volumes about his insecurity. And how, indeed, could Karajan feel secure, when his path to the Philharmonie and the Berlin Philharmonic was constantly being barred? Astonishingly enough, it was the Reich's Minister of Propaganda, Josef Goebbels, who repeatedly separated the two fighting cocks, describing as nonsense the popular arguments that raged in Berlin over their respective merits and observing: 'The variety of artistic phenomena should be seen as a source of pride.'

The war, meanwhile, pursued its disastrous course, abandoning art to fend for itself. The bombing raids which wrecked human lives, destroying churches and homes, also left the city's concert halls and opera houses in ruins. Among the very few buildings left untouched by the Allied forces was the radio station in Masurenallee, an act of early precision bombing designed to give them a voice as soon as the country capitulated.

In 1944, shortly before the end of the war, Karajan and the State Opera orchestra spent a day in the main recording studio at what is now the Sender Freies Berlin, recording Bruckner's Eighth for the Reich's Broadcasting Company. Thanks to Helmut Krüger, then rehearsal engineer with the company, this historic document turned into something of a sensation. Unknown to Karajan Krüger rigged up stereo microphones in addition to the usual monophonic equipment and recorded the work on what was then a new invention, the stereophonic tape recorder. The result was a recording of Karajan which is not only of astonishing artistic quality but a splendid example of the technological progress of the time.

After the war, Karajan's prominent role in the Thousand-Year Reich and his party membership card meant that he was compromised. Like Furtwängler, who, at the very last moment, was able to flee to Switzerland, Karajan had to wait a long time before being denazified and receiving permission to conduct again. But although he was banned from giving public concerts with the Vienna Philharmonic in the country of his birth, his contacts with the record producer Walter Legge proved to be highly lucrative. With Legge he made a number of recordings, including some with the Vienna Singverein, which in 1949 elected him its artistic director for life.

The ban was lifted on 26 October 1947, five months after Furtwängler, and Karajan – the unpolitical opportunist – returned to the concert platform. By 1948 he was conducting at La Scala, Milan, and working at both the Salzburg and Lucerne Festivals and with the Vienna Symphony Orchestra. Berlin, too, received a visit from Karajan and the London Philharmonia, a group of players that he succeeded in turning into a recording vehicle for high-quality export goods. In 1951 he was invited by Wieland Wagner to reopen the Bayreuth Festival, but in spite of his grandiose musical triumphs with *Die Meistersinger* and the *Ring*, differences of opinion over the staging led to a breach with Wagner's grandson within the space of a year.

In Berlin, Furtwängler resumed responsibility for the BPO in 1952 but could counter the lowering approach of the Karajan era with little more than sceptical toleration. When Furtwängler died on 30 November 1954, Karajan knew that his hour had come, the hour for which he had waited all his conducting life. He alone was in a position to take over the Philharmonic and lead them in triumph to America. But his Nazi past caught up with him – and not for the last time either. In New York there was a demonstration by Jewish immigrants outside Carnegie Hall, while, to the musicians' dismay, doves were released inside the hall. 'We go to America to bring music and beauty. We want only good and not hatred,' the maestro declared:

> I automatically became a member of the NSDAP when I took over the Aachen town orchestra in 1934, which was a state appointment. I have never been interested in politics – not in the slightest – and nothing apart from my music has any significance, nothing, that is, except for science, art and sport.

This was Karajan's defence at a press conference held in New York on 3 March 1955. He could not have known that not until after his death would the matter at last be laid to rest. According to a German Press Agency report dated 4 August 1989:

> During recent months the American Department of Justice has been investigating the Nazi record of the Austrian conductor Herbert von Karajan, who died in July. Joe Krovisky, one of the spokesmen at the Department in Washington, confirmed that the investigations of the Office of Special Inquiries had been suspended following the conductor's death. According to information given by Krovisky, enquiries had been initiated at the beginning of the year when accusations had been levelled at Karajan concerning his conduct during the 1930s and his contacts with leading National Socialist figures. The spokesman refused to say who the authors of the accusations were or to divulge details about the state of the investigations at the time of their suspension.

But certain American circles, to say nothing of the Israelis, could never find forgiveness in their hearts, not even after Karajan's death. It had always been the Berlin Philharmonic's declared intention to pay a visit to Israel after the war. Right up to the last, however, the Israelis refused the musicians permission to enter the country, precisely because of their chief conductor. A year after Karajan announced his decision to stand down in April 1989, the orchestra gave a series of concerts in Israel with Daniel Barenboim and Zubin Mehta, a visit already planned during Karajan's lifetime.

5
'More or less for life'
The controversial contract

In later years Karajan would conspicuously absent himself from Berlin at Easter, but for his forty-seventh birthday he had every reason to remain in the city. Following the Philharmonic's concert on 5 April 1955, the Minister of Education and the Arts, Joachim Tiburtius, stepped on to the platform and, speaking in the name of the Berlin Senate and of the enthusiastic audience, thanked the conductor for all he had done in recent weeks for the city's reputation. And with that he handed the maestro not only a replica of Berlin's Liberty Bell but, more importantly, the long-coveted contract.

The public could breathe again. They assumed, of course, that both parties to the contract had also appended their signatures. But as long as disagreements raged on either side, all talk of the contract being signed was over-optimistic. The Senate had the Furtwängler model in mind, albeit with certain modifications, since it was hoped to have the new chief conductor on hand for as many concerts as possible. But Karajan was still relatively young, and to bind him to the Berlin Philharmonic for life might later give rise to unforeseeable problems. Because of his interest in composition, Furtwängler had taken years to agree to resume control of the orchestra from 1952. A long-term contract, however, had struck him as altogether 'nonsensical'. Not so with Karajan, who, like his predecessor, wanted to conduct as few concerts as possible in Berlin but who, as a precondition, insisted that no time limit should be attached to the contract. The Senate received a warning shot in the form of a press agency report dated 22 March 1956, announcing that Karajan had assumed overall direction of the Salzburg Festival for a three-year period starting in 1957. And this on top of already extensive commitments as conductor and producer at La Scala. But what really set the alarm bells ringing was the news that talks had been taking place to discuss his future work with the Vienna State Opera, where the post of artistic director was vacant, following Böhm's resignation.

The sense of indignation in Berlin was growing by the day and the question now being asked was whether a fresh attempt should be made to find a successor to Furtwängler. Karajan did what he could to defuse the situation, assuring all who would listen that he fully intended to honour his commitments in the city. The affair pursued its complicated course: on 24 April 1956 the contract was signed by Tiburtius; Karajan added his signature on the 25th, and, on the 26th, the Minister of Finance, Senator Haas, added his.

All that the general public was told was that, during the 1956/7 season, Karajan would conduct six programmes in Berlin, each concert being repeated twice, in addition to which there would be two performances of Beethoven's Ninth Symphony to celebrate the seventy-fifth anniversary of the founding of the BPO. There would also be a second American tour involving thirty-two concerts, together with tours of West Germany, Italy, Switzerland and Austria.

At the press conference called to unveil these plans on 26 April, Tiburtius spoke of a contract 'more or less for life', to which Karajan added: 'With my signature I am demonstrating that, as far as I am concerned, it is my honest intention to continue the work until I can no longer do so, or until my death.' In announcing this, he was also declaring his independence of every future government, while ignoring the views of the players themselves. One could, of course, set out from the premiss that the Berlin players had not yet reached the level of emancipation they enjoy today and that, with joy in their hearts, they would all have agreed to a 'contract for life' – as Karajan always described it himself in later conversations. But none of them knew at the time what Karajan was planning for the years when he came of pensionable age. Not until 5 June 1984 would they read in the *Berliner Zeitung*:

> From his sixty-fifth birthday he has the right to retire at any time and at his own request. Such a request has to be submitted to the Senate in writing before the end of the season in question. Thereafter it is open to him to accept another post.

Only at a much later date, when the question of a 'contract for life' took on a broader aspect and became a source of lasting conflict, were questions asked with increasing insistence as to what the contract that Karajan signed with the Senate in 1956 had actually looked like. Since the terms of this secret document have never been fully divulged to the public, all we can do is attempt to piece the mosaic together from more or less unguarded remarks by ministers, intendants and musicians.

Let us begin with a fragment of information which, deriving from Tiburtius, was combined with a priceless caricature in the *Berliner Zeitung* of 13 June 1956, in which Karajan was depicted standing on one leg and simultaneously conducting the Berlin Philharmonic, the Vienna State Opera and the Salzburg Festival with both arms and his one remaining leg. Tiburtius said that the contract ('more or less for life') could be rescinded by the Senate if Karajan failed to show the Berlin Symphony the degree of commitment they expected of him or if he conducted fewer concerts than planned. It seems as though the Senate wilfully concealed this clause during the later years of crisis in order not to have to accuse the maestro of breach of contract. This interpretation receives support from the events of 1 May 1986, when Karajan spoke of an 'outright breach of contract', since the BPO was planning a concert without him in London's Royal Albert Hall. The intendant, Wolfgang Stresemann, rejected the charge out of hand. The two media representatives, he claimed, had wanted to hold a private concert with Barenboim, but the scheme had got stuck at the planning stage. He, Stresemann, had insisted all along that, if the concert went ahead, it must of course be offered to the orchestra's permanent chief conductor, but in the event that had proved unnecessary: 'As far as any breach of contract is concerned,' Stresemann continued,

> the contract which you signed with Berlin provides for six double concerts with you as conductor; the concerts at the end of the year are expressly mentioned here. I fully understand the reasons for the changes which you yourself have made to your commitments. But people who live in glass houses shouldn't throw stones.

This last remark was clearly aimed at Karajan, who was planning to spend New Year's Eve 1986 not in Berlin but in Vienna, conducting the New Year's Day concert there.

'Money does not interest me,' Karajan once remarked – but the words have a somewhat hollow ring on the lips of a man who left his wife and two daughters 500 million marks, not to mention forty-five unpublished video films and the undiminished royalties on several million records. On 25 November 1979 *Welt am Sonntag* published a comparison of the incomes of prominent Berliners. Karajan's budget for 1980 provided for fees and salary to the tune of 360,000 marks. A special contract additionally gave him an annual income of 25,000 marks. The only point of any real interest in this context is that, right up to the end, the 'artistic supremo', as *Welt am Sonntag* described him, continued to receive 10,000 marks for each of the concerts he gave in Berlin. For years this remained the upper limit for every conductor appearing with the BPO. Only at a much later date was this benchmark ignored, for otherwise the orchestra would have had to forgo the services of conductors like Abbado, Mehta, Ozawa and Giulini. From that moment onwards the fees for an evening's concert soon began to double, while Karajan – for tactical reasons – stuck with his 10,000 marks. His 'business trips' with the Philharmonic, especially those to the Salzburg Easter and Whitsun Festivals (for which the Berlin Senate continued to pay, with 'non-contracts' handed down from one intendant to the next), created so many advantages elsewhere that all he needed to do was to wait for the money to come rolling in. After all, the BPO later became a sort of private orchestra which, never short of food itself, did not allow its chief conductor to starve.

In an article in the Berlin *Morgenpost* on 22 July 1989, Volker Hassemer, Berlin's Minister of Education and the Arts from 1983 to 1989, announced, to the surprise of all concerned, that Karajan had felt 'betrayed' by Berlin from the outset: because he felt he had no contract, he had never tried to negotiate an increase in his fees in Berlin. According to Hassemer, Karajan had set out in 1955 from the belief that he should have been offered identical rights to those accorded to Furtwängler.

A clause in Furtwängler's contract had stipulated, in fact, that a new intendant could be appointed or dismissed only with his 'agreement'. With Karajan, the wording of this clause was slightly altered, and the word 'agreement' was replaced by 'consultation'. What this meant when translated into layman's language was that, in Furtwängler's time, Gerhart von Westerman could take up his appointment as intendant only if Furtwängler gave his consent. In Karajan's case, by contrast, it would have been enough for the Senate merely to inform him of any decision already taken. Moreover, the BPO's rules stated clearly: 'The intendant will be appointed and dismissed by the Senate after consultation with the orchestra.' Hence Karajan's feeling of 'impotence'. In practice, when things were going well, this meant that all the parties concerned – Senate, orchestra and chief conductor – would work together to find an ideal intendant. But life was not like that. After all, both Peter Girth and Hans Georg Schäfer appeared to be ideal for the post of intendant, and both their appointments were made with the full agreement of all concerned. Their departures, by contrast, were very differently managed.

Schäfer, as we have seen, finally left of his own accord. By contrast, Peter Girth was made to feel the full force of the clause which spoke of 'consultation'. Karajan refused point-blank to do without his services during the crisis-ridden year of 1984. It was all the more fortunate, then, that the Senate reserved the exclusive right to take decisions concerning his dismissal. Girth could be sent on compulsory leave and the orchestra's sense of self-confidence restored at a time of particular difficulty.

The regulations governing the way the BPO was run, dated 2 December 1952 and signed by Joachim Tiburtius, contain an important clause:

> In keeping with its politico-cultural role and longstanding tradition, the Berlin Philharmonic Orchestra has a substantial part to play in its own artistic organization. In particular, it is responsible for building up and developing the orchestra.

The meaning is unambiguous: the orchestra itself decides its own future make-up. As will be demonstrated in the case of the clarinettist Sabine Meyer, Karajan courted disaster each time he tried to introduce a candidate of his own choosing.

Against this background it is scarcely surprising that, after Karajan's death, the players themselves chose their own chief conductor for the first time in over one hundred years. The decision was reached after several hours of consultation, uninfluenced by the Minister of Education and the Arts, in the Siemens Villa at Lankwitz. A secret ballot was held and the result, as we know, was Abbado's appointment in the second round of voting.

6

'Eight wild years'

Director of the Vienna Opera

According to the *Tagesspiegel* of 24 March 1954, the latest news from Vienna was that

> Herbert von Karajan is said to have expressed his willingness to commit himself to the Vienna Opera for seven months of every year. Since he has also undertaken the artistic direction of the Salzburg Festival for the period 1957 to 1959, he will be at the disposal of Austria's musical life for a total of nine months every year.

Three months later the *Berliner Morgenpost* confirmed the report:

> Herbert von Karajan is taking over as artistic director of the Vienna State Opera . . . We in Berlin hear this news with feelings of some alarm. It was only a few months ago that the conductor signed a contract as director for life of the Berlin Philharmonic . . . It is because the post of director at the Vienna State Opera is a full-time appointment that the Viennese allowed Karl Böhm to go. Can they really have granted Karajan the very thing they denied to Böhm?

And a day later, on 15 June:

> Herbert von Karajan telephoned the intendant of the Berlin Philharmonic Orchestra, Dr von Westerman, last Thursday to assure him that his 'lifelong commitment to the Berlin Philharmonic would be fully honoured'.

For Karajan, his post in Berlin was initially only a sideshow, a sort of life-insurance policy offering highly favourable terms, providing, as it did, the greatest benefits in return for a relatively modest outlay and making sure that here, at least, his major conducting rivals were kept well out of the way – for life. The number of concerts he gave in the city was stipulated in the terms of his contract, while foreign tours beckoned invitingly – not only in Europe but, between 1955 and 1965, to America (four times) and Japan (twice). Willy Brandt – elected to office on 3 October 1957 – was a popular choice as the city's mayor, and was, in addition, on friendly terms with Karajan. A further calming influence, at least after 1959, was the orchestra's new intendant, Wolfgang Stresemann. Not only was he musically educated, he was also supremely diplomatic and loyal in his allegiances. Only once were he and his chief conductor on opposite sides of the barricades, when battle lines were drawn up in 1982, at the time of the orchestra's hundredth anniversary. Time and again he described the Berlin Philharmonic, the Philharmonie and Herbert von Karajan as an indivisible trinity, and he did more than anyone else to increase their reputation at home and abroad. From 1959 to 1986 he played a leading role in the annals of the BPO, earning a special place of honour, as the following narrative will show. It is he, as much as Karajan, who functions as the protagonist of the concluding drama.

If Berlin was described as a 'sideshow', it is only because the focus of interest shifts to Vienna from 1 September 1956 to 31 August 1964, eight wild years in Karajan's career. His contract with the Vienna Opera required him to spend several months of every year there, conducting some forty to forty-five performances scattered throughout the season. There were also plans to exchange productions with La Scala, Milan, and to appoint Egon Seefehlner to act as deputy director or 'general secretary'.

Karajan made his Vienna Opera début conducting his own production of *Die Walküre*. It proved a highly auspicious start to his new appointment. Writing in *Die Welt*, Heinz Joachim spoke of an 'instantly striking concordance of music, word and gesture, a correspondence that was also symbolic and deeply meaningful'. He admired the singers, the homogeneity of the performance and the 'instrumental splendour of the glorious Vienna Philharmonic'.

As head of the Vienna Opera, Karajan was of course required to put in an appearance at its principal gala events. It was always a source of bewilderment that Karajan never ceased to attract the attention of journalists and paparazzi, who were drawn like moths to a lamp, and yet there was no one who felt such hatred of gala occasions, balls and official receptions, with all the social pressures that they involved. Everyone, of course, desired his presence. But here he was only one among many, and lonely into the bargain – a frequent problem with domineering types. His sense of security came from his power. He needed only to enter the orchestra pit or hurry on to the concert platform and a palpable electric charge would run through the house as it fell beneath his charisma's all-constraining force. In February 1958, during his second year of office in Vienna, out-of-town commitments obliged him to miss the traditional Opera Ball, an absence that the Viennese took very badly. There were complaints at visits by La Scala, when Italian works were performed for weeks on end with all-star native casts, forcing local singers like Irmgard Seefried, Christel Goltz, Paul Schöffler and Anton Dermota to pursue their careers elsewhere.

In October 1958 the critic Manfred Vogel attacked the *stagione* system and demanded a return to the traditional Vienna opera ensemble, describing Karajan, in the *Kölner Rundschau*, as 'Rex Liquidator'. Elsewhere Vogel accused the director's personal assistant, André von Mattoni, of acting as manager, recommending the singers on his own books and pocketing a percentage of their fees. Karajan could take no more. He instituted civil proceedings in the district court in West Berlin, and Vogel was forced to make an official retraction. Since Karajan's former assistant had been placed – not altogether unexpectedly – in a somewhat unfortunate light, the conductor reacted by making Mattoni his private consultant and thus an *ex officio* member of the board of directors of the Vienna Opera.

Attention at this point turns to Karajan's home town where, in 1957, he had finally been appointed artistic director of the Salzburg Festival. And here the chronicler has to report a second lapse of etiquette which, following hard on the heels of the Vienna Opera Ball Affair, could not even be ascribed on this occasion to some other commitment elsewhere. The attack of neuralgia the conductor suffered in the summer of 1959, during the first night of his own production of *Tristan* in Vienna, required a rest-cure in Italy. He could, of course, have ended the treatment two days early but clearly he had no desire to attend the official opening of that summer's Salzburg Festival and offer himself for official duties. He simply failed to attend the meeting, omitting to send his apologies, and the seat beside the Austrian President, Adolf Schärf, remained unfilled. It was seen as a massive affront to the country's elected head of state and to Austria as a whole. But the country quickly forgave the conductor when, two weeks later, a photograph of him appeared in the national press showing him wearing a sportsman's cap and standing beside his latest acquisition, a 'Spyder with a Carrera GT engine', which he collected in person from Porsche's racing division.

Karajan was also the driving force behind Salzburg's Grosses Festspielhaus. Officially opened on 26 July 1960, it cost 230 million Austrian schillings to build (over £3 million at 1960s' prices). Yet it was not the number of seats that made it so exceptional but the huge dimensions of the stage, with its playing area of 1600 square metres and a maximum stage width of 30 metres (compare the Vienna Opera's 14 metres and Covent Garden's 13.5 metres). These dimensions fully accorded with Karajan's *mondo* concept. The artistic superlatives conjured by the conductor had to find their counterpart in wood and steel and concrete.

For the theatre's official inauguration Karajan had failed to find a producer in Salzburg willing to run the risk of directing a Mozart opera on the enormous stage – a factor which, in itself, was regarded as sacrilegious in the town where Mozart had spent so much of his life. The choice fell, therefore, on *Der Rosenkavalier*, in a staging by Rudolf Hartmann, designed by Clemens Holzmeister (who had also designed the building). But even here the hard-pressed taxpayer found himself disappointed: although the gala première should have been shown on television, Karajan turned a deaf ear to requests from the state and from Austrian Radio to allow the first night to be broadcast. As always, artistic reasons were said to be responsible – and, if one accepts the maestro's perfectionist streak, the excuse was perfectly valid. Television was as yet an untried medium where live broadcasts were concerned, and viewers would have had to make do, in any case, with black-and-white pictures. Karajan opted for quality and, once again, beat everyone else to the post. He obtained the relevant rights from Strauss's heirs in Garmisch and signed a series of contracts with the English producer Paul Czinner, who duly captured Hartmann's staging on film. Austrian viewers gazed disconsolately at their blank television screens, journalists gnashed their teeth, and questions were tabled in parliament. Karajan now spoke out in public, saying how much he felt he was misunderstood: 'I am saddened and hurt.' Of course, he could well afford to admit to such feelings, since the Salzburg committee of management had twelve months earlier refused permission for the production of *Der Rosenkavalier* to be broadcast live, a decision taken 'for artistic reasons'. More general needs were nipped in the bud in the form of an unsatisfactory compromise:

> It was agreed at a meeting to broadcast a programme about the Festspielhaus, its facilities and the rehearsals that have been held there, together with a live transmission from inside the theatre itself before [!] the start of the première, and that this programme will be followed by television recordings [!] of important scenes from the production.

Critics of the stage's size kept up their pitiful bleatings, and since he was still unable to prove its suitability for staging Mozart's works as well, Karajan used the official opening to announce his resignation as Salzburg's artistic director. He would, however, continue to be available as producer and conductor. Bernhard Paumgartner, the Festival president and Karajan's friend and foster-father, had a difficult time convincing the press that there had 'never been any differences between them'.

Among the conductor's basic characteristics was the fact that, whatever he did, he was always convinced that what he was doing was right. He himself, for example, never doubted for a moment that the size of the Grosses Festspielhaus pointed the way ahead. Nor did he suffer any self-doubts when, only a few months after his resignation in Salzburg, he hurried back to Berlin to lay the foundation stone for the Neue Philharmonie, an architecturally far more hazardous venture. Less than twelve months later, on 13 August 1961, the whole of the area round the Kemperplatz was turned into a building site, albeit without the maestro's doing, as the German Democratic Republic walled itself in and reduced the Philharmonie – intended as a focal point for East and West – to a role on the city's periphery. Within the political sphere, all eyes were turned on Berlin, but Vienna, too, was not without its tensions at this time.

The Concert Pitch War had recently broken out at the opera. Orchestras, it need hardly be said, tune their instruments prior to a concert or operatic overture. Not so the singers, who have to follow the woodwind and strings and for whom the distinction between a high C and a high C sharp is a matter of some importance. The Vienna Philharmonic were insisting on their chamber pitch of $a' = 448$ Hz, while the singers demanded a return to $a' = 440$. Karajan found himself caught in the crossfire. A memorandum then arrived, adding to his worries, as members of the State Opera ballet demanded longer working hours: at one time there had never been fewer than thirty-six ballet performances every season, whereas now there were only twenty.

But this was only a preliminary skirmish. The technical personnel were wanting a change in their working conditions, including a five-day week and more money. At that time a stagehand in Vienna was earning £30 a month. The lighting technicians found an effective solution by turning the lights off during a ballet rehearsal. The result was that Karajan – whose sympathies were all on the side of the stagehands – had to postpone the first night. By November 1961 the situation had reached the point where he had to inform the press that, because of the dispute with the stage crew, all new productions during the current season were having to be cancelled. He demanded that the body in charge of all the country's theatres provide an annual guarantee of 360 to 400 hours' paid overtime for each of the Opera's employees, in order that the company could continue to maintain its present artistic standards. Otherwise he would resign.

And, true to his word, he announced his resignation (the first of many such announcements in Vienna), when the theatres' governing body succeeded in playing a trick on him by signing a compromise deal with the stagehands to which he would never have given his name. 'The unique lustre that Karajan brought to the Vienna State Opera during the last five years has faded,' *Der Tag* announced on 8 February 1962.

Hardly a day went by without a report in the papers describing the mood in the opera house: artists and stage crew gathered on stage to arrange a sit-in supporting Karajan. Heinrich Drimmel, the Minister of Education and the Arts, could not, he said, accept that the opera-house staff should be better paid than their colleagues at Vienna's other state-run theatres. The Opera, he insisted, should put its house in order, since the post of general secretary had not been filled by Karajan following Egon Seefehlner's departure in May 1961. Finally – and this was surely the prosecution's principal argument – the State Opera could not be turned into some 'cog in a worldwide combine' if, as was claimed, the conductor was thinking of linking together some four or five of the leading houses in Europe and America and of 'liberating' Vienna.

Karajan's vision of the future was certainly on the grandest scale, as he himself admitted only a short time later, when explaining his ideas in public: 'The singers for five or six operas would have to remain in one opera house for a period of six weeks and would not be allowed to accept engagements elsewhere. They could then be exchanged for others.' In other words, he was trying to guarantee the very highest standards by attempting a form of *stagione* ensemble that had never been tried before.

Whenever Karajan caused a scandal in Berlin, the Viennese would celebrate – and *vice versa*. The maestro had scarcely resigned from Vienna when it was said he had opened negotiations with Gustav Rudolf Sellner, the intendant of the Deutsche Oper, Berlin. By flirting with Berlin, Karajan got what he wanted: by early March he was back in Vienna, returning in triumph to take up his old appointment, while singers and stage crew alike acclaimed him. Decisions had been taken at the highest level to alter the house's system of funding: instead of being administered by the Austrian theatres' governing body, it was now to be placed under the direct control of the Ministry of Education, thus clearing away a bureaucratic hurdle, which meant that contracts with solo singers and budgets for new productions no longer needed official approval. 'I am interested only in the artistic running of the Vienna State Opera,' Karajan had told Hans Heinz Stuckenschmidt in Berlin on 20 February. He was, however, prepared to compromise, and agreed to place the house's affairs in trustworthy hands. His favourite for the job was Walter Erich Schäfer, general intendant at the Württemberg Staatstheater in Stuttgart, who was duly granted a year's leave of absence to go and work in Vienna. By mid-April 1962 threats of resignation undermined Karajan's health and a journey from Paris to Milan ended up in Zurich, where a kidney infection was diagnosed.

In August 1962 a desire was expressed to strengthen the ties between the Vienna State Opera and the Salzburg Festival. Karajan was by no means disinclined to return to the scene of his youthful exploits and later artistic triumphs, but first a head had to roll. Karl Haertl was head of the Austrian theatres' governing body and, as such, was held responsible for Karajan's earlier resignation. He also sat on the board of directors in Salzburg – or did so, at least, until Karajan had him removed. But instead of filling the vacant seat himself, Karajan sent Schäfer to Salzburg to represent his interests and to settle another impending row: his rival Karl Böhm had expressed the wish to conduct a new production of Strauss's *Die Frau ohne Schatten* to mark the centenary of the composer's birth, but Karajan beat him to it by claiming the work for Vienna. Böhm's response was to threaten, once again, to resign.

Meanwhile, in Vienna, Karajan, too, was insisting on all or nothing. Although he had still not signed a contract in any legal sense of the term, he demanded total control of his allocated budget on all matters relating to personnel and finance. But a report in the *Berliner Zeitung* of 17 October 1962 sent shock waves all round the world: 'Herbert von Karajan has suddenly been taken ill. His doctors have ordered a complete rest and advised the cancellation of all his commitments until the end of October. No further details were made known concerning the nature of the illness.'

At the beginning of May 1963 Karajan was engaged in building work on his new house in St Moritz when he fell and, according to newspaper reports of the time, injured his back. Ordered to rest, he repaired to the island of Ischia, where ill fortune continued to dog him. Once again the events in question were hardly Karajan's fault, but they could not have been more welcome to those of his critics whose constant complaint was the slovenly way the opera house was run. *Die Meistersinger* was scheduled, but not a note of it was heard. The tenor Wolfgang Windgassen, due to sing the role of Walther, failed to turn up in time, and since the great Vienna Opera did not have a cover, the performance had to be cancelled. A hunt for those responsible was set in motion, but Karajan was nowhere to be found. And where was his director, Schäfer? Schäfer was suffering circulatory problems brought on by overwork and had been ordered to take a rest. The press went on the offensive: 'How to Ruin an Opera House' was only one of many headlines at the time.

Seven years had passed since Karajan had taken up his Vienna appointment and only now did he finally sign a contract with the Austrian Education Minister, who returned the honour by giving him the country's highest award for services to science and the arts. As an additional token of his gratitude he appointed Egon Hilbert, until then director of the Vienna Festival, to replace Schäfer following the latter's resignation. According to Curt Riess, Hilbert

> did not like Karajan . . . because, as a committed anti-Nazi, he had no time for a man who, long before the Nazis came to power in Austria, indeed, even while the party was still officially banned there, had joined the party illegally. To do that sort of thing one would have to be hugely enthusiastic about Hitler.

Back in Berlin, the Wall had imposed its presence on the city, an eyesore that ran barely half a mile from the Neue Philharmonie. The East Berliners had watched as Hans Scharoun's Expressionist structure reached completion and were looking forward to seeing the building's official opening ceremony on 15 October 1963 broadcast on their television sets. But the sequence of events which had taken place in Salzburg at the opening of the Grosses Festspielhaus was now repeated; and once again it was Karajan who proved to be the stumbling-block with his adamant refusal to allow the opening concert to be broadcast live on television. It was one against all, but the one was Herbert von Karajan, who always got his way: the artists' contribution, he insisted, would be compromised. And he certainly had a point. How often, in later years, when his *mondo* concept got the better of us, did we have to put up with television recordings for his musical 'testament'. Cameramen would wield their monstrous cameras, the balustrades around the hall would all be draped in black as though for some state funeral, and television lights would turn each concert into an ordeal for performers and audience alike – all at Karajan's bidding. And no one said a word.

This source of annoyance in Berlin was followed by another operatic scandal in Vienna in November 1963. This time Karajan found himself in conflict with the house's union representatives. What was the cause on this occasion? Every leading opera house is faced, at some point, by the need to employ a *maestro suggeritore*, a sub-conductor placed in the prompt-box to help the singers with difficult entries. The fact that this little-known subject became a matter for public debate was due to the cancellation of another of Vienna's first nights. The conductor and prompter Armando Romano had already worked with Karajan on a production of *La bohème* at La Scala, Milan, and Karajan now decided he needed Romano to work with him in Vienna. In the view of the house's committee of management, prompters are classified not as artistic appointments but, without exception, as members of the technical crew. In other words, if a foreigner was to sit in the prompt-box, it could only be with express permission of the local employment exchange. Karajan and Hilbert disagreed. They paid Romano £400 for four weeks' work in Vienna, and sat back to wait for the première. The curtain was due to go up at 7 o'clock. Five minutes later Hilbert had to appear in front of it to announce that the artists had gone on strike. A storm of protest followed, but Karajan managed to convince the audience that the fault on this occasion was not his. He embraced his director, Egon Hilbert, in the presence of the first-night audience, and the lights were then switched off.

The battles that were fought behind the scenes were rather less concerned with art than with politics pure and simple. The unions sought to provoke a series of scandals by stirring up anti-foreign feelings and thereby winning votes, a ploy for which Karajan, needless to say, had no time whatsoever. He conducted the new production of *La bohème* – without Armando Romano – and scored a sensation with it. At the same time, however, he asked the Austrian courts to settle the dispute, not least to avoid being sued for the cancelled performance. In June 1964 the Court of Justice duly ruled that Karajan had been justified in employing an Italian prompter for performances in Italian. There was, by now, a certain irony to the ruling, Karajan having resigned his position as Vienna's artistic director earlier that same year. But, once again, he had triumphed all along the line.

Whether his resignation was a victory or not is something history has yet to decide. It is worth, however, looking at the facts, before quoting Karajan's later public pronouncements and the Viennese auditor-general's balance sheet.

Early in December 1963 Karajan and his co-director, Egon Hilbert, called a press conference to announce their plans for the 1964/5 Vienna season. Apart from the 'normal repertory performances' with the Vienna ensemble, they also planned to present the first of what were called 'series productions': in other words, the conductor's élitist ideal was being touted again, albeit under a different name, with complete productions, including sets and all-star casts, joining the international circuit. The Italian repertory would be presented during the months of October and November, when both La Scala and the Met were closed: in other words, their singers would be free to come to Vienna. Further plans for cycles of Wagner, Mozart and Strauss were temporarily shelved.

Scarcely was the conference over when the telexes started up again: Karajan had to go into hospital. Acute circulatory problems required him to rest for at least a month. The Mattoni and Concert Pitch Affairs, the cancelled ballets and operas and the constant friction with co-directors, bureaucrats and the press had taken their toll at last. The breakdown of the conductor's health was real enough and forced him to accept his limitations. He barely managed to complete a European tour with the BPO, including a Brahms cycle in London, but then had to call a halt. There was, however, at least one piece of cheering news during his convalescence: on 2 January 1964 Karajan's wife, Eliette Mouret, a former leading model, had given birth to their second daughter, Arabel. Arabel had the honour of being goddaughter of the Berlin Philharmonic, a role the players expressly asked to assume, to repay an old score with their colleagues from Vienna, who, on 25 June 1960, had stood sponsor to the Karajans' first daughter, Isabel.

For over two months Vienna saw nothing at all of its operatic supremo and once again there was talk of an imminent crisis. The rumour seemed to gain support from the fact that the Minister of Education, Heinrich Drimmel, an increasingly staunch supporter of Karajan in the past, had been removed from office. His successor was Theodor Piffl-Percevic, a man, it was said, whose previous expertise had lain in the agricultural field. When Karajan returned to Vienna in March 1964, he made no attempt to deny that he and Egon Hilbert no longer saw eye to eye, though his greatest wish for the coming weeks, he told waiting journalists, was 'to be allowed to work'.

By the end of the first week of May, however, Karajan had resigned. His telegram of resignation, sent from Zurich, arrived on Piffl-Percevic's desk on 8 May and, according to the *Hamburger Abendblatt* of four days later: 'A final medical examination has shown that, for reasons of health, he can no longer perform the duties of an artistic director. It was with "the greatest possible regret" that he saw himself obliged, therefore, to resign.' The opposing positions are best summed up by two of the episode's principal witnesses. First the Danish tenor Helge Rosvaenge, a former member of the Vienna ensemble:

Apart from a few individual performances, which reached festival standards and which Herr von Karajan himself conducted, standards at the Vienna State Opera in recent years were no different from those elsewhere. Regular audiences stayed away in ever greater numbers. It was very much the function of the old-style ensemble theatre not only to provide an integrated ensemble for every new production but to have a second cast which, made up, for the most part, of younger singers every bit as competent as their elders, was ready to cover at a moment's notice. This is something that Herr von Karajan failed completely to do. When singers were ill or had to cancel, the grotesque situation would often arise whereby hurried recastings would undermine whatever artistic merit the performance might have had, always assuming it went ahead at all and that the audience was not simply turned away.

Two weeks after Rosvaenge's letter appeared in *Der Spiegel*, Karajan was interviewed by one of the magazine's reporters and publicly revealed the background to his resignation: 'If I have to engage a singer overnight, I cannot wait six weeks for an official decision on the matter.' As for Egon Hilbert, whom, as we know, he had publicly embraced only a short time before:

It became necessary to find a new organizational manager. From the whole of the Vienna area, this one person seemed to commend himself simply because everyone said he would save the situation. So I went to him and said to him: 'Dr Hilbert, it's like this, this is my plan, I dare say you've already read about it, but I'll explain it to you again in detail.' But either he didn't understand what I meant, or he understood and said to himself: 'I'll do the opposite.' It became clear very soon that he simply didn't want or didn't like what I had in mind, but that all he wanted was the old-fashioned type of ensemble theatre, which, as far as I'm concerned, is only another synonym for gas lighting.

The affair flared up again briefly – and pointlessly – when Karajan issued an ultimatum, stating that if, within twenty-four hours, the Minister of Education had not relieved Hilbert of his post as co-director of the State Opera, he would never again conduct in Vienna. At the same time he proposed Dr Emil Jucker (later to become his longstanding factotum) as Hilbert's successor. Hilbert, however, remained in office. Indeed, he was shortly awarded the city's gold medal, no doubt a calculated insult to Karajan. The latter made one last attempt to salvage his old position by sounding out the producer, Oscar Fritz Schuh, then general intendant of the Schauspielhaus in Hamburg, as potential co-director. This latest move was all the more remarkable in that, only eight years previously, Schuh, together with Böhm and a number of others, had threatened to walk out of the Salzburg Festival because, as Schuh said at the time, 'Karajan's aim was clearly to arrogate all the decision-making powers to himself.' By 1964, however, it seemed to be a question of 'if the Schuh fits . . .' At all events, Karajan must have made his peace with Schuh and was able to ask Dr Piffl-Percevic to negotiate on his behalf. The result, however, was negative. According to *Der Abend*, 'The legal position at present makes it impossible for either side to make a concrete offer.'

Karajan duly called down his curses on the country as a whole: 'After eighteen years' activity in the concert hall, sixteen in Salzburg and eight as artistic director of the Vienna State Opera I shall cease working in Austria on 31 August 1964,' he told *Die Welt* on 25 June. That this was not intended to be for all time became clear within a matter of weeks. By 7 August *Der Abend* was able to announce:

> Star conductor Herbert von Karajan has joined the Salzburg board of directors. The Festival operates the *stagione* system, an idea which he himself has always advocated and which, he insists, so fully accords with his own ideal that he has decided, for artistic reasons, to continue working in Salzburg after all.

In taking this decision, Karajan also sowed the seeds for the Salzburg Easter Festival, which he was later to call into being with the Berlin Philharmonic, beginning with a concert in the Grosses Festspielhaus on 19 March 1967.

By way of a postscript to the conductor's years in Vienna, it is worth recalling what the auditor-general had to report in an article published in the *Wirtschaftszeitung* on 30 October 1964. It examined the co-directors' financial activities during the whole of 1963 and applies, therefore, to Schäfer's period of office rather more than it does to Hilbert's. Be that as it may, the list of sins that figures here contains the following points:

1) The State Opera's expenditure amounted to £1 million. (By way of comparison, it is perhaps worth adding that Covent Garden's budget for the same period was £1,809,660.)
2) Between 1962 and 1963 there was an increase in expenditure of £210,000.

3) The estimated budget for the new production of *Tannhäuser* was £22,000, whereas it actually cost £30,000.
4) At the time of writing, the Vienna Opera's public liabilities amounted to almost £123,000.
5) It was often not only the artists themselves whose travelling expenses were reimbursed, but the persons who travelled with them.
6) Fees paid to foreigners were not taxable in Austria.
7) Sets loaned to La Scala – which, experience showed, lasted only a year there – were later bought back by Vienna for 80 per cent of their production costs.
8) Foreign artists who were engaged as covers received a full performance fee even if they did not appear.
9) André von Mattoni was on a fixed contract even though he continued to work as Karajan's private secretary.

When Karajan gave an interview to *Der Spiegel* in July 1964, it appeared under the headline, 'That sort of thing you do only once'; a similar piece in *Quick* was headed, 'I couldn't breathe any longer'. It was, however, a cause for universal rejoicing to know that Karajan could breathe again – and here were some fetching photographs to prove it: Karajan in bathing trunks, with a visible paunch, stroking his daughter's chin; Karajan in a rowing-boat with his third wife, Eliette; and Karajan on a scooter, or standing proudly by his aeroplane. His journey took him from Vienna to Salzburg and here, in his native surroundings, he founded his Easter Festival, the fulfilment of his operatic dreams. It was becoming increasingly clear that his first and only love was the Berlin Philharmonic Orchestra, a love which – very nearly – lasted the whole of his life.

7

'The Karajan Circus'

Berlin's Neue Philharmonie

In discussing the official opening of Salzburg's Grosses Festspielhaus, we had occasion to comment on some of the building's dimensions. It is all the more essential, therefore, to describe the special features of the Berliners' Philharmonie. According to its architect, Hans Scharoun, the structure was intended to set up certain tensions, but it was tensions of a different order which increasingly made themselves felt during the 1980s, when art and politics met head on, making it clear that high artistic ideals are always bound up with basic human problems.

The Neue Philharmonie stands on the Kemperplatz in the heart of the city's so-called 'Cultural Forum'. Opened in 1963, it set the style for a series of public buildings, none of which, however, was able to rival the brilliance of Scharoun's design. It was, so to speak, a sun that rose on the cusp between West and East, a sun that many lesser but no less interesting planets were to orbit, including the Kleine Philharmonie or Chamber-Music Room, the Museum of Musical Instruments, the National Institute for Musical Research and the National Library, all of which were designed by Scharoun with the help of Edgar Wisniewski. Across the road is Mies van der Rohe's National Gallery and, in front of it, the neo-Classical outlines of Stüler's St Matthew's Church, whose brick-built façade provided the inspiration for Rolf Gutbrod's Kupferstichkabinett, his Library of Art and, south of the Tiergarten, his strangely austere Museum of Arts and Crafts.

With its daring angles and soaring curves, the Neue Philharmonie suggests a sense of constant and creative thrust. Its roof, which rises to a height of 34 metres, is crowned by Hans Uhlmann's winged sculpture. In the foyers, art is deployed only sparingly, since the building itself is a work of art. Thus Alexander Camaro's coloured glass walls and the floor mosaics are among the subcutaneous comforts the building has to offer. Even Bernhard Heiliger's abstract sculpture rarely comes to mind when visitors to the Philharmonie are asked to describe its interior.

The hall itself, to which we shall often have cause to return, can seat up to 2218. With its interlocking pentagons, its form is so hard to fathom that visitors never tire of it. The tent-like structure of the ceiling mirrors the building's outer shell, and even the safety-net added in 1989 and 1990 to protect the musicians from falling debris fits the concept of a big-top, housing the Karajan Circus.

The gently rising tiers have always been described as 'vineyards'. In contrast to the chamber-music room, they allow the assembled audience to identify itself as a group, sharing a sense of well-being. The concert-goer feels drawn into such a space and would happily choose to remain there. It calms and inspires at once. If his eye is drawn to the organ, it is not unavoidably so, as in the Leipzig Gewandhaus, but incidentally, as though by chance: perhaps because solo organ recitals are hard to imagine in such a dry and unchurchlike acoustic, Karl Schuke's priceless instrument is positioned to one side of the hall, just beneath the ceiling. Not until two years after the building was opened was it heard at one of the Philharmonic's concerts and not until 23 January 1966 was it used for a solo recital by Helmut Walcha.

We must not, however, forget the building's artistic director and the famous Tale of the Bathtub. Scharoun had designed a special – and not unattractive – room for the Philharmonic's chief conductor, a holy of holies adjacent to the room which normal conductors had to use and which was windowless and sparsely furnished, and thus entirely suited to itinerant musicians. But Karajan's quarters had no bath, the architect having decreed that, after a concert, the maestro would have to impose on his neighbour's facilities. He applied, therefore, for a bath of his own, but encountered opposition all the way up to the top. Finally Willy Brandt, Berlin's ruling mayor, was asked to look into the matter, an investigation that prompted him to remark, in a radio interview on 21 March 1965:

> Those who allow their view of Berlin to be affected by a bathtub at the Philharmonie do us an injustice. One shouldn't imagine that, just because Berliners need the help of the greater part of free Germany, they should run around in sackcloth and ashes.

Karajan bided his time and finally got his way. The bath was duly installed and, during the interval at a Sibelius concert, he invited the city's music critics to inspect the facilities for themselves, an invitation many might well have found *de trop*, since they all had baths of their own at home. But at least they were present to hear a remark on the maestro's lips which put an end to the whole embarrassing incident once and for all:

Berlin's Neue Philharmonie

Anyone who thinks he can scare me away from Berlin and the Philharmonic by means of malicious articles in the press is well and truly mistaken. I have grown very close to this orchestra over the last ten years and hope to conduct in this house for another twenty. So let's get on with the concert.

8

'A perfectly outrageous affront'

Philharmonic manoeuvres in Berlin and Vienna

In the eyes of every leading musician for whom the city ranks as second to none – or second, perhaps, to Berlin – Vienna is synonymous with the Vienna Philharmonic, an orchestra which still fulfils its original role of accompanying performances at the Vienna State Opera but which also performs in the world's leading concert halls. It was on 28 March 1842 that Otto Nicolai brought the Viennese players out of their opera-house pit and gave them that sense of self-importance which inspires due respect in their opposite numbers in Berlin, where the local Philharmonic was a concert orchestra from the outset.

For the members of the Vienna Philharmonic, 'government employment' means working at the opera, which in turn means the Vienna Opera. But this job description covers only a part of the orchestra's range of activities. The real money-spinner for them is their membership of the 'Vienna Philharmonic Society', which governs all their private activities, including subscription concerts, the Nicolai and Furtwängler Memorial Concerts, the internationally regarded New Year's Eve and New Year's Day concerts, concert tours, festival appearances, especially those in Salzburg, and all records and television recordings. It is from here that the Vienna Philharmonic players derive their lucrative private income, here that they form a corporate body enjoying autonomous rights and running their own affairs. Neither women nor chief conductors have any place in this scheme.

In 1942 the VPO celebrated its first hundred years as an independent orchestra. Furtwängler marked the occasion by making a speech in the course of which he uttered the following memorable words – words which have never ceased to resonate in the ears of the Berliners:

> This whole many-headed monster, this band of high-class virtuosos, is made up of sons of a single setting, sons of a single city. There is nothing like it anywhere else in the world. More than anything else, it is this uniformity in its composition which also conditions and shapes the characteristic features of its musical physiognomy. Herein lies the reason for the peculiar fullness, roundness and homogeneity of the sound of our Viennese players.

If we turn our attention briefly to the biographical details of the three last chief conductors of the Berlin Philharmonic Orchestra, we shall be struck by certain remarkable but none the less enlightening parallels:

Wilhelm Furtwängler – first conducted the Vienna Philharmonic in 1922 and was their permanent conductor from 1927 until 1930. In 1928 he turned down an invitation to direct the Vienna State Opera in favour of an appointment in Berlin, but in June 1939 resumed his former position with the Vienna orchestra. From 1947 until 1954 he appeared regularly at the Salzburg Festival, a commitment which ensured that he was better known to the Viennese players than any other opera conductor. His final gramophone recording, of Wagner's *Die Walküre*, was made in Vienna in October 1954, and featured the Vienna Philharmonic.

Herbert von Karajan – was born in Salzburg, where he first conducted the VPO in 1934. Even before his sensational success in Berlin he had already conducted *Tristan* at the Vienna State Opera on 1 June 1937. Furtwängler had become concert director of Vienna's Gesellschaft der Musikfreunde in 1921, a position which Karajan himself took over in 1948. His commitment to the Vienna State Opera was not, of course, limited to the years between 1957 and 1964 but remained right up to the end. The same is true of the Salzburg Festival, the chief orchestra for which had been the Vienna Philharmonic since 1877. It was a role they continued to play under Karajan.

Claudio Abbado is the third member of the group. In 1965 he delighted Salzburg audiences with his performance of Mahler's Second Symphony – with the Vienna Philharmonic. Since 1971 he has been their chief conductor in Vienna and, in his capacity as the city's general music director, head of the opera and the leading figure in its concert life.

There is also a direct line of succession linking all three men as chief conductors of the Berlin Philharmonic. It is scarcely surprising, therefore, that this double life of theirs not only brought them happiness but time and again caused envy and resentment on both sides. There were problems even in Furtwängler's day and when, in the course of an interview on 30 March 1983, *Stern* put it to Karajan, 'You yourself once conducted two orchestras at once, the Berlin and the Vienna Philharmonic,' Karajan freely admitted, 'It wasn't a good idea: one orchestra is always played off against the other'.

Shortly after being installed in Berlin, Karajan made up his mind to show the Austrian capital how their beloved Mozart should sound. And so he used the 1956 Mozart Celebrations to parade the BPO before the Viennese. It was clear in advance that the press would refuse to forgo the chance to draw comparisons between the two. The critic of the *Salzburger Nachrichten* came to the conclusion that

> The Berliners are musical labourers – they give more of themselves, which may be the reason why the impression they make is somewhat ponderous. With us a sense of ensemble is achieved by simply playing together, with the Berliners, by contrast, it comes from working together. This is perhaps the best way of characterizing the difference between the two orchestral styles.

Once Karajan was convinced of something, there was never any going back: critical articles in the newspapers certainly made no difference. The artistic director of the Vienna State Opera and artistic supremo of the Salzburg Festival had taken it into his head that his home town of Salzburg should also reap the lifelong benefits of his artistic directorship of the BPO. And so, for the first time in its history, the Berlin Philharmonic was brought to Salzburg to play at the 1957 summer Festival. They stayed for two weeks, during which time they were conducted not only by Karajan but also by Rafael Kubelík, Wolfgang Sawallisch and George Szell. Three years later this act of shameless presumption was perpetrated yet again, this time under Joseph Keilberth and Dimitri Mitropoulos, with Frank Martin's *Mystère de la nativité* as the final straw. The Vienna Philharmonic had had as much as they could take: for eighty years their claims on Salzburg had gone unchallenged, and now they had increasing cause to fear not only for their reputation but also for their precious private incomes. A storm began to brew and wild attacks were mounted against the conductor seen as the cause of all the dissent. It was said the Berliners were taking work from the Viennese and that Karajan wanted to 'raise the Berlin Philharmonic's international standing at the expense of the Vienna Philharmonic'. He intended to bring the Berliners to Salzburg every other year from now on and to give them more and more work. 'Let it not be misunderstood,' *Neues Österreich* assured its readers on 14 August 1962: 'top-notch foreign forces have always been welcome here ... but the Festival's Austrian character must not be allowed to suffer.'

As a result of the Festival's much-expanded programme, however, the Vienna Philharmonic was no longer in a position to carry out all the duties involved. Karajan, therefore, was as good as his word and engaged the Berliners for five further concerts in 1964 and five in 1966, all of them under leading conductors. Their expenses were paid by the Berlin Senate.

*

By May 1964 Karajan had finally resigned from the Vienna State Opera, bringing an end to eight star-struck, star-crossed years. Since Salzburg's Grosses Festspielhaus was closed at Easter, the town's illustrious son hit upon the idea of founding his own Bayreuth Festival there, inviting Karajan fans to lavishly mounted operas, to choral and orchestral concerts, and bringing a little warmth to this paradise for skiers. But which orchestra would offer him its services?

A palace revolution was reported in Vienna when Karajan, not unnaturally, turned to the local players for help. As the Vienna Philharmonic they would, of course, have been only too pleased to follow the summons to Salzburg, not least because, as already noted, their aim had always been to keep Austria for the Austrians. But *Der Abend* announced on 5 January 1966:

In consultation with the director of the State Opera, Dr Egon Hilbert – an old enemy of Karajan's – the Austrian theatre authorities turned down the invitation to go to Salzburg. In justifying the decision, the committee argued that the Philharmonic was exclusively the orchestra of the Vienna State Opera and that it could not take part, therefore, in opera performances outside Vienna. The only exception was the official Salzburg Festival.

The Berliners were not so prevented, with the result that, from Easter 1967, audiences in Berlin had to forgo their local orchestra, while the Senate sent its choicest players to Salzburg. The Berliners, moreover, insisted that when they performed in opera, they were paid out of private funds (whereas for concerts and choral works they played as Senate employees within the terms of their contracts). It is no wonder, therefore, that this altogether unique opportunity to perform in top-class opera was not only a source of artistic pleasure for them; it also meant an appreciable extra income. The taxpayer footed the bill.

The first of the Easter Festivals opened on 19 March 1967 with a performance of *Die Walküre*, which received no fewer than thirty curtain calls. The Ride of the Valkyries echoed far and wide, causing confusion as far afield as the Vienna Opera orchestra pit, where the players began to plot revenge, finding a suitable weapon in the person of Karl Böhm. They began by appointing him their honorary conductor and followed that up by inviting him – and him alone – to conduct the celebrations held to mark their 125th anniversary. According to *Express* of 30 March 1967, Karajan found their behaviour 'a perfectly outrageous affront', but the Viennese, with their infinite charm, declined to see it in such terms and sent an invitation to Karajan's private secretary, André von Mattoni.

How much the maestro himself missed Vienna was more than amply demonstrated by the celebrations held to mark the centenary of the Vienna Musikverein. After six years' self-imposed abstinence, unable to resist the magical draw of the Goldener Saal, he prevailed on Rudolf Gamsjäger, general secretary of the Verein, to invite him to the ceremony and, to scenes of universal rejoicing, brought the Berlin Philharmonic with him. Prominent personalities from the world of politics, business and even culture were regaled with a Beethoven programme: the Overture to *Coriolan* and Symphonies No. 5 and 6. 'In spite of the almost unbearable heat in the hall, the applause grew more and more frenzied and went on so long at the end that after twenty minutes the lights in the hall were turned off,' the *Telegraf* reported on 11 June 1970. All who were present interpreted this as a demonstration intended to lure the conductor back to Vienna.

There was, however, still some way to go. At the Salzburg Easter Festival Karajan went on working with the Berlin Philharmonic, conducting and staging the *Ring*, *Fidelio* and *Tristan und Isolde*. From 1972 he reduced the orchestra's summer commitments to only a couple of concerts under his baton, spending the time that he saved in this way by preparing a further powerful blow against the recalcitrant Austrians. Easter was not enough for him: there had to be a Whitsun Festival too. And so, on 9 June 1973, the Berliners gave a performance of Bruckner's Fifth, ending the solemnities two days later with the same composer's Eighth. On the intervening day two events had taken place. In the morning there had been a performance of Mozart's Requiem and Bruckner's massive *Te Deum* with the Vienna Singverein, a choir which, unlike the BPO, remained loyal to Karajan all his life. And in the evening, the former pianist Herbert von Karajan joined forces with Justus Frantz and Christoph Eschenbach to play Mozart's Triple Concerto, rounding off his miniature Whitsun Festival with a performance of Bruckner's Fourth, the 'Romantic'.

Karajan – freeman of Berlin and holder of the German government's highest decoration – continued to haggle with Vienna but, as if in compensation, developed an unexpected interest in the Second Viennese School. And once again it was the Berliners whose name appeared on the box of records that proved to be a best-seller. Even Böhm offended the Viennese, as he himself was the first to admit, when he made the first complete recording of Mozart's symphonies with their rivals in Berlin.

A change in Karajan's relations with Vienna and Berlin came on 22 December 1975 with the first of the operations to his vertebral column. He had still not fully recovered his strength by the following Easter Festival, with the result that the sixty-eight-year-old maestro made a number of serious miscalculations. Immediately after the first performance of *Lohengrin*, held to mark the tenth Easter Festival, the tenor René Kollo, who was singing the title role, walked out of the production, whereupon Karl Ridderbusch announced that he too was resigning his role. Even with the Berlin Philharmonic the situation became intolerably tense. Writing in the *Frankfurter Allgemeine Zeitung*, the critic Hans Heinz Stuckenschmidt spoke of 'poor ensemble' between the pianist Alexis Weissenberg and Karajan's conducting; his interpretation was said to be an 'outrage'. In his annoyance the maestro let fly and threatened to replace the Berliners with the Vienna Philharmonic, openly proclaiming that the two were interchangeable, a claim in which he saw himself vindicated by his well-prepared return to Vienna and its State Opera. But, as so often, the threat was not carried out.

Karajan soon recovered his strength and realized that in future a second support would be of use. He also had to admit that the Berlin press was much better bred than its colleagues in Vienna, where *Neues Forum* had published the following quatrain, lampooning the famous conductor:

> At each wrong note Herr Karajan, I'm told,
> Beshits himself (the maestro's so attentive).
> But then he bathes his arse in liquid gold,
> For high-brow art should be anal-retentive.

These lines were the work of the Secretary for Cultural Affairs, Fritz Herrmann, who had used the state-subsidized *Neues Forum* to put them into circulation. The Austrian Minister of Education, Fred Sinowatz, expressed his deep regret at his own adviser's unfortunate slip and assured the maestro that 'such lapses would not be tolerated in future'. The celebrations were therefore able to go ahead without any further disruptions, and on 8 May 1977 the Vienna Opera shook with applause as Karajan took his place on the podium for a performance of *Il trovatore*. It was thirteen years since he had last stood there – a 'terrible time, a time without Karajan', some had described it – and now the city accorded its prodigal son a standing ovation.

9

'The best and finest place to work'

Karajan at sixty

Karajan was always a master at denying his age: at least he always avoided Berlin when his birthday came round. Unlike Furtwängler, he never owned a home in the city, so there was never any question of his seeking domestic comforts there. Instead he preferred to live in Saint Tropez on the French Riviera, in St Moritz in Switzerland or in the village of Anif outside Salzburg. Only working visits brought him to Berlin, where he stayed at the Savoy Hotel or at the Kempinski a few doors away. When the Salzburg Easter Festival began in 1967, Berliners had to accept that their leading orchestra, too, would be absent for longer periods. Since Karajan's birthday fell at a time when he was producing and preparing operas, he had neither the time nor the leisure to celebrate or think about himself. Shortly before his sixtieth birthday on 5 April 1968, he once again fell seriously ill. In addition to viral influenza and pneumonia affecting both his lungs, a further attack of polyneuritis was diagnosed, a painful illness caused, it was thought, by a chill but also, no doubt, by constant over-exertion. 'The world of music holds its breath,' *Die Welt* reported on 3 March 1968. But Karajan refused to let things get him down.

The second Salzburg Easter Festival provides a good example of his schedule. Karajan had just turned sixty and been given the freedom of the town. The Vienna Philharmonic had showered him with presents, while their rivals in Berlin gave him their Ring of Honour. In Salzburg a new production of *Das Rheingold* was added to the previous year's inaugural *Walküre*, while the choral and orchestral concerts which he offered subscribers to his private Festival included Brahms's *German Requiem* and Beethoven's Overture to *Coriolan*, together with the same composer's Sixth and Seventh Symphonies. The Festival lasted from 7 to 15 April 1968, its mood summed up by Karajan himself in an interview broadcast on Austrian Radio:

> I'm spending my birthday working, which is how I always like to spend it. We're now engaged in our final rehearsals and you know that my work here is something that lies particularly close to my heart. The greatest perfection possible is on offer here, where performances can be mounted with a degree of calm and care which is

simply out of the question in any other theatre. This is such a wonderful birthday present that I can't imagine anything better. So far we've planned a new production of the *Ring*, but there'll be other Wagner operas, too. *Tristan* will certainly be next. With a *Ring* cycle, which has, of course, to be given twice, you're already on the slippery slope to repertory theatre. It needs only a small thing to go wrong and a chain reaction follows, but that can't happen now. Because the subscribers come for four evenings, I could, for example, simply change the dates round if someone were to cancel, giving a concert first and then the opera, which would allow the artist time to recover. Moreover, I'm firmly convinced that Salzburg's Grosses Festspielhaus, with a stage which, in terms of today's theatre technology, really is the most perfect in the world, to say nothing of its sight-lines and the whole vast space available, combined with the Berlin Philharmonic and the best singers you can possibly get – for me, all this is the best and finest place to work. *Die Walküre* is one of Wagner's most important operatic works, one on which I've effectively worked the whole of my life and one which is really very close to my heart. It's something I want to realize here.

10

'It's not because of the speed'
The Herbert von Karajan Foundation

On 25 September 1968 Herbert von Karajan duly signed the charter setting up the Foundation which bears his name. According to paragraph 2 of its constitution, 'The aim of the Foundation is to encourage young artists, support scientific research and foster international understanding in the field of music.' It has often been suggested that Karajan brought no more than his glorious name to the Foundation. But as his physical strength began to wane, it became increasingly clear that it was only thanks to his authority and presence that projects were taken in hand and any progress made. Only after the total collapse of the competitions for conductors and youth orchestras, which he himself began in Berlin, did it finally dawn on all concerned that no one else was in a position to carry on his work with the same insistence on quality. It was thanks to Karajan that courses for young conductors became the rule in Berlin shortly after he took up his appointment with the BPO: this much, at least, is clear from a newspaper article published in *Der Tag* on 18 May 1958 and signed by a certain 'Rudolf Nestler', who evidently had an insider's knowledge of the situation. Karajan, it was said, was giving lessons free of charge, lessons which, intended to encourage a new generation of conductors, were undogmatic in their approach:

> Each of the sessions lasts around two and a half hours and in the course of it each of the six to eight candidates is gently taken in hand . . . A considerable number of participants came from the school for conductors at the Berlin City Conservatory, whose director, Herbert Ahlendorf, was asked by Karajan to select and prepare the applicants. Ahlendorf was also required to assist on the courses.

Since the same report appeared five months later in *Die Welt*, this time under the name of Ahlendorf himself, it became clear at last who 'Rudolf Nestler' was.

Also of interest in this context is the fact that the master-classes at the City Conservatory were becoming more and more international and that a small orchestra, specially assembled for the purpose, was being placed at their disposal. Karajan, at all events, was clearly prepared to take on these strenuous duties at least four times a term. If his active encouragement of young conductors later took the form not of classes but of competitions, the change was no doubt due to impatience on his part: he suddenly wanted to bring the world's most gifted conductors to Berlin and have them tested by a jury, believing perhaps that the dearth of conducting talent could thus be countered within a short space of time.

Whenever the maestro wanted something from the press, journalists were most warmly welcome, even with their flashlights. He could then be utterly charming as a raconteur, expansive in his oratory and totally in control. And so it was on 1 October 1968. He had just completed a cycle of Brahms's works, ending with a performance of the *German Requiem*, at which the soloists, tried and tested at that year's Salzburg Easter Festival, were Gundula Janowitz and Dietrich Fischer-Dieskau. It must, therefore, have been the morning of the final concert when he called the press to the Philharmonie and spoke for half an hour, barely drawing breath, about his proposed Foundation. As always with Karajan, his enthusiasm was infectious:

Ladies and gentlemen, may I welcome you here most warmly once again and thank you for giving me the honour and pleasure of your company at the conference to which I've invited you. Two days ago the Senate gave its approval to the Foundation which I've been planning for three months. Something similar is in preparation in Austria or, more precisely, in Salzburg.

In spite of what people have said, the aim of the Foundation is not just scientific research. No, I want music to be performed, produced and interpreted in the best way possible and to be made available to a group of listeners which is not only well prepared but, at the same time, as large as possible.

We must think back to the past. You see, when I began to study music, a concert in Salzburg, for example, was attended by two or three hundred people at most. It was said at the time to be for connoisseurs and music-lovers. And the audience listened to it as though it were some esoteric affair, and that was the end of the matter. The masses were simply not interested. When you consider how this has changed in the last few years, it seems little short of a miracle. Concerts are no longer directed at a small circle of listeners but have something to say to the whole of humankind. They've carried the joys of music all round the world and, above all, they've taken in sections of the public which had previously never been thought of.

I'll tell you a little story. For my first recording contract with Columbia we began with a Beethoven symphony. To follow it up, I asked the then manager if I could record a Brahms symphony. And he said to me: 'Listen, I simply can't suggest that to my directors; they'd think the two of us had gone completely mad.' That was in 1949. Today there are probably seventeen different versions of a single Brahms symphony. We owe this to the introduction of LPs and stereo records. As with so many other cultural things, it isn't an industrial invention that has changed everything, it's people's needs that have created the media. Many more people now want to listen to classical music, either live or on record. The technical means will then be found to make it possible. That's simply a statement of fact, although I don't know whether anyone has ever tackled the question of why that's the case – why symphonic music attracts so many people.

I've thought about it a great deal. Take, for example, today's spoken theatre, which is much more problematical in its aims and which normally leaves the audience with a big question mark. Think of all the symphonic works you know and ask yourselves how many of them end on a negative note. I doubt whether you'll find even three. I know two that come to a genuinely tragic end. But all the others allow the listener to enter a better world, where he's freed from the pressures to which he's exposed in everyday life. I think this form of music naturally provides an element of strength, and there are more and more people who swear by it, because it has so much to give them.

It is curious, though not entirely fortuitous, that this week marks the fortieth anniversary of my début as a conductor – not that I shall be celebrating it. I have often asked myself in recent years: 'What do we really know about the laws of listening, of listening to music? What do we feel and why? What are the purely psychological factors?' This brings us on to the question of whether it is right and proper to know too many things, when there's the danger that they'll be too closely analysed. But the danger really only exists for us, not for the audience. I'll come back to this later, since I've got something I want to tell you about the way we listen to music.

It's clear that we know many things and that there are many others about which we still don't have the first idea. It has, for example, never been conclusively explained why people can hear things vertically, even though it remains an empirical fact. As far as the organ itself is concerned, we know perfectly well that the ear is not primarily sensitive to vertical impressions. You can hear things to the left and right of you simply as a result of the different angles and times at which the sound reaches you. But the same isn't true of sounds reaching you from above and below. This is one of many topics that need to be discussed if we want to account for the exact sequence of listening to music.

People keep telling me that what I want is by no means new. Certainly. A great deal has already been written on the psychology of listening to music, some of it with vast numbers of experimental subjects. Only one thing is missing here, I think, and that is to correlate their findings with the way music is interpreted. If you look through these studies, you'll see that it normally says the test subjects were played such and such a piece of music. It never says the same piece of music in different interpretations. But it's precisely there that the big difference inevitably lies. I know only one experiment that was carried out a long time ago and, it has to be said, using primitive resources. Three great pianists were asked to play a note on the piano. The oscillations of all three notes were recorded on an oscillograph and a fourth sound was added in the form of an umbrella being dropped. All four oscillograms were identical. Well, of course you can say it was only a single note that was struck. We know very well that what we call attack is not only the resistance which I produce in the keyboard, causing the hammer to hit the note, but that it is also the connection between one thing and another, just as a note grows out of the one before. It is this that constitutes what we call attack and, ultimately, that also means phrasing. If the experiment I've just described were to be carried out using today's techniques, it would look very different.

You know that the galvanic skin reflex is one of the chief measurements that used to be used in lie-detecting, since emotions affect this skin reflex very considerably. The director of the Regional Hospital conducted some very interesting experiments at the Neurological Clinic in Salzburg. He showed that people who were played Dixieland jazz react in a completely different way. Their cardiac activity changes at once, they stop breathing, and so on.

As I say, a lot of work has already been done on the subject. What matters now is to relate these results to what we know – or think we know – about what way music is interpreted. We know, for example, that music can be used to calm people down. What is important, however, is the way in which the piece of music with which you are bombarded in order to calm you down is played. If, for example, you were to take a single analysis of one the best-known pieces used in these experiments, Bach's Air in D major, you'd have no difficulty in showing that not even the bass line moves at a regular pace. But how can a person be calmed by an irregular rhythm? It's things like this where you have to apply far more precise standards in order to see what it is that makes so many people react in the same way. That's one of the points that seems to me to be very fundamental.

What will happen is that individual committees, having set themselves a common goal, will divide the specialist topics among themselves, leaving each group free to undertake its own research . . . A number of people have already asked me what are the results of our research. Well, at present there aren't any. We have only just reached the legal stage of the operation and are beginning preparations which, in the scientific field, are bound to take a very long time. The people who are carrying out these experiments will also attend our orchestral rehearsals and see, for example, how we work and how it is all done. They'll see what it is that is so essential to that work. Ultimately, of course, the joint result will serve only music and a better way of performing music.

If we accept that there are large numbers of healthy people who lead happier and more fulfilled lives as a result of music, how much more is it our duty to provide an opening for music in the lives of those who are sick – children, for example, who are maladjusted and difficult to handle. For we know from previous experiments that children in particular can relate to music immensely powerfully and lose many of their complexes. I don't know if you're aware of an experiment that was carried out recently, in which a mother's heartbeat was recorded before the birth of her child. After the child was born – it was evidently a difficult child that cried a lot – it became completely calm when its mother's heartbeat was played back to it. Heartbeats were then played to it involving very slight variations in their frequency, and the child remained completely reactionless. This single heartbeat demonstrates the importance of the pulse with which the child was associated for so long. But, of course, our susceptibility or receptivity to a particular rhythm stays with us throughout the whole of our lives.

We know, for example, if you analyse Bach's music closely, that there are, in fact, many tempi here that all work out at around 72 beats a minute, which is exactly how many times a pulse beats. And I know from my own experience that there are certain tempi which some days come entirely naturally to you and which you know are correct. You then feel immensely happy, because you are then working in correlation with what your own blood is saying. Of course, there are also certain ratios such as 3:5 which can have the same effect. Certainly, the harmony of the spheres has been a perennial topic ever since the Greeks, and harmony in relations is, of course, provided by the scale itself and undoubtedly has an immense influence on people's inner lives . . .

As far as musical education is concerned, I have to say at the outset that I think children should receive identical schooling throughout the whole of a given country. Carl Orff once told me about his difficulties in this respect. He told me that the Orff Institute in Salzburg was not really for pupils but was designed to train teachers. If he didn't have at least twenty or thirty teachers to be divided up across the whole of Germany, his institute would remain an isolated phenomenon.

I saw this for myself at home when my daughter, who is now seven, began to play the piano. She was four at the time. It is exactly the same kind of teaching that we've always had: a private tutor turns up and proceeds to give the most primitive of music lessons. The first time she played me something, she came to a difficult passage and suddenly slowed down. I said: 'Child, what are you doing?' – 'Well, I can't get my fingers round it . . .' – 'All right, then, play it twice as slowly, but keep in time.' My wife was horrified and said I'd give her a complex. Certainly not, I said, she's an extremely intelligent child. And I spoke to her for three quarters of an hour, she took it extremely seriously and then said: 'Daddy, I still can't play it exactly in time, but now I'll play it slowly.' I believe this is a crucial point that must be brought home not only to the younger generation but also to practising musicians.

Whenever we have an audition here with the Philharmonic – you know the whole orchestra always sits in on it – people come from large and very famous theatres (I'll not mention any names) who are incapable of playing ten successive quavers in time . . . We've a standing joke: whenever the orchestra plays something too slow or too fast and I break off, one of them will say that that's why I've set up a foundation.

People have already put a great deal of effort into this. After all, I've now been here twelve years – twelve years of hard work, love and boundless happiness – and I'd like it to continue. My successor will at least have a rough idea where his players are being recruited from. If you're reduced to assembling your orchestra from six different towns, you always end up asking yourself: 'Should we take him? Should we inflict an irreparable loss on that town? Better to leave things as they are.' It's nothing to do with musical standards. And I'm sure – but this really *is* just a question of money – if the resources are available (and I'm confident that they will be), then the members of the Philharmonic who work with me here ought to be able to pass on their knowledge to younger players who would also attend our rehearsals. They would sit at the second desks when the parts are doubled and, in that way, grow to be part of the orchestra, so that at the end you would have the best available talent – just as you draw the cream from the top of a bucket of milk when you need it. They'll already be sitting there, fully prepared. And I'm also certain that, given the name of this orchestra, there'll be no shortage of people interested in attending this orchestral academy. We'll be able to choose on a totally different basis from the one that exists today, when you're grateful if a player knows which way round to hold his fiddle. You wouldn't believe the headaches it causes us, trying to fill a vacancy in the orchestra. As you can imagine, our players are extremely demanding in this respect, and justifiably so.

It's certainly one of the functions of the music we interpret that we should pass on the tradition from within our own ranks. It's a tradition, after all, which all of us, my three great predecessors included, have worked and fought for and one which we can perhaps also feel very proud of.

It's understandable in this context that my particular attention should be directed at the next generation of conductors. It's a real tragedy that so many famous conductors have died recently – twenty-five or thirty of them, beginning with Koussevitzky. A real gap has arisen that urgently needs to be filled. It's also clear why it arose: there were simply not enough people after the war who were able to afford to undertake the sort of study needed to become a conductor. And worries about finding any kind of job meant that many potentially gifted individuals were not given the chance. That must now be changed and the Foundation's first practical step is a competition for conductors, which is planned to take place at about this time next year and which will, of course, be international and, I hope, attended by conductors from all over the world.

The winner, or the two winners (always assuming that the competitors are sufficiently talented), will be offered the chance to conduct one or two concerts here and to continue working with me by attending my rehearsals. This seems to me to be very important, not least because it offers us another means of filling a gap.

As you can see, the Foundation is extremely diverse and will need time, patience and a great deal of love to co-ordinate all these things. Of course, as I said earlier, we are addressing ourselves to a small group of people. But you know that, partly out of necessity, I began to move into completely different areas two years ago by making symphonic films. Wherever these films have been shown the results have been quite astonishing. When the Beethoven symphony was first broadcast, I was in Munich, about to set off on tour. My wife, who was driving over from St Moritz to be with me, broke down in her car outside Garmisch and telephoned me. Obviously I'd have to go and collect her. She was standing in a call-box and said: 'There's a man standing beside me here, waving his arms about wildly, indicating he wants a word with you.' He said: 'Herr Karajan, I just wanted to tell you that I've never *heard* the Fifth Symphony played as beautifully as it was last night.' It's simply the medium, people now think in visual terms, I've spoken to many people who watch it. In particular, people who are completely unbiased say that seeing has led them on to listening. I was recently in the Almental near Salzburg, when a farmer jumped down from his tractor and said: 'It was so good, what you did on television.' – 'Why did you watch it; it was boring,' I said. – 'No!' It was a completely new world for him. You shouldn't dismiss it out of hand on musicological or aesthetic grounds, and say that it's rubbish. Otherwise you'd have to issue people with blindfolds when they went to symphony concerts. They'd have to wear them in order not to be distracted by what they saw. At a normal concert the subscriber sees the conductor's back from an angle of thirty degrees, and his conducting takes on more and more of a sheen as his tails get older and older. We're doing all we can, and have more or less reached the point that the cinema had reached some time ago, with all the difficulties that that involves – difficulties you simply have to discover for yourself and laws you have to invent as you go along. What I imagine is a visual interpretation of what is heard, and there's no doubt that, until now, we've had only a small club of some two or three thousand people. But once there's a fixed satellite over Europe, 150 million people will be able to see and hear it. I believe that, especially with people who are hearing a work for the first time, it can never be good enough. The biggest mistake, in my own opinion, is to say that people who don't know a work can therefore be fobbed off with something inferior. No, what holds their attention is the fact that you're doing something special. And I don't think there's anyone who can resist that appeal. That's the fascination, whether in art or in sport or whatever. It's the fascination everyone feels – even before the start – at how much intensity, how much tension and how much love have gone into it. It's something you can sense, without knowing. And the result is that the dentist, for example, returns home from the concert and treats his patient better, more lovingly and more carefully.

People have always said, for example, that I have a mania for driving fast cars. It's not because of the speed. It's because I'm holding something in my hand which is normally regarded as the ultimate in what a person can think up with his brain and what such and such a number of people can create with their hands. It's an instrument of perfection. If you have it in your hands five minutes before the start of the rehearsal, you can ask yourself: 'Are you really as prepared or as concentrated as the people who made it?' For me, it's rather like someone taking drugs. I'm against drugs, I prefer a simple life. But it's a sign for me that, if a whole number of different things turn out well and if the circumstances are right, you can achieve the sort of thing that we're all somehow seeking to achieve. At the Easter Festival, for example, I'm lucky enough to be able to choose from what's available – so that when the performance actually takes place, there's only me to blame if it goes badly.

The committee appointed to run the Herbert von Karajan Foundation naturally included the founder himself, together with the intendant of the Berlin Philharmonic Orchestra, Wolfgang Stresemann, and Peter Csobádi, a naturalized Austrian journalist. When Karajan took the orchestra to the Soviet Union in 1969, Csobádi accompanied them and recorded the conductor's impressions of Leningrad.

I've really been looking forward to this tour for a very long time. The feeling was justified because I believe there's something special about coming to the Soviet Union for the third time and coming, moreover, with an orchestra which is really my own or, as I keep on saying, an extension of my arm. And the expectations which the players had of the journey have also been fully realized. The highlight of the tour for us was being able to play Dmitri Shostakovich's Tenth Symphony in the composer's presence. You know I've worked a great deal on this symphony with the orchestra and it's now also been issued as a recording. I'd always had the idea of playing it to him as he may have dreamt hearing it played or perhaps not even imagined it in his wildest dreams. It was very moving when he came on to the platform at the end and I sensed he was actually trembling with emotion. He's someone who's very shy and who says very little. But I sensed that he was well satisfied. The orchestra really performed wonders of interpretation . . .

I knew the audiences from my last two visits. Their warmth and sincerity really provided the counterbalance that we needed on this journey in order to be able to say to ourselves that, in spite of all the difficulties which kept on occurring, we had met with really genuine contact and a sincere sense of community. I must also mention in passing that never in forty years have I seen such a full concert hall as yesterday. They gave away an additional 1500 tickets for standing room. People virtually broke down the doors but they listened in almost reverential silence, and their understanding and sympathy gave us enormous pleasure.

In Moscow I met the Minister of Culture, Mrs Furzeva, whom I'd got to know in Vienna when I was artistic director there. She had come as part of a state visit and we'd had an extremely lively discussion that went on for an hour. The impression has now deepened. She has great foresight and certainly thinks big. Musical education is of immense importance to her. She took up my offer immediately when I said I'd be happy to make myself available in order to get to know the conductors here and hold a class. The whole thing was organized within a day and twenty conductors were brought to Leningrad from distances of six to seven thousand kilometres, all of whom already conduct orchestras here. We had the second Symphony Orchestra at our disposal – an excellent group of players – and I think I was able to give them something . . .

I discovered three exceptionally talented conductors who will be coming to Berlin or Salzburg on a regular basis. They won't have lessons but will simply attend my rehearsals. And I'm convinced that we've found further valuable additions to the ranks of young conductors.

You know the Foundation is a particular concern of mine at present. We've had our first scientific and medical conference in Salzburg, when the main challenges in the field of medicine were mapped out for the future. The second conference – on philosophy – will be held in August and I already know that the lecturers will include three Nobel prizewinners.

The German side is particularly well represented in the Foundation by the fact that the competition for conductors will be held in Berlin this coming September. It's the first major event to be held in public. Mrs Furzeva was very impressed by the whole idea and I invited her to send us young conductors to take part in the competition. So far we've had 235 enquiries, though, needless to say, we'll only be able to consider a fraction of them. It's been decided that, in order to be accepted, conductors must be able to show that they've worked with an orchestra. Otherwise, we'd probably need three months just to make a preliminary selection.

11

'Completely self-taught'

The first conducting competition

If the opening of the Easter Festival in March 1967 was a major event in Salzburg's annals, a similar sense of occasion was felt two and a half years later when the first of Karajan's conducting competitions was formally launched in Berlin. Once again the maestro had staked everything on a single card. A large-scale spectacle had been announced, eliciting nationwide approval. Even the lavish programme booklet showed that not only the next generation but industry too had been mobilized in support of the whole vast undertaking.

Three halls were made available to the young conductors taking part – the University Hall, the main concert hall of Sender Freies Berlin and the Philharmonie itself – while the preliminary, intermediate and final rounds were held in the concert hall at the city's College of Music between 18 and 25 September 1969. The orchestra was the Berlin Radio Symphony Orchestra which sought, in an access of self-sacrificial devotion, to meet the candidates' more or less coherent demands. The same was true of the final heat, held in the main studio of Sender Freies Berlin, when the jury agreed the names of the three prizewinners, simply announcing the final positions for the benefit of the invited audience, who were not allowed to vote.

The high-point was the final concert, held two days later in the Philharmonie, when the Philharmonic – no less – graciously deigned to play. On this occasion Karajan's only contribution was a speech, delivered as part of the eagerly awaited prize-giving ceremony.

The prizes themselves were listed in the programme: the Herbert von Karajan Gold Medal included a prize of 10,000 marks, the silver medallist took away 7500 marks and the bronze medallist 5000 marks. Even more valuable, of course, were the contracts that the winners signed (and which were later much reduced in number): the opportunity to work alongside the maestro as his assistant conductor, a complete subscription concert with the BPO, concerts in Cannes and Vienna (the latter with the Gesellschaft der Musikfreunde) and a recording contract with Deutsche Grammophon.

It was not only the founder himself who provided all these benefits but the members of the international jury, which included Elsa Schiller, Sir John Barbirolli, Franco Ferrara, Wolfgang Fortner, Rudolf Gamsjäger, Karl Höller, Lovro von Matačić and Hans Heinz Stuckenschmidt. The chairman of the jury was Wolfgang Stresemann, who held the undertaking together. Among the very first competitors was the Czech conductor Jiří Bělohlávek, the Spaniard Garcia Navarro (at that time still calling himself Luis Antonio Garcia-Navarro) and the Russian Dmitri Kitaienko, who has now succeeded Eliahu Inbal with the Hessisches Rundfunkorchester. It must be said, however, that the two first-named conductors did not win a prize, yet still succeeded in making careers for themselves.

The prizewinners of the first Herbert von Karajan Foundation Competition for Conductors were presented to the public at 11 o'clock on the morning of 28 September 1969. Shortly beforehand, Karajan himself held a press reception, convened in the hope of creating a good impression on all concerned. His bold suggestion that the Philharmonic be used as a permanent practice-ground for his novice conductors was one to which he never returned.

One shortcoming has already emerged and it lies in the very nature of the exercise. There were 250 applications. To find the necessary thirty conductors out of 250 – and even thirty may already be too many for one heat – is really an extremely difficult task. Of course, we knew as soon as we saw the vast influx that we'd have to limit the numbers in some way. We did this, first, by age and, second, we said that, in the main, we'd consider only those conductors who'd already had jobs as conductors. However, it turned out – and this is what is so decisive about this morning – that the best conductors were in fact those who had not previously worked as conductors.

The first prizewinner is completely self-taught. He's never had any lessons but has had to win through on his own. It's a fate that I share with him, though neither of us has done too badly. That's the main thing. He'll now remain in contact with me, of course, and I hope I'll be able to help him. Right at the outset I told the gentlemen of the jury that it wasn't a question of filling a second conductor's post but of finding an explosive new talent. Whether that talent is already fully formed or not is completely irrelevant. We wanted to find someone who has a genuine feeling for music and a genuine feeling for communication. Life and practice will do the rest. And these conditions were met by all three.

If we decide to go on with the competition, I'd like to try something different next time. I'll suggest to the orchestra that I give up five minutes of every rehearsal, we'll take five minutes off the break, and I'll pay them an extra ten minutes. In that way we'll have twenty minutes. I'm here sixty or seventy times, which makes 1400 minutes, or around twenty-two hours. During that amount of time I can hear at least eighty to ninety conductors. Three minutes with my orchestra is all I need to tell whether someone is capable or not – and, of course, he'll then enter one of the competitions. The jury will tell you that even before someone's begun to conduct, you already have an idea what's in them. As a result we'll then be in a position to organize the initial round in such a way that we have much more time to test them thoroughly.

That's my suggestion, though of course it's practicable only if we hold the competition every other year. It's too difficult to organize it annually, but I also think it's better, so that during the run-up year you not only know whom you intend to have but also that you are in fact able to bring off the competition during the second year.

With these words still ringing in their ears, the assembled press corps entered the concert hall at the Philharmonie. Expectations were running high. Tickets had sold out quickly, since there had never previously been an opportunity in Germany to sit in on the results of a competition for conductors. The jury was unable to decide between the twenty-three-year-old Belgian conductor François Huybrechts and the twenty-nine-year-old Russian Dmitri Kitaienko, and so two second prizes were awarded. Huybrechts opened the proceedings with Mozart's 'Jupiter' Symphony, followed by Kitaienko with Strauss's *Don Juan*. But the real sensation came after the interval, when Beethoven's Fourth received a performance as vibrant and as beautiful as anything that the maestro himself could have conjured from the BPO. The conductor in question was Okko Kamu from Finland – twenty-three years old and 'completely self-taught'.

Karajan breathed a sigh of relief and brought forth a few emotional words, celebrating the competition's success, a success in which fortune and the Berlin Philharmonic had played a not inconsiderable part. The sixty-one-year-old maestro took his three charges into his arms, telling both them and his audience of the high objectives which the competition had set itself:

May I begin by welcoming you most warmly and thanking you for the interest you have shown our Foundation. I should also like to take this opportunity to thank not only the Senate for its active support but also the patrons and friends of this event; and let us not forget the Berlin Radio Symphony Orchestra and the Berlin Philharmonic, whose selfless commitment has made this competition possible. If I may make a personal observation, it is that today has made me very, very happy. My greatest wishes have been fulfilled if not surpassed. It has been possible to present the musical world with three young and talented musicians of extraordinary gifts, and I have no doubt that they are destined to play a decisive role in the musical life of the coming decades.

This competition for young conductors, on which I have expended a great deal of love and even more effort – supported by Professor Ahlendorf – will now be continued.

It is my greatest hope that, among the ranks of the prizewinners, I shall one day find the man who is destined to succeed me, so that, free from care and with joy in my heart, I can entrust him with what has been the most precious possession of my life as an artist, my friends, the Berlin Philharmonic. [*Cries of 'bravo', rapturous applause; turns to the young conductors*:] The presentation of this prize is certainly a milestone in your lives. It is a source of pleasure, but it also places you under an immense responsibility. Each time you appear before an audience, people will observe you with much more critical eyes and ears, precisely because you won here. It should be your innermost effort to meet this challenge.

Go forth into the world. My warmest congratulations and very best wishes attend you. If any of you finds himself in difficulties, come back to me as you would to a father. I shall help you as best I can. I wish you well, and do not forget that you are destined and chosen to serve our great art, the art of music. [*Shouts of 'bravo', applause.*]

Although one half-expected the ceremony to end with the laying on of hands, there was no mistaking the laudable aim and positive energy shown. A highly important initiative had been started which continued to bear fruit until 1985, producing no fewer than twenty-five prizewinners. None of the winners, it is true, became an Ozawa, a Mehta or a Muti – in other words, a conductor of the very highest order – but many candidates knew how to seize their opportunity. Karajan's wish that his successor would emerge from one of the Foundation's competitions was not, of course, fulfilled. And his later suggestions for Tennstedt and Semyon Bychkov were as far from the mark as Furtwängler's supposition that *his* place would be taken by Karl Münchinger.

The problems associated with conducting competitions will be discussed elsewhere in other contexts, but it is worth quoting two of the 1969 prizewinners here who, ten years later, told me about their later developments. The first is Dmitri Kitaienko, who in 1976 became chief conductor of the Moscow Philharmonic. When I spoke to him in Berlin in February 1978, he told me:

Immediately after the competition, I was offered work at the Stanislavsky Opera Theatre in Moscow. I rehearsed *Carmen* there in Walter Felsenstein's production. Within a year I'd been appointed the theatre's general music director. I conducted very many works there, including ballets and operettas. The competition made things easier for me, since I was immediately able to take on many concerts in Russia and in almost every country abroad, the only exception being Australia. But it wasn't until last year that I undertook my first foreign tour with my orchestra, the Moscow Philharmonic, when we visited Germany, Switzerland and Austria. We were away for a whole month.

Okko Kamu, who carried off the first prize in 1969, struck me as equally sympathetic when I met him in October 1978, but was far more restrained in his praise. A year after his unimpeachable triumph he had been offered a concert with the BPO at the 1970 Berliner Festwochen. In a programme of works by Rautavaara, Beethoven and Sibelius he had shown himself to be completely out of his depth and suffered a real defeat, a shock from which he has evidently not yet fully recovered. At all events, he has not been invited back to conduct the Philharmonic. It is easy, therefore, to understand what he meant when he told me in October 1978:

> I think your career is speeded up as a result of the competition, but I don't know how much that actually helps. Sometimes such help can have a negative effect, since you take on difficult pieces too soon and have no time to develop. It's very important for a conductor to develop naturally and that development shouldn't be disturbed by winning a competition too early in your career. The first few years that followed it were very, very hectic for me. I had too many concerts and had to rehearse too many works in too short a space of time. It's only now that I have time and can work without panicking. My contract with the Oslo Philharmonic ends in the spring of 1979. I'll then take a year off. What will happen after that I don't know.

Of course, such warning cries reached Karajan's ear at a fairly early stage, so that the pressure to make a success of competitions which, by now, were being arranged on the grandest scale waged a permanent war on his sense of moral responsibility.

12

'In the service of beauty'

The first competition for youth orchestras

Karajan's own problems during the early years of the Berlin competitions were of a wholly different order. Following the sudden death of the conductor Charles Münch on 6 November 1968, he had been urged to take on the role of temporary artistic director of the newly founded Orchestre de Paris. Karajan agreed but could not begin to meet the orchestra's wishes in terms of recordings, concerts and tours. The beginnings of the video boom and huge recording contracts with DGG and EMI had absolute priority. And for these he needed the Berlin Philharmonic. It was hardly surprising, therefore, to read in *Die Welt* on 22 May 1970: 'The French Minister of Education, Edmond Michelet, has issued Karajan with an ultimatum: he should either spend more time with the Orchestre de Paris or resign'. The orchestra's *conseiller musical* resigned – and just in time, for he was needed in Berlin for the second great showpiece of his Foundation, the 'International Meeting of Youth Orchestras'.

The competition, involving eight symphony and chamber orchestras from all over the world, took place between 19 and 27 September 1970. They played full-length concerts in the University Hall and, as might have been expected, the Moscow Tchaikovsky Conservatoire String Players carried off the prize. Under their conductor Mikhail Teryan, they despatched a Tchaikovsky serenade with an opacity and vehemence which even Karajan himself had never managed. Even *he* was taken by surprise. His real task, however, still lay ahead: he assembled an 'International Youth Orchestra' from the pick of the players present and, in a handful of rehearsals, prepared Brahms's Second Symphony with them. And even if some of the players – especially the horns – were audibly overtaxed by the final concert, we were none the less struck by the way in which Karajan managed to produce his characteristic sound in such a short space of time. At the end of the performance, on 27 September, he addressed a few words to the Philharmonie audience:

> Members of the Senate, ladies and gentlemen and, above all, dear music-lovers, this final concert brings to an end the first meeting of youth orchestras. Before I present the medals, I should like to thank our jury, which, with true self-sacrifice,

has undertaken the complex task of judging and, above all, of selecting the International Youth Orchestra. I should also like to offer my warmest thanks to my dear colleague, Professor Ahlendorf.

Permit me to say two final words. For me personally it has been a source of tremendous happiness and a very real privilege to have been able to take part in this event, not least because it has brought me into contact with an orchestra made up of very young people.

We have been here together for seven days, and members of every nation from every corner of the world, with different views, different opinions and differing tastes, have come together to work for a single goal: to serve beauty and music, which, as far as humankind is concerned, is without doubt the most international of languages. I am sure that, as you return to your own world, you are somehow inwardly transformed. You have shared in a single experience, which shows how so many conflicts can be reconciled by an overriding idea. If that was at least minimally possible here, we are richly rewarded for our efforts.

13

'How do people listen to music?'

Panel discussion at the College of Music

Competitions for conductors, competitions for youth orchestras: the reader might be forgiven for thinking that that was enough. Not, however, for Karajan. The Orchestral Academy of the Herbert von Karajan Foundation was the next of his projects for Berlin. As with all his other attempts to encourage a new generation of players and conductors, it was, of course, his foremost concern to ensure the future of his own orchestra. After all, as a wise man once said, conductors come and go, but orchestras remain.

By 1972, thanks to the help of a number of sponsors, the money had been collected and the initial entrance examinations held. Candidates were required to have studied music at least to degree level and were expected to concentrate on chamber music with the director, Horst Göbel. In itself, the size of the grant on offer would scarcely have candidates flocking to Berlin, but a chance to study with some of the finest Philharmonic players and to be assimilated into the orchestra was, of course, highly attractive. By the time of Karajan's death, it has to be said, few had attained the highest goal and joined the BPO, but the 300 or so musicians who completed the two-year course were always in demand throughout the rest of the world.

Berlin's Lessing University was twice able to persuade the conductor to explain his pedagogical aims in public. The first occasion was a highly enjoyable afternoon, in January 1972, in the concert hall at the Berlin College of Music. The hall was packed to the rafters, since few of those present had ever been able to hear the conductor speak. It soon became clear that Karajan's gifts as a listener were musical rather than verbal, a fact that gave Walther Schmieding the thankless task of acting as moderator. Only a ten-year-old boy managed to stop the conductor in his stride:

KARAJAN: What kind of music did you listen to first?
YOUNG BOY: My mother used to play to me on the piano – old works.
KARAJAN: You mean Mozart?
YOUNG BOY: Yes, Mozart, sort of classical.
KARAJAN: And . . . ?
YOUNG BOY: And what you said here isn't completely true. People

shouldn't prefer one thing or the other, classical music or beat music. But I don't want to say anything more on that, because it's a matter of taste [*laughter and applause*]. But to come back to the question 'how do people listen to music', I'd just like to say one thing. There's music that puts you to sleep and there's music that carries you with it. An important element in music that carries you with it is the tension set up by the chord of the dominant seventh, by lots of dissonances, transitions and other things besides, whereas . . .

KARAJAN: Yes . . .

YOUNG BOY: . . . whereas with music that sends you to sleep, it's generally around 70 per cent harmony and, say, 30 per cent dissonances [*astonishment, applause*].

KARAJAN: How old are you?

YOUNG BOY: Ten.

KARAJAN: And you play the piano yourself?

YOUNG BOY: For five years.

KARAJAN: You've been having piano lessons for five years?

YOUNG BOY: Yes.

KARAJAN: Well, I too was five when I began.

How do people listen to music? That was the topic for discussion at the College of Music that January afternoon. Most of those who were there, of course, really wanted to know how Herbert von Karajan listened to music. Once again his knowledge of science proved to be good, if never excessively deep:

The Salzburg branch of our Foundation is attached to the University and throws light on the way we listen to music from the medical aspect. We have a team of researchers working there who are looking into the way that music affects the individual person, for example. They've a piece of equipment, rather like the thing that astronauts have, but with cables attached, though we'll also be getting some without. I've tried experimenting on myself with it to find out how brain activity is affected when we listen to music. Then there's an ordinary ECG. Most important of all is a test designed to measure the physiological electric tension of the skin. This is sometimes also described as a lie-detector, since it's completely independent of the individual's will: in other words, the pointer moves whenever you are in a state of mental excitement or receive a powerful impression. We've made some extremely interesting discoveries here. During one of the dress rehearsals for *Siegfried*, for example, when there was no audience present, I carried out the following experiment: we began in Act III with the passage normally described in the concert version as the *Siegfried Idyll*. I must emphasize once again that there was no one at all in the auditorium and that I was at liberty to start and stop whenever I wanted. Needless to say, I felt no fear or any other emotional excitement. The music began very quietly and slowly with a passage for strings involving no intonational difficulties – in other words, the simplest thing imaginable.

The apparatus showed the following: I have a relatively low heartbeat, in other words, between sixty-seven and sixty-eight. Three seconds before the music began, my pulse shot up to 148. Remarkably, however, it calmed down again immediately the music got going. The test continued and we came to a passage where the soprano – it was Frau Dernesch, who was singing the part for the first time – goes up to a top C. This was also a problem for me, of course, because if she didn't manage the passage, she'd develop a complex before the high note and since the first night was imminent, it was possible that she'd start to suffer from nerves. I was very keen, therefore, for her to hit that top C. The curve on the physiological test rose steeply just before the C and, of course, it fell away again after she had sung a wonderful top C.

But now comes the remarkable part of the story. After this first test had been done, I was placed on a sofa, similar to a psychiatrist's couch, and the whole passage was played back to me on tape. You can believe this or not, but although I knew that it was in the bag and that nothing could go wrong, I still had exactly the same reaction. And so you see, there are many things that can't be controlled by will-power or by reason.

One of the results of the experiment was crucial: the greatest strain on a conductor is not the energetic phrase in an Allegro – in other words, muscular effort plays absolutely no part. Far more demanding are the pauses where there is nothing, where you have to wait; from a purely psychological point of view, it is these that place the greatest strain on the conductor. We could tell this by observing heartbeats and, especially, physiological skin reflexes. This explains, for example, why two conductors suffered a heart attack at almost the identical passage in Act III of *Tristan.* When Tristan wakes up from his faint, there is a bar of orchestral playing, two whispered words, a rest, and so it goes on. We know from experience that this is a tricky passage. If the singer makes a mistake, the orchestra will come in late, or both will sing at the same time, and then you'll have two bars' rest. It's a moment of incredible tension . . .

Of course – and here I come to what is really the main subject of this afternoon's discussion – we want to know how people hear music and how they react to it. First of all, there's the physiological aspect: what happens during the actual auditory process, a process that ultimately involves no more than a finely differentiated, extremely subtle sound pressure on the ear? Just think for a moment how immensely complicated and complex a concert is.

The music you hear is rooted, first and foremost, in the composer. This intellectual property is translated into certain forms which, depending on the age you belong to, are typical of a stylistic period. In other words, the composer expresses himself in the form of his time. And this brings us to the decisive point: what happens to a person, physiologically, when a sound enters his ears?

Although it takes us away from the matter in hand, I want to tell you about an extremely interesting experiment undertaken by Professor Cremer, who was responsible for the acoustic arrangements at the Philharmonie. A few weeks ago he and his team of researchers accompanied us on a tour of Germany. They constructed six or seven dummy heads of the kind you see in shop windows. They could be taken apart and were fitted with an auditory canal which was correct in every anatomical detail. Two microphones were fitted to the end of the auditory canal, at the point where the eardrum is located. In other words, the sound had to pass through these two winding canals in order to reach the microphones.

Now, I'm sure that all of you know what happens when you hear something from one – or two – loudspeakers. Imagine you were wearing headphones. When we heard the first stereophonic recordings, we turned round spontaneously, thinking the sound was coming from behind us. These are acoustic phenomena which have not yet been fully explained.

Professor Cremer asked me to join him after an orchestra rehearsal. It was a very narrow room. He placed a set of stereo headphones on my head, and as soon as he played back the recording that had been made on the dummy-head microphones, I had a completely new sensation of sound. It felt as though the sound was not so much entering my head as starting out from inside it. I don't know whether this microphone technology will ever be commercially viable but, for me, it offers the sort of sound I ideally want to hear when listening to a piece of music. I can compare it only with the sensation I have when standing on the conductor's podium, where you also have the feeling that the sound you want to hear comes from inside you and that the orchestra is a natural extension of it.

We come now to an extremely fundamental element of music in general: rhythm. I was once in Cuba, in a suburb of Havana, where only local music is played. I often went there with a stopwatch. People would normally arrive at the place around 12 o'clock with bloodshot eyes – they were clearly high on marijuana – and would sit down and make music for the next five hours. Within the space of around sixteen bars you could observe no more than a hundredth of a second difference. Every musician is better than a metronome. They have such a feeling for this particular rhythm – it must be innate. During the Cuban Carnival, two-year-old children emerge from their homes dancing – and they've already got the right rhythm, they've never learned it. Ask yourselves: why is the need for rhythmic music greater now than ever before?

I once made an experiment in a discothèque. There was a girl there who was a wonderful dancer; she had the rhythm in her bones. During a break I went over to her and said: 'Can you give me five minutes of your time and beat this simple rhythm for me?' And just imagine! The result was completely unrhythmical. Do you know why she was dancing? It was because, in doing so, she'd found the rhythm she didn't have inside her.

The other example is the military march. It's clear that this particular rhythm is infectious or, rather, that our fathers found it infectious. The same is true of the waltz, of course.

But what is curious – and it's this that really sets us apart from the Slav races – we completely lack their attitude towards syncopation and, above all, to irregular rhythm. Even without any musical training, a Yugoslav girl can sing you Yugoslav folksongs written in 3/8, 11/8, 4/8 or even 7/8 as if it were the most obvious thing in the world. They simply aren't aware of what they're doing. In other words, it may be that what strikes us as irregular is entirely self-evident. With us, syncopation is essentially felt as something alien. When you learn it, people will say: 'Watch out, there's something very difficult here.' And so you stumble over it.

Let's take something far more difficult. You're told, for example, that you have a metronome mark of 80 and that you have to play crotchets, then quavers and finally triplets at this tempo. That's something that every orchestra can basically manage to do without difficulty. But black notes are difficult for the student of music and he automatically speeds up. You see how much we're influenced: first, by childhood impressions and, secondly, purely by the visual aspect of the notes.

I'm convinced that – if I were to find the time to get together with a publisher – I could publish an edition of Beethoven's symphonies which would be printed in such a way that the most serious mistakes would, in principle, be avoided. Sheet music is in fact printed with an unbelievable degree of carelessness. I noticed again recently when I was looking at a score. You'll find bar-lines there which are set at the same distance apart, and then you suddenly get a harp glissando in a bar. All the notes have to be written out and so the bar is much longer. Every orchestra in the world slows down when it reaches a passage like that.

From a strictly scientific point of view, of course, music notation is absurd. For every scientific system of co-ordinates is built up on the fact that when the speed and distance are covered in the same time, you begin at nought on the graph. But we begin not at the bar-line but on the first note of the bar, so that that note always comes in too late. It's a problem that may be solved some day with a new system of notation.

In one of the Beethoven symphonies there's a particular passage where the rhythm is wrongly played throughout the entire world. I didn't think it was possible and so I asked to see the part. And it was clear that the typesetter must have told his assistant that they needed nine bars at this point instead of six. The assistant did as he was told and, of course, he placed the final upbeat very close to the bar-line, as a result of which players always play it too short.

Human beings are first and foremost visual creatures and only secondarily are they acoustically influenced. Many people, including myself, close their eyes when they have to, or are able to, listen to music – they find many things disturb them if, at the same time, they have a powerful acoustic impression.

I'd now like to move on to something practical and say something about the Three Pieces for Orchestra op. 6, by Alban Berg, which were written in 1914 and which you were able to hear at yesterday's concert. Why is this music now much closer to us? Of course, one could say that it's because we've played it so often. Because there are so many imponderables to it, it's a work that involves enormous difficulties. Although they're there in the score, they often have to be fully subordinated, otherwise you can't hear the most important things. I think that where modern or contemporary music is concerned, everyone made the mistake of organizing music festivals after the war – perhaps to please the press. In Vienna, for example, ten concerts were given by the same orchestra within the space of a week. They'd scarcely enough time to absorb the music, before offering a rough and ready performance of it.

If, for example, you had a modern orchestra of average ability and asked it to sight-read the 'Eroica' Symphony, the result would be highly suspect. But this is what people have done with new music, thinking they can increase understanding of it in this way. I think that exactly the opposite has happened. I'd never have dared perform a work like that with only one or two rehearsals. In our case we normally spend a year preparing a piece. Recently, for example, we considered the character of a seventh or a ninth in the tone-rows found in Berg's orchestral pieces. How can they be played so that they strike the listener with the greatest possible aesthetic beauty? It's astonishing, but if you rehearse eight bars only from this point of view, the whole thing suddenly sounds like Mozart. The acidity has been introduced quite unnecessarily because musicians have told themselves that it sounds ghastly in any case, so that they then make no attempt to play it beautifully. I told the orchestra I was very grateful to them for their appreciation but we hadn't reached that point yet. I expect we'll continue working on this piece for six or seven years, just as we would play a divertimento by Mozart until everyone believed he was playing his own violin concerto. From the player's point of view, the creative moment really only comes when he can distance himself sufficiently from a piece not to need to look at the music any more.

I firmly believe that a lasting effort to get to know a masterpiece – whether in painting, poetry or music – wakens things that are hidden. After all, you know that, according to yogic lore, once a thought has been thought, it remains in the universe for ever. And the man who makes a real and constant effort to understand it, thinking about it and meditating, comes much closer to the heart of the matter, so that, at some stage, he'll finish up by understanding it.

I just want to tell you how thinking and feeling in music have been transformed for me. The 'Bible' for all concert-goers at that time was the *Concert-Hall Guide* by Hugo Botstiber, general secretary of the Vienna Konzerthausgesellschaft. Every symphony was explained exclusively in images, using a vocabulary that had emerged during the post-Romantic age. It was through him that people were introduced to Bruckner's works, for example, a composer who, at that time, was really having to struggle for recognition. I remember my father telling me that he had attended a performance of the Eighth Symphony by the end of which there were only thirty people left in the audience. I can still recall the concerts that Webern conducted and Alban Berg attended, when there were perhaps sixty people in the hall.

My own generation and that of my parents always thought of music in visual terms. But the path my own career has taken means that I now hear music only as music, and this is true whether I hear it performed by others or whether I conduct it myself. Of course, form – in other words, the way that something starts and is rounded off at the end – is something absolutely fundamental for me. But I couldn't associate it with any conceptual content or anything else. I believe that, unless I'm much mistaken, the youth of today has a much deeper feeling for music, otherwise how do you explain that the number of concert-goers has increased not just tenfold but probably a hundred-thousandfold? What's the reason for this genuine need? It might of course be that – if you want to draw a comparison with Jung and his archetypes – music touches on very particular basic emotional situations which affect the individual listener at his most vulnerable point and which give him, therefore, a genuine human experience. That's really the point of every art.

I remember a case from my own field of experience: I was about nineteen when Toscanini came to Vienna for the first time with La Scala, Milan. It was a long-awaited visit. We then discovered what the programme was – Donizetti's *Lucia di Lammermoor* which, for us, was a completely unknown quantity. I went off to the local library, got hold of a copy of the score and played it through with some friends. After half an hour we said: 'What can the man find in this piece? How can he inflict this barrel-organ music on us?' But within four minutes of Toscanini's starting to conduct the work, we were held as though by a magic spell. Ultimately it's a miracle – the work is transformed by the fact that a group of people or an individual is so convinced by a thing. You can see it with pictures, you can see it with statues, that people who are not at all artistic but who, at a propitious moment, can approach a work with an open mind suddenly receive a tremendous impression from a work of art, without knowing a thing about it. That, I think, is the most important thing.

After all, there are things that remain with you for a long time and others that are suddenly lost. Now you can perhaps understand the difficulty with which we have to contend. For even something that appeals to you directly has to be repeated over and over again during the two or three months you are working on a production, for example, until it becomes meaningless. In this profession there is a great deal of purely mechanical work. Everything has to be thoroughly cleaned up, so it contains no technical or audible mistakes. How much idealism is needed to prevent the inner spiritual vision from being clouded, so that, when you finally play the music, it's performed with the requisite freshness?

It's fortunate that, the further you go in life, the clearer things become, which also gives you the chance to change everything. The orchestra and I have now become one heart and soul, thanks to all the effort and love involved. I'm grateful to the orchestra for this, for it's made life worth living for me. I remember, in the past, having to fight for everything, whenever I was invited somewhere for a single guest appearance, but that's something I gave up long ago. What can you hope to achieve with an orchestra in three rehearsals? You'll never come to a mutual understanding in such a short space of time. Well, after sixteen years everything is really bearing fruit, and one knows how one does it and how the orchestra responds. It's the sense of community between *a single* partner who stands opposite you and yourself. Each respects the opinion of the other and something emerges that's possible only if there is harmony between the two of them and between them and the work of art, and if that harmony appeals to you for one brief moment. That's the finest moment *we* can have.

14
'Quality comes first'
First interview with Karajan

I first met Karajan on 27 September 1972. It was late one afternoon, a few hours before the final round of the second youth orchestra competition, which was the fourth of his competitions to be held in Berlin since 1969.

We all knew, of course, that Karajan was especially interested in medical matters, an interest due not least, perhaps, to the fact that his father had been a doctor. It occurred to me, therefore, that the Salzburg centre for research might like to see the result of some of my own investigations and so I took with me to the Savoy Hotel a copy of my dissertation on *The Male Voice Before and After Breaking*. I was curious to see the sort of reaction the subject would provoke in him and, as I had hoped, it roused his immediate interest. He promised to show the dissertation to the University and at once began to talk about himself. As a small boy he had sung in a choir in Salzburg but had had to have an operation to remove nodules from his vocal cords. When I first met him, he said nothing about the effect this had had on his way of speaking; only at a much later date did he comment on it, even going so far as to make a joke about the rasping voice we knew so well. In September 1985 I sat in on a course he was giving for young conductors at the Berlin College of Music. 'I've been croaking for more than sixty years,' was his comment on hearing a young Korean singer croaking out a melody.

Central to the discussion on this first occasion was the interrelationship between the various elements of the Herbert von Karajan Foundation, and it soon became clear that here, as in every other discipline, the conductor was keen to champion his super-élitist principle: his power and his international reputation had grown so unassailable that all of his plans were now designed to involve and improve the whole world.

LANG: The competition for conductors and the meeting of youth orchestras which ends this evening are both part of your Foundation. What do you see as your specific role at these international meetings in Berlin?

KARAJAN: I'd say the most important thing is that they take place here in Berlin. Berlin, after all, is the centre of my activities, and so my function is to get things moving and provide the organization.

LANG: People have often expressed the wish that you yourself should be on the jury.

KARAJAN: No, I think that would be wrong, since I'd then be biased. That's why I've appointed a jury which, as you know, is made up of particularly outstanding figures from the world of music whose function is to decide the matter for themselves. I've no vote on the jury.

LANG: Should there not also be some younger critics on the jury?

KARAJAN: But what do you understand by a critic in that sense?

LANG: Are there no longer any younger people today who could judge such a competition?

KARAJAN: Yes, but I think you'd then have to go much further and take in the public at large. Think of that splendid line in *Die Meistersinger*: 'Then let the folk the judges be, / With the maid, I'm certain, they'll agree.'

LANG: What connection do you see between the youth orchestras and your orchestral academy?

KARAJAN: The main connection – and it's one that has not yet really been sufficiently emphasized in public – is that all the young players are offered the opportunity to audition for the academy.

LANG: Are there also plans to form an orchestra made up of members of the academy?

KARAJAN: No, that wouldn't be in the spirit of the thing. Look, as far as the orchestral academy is concerned, the plan is to accept only highly qualified musicians – graduates from our universities or from abroad – and to accept them, moreover, regardless of race or colour of their skin. They must be able to prove that they are potentially in a position to become valuable members of the Berlin Philharmonic Orchestra. They'll then receive two years' training here, receiving musical encouragement from the principals and leaders of the different sections and also sharing all the orchestral duties with them. The aim is partly for them to listen in and partly to join in the rehearsals so that their musical personality is fashioned by the orchestra, by me and also, of course, by their teachers. It's a perennial problem, since we very rarely get potentially good players at the auditions. Generally, they're not correctly trained to play in the particular way that we play. That's the aim of the orchestral academy.

LANG: Were you involved in choosing the orchestras which came to Berlin for the competition?

KARAJAN: Only indirectly, in fact. The competition is internationally publicized and we then receive a certain number of applications. I believe everyone was accepted who wanted to come.

LANG: Children's orchestras, amateur orchestras and highly qualified music students all took part. Can a competition like that be fair?

KARAJAN: I think it was extremely fair, but let me say one thing: we're always being told that it should be done in the framework of a convention. But we've neither time nor money for that kind of mateyness – if you'll forgive the expression. Only one thing counts with us, something I shall always uphold, and that's the quality of the Berlin Philharmonic Orchestra. Everything is subordinate to that. And if I invite youth orchestras to Berlin, if I give courses for conductors or whatever else we do here, including the orchestral academy, it involves a real performance test. Anyone who doesn't want that shouldn't come here in the first place.

People have repeatedly tried to say in their somewhat discriminatory way that the Symphony Orchestra of the Moscow Tchaikovsky Conservatoire is a professional orchestra. That's simply not true. I made enquiries two years ago and again this year. There are people there who have no intention of becoming professional musicians. They study for four years and you have to admire the way they're trained. It's fabulous. The results speak for themselves. Yes, I'm all in favour of others coming who are not so good and who are confronted by the highest standards that can now be reached with youth orchestras. Only when judged by those standards will performances improve.

It's always being said during the Olympic Games that what you have there are professional sportsmen. Believe me, this professionalism is absolutely necessary. Of course, one can ask oneself whether you couldn't also do it with an amateur system. I can give you an excellent musical example of this. The Vienna Singverein was here a week ago – and I believe that those who heard it will agree with me that it's by far the best mixed choir in the entire world, whether professional or amateur. The Singverein consists entirely of professionally employed people who, in special cases, have the cost of their tram fare reimbursed because they can't afford it themselves. These people, who work late into the evening and then attend rehearsals twice a week and, if necessary, on Sundays too are pure amateurs. This, I think, settles the whole question once and for all.

LANG: One can certainly compare the Moscow orchestra with the Berlin

Top: Karajan conducts his first symphony concert in Ulm, 1932. *Above left:* Hans von Bülow, *c.* 1865, after an engraving by Weger. *Above right:* Arthur Nikisch, *c.* 1900.

Wilhelm Furtwängler with Wilhelm Kempff and Conrad Hansen performing Bach's Triple Concerto in D minor, 2 October 1940.

Herbert von Karajan during his years in Aachen, *c.* 1935.

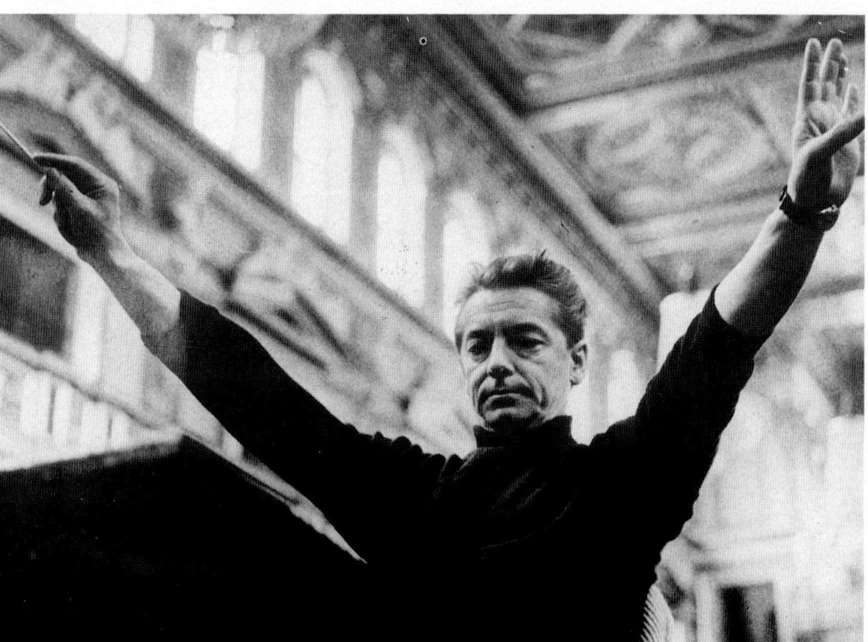

Top: Herbert von Karajan rehearsing in Berlin's Titania Palace, September 1954. *Above:* Karajan rehearsing in Vienna's Musikvereinssaal.

Joachim Tiburtius handing Karajan a replica of Berlin's Liberty Bell, 5 April 1955.

Top: Gustav and Käte Stresemann on their silver wedding anniversary with their sons Wolfgang (left) and Joachim, Wiesbaden, October 1928. *Above:* Gerhart von Westerman steps down as intendant, seen here with Joachim Tiburtius (left) and his successor, Wolfgang Stresemann, 23 October 1959.

Top: Eliette and Herbert von Karajan at the foundation-stone ceremony at the Philharmonie, 19 September 1960. *Above:* The official opening of the Berlin Philharmonie, 15 October 1963: Eliette and Herbert von Karajan with the director of the Berliner Festwochen, Nicholas Nabokov and the Mayor of West Berlin, Heinrich Albertz.

Karajan with the architect Hans Scharoun and (right) the sculptor Bernhard Heiliger with his sculpture 'Upbeat', 1963

Student Orchestra. But how do you explain the fact that our university orchestra came last?

KARAJAN: That's the jury's decision. I don't think there's any reason to criticize it. If others are better, they should come first.

LANG: Do you blame the system of education in Germany and, specifically, in West Berlin?

KARAJAN: There you've put your finger on a question which is becoming more and more of a burning issue. Training – and, above all, basic training in music – is really very bad. I've even seen it for myself in the way my own daughter's education has developed . . . I'm now trying to get together an international committee – it can only be done on a world scale – and getting them interested in some way – using the mass media – in children's basic education. Children must be taught in such a way that no damage can be done at a later date. For what's done badly at the beginning can never be put right later. We can see, in fact, that what we're dealing with are not so much musical problems as basic principles concerning length, shortness, tempo and keeping in time. It's this sort of thing that isn't properly brought home to children at the beginning and which has devastating consequences at a later stage.

LANG: Can you tell me something about the relationship between supply and demand in the Berlin Philharmonic Orchestra. How many vacancies are there?

KARAJAN: You see, that's the real reason why this orchestral academy has been set up. We get, say, fifteen or sixteen applicants for an audition, and, time and again, it's happened that we've had a completely negative result. Sometimes the candidate showed a certain ability on his instrument. But the musical nature of the interpretation was simply not of the standard we need. But, moving on to another subject: I've been reproached in recent days for having found too little time for the youth orchestras. But please remember that, during this one week, I've not only conducted three concerts but been working six hours a day, every day, with my orchestra. And there was also the organization for this new orchestral academy. I think that was quite enough. But my rehearsals with the Philharmonic were open to all the orchestras and, I have to say, practically no one came. I don't think it's up to me to go running after people. Don't forget that I cycled all the way from Salzburg to Bayreuth in order to hear Toscanini rehearsing. And here it's only five minutes on foot or by car to the Philharmonie. The fact that the participants didn't bother seems to me to show a certain lack of interest on their part. There were a lot there today because it was the final concert; yesterday there were perhaps twenty-five or thirty. Of course, I immediately took the opportunity to speak to them. We discussed particular problems of orchestral technique and I asked if anyone was there from the Washington Youth Orchestra. I was told that no one was. So they'd nothing else to do.

LANG: Do you see any other opportunities for musical collaboration – apart from forming the 'International Youth Orchestra'? What about an exchange of conductors or music groups, for example?

KARAJAN: Yes, we're currently trying to establish whether, at the next competition, we could perhaps form two large orchestras out of the ten orchestras that take part. The individual conductors accompanying them, and perhaps others, too, who would in any case be under my supervision, would then have the chance to spend, say, two days working with them. We could then see whether they'd not just been well drilled but how far someone, as conductor and teacher, could impose his ideas on an orchestra in a relatively short space of time.

That's our next job and I believe it really has to be done differently. We'll probably have to find another time of year, since there's simply too much going on during the Festival in September. It should take place at a quieter period. A preliminary selection of conductors would have to be made which, in that sense, would not yet involve the jury. But they'd then see how the individual conductors worked with these orchestras. It would then be a competition both for the orchestras and for the conductors. I expect this will be what happens two years from now.

LANG: What practical results have the competitions achieved so far in Berlin?

KARAJAN: First, there's the human contact that one has with the contestants, especially at the competition for conductors. That's one of the finest things one can experience. I keep in touch with these people and meet them all over the world. They come and see me and we then talk about their careers. Many of them attend my rehearsals or recordings on a regular basis, and the contact continues. From a purely practical standpoint, however, a very great deal has in fact happened. The first prizewinner, Okko Kamu, began his career somewhat over-hastily, but it's now been channelled in the right direction. I've personally assumed responsibility for the career of Gabriel Chmura, who won last year, since I was afraid he'd be exploited by agents and that he'd burn himself out. He's preparing himself very slowly and gives approximately one concert a month. He spends the rest of his time here, studying with me, and it's really looking very promising. Things naturally need a certain time. Take the case of Dmitri Kitaienko, who won second prize here at our first competition: I wrote a letter to the minister, Mrs Furzeva, saying: 'You have a colossal talent that has revealed itself here; give him the work that suits his gifts.' What they offered him was not the Bolshoi but Moscow's second opera house, but even that is a tremendous challenge for a young person. He's continued to develop and has now made it right to the top as a really good conductor. Basically, then, there are now about ten people who owe their appointments all over the world solely and exclusively to the competitions. I think that's good. It will go on, since I, in particular, am of the opinion that the more talented people you produce who can pit themselves against one another in the most demanding competition, the more they'll encourage each other in what they achieve.

LANG: We saw once again with these youth orchestras that more than 50 per cent of the contestants were women. Isn't it rather sad for them to see that there's not a single woman in the Berlin Philharmonic – perhaps the most outstanding orchestra in the world?

KARAJAN: Why would you say it's sad?

LANG: Do women stand any chance of being accepted by the Berlin Philharmonic?

KARAJAN: If they're better than the men, they stand an enormously good chance. We've left it open at every audition. It doesn't matter to us in the least whether it's a man or a woman. They only have to be better, otherwise it's pointless. No one can sit there simply as an ornament. That's not why we're here.

LANG: What do you think of the idea of holding auditions behind a curtain?

KARAJAN: It's often been tried, but we've come to the conclusion that it's better without a curtain. You know that all the members of the orchestra are present at auditions. They attach great importance to getting to know the sort of person they'll be working with over the years, so that, quite apart from the purely musical aspect, there's also the character of the person involved which has to be taken into account. As you know, we do a lot of touring. And, when we're touring, what's essential is not just the musical quality but also the sort of person he is. Don't forget that it's really one big family. An alien presence is extremely harmful since it can undermine the whole sense of morale. This orchestra has an absolutely instinctive ability to say that such and such a person would make a good colleague, while another one wouldn't. That's really the main reason why the auditions are as they are – so that one can see what the other person is feeling when he plays. With a curtain that's not possible, otherwise you'd then have to go on to ask why concerts weren't given behind a curtain. It would be exactly the same.

15

As others see him

Karajan at sixty-five

Since Salzburg had marked Karajan's sixtieth birthday by making him a freeman of the town, Berlin resolved to follow suit and offered him the keys to the city on the occasion of his sixty-fifth birthday.

At an age when most men think of retiring, Karajan showed no sign of letting up: his pension could clearly wait. But in founding the Salzburg Whitsun Festival, he had mapped out his final field of conquest, circumscribing the confines of a world to which he remained firmly bound through the remaining sixteen years of his life.

His imminent birthday provided the opportunity for a thorough reappraisal. This time, however, it would not be Karajan whom I interviewed but those who had known him over the years and been his constant colleagues. I chose the five-week period from early December 1972 to early January 1973 to speak to a number of leading musicians and other figures active in the musical world, in order to paint a composite portrait of the conductor.

Of the people I interviewed, Böhm was an obvious candidate and yet I hesitated for a long time before asking him questions about his fellow countryman. In the end I used the old trick of first discussing conducting, composing and even the way that batons were made. Finally he fell into the trap and I started to ask about Karajan until, emboldened by the directness of my approach, I felt the need to apologize. 'You've an honest face,' was Böhm's reply. Were his answers all so honest, I wondered . . .

'Let's be happy that we have both'

LANG: Professor Böhm, you and Herbert von Karajan were both born in Austria. When did the two of you first meet?

BÖHM: I think . . . yes, I know exactly when it was. It was a rather dramatic moment when Herbert von Karajan, my colleague Herr Karajan, called on me, here at the State Opera, where I was conducting a concert. I can remember exactly what happened. The final piece was Brahms's Second Symphony and I had to stop the performance during the second movement, right at the point where the tempo changes to 12/8 and the clarinets enter, since one of the most terrible air raids was going on outside. I believe the imperial palace and the whole of the inner city were destroyed in that particular raid. We were with the Philharmonic in the State Opera foyer, but luckily, the building was untouched. I'd only three hours before the concert was repeated in the afternoon. I couldn't get anything to eat – I'd been staying at the Adlon Hotel – and so I had to conduct this concert and had virtually got to the end of Brahms's Second. To my astonishment almost the whole of the audience stayed. During the concert things were going on all round me, it was like a circus. Then my colleague, Herr Karajan, came up to me and said: 'It's all right for you in Vienna. In Berlin we've been having these air raids for weeks.' That was my first meeting with him.

LANG: Have you attended opera performances or concerts conducted by Herbert von Karajan?

BÖHM: Yes, often, of course.

LANG: Do you see yourself as another generation? After all, you're fourteen years older.

BÖHM: What do you expect me to say? There's an old proverb: 'You're only as old as you feel.' If you look at my diary and see what I can still manage to do today and what I've been managing to do during the last few years ... I've just got back from Paris, where I conducted ten performances of *Die Frau ohne Schatten.* I then went straight into rehearsals for *Così fan tutte* and conducted six performances of that. I'll then be flying to Vienna to conduct a new *Salome* with Frau Rysanek, then on to Rome, where I'll conduct six concerts, I then fly directly from Rome to New York, from New York back to Berlin for just one concert, and so on, and so forth. All I'm trying to say is: 'Why should I draw a distinction?' Herr Karajan doesn't work quite as much as that but, on the other hand, he makes a lot more records than I do. But I think we're at least level pegging when it comes to the way we work.

LANG: How would you describe the difference between your interpretations?

BÖHM: Look, I can't start criticizing a colleague. That I hear many, many things differently from my colleague or interpret them differently is something I've every right to do. I remember, on my seventy-fifth birthday, someone asked a similar question to the one that you've just asked. On that occasion I said: 'Fortunately all men don't throw themselves at the same woman; that would be terrible.' And it's the same with music. Some people prefer one interpretation, others prefer a different one. The way I put it was: 'One person prefers that nose, while another person prefers this nose.' I'm often asked whether I prefer Beethoven or Mozart. My only answer to that is: 'Let's be happy that we have both.' And I'd like to say the same about Herr Karajan.

LANG: Did Herr von Karajan see your *Figaro* in Salzburg?

BÖHM: I really don't know, we never spoke about it. I assume he was there, at least for some of the rehearsals.

LANG: Your *Figaro* was the finest there's ever been in Salzburg. Why did there have to be a new one?

BÖHM: That's something you'll have to ask the directors of the Salzburg Festival, not me. It wasn't I who arranged it.

LANG: Have you seen the new *Figaro* in Salzburg?

BÖHM: No, there was no way I could see it. Last year I was conducting *Wozzeck* and during the run I had to go to Munich twice, I was also conducting seven performances of *Così fan tutte* and two concerts. It simply wasn't possible. But the *Figaro* is being repeated at this year's Festival and I'll definitely see the production then. However, I'm sure I'll be less surprised by Herr Karajan's tempi than I will be by the production.

LANG: What sort of contact do you have now with Herbert von Karajan? Do you meet regularly or only by chance?

BÖHM: Not regularly, but I always call on him, since he was, after all, born in Salzburg and more or less lives there. We're on friendly terms.

LANG: What do you wish Herbert von Karajan on his sixty-fifth birthday?

BÖHM: That he can continue to conduct for as long as I have.

'Music is music'

I was able to go into greater detail with Wolfgang Stresemann, who, at the time I spoke to him, had been intendant in Berlin for thirteen years. Throughout that time he had worked for the good of the Philharmonic concerts and remained on the best of terms with his chief conductor.

LANG: From time to time, people attending Philharmonic concerts are bound to ask themselves how this combination of conductors, soloists and programming comes about. What part do you have to play as intendant and how does Herr von Karajan influence the scene as chief conductor of the Berlin Philharmonic Orchestra?

STRESEMANN: Well, things are relatively simple. Herr von Karajan generally informs me, in the course of a season, which works he would like to conduct or, let's say, which works should be reserved for him. That's done as a matter of course. These programmes are then fixed in detail, and, where relevant, soloists and chorus are engaged. It's then my job to co-ordinate the programmes of the other conductors with Karajan's programmes. Of course, we try to ensure that a major work such as a Brahms or Beethoven symphony turns up only once in the course of the same season. Then we have to see that the overall programme contains those central historical works which we can never forgo, not least in the interests of the younger generation. And it's also important to ensure that a number of contemporary works appear, and that they're taken up into the programme both by Herr von Karajan and by our guest conductors.

I make it my business to find out exactly how the orchestra reacts to a guest conductor. It's certainly not the case that every conductor fits in with our orchestra, which of course has its own personality. I know one or two conductors who've never hit it off here, even though they've been brilliantly successful elsewhere. That says nothing for or against either the conductor or the orchestra. When a guest conductor works with an orchestra, it's like a brief marriage. You may not have enough time to get to know one another. That's why guest conducting is always so problematical. But it may also be that the personality of the orchestra is such that it does not blend with the conductor and the result is that one prefers to choose other conductors who can work better with the orchestra.

LANG: What were the functions and duties that Herbert von Karajan took over as chief conductor of the Berlin Philharmonic Orchestra? Is there a fixed number of concerts that he has to conduct?

STRESEMANN: There is, of course, a contract which Herr von Karajan signed when he became Resident Conductor of the Berlin Philharmonic Orchestra, to quote his official title. It was said then that he would conduct six concerts in Berlin and also take charge of the orchestra when it went on tour, which would involve some twenty additional concerts. This contract still exists. However, over the years Herr von Karajan has taken over many more concerts, both here in Berlin, where he's conducting twenty-five concerts this season, and on tour, now that the orchestra's touring more often.

The ties between Karajan and the Berlin Philharmonic have grown closer over the last five years. From now on our orchestra will be conducted exclusively by Herr von Karajan when it's performing away from Berlin. We're particularly pleased at this, since under Herr von Karajan this orchestra gives of its very best and, of course, we want to show people, especially people outside Berlin, what the orchestra's ultimately capable of achieving.

LANG: Does Herr von Karajan have a deciding vote when it comes to filling an orchestral vacancy?

STRESEMANN: What happens here is that anyone wanting to join the orchestra has to play in front of the entire orchestra. It's certainly a very tense situation when a young man shows off his abilities to the Berlin Philharmonic Orchestra. Herr von Karajan is always there, above all when it's a question of filling important solo positions in the orchestra.

LANG: How often do such auditions take place?

STRESEMANN: It depends on how often we need someone. But Herr von Karajan has, in any event, a right of veto. He can say to the orchestra, for example: 'Although you may like this horn player or oboist or clarinettist or bassoonist or violinist very much, I find that he doesn't fit in with me and my views, I'd prefer someone else.' He has this right of veto; it's in his contract. But what's the point of appealing to one's rights in trying to get something done? That's never good policy.

LANG: Are there any festivities at any time of the year when Herr von Karajan celebrates with the players?

STRESEMANN: From time to time there are receptions and also official welcomes for other orchestras that come to Berlin. Herr von Karajan also attends these occasions. But, you know, celebrations are formal affairs. It's not a matter of the orchestra saying twice a year: 'Let's organize a real party and have a drink with Karajan.' Our celebrations are our concerts and – I don't know – there simply isn't anything finer. The idea that you have to lay on some vast celebration afterwards is one, I think, that appeals neither to the orchestra nor to Herr von Karajan.

On a smaller scale, Herr von Karajan may, for example, invite a few of the players to St Moritz, where there's more of a private atmosphere. I'm told that he often spends time with members of the orchestra there, showing them the beauties of nature and his house, and getting to know them better. But don't forget that we've 120 players. An official get-together doesn't mean that all 120 members suddenly start to rub shoulders with Herr von Karajan. Contact is forged through rehearsals and concerts, which I'm sure is the best way.

LANG: Is it important for a chief conductor to know his musicians' private problems?

STRESEMANN: He doesn't have to know them all. Certainly he can't act as a sort of father confessor or go around massaging people's egos on a grand scale. Everyone has problems, but sometimes the individual player may have difficulties that affect what he does in the orchestra. And in several cases Herr von Karajan has attempted, with considerable success, to solve these problems with the musician concerned, including physical problems. Physically, musicians are much more prone to illness than other people, and Herr von Karajan – who has always been very interested in medical matters – has been able to offer several musicians positive help.

LANG: You've often accompanied Herr von Karajan on concert tours at home and abroad. Can you think of any incident that sheds light on the human relationship between the members of the Philharmonic and their chief conductor?

STRESEMANN: It's always wonderful to see Karajan saying goodbye to his orchestra after a tour. What I particularly liked was his word of thanks – I think it was after an American tour – when he said: 'You see, we've now grown so close to one another that I'd like to describe you as an extension of my own arm. One consequence of this is that if anything goes wrong, then it's me who's to blame, not you.' I thought that was a very nice thing for him to say: we were all touched by it. It's also an example of the real Karajan, who sometimes seems rather distant from the outside but who, deep inside him, feels a great love, and that is his love of the Berlin Philharmonic.

LANG: What is it that makes Herr von Karajan so exceptional a conductor when he appears before his orchestra?

STRESEMANN: I wish I could say. Wherein lies the magic of a personality? All we can do is say that it's there. But why is it so? It's like asking why a mountain looks so wonderful, why the weather's so fine, why an actor has true greatness. It's the secret of the personality and it remains a secret. As Goethe said: 'Personality is the greatest happiness of the children of this earth.' Of course, it's the result of a happy chance. But why it should be so is beyond our analytical powers. We can't analyse why it is that, when Herr Karajan takes his place in front of the orchestra, the orchestra, even before it has struck a single note, is already playing half a class better, so to speak, than it would under most other conductors. There's something mysterious, mystical, astonishing about it which defies logical explanation – and thank God that it does is all I can say!

LANG: How could one characterize his interpretations? In what are they typically Karajanesque?

STRESEMANN: What a terrible word! It's one I don't care for at all. It really is most unfortunate to brand people in that way – whether they're conductors, actors or whatever – and to say that they're somehow typical. But Karajan, as we all know, is regarded as a sound merchant. He has, of course, a wonderful ear for beautiful sound. But that's something which others have had and still do. As you know, he closes his eyes – not as a pose but because, as he rightly says, his ears are particularly responsive when he closes his eyes to conduct. Karajanesque? Yes, it's said that everything's bathed in a golden sound. But that's not right. Of course, he produces the most glorious sounds that an orchestra is capable of producing. But it's not just a question of sound. What about when he conducts a fast movement by Bruckner or Beethoven? It's then a question of rhythm, temperament and real dynamics. And all these qualities are present in his conducting. Or take the Adagio from Bruckner's Eighth, where he shows a great, deep inwardness, more beautiful than anything you could ever imagine. Of course it all sounds good, but that's really only a precondition. You can't say there's something specifically Karajanesque. Perhaps he has a particular affinity with composers like Richard Strauss but, when all's said and done, he lived at the same time as Strauss. But he also conducts Brahms, Bruckner, Beethoven and Mozart: it would be wrong to say that, because of his affinity with Strauss, he can't achieve equally brilliant results with other works. He's not simply a phenomenal conductor, a quite outstanding personality, he's also, of course, a great musician, otherwise it wouldn't be possible to get to the top and to stay there.

LANG: On the wall here above us are two portraits of Wilhelm Furtwängler and Herbert von Karajan, hanging peacefully side by side. How would you describe the essential difference between these two chief conductors?

STRESEMANN: Well, of course, I heard Furtwängler in my youth. But I was very much younger then and, although I was aware of Furtwängler's greatness – which no one would deny – I never really understood it. It's very difficult to sketch out the difference in any greater detail. Like many of his contemporaries – and this is true of Bruno Walter and others – Furtwängler set out from what lay behind the music. He was particularly concerned with the emotional structure that sounded forth from this music. More than anything else, his aim was to understand and reproduce what, in Furtwängler's view, had motivated the composer to write the piece, in other words, his – the composer's – inner experience when composing such a work.

At risk of exaggeration, I think Karajan would say: 'Music is music. Full stop.' But Furtwängler, too, reproduced what he found in the score, above all in more modern music. And a conductor like Karajan must, of course, consider the question where this music comes from. He's going to write a book on the subject – he's already said so in public – and explain who his two great models were, or from which two conductors he's learned the most. All right, one of them was Toscanini, but the other one was Furtwängler – so you can't say that Furtwängler was completely different, and that Karajan has absolutely nothing in common with him. But this is equally true of composers, of course. Each of them starts out from the point where the other one left off and, ultimately, it's a historical development. It rarely happens that someone composes or interprets music in a completely different way. So it's very difficult and even dangerous, in fact, to speak of vast differences. They've never been as big as that.

LANG: What sort of relations does Herr von Karajan have with the press? Does he read what's written about him?

STRESEMANN: How could he? Where would he find the time? No, he doesn't. He says there's no point. He's convinced that the press has very interesting things to say, but that if he were to follow up all their suggestions for what he should or should not do, it'd simply be confusing. You know, this man – it's as true of him as it is of every great man: 'Here I stand, I can do no other.' He has to conduct and interpret works in the way that he does. If he were to start studying every press cutting after every concert – and don't forget how many concerts he gives away from Berlin, each of which is reviewed in detail – well, even if he *were* to read them all, what would it achieve? In the final analysis, a man who, let's face it, is not the youngest of men must know for himself what he wants. And Herr von Karajan has known for a long time what he wants.

LANG: Why have concerts become so short?

STRESEMANN: Like every man of genius, Karajan, too, is sometimes ahead of his time – as he also is in the field of technology, including the way music is shown on television. And so all his concerts have become somewhat shorter. If a concert starting at eight isn't over by ten, people start to get restless. That wasn't the case earlier. Karajan felt quite clearly that people no longer want these long programmes. Perhaps he's gone a bit too far, though we shouldn't always judge in terms of minutes. If you give two great works – and even if they both last only thirty minutes – the audience will be well satisfied, so that an overture would be no more than an apology. To take an example: Honegger's *Symphonie liturgique* and Beethoven's Seventh Symphony – a famous Karajan programme – last sixty-four minutes in all. From the usual standpoint, that's too little. And yet it's a perfectly satisfactory programme. Why do you want more than two such powerful works? Can you absorb any more? Karajan is more and more inclined to include two great works in a programme, contrasting them and separating them by an interval. But there has to be some inner relationship between them.

LANG: What do you wish Herbert von Karajan on his sixty-fifth birthday?

STRESEMANN: That he remains as young and as active as he has been till now. And that he continues to derive as much pleasure from working with the Berlin Philharmonic as he has till now. And that people don't talk such dreadful rubbish about a birthday which, for a man as energetic and youthful as Herr von Karajan, really has only a rhetorical significance.

LANG: Herr von Karajan is very sad that he can't come to Berlin in his private jet.

STRESEMANN: Yes, that reminds me: there's one particular wish I have for his birthday, though it's somewhat political in character, and that is that he may very soon be allowed to fly into Berlin with his aeroplane.

LANG: Is there any chance of that?

STRESEMANN: Not at present. It's in the hands of the Allies and, as you know, no one's been allowed to fly into Berlin privately until now. But it's very much my wish that, in the wake of détente and peaceful developments, he may be allowed to land his private plane at Tempelhof or Tegel. He's always on the move and lands in Belgrade, London, Paris and wherever he can. He's passionately fond of flying, it's an extraordinary form of relaxation for him. In America, too, when he's been on tour, he's often flown in a plane which he himself has chartered. He's taken members of the orchestra with him, I even flew with him myself on one occasion. It's a marvellous feeling. Afterwards he's in the most wonderful mood, he gets endless pleasure from being up in the air. He's right, you know, when he says that it's too dangerous for him on the ground – he used to be a famous car driver.

LANG: Does he have a co-pilot?

STRESEMANN: Yes, of course. But it's he who flies, and the co-pilot sits next to him. He's particularly fond of his co-pilot since he knows it's he who's really the great expert, whereas he himself is not much better than a schoolboy. But over the years he's acquired sufficient mastery for us to feel proud of his achievements. This machine flies very very fast and at the same height as other jets.

LANG: What chance is there then of Herr von Karajan being able to fly here to Berlin? How can it be arranged?

STRESEMANN: It's all bound up with the flight situation in Berlin, which is really very complicated. The Allies would have to give special permission, which would then, of course, have to be given to others too. It's not possible at the moment. Karajan tried to get something done through our mutual friend Nicolas Nabokov, who has good relations with the Russians. But he's had no success so far.

'The most versatile of conductors'

I reserved the most obvious questions for Michel Schwalbé, the leader of the BPO. The lively Pole had lived in Berlin since 1957 and taught at the city's College of Music. For almost thirty years he was one of Karajan's staunchest supporters, retiring in 1986, when his services were recognized by the Order of the Federal Republic of Germany and by a gold watch from the maestro:

LANG: You've been leader of the Berlin Philharmonic for sixteen years. What was it like when Herr von Karajan said, 'I want him and nobody else'?

SCHWALBÉ: In fact, I'd already known Herr von Karajan for many years before I came to Berlin. I first got to know him in 1947, soon after the war, when he returned to the concert platform at the Lucerne Festival, appearing alongside Furtwängler. It was a great, sensational launch.

From the very beginning my contacts with him were excellent, so that it was really *he* who had known *me* all these years, before appointing me here in Berlin.

LANG: Was there an audition?

SCHWALBÉ: Yes, I couldn't get out of that, since it's a tradition with the Berlin Philharmonic that every new member has to audition, to say nothing of the leaders.

LANG: There was then a one-year probationary contract. What happened during that time?

SCHWALBÉ: No, there was no probationary year. I was invited to the audition, which Herr von Karajan and virtually the whole orchestra attended. I had to play the first movement of the Brahms concerto and also Paganini's Twenty-fourth Caprice. I still remember playing the infamous pizzicato passage in the Paganini particularly fast and, instead of using my bow and left hand, I played it with both hands and without a bow. When I'd finished the variation, I suddenly heard someone laughing. I turned round and saw Herr von Karajan with his arms raised heavenward. He said: 'What more do you want? Enough, enough. Don't go on.' I thought at first that they hadn't liked it. But it soon became clear that they were all very enthusiastic. As you can imagine, it made me very happy. As far as a 'probationary year' is concerned, I should perhaps add that – in spite of the quality of the Berlin Philharmonic and my excellent relationship with Herr von Karajan and the admiration I felt for him – I had great difficulty making up my mind to leave Geneva, where I had the most senior professorship in the town and, indeed, in the whole of Switzerland. I had six professors under me and was in charge of the concert-training course, which Joseph Szigeti used to run a long time before me. Well, lots of letters passed between me and the then intendant, Dr Westerman, with Herr Karajan begging him to do everything he could to get me here. In the end I decided to leave Geneva and come to Berlin.

LANG: Is it essentially the case that you play with the Philharmonic only when Karajan is conducting?

SCHWALBÉ: That's the basis of our arrangement. But I was always happy to allow the other leaders, Thomas Brandis and Leon Spierer, a chance to lead the orchestra when Herr Karajan was conducting. And I also enjoy playing the odd concert conducted by old friends such as Zubin Mehta.

LANG: You've played under a lot of different conductors. What would you say is so exceptional about Herr von Karajan?

SCHWALBÉ: That's a complex question. In my view he's the most versatile of conductors, with an absolutely compelling sense of clarity and a brilliance I've certainly never encountered on any previous occasion in my life.

LANG: Is there anything special about his conducting technique?

SCHWALBÉ: Yes, I've never met a conductor who's so sparing in his gestures. I remember once taking part in a course he was giving for conductors, with a tiny orchestra. He was very pleased with what I was doing, but he interrupted me, saying: 'Why are you giving such clear entries?' At first I was extremely surprised by the question, because I thought that's how it should be: it was right, I believed, to help the orchestra. But he said: 'It's all very nice. But you'll spoil people by giving them such clear instructions. What will happen at the concert in the evening, if you don't repeat a certain passage precisely the way the players expect it? Believe me, it's much better that you leave them in some uncertainty and train them to listen to each other.' That's basically very, very sensible and speaks for his immense experience. You understand? He forces the different sections to perform a piece as though in a chamber orchestra, in other words, as though it were chamber music, and to get used to that approach. That's extremely important, because it doesn't work to have everyone sitting there as though hypnotized by the baton and unable to play unless there's someone visibly beating time. There should be both: the ability to listen to one another and the willingness to be led by a conductor of genius.

LANG: When you rehearse a new work with your chief conductor, do you also discuss the piece from an analytical point of view?

SCHWALBÉ: Yes, we have done, for example, with new works by Alban Berg or Schoenberg, where it's only natural that Herr von Karajan should offer us some words of explanation. But that wasn't the case with Richard Strauss's *Sinfonia domestica* which we're playing tomorrow and the day after. It's not exactly a new work for us, and the precondition for any expert – and, God knows, the orchestra is made up of a selection of the finest musicians in Germany and beyond – is naturally that he should know the history of music. Well, we all know more or less how the *Sinfonia domestica* came to be written, so it needs no more than a few words of explanation. You know, Herr von Karajan is extremely economical with his time, with us, and unlike so many other conductors, he's never boring. That's something else that sets him apart. It's always exciting being with him, so exciting, indeed, that for the next one or two weeks you're virtually incapable of doing anything else.

LANG: How would you describe the difference between the Mozart interpretations of Karl Böhm and Herbert von Karajan?

SCHWALBÉ: Ouch, that's a difficult one. Of course, everyone has his own idea of how something should be interpreted, especially the tempi. Karl Böhm is an old opera conductor – an old hand, as they say, an old expert with immense experience. He gives such a paternalistic impression and often prefers broad tempi, perhaps a little too broad in a rather more expressive, Romantic way. Of course, many people like that, people who are, perhaps, slower-thinking. My God, most of them aren't what you'd call quick or lively. But to come back to our chief: you know, one thing that sets him apart from others is the fact that he doesn't make life easy for himself, in anything. He has an extremely pure, Classical outlook, with brisk tempi, and never allows himself to be misled into driving the players too hard or indulging in ritardandi. Everything is very concise, which tends to strike many people as too fast. One person sees it like that, the next person sees it differently. If everyone were to do the same, the world would be a very boring place.

LANG: How much work does Herbert von Karajan put into a concert in relation to the rehearsals?

SCHWALBÉ: It's a completely different type of work. At the rehearsals – apart from the final one – the emotional side is generally excluded. Only his intellect is at work then, together with his instinct, and his ears, of course, and his memory: in other words, the human machine. Needless to say, his psyche is also involved. He has a fantastic idea of colours, for example. You can see a wonderful example of this with the French Impressionists, but also with Wagner's operas. That's my opinion and that of all my colleagues, and one which we've often discussed among ourselves.

He's his own boss at the Wagner performances at the Salzburg Easter Festival – a unique figure, almost imperial. It's really fantastic. He knows every last detail, and not only in the orchestra; he knows every entry on stage, every word, how and what people have to do. It's absolutely great. But, to come back to your question about his rehearsals. He rehearses better and more than almost anybody else.

He notices the tiniest, briefest detail with electronic speed – nothing escapes him, whether to the left or the right, in front of him or behind him. It's as though he could see in every direction at once. And at the evening's performance, the emotion is automatically switched on, of course; he's no longer self-conscious but simply launches into it. But it's like that with every conductor and soloist.

LANG: Is it different with gramophone recordings?

SCHWALBÉ: Yes, there's no doubt about that. Any soloist who's involved in a recording is somehow obsessed by the presence of the microphone. The microphone is something inexorable, whereas an audience is made up of human beings. That's something we can feel. You can say the same about broadcasting in the age of airwaves. You can't see anything in the air, but you can hear it on a small radio. In other words, these waves exist. In the case of television, you can even see something. In exactly the same way, I believe, waves exist between people. Psychiatrists are increasingly interested in this dimension, which is still little known. I myself am firmly convinced that there's something like a transmitter and a receiver in every human soul.

The audience – in other words, the presence of so many people together – creates an atmosphere which a recording studio can never offer. And so, basically, it's very dificult for any artist – to say nothing of a conductor who is, after all, ultimately dependent on his entire orchestra – to abstract himself from all that and to work himself up into the right emotional state. I often took part in recordings, including ones of the Beethoven and Brahms symphonies and Wagner's *Ring*, where, after detailed rehearsals, we finally moved on to the actual takes and I then found Herr von Karajan to be often very, very emotionally involved.

LANG: But wouldn't it be better to make live recordings instead of ones that are studio-based?

SCHWALBÉ: Of course – as, indeed, has already been done. But all sorts of minor things happen at these concerts which you can't then put right and which it would be wrong to immortalize. For the acoustics wouldn't be the same if you were to try to make corrections in the same hall without an audience.

LANG: You and the Berlin Philharmonic Orchestra now go to Salzburg not only at Easter but also at Whitsuntide. Are you happy that the Berlin press and the Berlin public are against it?

SCHWALBÉ: It's good of you to give me the chance to say something on the subject. I've enough courage to stand up for my beliefs. When I've had my say, you can shoot me, or crucify me, I don't mind which. But I'll be spending a few more years in Berlin and would like to state my views. Let me begin with a small comparison based on names: Berlin Philharmonic – Vienna Philharmonic. I'm sure you know that the Vienna Philharmonic even has a street in Vienna named after it. Far more important, however, is the whole conduct and relationship of the audience and the authorities to the Vienna Philharmonic. A member of the Vienna Philharmonic is treated as a real *persona grata*, he receives assistance and is always made to feel welcome in shops, restaurants, ministries and so on. In Berlin, by contrast, there's nothing but envy towards the Berlin Philharmonic – as I've discovered from audiences and others alike. There's often a sense of admiration as well: 'My God, you're wonderful!' But also: 'My God, you're lucky to be able to travel around so much and see the world. You must be well off!' That sort of envy leaves an unpleasant taste in my mouth. What do they mean when they say 'a lot of money'?

There are people – businessmen, doctors and so on – who earn a lot, lot more. If the Berlin players get a couple of thousand marks a month, so what? After all, they have to have a very high standard of living, and basically no amount of money can ever make up for the sort of work they have to do. It's extremely difficult work and the travelling conditions often involve them in a degree of strain of which the general public has no idea. If the man in the street was asked to put up with that sort of thing, he'd refuse point-blank.

We've just got back from London, where we played two Beethoven symphonies – the Fourth and Fifth – to mark Britain's entry into the Common Market, the so-called 'Fanfare for Europe'. It was at the Royal Albert Hall in front of around 8000 people. There were perhaps one or two thousand young people between sixteen and eighteen years old standing in the arena, immediately in front of the orchestra, packed together like sardines in a tin. They gave us an unforgettable welcome. They roared their enthusiasm – it was as if a revolution was about to break out. It put the whole orchestra, including Herr von Karajan, in such a festive frame of mind that we played magnificently for them.

It's a shame that more isn't done to encourage young people here in Berlin. I'm thinking, for example, of the famous televised concerts with Leonard Bernstein. He'd go over to the piano, play a number of themes to show what they meant and then get the orchestra to play them.

LANG: Would Herr von Karajan be prepared to do that sort of thing?

SCHWALBÉ: I don't know, but you could always ask him. He's extremely interested in young people and in the future. He's not a bit as people imagine. There are many young people and others who are simply ignorant who've no idea what his aims are. His interests are extremely varied. I'm sure you could put that question to him without difficulty. You ought to ask him yourself.

LANG: What have been your finest memories of the many years you've worked together with Herbert von Karajan?

SCHWALBÉ: Do you know, there are so many that it's difficult to know where to begin. We had fantastic times in Lucerne, Salzburg, London, Paris and Japan. But I remember two stories in particular which concentrate rather more on my personal dealings with Herr von Karajan.

I'm thinking of the time when Herr von Karajan had great problems with the Vienna Opera. I don't know if it was simply a question of power. At all events, he had plans for performances which, rehearsed to the highest standards, would be repeated with the same singers in Milan, Berlin and London. There was a great deal of local resistance to the idea, perhaps because they were afraid of such high standards, I don't know. At any rate, it was a difficult time for Herr von Karajan. He came in for the most extreme criticism in Vienna, and there was certainly a great deal of envy involved.

It was at precisely this time that we were invited to play at the Festwochen in Vienna. I still remember that, in addition to a number of Brahms symphonies, I also had to play the great violin solo in Richard Strauss's *Heldenleben.* I put everything into it that I could, because I wanted Karajan to have the greatest possible success in Vienna. He, too, gave it everything he had and was completely exhausted at the end.

After one such concert I went to his dressing-room and found that he, too, was bathed in sweat. We were both still caught up in the heat of the battle. I said to him, 'Herr von Karajan, I'm so glad you've had such a fantastic success in this city just now.' He took me in his arms there and then and thanked me very, very warmly for my help. That was one particular high-point.

The other happened on our trip to Russia. You'll recall from reports in the Berlin press that initially there were certain difficulties over what to call the orchestra. We were described as 'A Symphony Orchestra', and underneath, in tiny letters, were the words, 'From West Berlin'.

LANG: And you were annoyed at that.

SCHWALBÉ: Of course we were. In itself, it was remarkable that we'd been invited at all. But when we arrived and saw these difficulties, we were determined, in spite of everything, to give of our best. Even in the hall itself we felt a great coolness towards us, but also a great sense of expectation. Although we'd not discussed it in advance, we'd all made it our watchword to give the very best we could. I still remember playing like a man possessed, and it's a complete miracle I didn't have a coronary. Although the first concert involved only Beethoven symphonies, I was asked to act as joint-leader. Then, at the second or third concert, we played a symphony by Shostakovich. He was there in the hall and at the end came up on to the platform and embraced Karajan and me. He was almost in tears, he was completely beside himself and said that never before had he heard an interpretation of his symphony like it.

We then played Strauss's famous *Heldenleben* and I think I played better than I'd ever done before, so that I could almost see tears of emotion in the eyes of many of my colleagues. Afterwards, at a reception arranged by the German ambassador, I felt just as Fritz Walter must have felt when he led the German football team to victory in the World Cup. That just about sums up what I was feeling, and I still remember Karajan leading me back on to the platform on my own. The audience was extraordinarily enthusiastic at this fantastic achievement of his and of the orchestra. The ice had been broken.

LANG: One final question. What do you wish Herbert von Karajan on his sixty-fifth birthday?

SCHWALBÉ: First of all, of course, that he retains his health and remains at the head of our orchestra for many years to come. We simply can't imagine doing anything without him. But if I could express a very personal wish, it would be for something unreal: if I could be a magician with a magic wand, I'd make a wish that Herr von Karajan could be taught to play the violin in a matter of seconds.

LANG: Why ever do you wish that?

SCHWALBÉ: It's not enough to think you've always got the right idea of a piece from a purely musical point of view. It's very, very important to know the instrument yourself, from the point of view of the different fingering, the colours, the strings or the bowing. And so it would be good if Karajan were able to discuss our difficulties with us from a purely professional point of view and if we could understand one another better in this respect. Sometimes I've joked with him and said, 'Dear Herr von Karajan, how would it be if I were to give you my Stradivarius, you'd play it, and I'd be happy to conduct for a bit.' And he'd say, 'Go ahead, why don't you conduct? But whether I could get any sounds out of your violin is another matter.' You know, he's a great sportsman and often treats us as colleagues. It's a fantastic relationship.

16

'I always look grim'

Karajan's dealings with press photographers

Press photographers in theatres and concert halls have an unenviable time. On the one hand they merely want to go about their rightful business while, on the other, they generally cause disruption simply by carrying out their professional duties. If they use a flash, they startle subjects with over-sensitive eyes, while the click of their shutter release would disturb the heaviest sleeper. In short, they are a burden to the very group of people that clamours to have their photographs. The taking of photographs during concerts and opera performances has rightly been forbidden and photo-calls have been introduced instead. That Herbert von Karajan needed photographers is something no one will seek to deny who knows the conductor's publicity shots or the covers and sleeves of his books and records.

Anyone wanting to know what Karajan looked like around the time of his appointment to the directorship of the Berlin Philharmonic would do well to turn to a volume of photographs taken by Roger Hauert and published in Geneva in 1956. Just look at him standing there, his forehead furrowed with lines which annoyed *him* more than they did other people. Or look at him posing, baton in hand, like a magician, his fist tightly clutched or his eyes upraised as though in prayer. Even at that early date he already wore his watch on the inside of his wrist, with only the leather strap visible from the outside. 'Listening to one of his own records' – thus the caption to one of the photographs – shows him bending his head right down to the stylus – not to the loudspeaker, as one might in fact have expected from a hi-fi buff like Karajan. He closes his eyes when conducting, that's clear enough; but when he holds the baton to his neck, as though to decapitate himself, or points it at his own body, as though to stab himself with it – who would not go into raptures at the sight? Wilhelm Furtwängler's widow, Elisabeth, was certainly right when she said: 'It's a blessing having a husband who isn't vain.' It was she who, at Clarens on 18 November 1988, gave me Hauert's slender volume with its photographs of Karajan, adding the dedication: 'Wrenched from my heart.'

Or take down a couple of more recent record sleeves from the shelf and what do we see? Karajan as an angel soaring on high (Dvořák's Eighth Symphony); Karajan wearing a roll-neck pullover and leather jacket interwoven with laser beams (Strauss's *Ein Heldenleben*); or Karajan wearing a bangle (Stravinsky's *Circus Polka*). A rather more serious lapse in matters of taste is revealed by the front and back of Vivaldi's *Four Seasons*. On the front of the cover is Anne-Sophie Mutter, seated artistically in the greenwood, with violin and bow resting on her lap, while a bright red pullover, idly draped around her shoulders, barely covers her plunging neckline. Turn over the record sleeve and what do you see? The wood is now much darker: the seventy-six-year-old maestro is standing on his own, leaning against the trunk of a mighty oak, only his face and hands stand out from the all-pervading gloom. But what is this? Around his shoulders is draped the same – or at least a similar – bright red pullover, its redness caught in the sun's glaring rays. These lasting impressions we owe to Lord Snowdon, though the staging of the drama was no doubt Karajan's own.

For his seventy-fifth birthday Deutsche Grammophon issued a boxed set containing the BPO's recording of all Tchaikovsky's symphonies and accompanied by an equally unctuous book of photographs. Since then there can have been no question in our minds that Karajan was a reigning monarch of truly philharmonic stature: he is seen embracing even Böhm and Fischer-Dieskau, has time for his dog and family, is photographed at the controls of his yacht and private jet, subjecting sports cars and motor bikes to the same degree of control as his dearly beloved Philharmonic players. What a great guy he must be to give so much time to his public. A hundred conducting poses on a single record sleeve! At least in that respect he has never had any imitators.

The whole of Karajan's life was made up of contradictions, a statement as true of his treatment of photographers as it was of the way he would open or close his clear blue eyes when conducting. In general he would close them, the better to hear the music or, as certain malicious tongues would have it, in order not to be forced to watch the musicians. If, however, there were television cameras present, he would keep his eyes open, perhaps to prevent younger viewers from asking their grandparents whether the man with the stick was blind. Where should one look for logic in the case of a man who spends half his life making video discs and who edits the films himself but who, in the very same breath, insists he hears best when he closes his eyes? Why has he made 800 sound recordings if his films are of far more interest to him? Did audiences go to Karajan's concerts because they did not want to see him? Or did they not rather keep their eyes open in order to watch the maestro in action as he conjured up a world of sound – watching him keep his eyes closed?

It is worth recalling Karajan's dealings with press photographers during the period stretching from 1956 to 1964. Remarkably enough – or perhaps, after all, it is not so strange – these were the years when Karajan was director of the Vienna Opera, a period when he was often accused of 'creative hubris'.

This choice chapter begins in Berlin in the concert hall of the city's College of Music. According to the *Depesche* of 26 November 1956:

> A minor incident took place at the weekend at the College of Music when the conductor of the Berlin Philharmonic Orchestra, Herbert von Karajan, refused to be photographed. The President of the Republic was among the audience. When photographers attempted to take flashlight photographs of the President and Karajan, they were prevented from doing so by the conductor's manager, since it was said that Karajan's eyes could not tolerate flashlight photographs. The conductor even threatened to abandon the concert after the interval if the photographers continued 'flashing'. During the interval a woman photographer touched the release button of her flash, whereupon her particulars were taken down by a policeman.

The following year the atmosphere in Salzburg was equally oppressive. Karl Böhm had conducted a highly successful new production of *Figaro*, a production Karajan wanted to take to Brussels in order to present it there himself as part of the World Exhibition. The plot misfired and Karajan was furious. This was in any case a difficult time for him, since he had to face the Vienna Philharmonic and explain his reasons for bringing their rivals from Berlin to Salzburg's hallowed halls. Nerves grew more and more frayed and Karajan hit a photographer. His own account of the incident, according to a press agency report of 31 August 1957, was as follows:

> I have explained many times that I suffer from hypersensitivity of my optic nerves, so much so that if I am photographed from very close quarters using a flash, my vision is temporarily affected, a problem which once forced me to interrupt a performance for half an hour. Ignoring this fact, Herr Harrer slipped into the tunnel connecting the Toscaninihof with the Felsenreitschule (a passage closed to the public) before the start of the second act. As I was making my way through this passage in the company of my assistant, the orchestra's first violinist, the orchestral attendant and the general secretary, Dr Nekola, before the start of the second act, the photographer leapt out of his hiding-place and, in total darkness and from extremely close quarters, fired his flash at the group. In an understandable attempt to defend myself I struck out at the light. It was not, however, the light source which was struck by the blow, but the man. I cannot pretend to regret what I did, since

anyone who, in pursuit of his goal, avails himself of methods normally associated only with highwaymen, must be prepared to accept any accidental consequences which may arise from his actions.

Karajan's scarcely credible self-defence was followed by a boycott of all of the thirty-eight press photographers present in Salzburg for the Festival. They almost literally had to force their way into a *Falstaff* rehearsal and even then there were only selected scenes which Karajan let them photograph. Perhaps the move was prompted less by Karajan's business-mindedness than by his well-known perfectionist leanings, a quest for perfection which also affects his photographs and which certainly is at odds with the snapshot realism of photo-reporters.

Anyone thinking the Salzburg boycott would have any lasting effects has only to glance at the papers published three years later. A few days before the Grosses Festspielhaus was officially opened on 26 July 1960, thereby fulfilling one of Karajan's major ambitions, a further outcry threatened to disrupt proceedings when the press photographers present protested against the 'undemocratic and dictatorial measures' taken by the artistic director of the Festival. He had had the foolhardy notion of allowing no more than two photographers to work in the Festspielhaus, one of them German, the other Viennese. Both, moreover, had to be women. Massive protests ensued, persuading him to extend his generosity and admit two further photographers from Salzburg and Vienna. All of them, however, were required to submit their work for approval before it could be published. Only when Austria's photo-journalists, in a gesture of solidarity, prepared to turn their backs on Salzburg was Karajan forced to revoke his absurd instruction.

Ten days later, however, press photographers were once again excluded, this time from a rehearsal of *Don Giovanni*, at which only two in-house photographers (both of them women) were authorized to work. Some thirty foreign and local photographers picked up their tripods and left, informing their clients that this production would not be covered.

The Festspielhaus in Salzburg had scarcely been officially opened when Karajan – on the move as ever – was involved in another building project. On 19 September 1960 the foundation stone of the Philharmonie was laid in Berlin, a move that the maestro had been demanding ever since his first American tour. The stone was duly laid, whereupon he hurried across to the College of Music and conducted the opening concert of the tenth Berliner Festwochen. Photographers were warned that he would immediately interrupt the proceedings if he saw any cameras in the hall. No doubt one reason for the highly charged atmosphere was a threatening letter which Karajan had received, containing a photograph showing him in Vienna with the Soviet leader, Nikita Khrushchev. The anonymous sender claimed the conductor was far too friendly towards a man 'who wants to strangle us all'; he should henceforth avoid setting foot on the concert platform in Berlin. According to a report in the *Kurier*, 'Throughout the Berliner Festwochen, the chief conductor of the Berlin Philharmonic Orchestra was accompanied at his concerts by an escort of three powerfully built detectives.'

In mid-April 1962 Karajan had to undergo renal surgery in Zurich but beforehand he paid a visit to Oslo, where the local people learned at first hand of his ban on photography:

> A further scandal in the life of the world-famous conductor, Herbert von Karajan, was narrowly averted this weekend. A press photographer from the *Arbeiderbladet* had been taking photographs during the first part of a concert given in Oslo with the Vienna Philharmonic, although Karajan had earlier forbidden the taking of photographs. During the interval the conductor cornered the miscreant and demanded that he hand over his film, adding that, if he refused, he would not continue the concert. The journalist declined to do so and an argument broke out which was described by those who heard it as extremely heated. The photographer is said to have used language which one would not expect to hear being used with an artist such as Karajan.

Morals are strict in Norway and the villain was banned for a year from using the Oslo Club for Photo-journalists.

Scarcely six months after Karajan had stepped down, 'for reasons of health', as director of the Vienna State Opera, he conducted *Il trovatore* at the Deutsche Oper in Berlin, a self-orchestrated triumph described by *Die Welt* as a 'highlight in the city's cultural life'. But, once again, the press found nothing to celebrate. Even Klaus Geitel, Karajan's loyal supporter, described the Austrian maestro as the 'inventor of a photographic cacophony': 'There are people who want to have their finger on every button, including the camera's shutter release,' *Die Welt* reported him as saying on 27 October 1964.

Dr Goerges, chief dramaturg at the Deutsche Oper, preferred to place a different interpretation on the matter, repeating the old familiar adage: 'If Herr Karajan said that the stage and the singers, rather than he himself, should be photographed, it was because of his eye complaint which, as you know, makes him particularly sensitive to flashlight,' *Die Welt* reported on 6 November 1964.

On 5 May 1966, however, we read in *Der Abend*:

> Halfway up the gangway the sun begins to rise. Herbert von Karajan, standing on the uppermost steps and looking like a Roman emperor, starts to smile, a little timidly, it is true, but a smile it is, none the less – and not even, this time, through pursed lips. Although he will shortly be flying on to Munich together with his wife Eliette, the maestro is untroubled by all the questions he faces or by the photographers' flashes. The Berlin Philharmonic Orchestra's four-week tour of Japan comes to a glorious end on the tarmac at Tegel Airport.

Six months later, writing in the *Bildzeitung* of 28 November 1966, Margarete Roemer had similar marvels to relate:

> What is the matter with Herbert von Karajan? It often used to be said of this most widely discussed but always wildly acclaimed conductor that he hated the press and that he was camera-shy, excitable and arrogant. That is how we found him in the past. But now we find him kind and obliging, tolerant of the press and no longer shy of photographers.

In September 1984, when Karajan wanted to make his peace with his players in Berlin, he was photographed getting out of his car, an incident that provoked a third report which, quoted in the *Morgenpost* of 26 September 1984, was a source of potential pleasure:

> In spite of being visibly tired, he appears to be fully alert and unexpectedly mild of manner. No irritation, none of the usual objections to floodlights, flashlights, questions and unwanted publicity.

What had become of his 'scintillating scotoma, a type of migraine affecting the eyes', to quote a report in *Hör zu* of 4 April 1978?

In an interview published in *Stern* on 6 April 1978, Karajan himself had the following comment to make: 'I find I look impossible in photographs. The only good ones are those which show me at work, because only then do I agree with what I'm doing.' When Axel Hecht and Jürgen Kesting asked the maestro why he always looked so stern while conducting, 'It's my way of concentrating,' was the reply. 'I always look grim; it reflects the fact that I make life difficult for myself.'

17

'That's not so funny'

The third youth orchestra competition

During the 1970s all was well with the world, or at least with the world of music that revolved around Herbert von Karajan. The third of the youth orchestra competitions organized by his Foundation was held in September 1974 and once again it was the Russians who walked off with the gold medal in the symphony orchestra category. For the final concert it had been decided to perform Mozart's Concerto for three pianos with the International Youth Orchestra. The three soloists were Bernard Pommier, Justus Frantz and – Herbert von Karajan. In view of the modesty of his own contribution Karajan delayed his appearance until the final rehearsal, which left the young musicians feeling somewhat disgruntled, since they had expected to work extensively with him. In 1970, when Brahms's Second Symphony had been on the programme, there had been time for seven rehearsals. Now everything had become mere routine, an empty ceremony. When Karajan stepped over to the microphone on 22 September, there was a strained atmosphere in the hall. Of course, he knew very well why he was being criticized, but he had no interest whatsoever in defending himself in public. Instead, he took advantage of the fact that the vast majority of the audience were in the dark, and turned the tables on his critics. It was a shabby trick but, at the same time, a typical autocratic reflex. For a full ten seconds he had to struggle to maintain his authority, but after that the matter was decided in his favour – or so it seemed at the time.

Ladies and gentlemen, this is the sixth event organized by the Foundation and the third one for youth orchestras, and I must say that it always gives me particular pleasure to be involved in preparing these events and seeing them through, since I believe that what is of most significance in our lives should be passed on to the younger generation. You've seen for yourselves the immense commitment which the orchestras have shown today in the good cause of music. For my own part, I have to say that it has given me particular pleasure to see our young friends here and to make contact with them at a rehearsal when I sensed their genuine enthusiasm. [*Guffaw from the audience.*] I really don't think that's so funny. [*Long pause interrupted by a brief catcall.*] You see, whenever you put your heart into something, you'll always get something out of it. It doesn't have to be ridiculous, it's – I mean, it's very valuable that we should incorporate it into our lives. [*Lively applause.*] I'm sure I'll keep things as they are in future. There's no point in beating about the bush. In the end it's the best man who wins. There are no compromises, either in art or anywhere else. I hope everyone here has gained this impression for himself. You're returning home to your own countries. Be proud of what you've done, and serve music as you've served it until now. [*Applause.*]

18

'My career went very slowly'

Second interview with Karajan

Karajan suffered constant pain throughout his final fifteen years. By late December 1975 an operation on his back could no longer be deferred. Not until some time later did he give away any details in an interview with Felix Schmidt in *Die Welt am Sonntag* of 16 October 1977: 'It is said you looked death in the face,' the interviewer asked. 'You must ask the surgeon,' Karajan answered. 'But I remember him saying one thing to me particularly: "Five days later I would not have been able to help you. You'd have been paralysed."' Schmidt probed deeper: 'You were in hospital for seven weeks.'

Yes, from the beginning I thought of only one thing – that I had to get out of there, as quickly as possible. And so, on the third day after the operation, I began gymnastics exercises in bed, so that I wouldn't go into a complete decline. By the fourth day I was able to read and move. But I was in constant pain. Apart from the pain caused by the operation scars, there was also the pain brought about by seven kidney stones. The last of the stones held out until I was released from hospital. I thought a great deal about myself and my way of working, and during these weeks I underwent a process of change. I felt it, though it's not something I can put into words.

Anyone reading this account must find it hard to imagine the kind of effort Karajan was forced to make in order to stage the Easter Festival barely three months later, in the course of which he conducted three performances of *Lohengrin*, two choral concerts and four orchestral concerts, all of them before an international audience. Such a degree of self-discipline could not have come from anyone else. It is scarcely surprising, therefore, that, as mentioned above, he found himself at loggerheads not only with two of his singers but also with the BPO. It is this, more than anything else, that constitutes the 'Karajan wonder', first hailed as such on 21 October 1938.

By 15 February 1977 Karajan had recovered from his first serious back operation, and the previous Easter's major row with Kollo, Ridderbusch and the Philharmonic was all but forgotten. Preparations were in hand at the Philharmonie for the first performance of Mahler's Sixth Symphony under the orchestra's chief conductor, an event awaited with eager anticipation.

The afternoon rehearsal was timed to start at ten past four. The orchestral manager, Heinz Bartlog, had the players at their desks, ready to begin. He put on his black beret and opened all the doors to the rear entrances to the hall. Wolfgang Stresemann arrived and, his hands behind his back, inspected the stairs and passageways. No red carpet was rolled out.

16.13: a black Mercedes drove up. Bartlog opened the rear door. Karajan stepped out, refusing offers of help. I managed to catch him outside his dressing-room. He held out his hand. I asked when I could interview him. 'Subject?' – 'Conducting competition.' (A spurious answer) 'Agreed.' – 'When?' After reflecting at some length: 'During the interval at tomorrow morning's rehearsal.'

The following day I turned up with my tape recorder. Karajan arrived relaxed from the rehearsal and invited me into his private room – the one with the bath. There are comfortable chairs, paintings, a grand piano and a charming little desk, with a pair of sunglasses on it. He freshened up behind a curtain and then invited me to join him on the sofa. 'What do you want to know?' I'd been prepared for this and began by reading out thirty questions, one after the other. At the tenth question he interrupted me: 'That's certainly extremely interesting and intelligent, but we'd need six and a half hours to answer it.' He was in the process of writing a book on the subject, he went on – an excuse that never varied throughout his life. The publisher would object if it had all been said in advance.

My brain rattled on, as my tape recorder grew impatient. Was I to go away empty-handed? Karajan asked in detail about my profession and activities. A long discussion developed on the theatre, musicology and television – 'that's where the future lies. I can see you'll be wanting to do something yourself.' That's right, I thought, but all I want to do just now is to feed my tape recorder, ideally with an interview with Karajan.

The break was over and the players could be heard tuning up. I wondered what I should do. Finally I managed to reawaken the conductor's interest in his favourite subject, and again he invited me to come to the Philharmonie during the break at the following morning's rehearsal.

LANG: This is the fifth time that an international competition for conductors has been held here under the aegis of your Foundation. Up to 1975 a total of thirteen gold, silver and bronze medals have been awarded. Have all the winners fulfilled the high expectations that were placed in them?

KARAJAN: Yes, I believe they have. The whole result has made me very happy. It's showed that we're on the right road. Well, I suppose you can question the merits and demerits of such competitions. What happens on these occasions? Do the people concerned benefit? There are two things I'd say to this. There are of course people who develop extremely quickly, but there are others who need a very long time to come out of themselves and to be able to express themselves. Naturally we help many who are somewhat slower but who find their feet in time. We know instances of the opposite from history. The classic example is Toscanini. He played the cello – in the orchestra in Rio de Janeiro, I think. And at one performance the audience angrily refused to accept the announced conductor. So Toscanini stood up, walked over to the conductor's podium and conducted a work for the first time in his life. The whole of *Aida*. I think he even did it from memory. So there are people who are simply born with it. They've no need to find their way slowly. People like that – how shall I put it – people like that don't need our help.

LANG: Yes, if one thinks of your own career, it began quite differently. You were eighteen when you conducted *Figaro* and by the time you were twenty-one you were first conductor in Ulm. After that you were general music director in Aachen for seven years. There were no competitions in those days.

KARAJAN: It wasn't quite like that. People always think I shot to fame, but my career went very slowly. Don't forget that, coming from the piano, I naturally knew a great deal of the repertory. Then there was my first concert in Salzburg. The intendant in Ulm at that time saw me and took me on. It wasn't what's normally called a guest performance, with a view to being taken on permanently. I was invited to work on a production. And so I had six weeks to prepare, in other words, about twelve orchestral rehearsals. You could really work your way into the material then. It's much more difficult to give a guest performance when the company has already been rehearsed and you have to conduct the orchestra without a rehearsal. I'm totally against it, since it never reveals the conductor's real merit. There are run-of-the-mill conductors who can rattle off any opera for you, but nothing worthwhile emerges from it all. People find it wonderful that they can do it without a rehearsal, but they should never do it without a rehearsal.

LANG: Are you not thereby criticizing your own conducting competitions? After all, the young people who come to work with you in Berlin are often completely inexperienced. Take Herbert Gietzen, for example. He won the bronze medal here but previously he'd only ever conducted Stravinsky's *Rite of Spring* from a gramophone record.

KARAJAN: Of course. But they have a relatively long time to show what they're capable of. It's not as if they've only one chance. There are rehearsals at which we make an initial choice, after which they work with an orchestra to show what they can do with it. We don't demand a perfect performance from any of them. The question is how each conductor manages to realize his ideas with an orchestra in the time at his disposal. I'm certainly enormously interested in teaching, since I myself have never had anyone to tell me anything. Furtwängler and Toscanini were demigods for us. We daren't even go near them. We had to hide if we wanted to listen to them rehearsing. But a discussion between teacher and pupil – that's something I've never had.

LANG: How did you learn then?

KARAJAN: I really missed the sense of contact and had to learn it for myself, the hard way. If I teach today, it's perhaps only by way of compensation. But I'm certain that, with correct instruction, you can not so much eradicate mistakes as the sources of later mistakes. Let me give you a technical example. When we were with the Philharmonic in Leningrad, we had a day off and I held a class with some young Russian conductors. There were twelve of them, with a very good orchestra. One of the professors there told me he had a hopeless case, someone who was so tense that he simply didn't know what to do with his hands. I told him it was perfectly clear that the reason for the tenseness was the difference in standard between intention and achievement. It also expresses itself in the face or in the hands or arms. I asked the young man what was the matter. 'Well,' he said, 'this melody isn't singable enough.' I said, 'Singable? You can't explain things like that. You must say to an orchestra, "That note's too long, too short, too high, too low." Or, "Those notes are not tied or, rather, you're holding on to them too long." You first have to rehearse a melody before you can conduct it; ask yourself what's wrong with it and what can be improved. Every note must be sustained as long as it possibly can. It must be related to the next note. What matters is the phrasing and the slurs.' We worked on this piece for half an hour with only one section of the violins. He was then completely relaxed when he conducted, and the whole feeling of tenseness was gone. I've just done another course in America and there, too, I said: 'I'm not going to teach you any tricks, I won't be showing you how to conduct, for example. But I'll tell you what you have to listen out for and what you need to improve. At the very first rehearsals you peer into the orchestra as though with a microscope, and detect even the most hidden mistakes. If you can remedy that, the main mistakes simply won't be made. I think that's something we can show them here. Of course, they're assessed by a jury, but I've always told the members of the jury that we're not interested in finding a run-of-the-mill conductor. What we're looking for is someone with genuine talent, rough-hewn perhaps, but who can ultimately express himself. The only thing that can't be replaced by anything else is the ability to be convinced of one's own abilities. That's something you've got to be able to express because without it you'll never become a conductor.

LANG: But let's look back at the results. The three prizewinners Okko Kamu, Mariss Jansons and Gabriel Chmura were all appointed as general music directors immediately after their victory, at which point the real problems started to emerge. Let's take Gabriel Chmura. He became director of the opera and symphony concerts in Aachen. He'd never previously conducted an opera.

KARAJAN: Yes, that's true. I'm very friendly with him, and I believe I've been able to help him a great deal. I told him, 'You must arrange things in such a way that the operas you have to give can be prepared as thoroughly as possible.' My own association with Aachen lasted seven years, and I still have a great many friends there. I now hear from all sides that they're very happy with him.

LANG: But how can he engage singers if he doesn't know them?

KARAJAN: Normally the intendant is still the dominant figure in all the larger German provincial towns. He's responsible for the budget and has the task of engaging singers. Chmura has heard a great deal in the meantime and travelled around as conductor. It's obvious that he's always coming into contact with new people. Of course, it takes a long time to train a singer. And it's that that I miss, unfortunately, in today's young conductors. First, they don't play the piano enough and, second, they don't know how to deal with singers. Those of us who went through the hard school of provincial opera houses were of course dealing with extremely mediocre singers or even complete beginners. Unless you managed to show them how to make better use of their vocal qualities, the standard simply suffered. And at that time the conductor was everything rolled into one. There were two of us co-ordinating things. Each of us was conductor, répétiteur and chorus master at one and the same time. I'm surprised we didn't have to sweep the stage as well.

LANG: You conducted operas and concerts?

KARAJAN: There were no concerts at that time. We were happy if we managed to perform our operas. Don't forget that we had people coming to see us like the one who was due to sing Ochs in *Der Rosenkavalier*. He said, 'I'd better tell you straight away that I can't read music. I know when it goes up, the voice gets higher and when it goes down, it gets lower. But that's all.' I taught him the part and can still remember it exactly. We had a hundred hours of rehearsals: after thirty hours I already knew the score by heart. You can still wake me up at four in the morning and I could sing any one of these repertory operas to you beginning at whatever point you like. It's so much second nature to me that I don't need to think about it. You see, that was the advantage for us, that we learned it so thoroughly. But a career – during which time you conduct these forty or fifty popular operas not just once but twice *and* take an interest in what's going on on stage – that takes fifteen or sixteen years.

LANG: As a rule today's young prizewinners are faced with symphony orchestras: in other words, they may never learn to conduct operas. How can they then accompany singers?

KARAJAN: They probably can't. You see that in very many cases. Certainly, they make life very difficult for themselves. It's a completely new world for them. After I'd left Aachen, I gave a series of guest performances at La Scala, Milan. It was the first time I'd done that sort of thing, but at least I'd years of experience behind me. I conducted the *Ring* and the whole of Wagner, but I lost three days simply because the dimensions there were too big. Imagine having a singer twenty-five metres away from you. He no longer reacts to your beat. You have to wait for the sound to reach you and then accompany him with the orchestra. Unfortunately, a number of conductors have come to grief since they didn't have the necessary experience. As long as things go well, it's relatively simple. But if a singer loses his way or if something else goes wrong, you need a lot of experience and hard work to get it together again.

LANG: Let me ask you again: can one learn to accompany other performers in the concert hall? Do you really think that's possible?

KARAJAN: Everything's possible, of course. But there are some things that are particularly difficult to accompany. There's one thing you mustn't forget: in the concert hall you've got the soprano eighteen inches away from you, in other words, you can always shut her up if the worst comes to the worst. But you can't do that in opera, since she's too far away. So what do you do if she doesn't appear? It's happened to me several times. You know, even while I was still very young, certain reflex actions became ingrained. On an unconscious level, I'm always waiting for something to happen, whereas others simply lose their heads. But, as I say, that's something you've got to learn for yourself, and for that you need time. The difficulty and the danger of the conductors' course is that once the prizewinners are known, there are already five or six engagements lined up. Since good conductors are in such short supply, all the concert promoters throw themselves at the winner. They all want to exploit him as much as possible, since they say to themselves, 'My God, perhaps there'll be another one next year.' And they give him a post for which he's not yet ready.

LANG: For example, because he doesn't yet have a repertory.

KARAJAN: Yes. There's a young Israeli here, who's being very sensible about it all. I told him, 'You have to work on every programme from scratch. For that you need at least three to four weeks of inner preparation, even if you know the works. So conduct very little. You'll see that that's much better than conducting four times as much and rushing from one thing to another.' A man like that can't be pumped completely dry; he needs to be kept topped up.

LANG: You're talking about Daniel Oren?

KARAJAN: Yes. During the last twelve months in particular I've watched him change completely, so that he's now much more mature. But who, in normal circumstances, has the strength to say no when they're offered everything? It generally means that young conductors travel the world with five repertory programmes and have no time to learn anything new. That's a real danger, since you can't learn an opera at the Salzburg Festival. I've always said, 'Try and work on it away from the public eye, so to speak. Conduct these things ten times in a small town.' Gabriel Chmura is now much better placed. He's learned every opera with his own forces in Aachen. Once he's gone through the whole programme once, he'll be ready to tackle it at a larger theatre.

LANG: Do you think it's right that the young prizewinners are in constant contact with the Berlin Philharmonic?

KARAJAN: Yes, it's a source of great pleasure to me. Above all those who already have some experience keep on returning and we discuss things together. It's far easier for me to advise a conductor if I know his problems when conducting. Then I can really help. It's always nice when all my children come and stay here for perhaps a week. Above all, they learn to listen. At home they work with their own orchestras, which are naturally not of the same high quality as the Philharmonic, so that they're easily inclined, let's say, to become more tolerant. And then they come to Berlin and hear that you simply can't let up but have to ensure that you get only the best out of your players. And with that they leave: it's like a kind of fix. Most of them then write and thank me. It's a form of contact that binds us together and will probably last for ever. I hope so, at any rate.

LANG: But there is, of course, a great danger that, having won the competition and been invited back for a subscription concert, they then prove a failure with the Philharmonic. It may be that they then won't be asked back for years.

KARAJAN: Yes, but, for heaven's sake, that's a risk we all have to take in this profession. There's always the danger that someone whose career moves quickly will suddenly sink without trace – basically because, with any major talent, the expectations of the audience and orchestra are boundless. Someone takes over at the last minute and scores a great success. He comes again and he's hyped up to a point which neither he nor anyone else could ever reach. He has to be better than everyone else before him. He senses that, the responsibility is too great and, in any case, he may not have the ability to get the best out of the orchestra. It's then a downward spiral, and outward success eludes him. If you say to people like that, 'Let's wait another three years', it's a shock, of course, which some of them never get over. I know a couple of cases where a career which, in itself, was very promising, simply petered out, through no fault of their own. You see, in the past there was never today's type of manager and impresario. There were people who saw to the business side of things, but they were also a friend of the artist. Fortunately, I had just such a person many years ago in Berlin. If things went wrong, he would say, 'Let's go to the Grünewald and have a long talk.' We'd then discuss what had happened, and I had the feeling that the other person wanted to help. That's become very difficult now, since the only thing most agents think about is how to exploit their clients.

LANG: We've had a very interesting example of that here. I'm thinking of Christof Perick, who used to be general music director in Saarbrücken. He won first prize at the youth orchestra competition with the Young German Philharmonic, and he's now going to Karlsruhe. In your view, has he gone the right way about it?

KARAJAN: He's not only going to Karlsruhe. Only today I read with great pleasure that he'll be conducting here in Berlin at the Deutsche Oper. I first got to know him here with this Mahler symphony. It was genuinely professional – that's the only word for it. He understands his craft. The way in which he rehearsed the orchestra showed that he's a real expert, not an amateur who waves his baton around and produces nothing. I told him, 'Use me as a referee, whenever you want.' But he really didn't need my help. He's now on the road to a proper career.

LANG: Do you think Christof Perick would have won a conducting competition?

KARAJAN: I'm sure he would. He'd have made the orchestra play in a completely different way from most of the others. For a jury which pays particular attention to the way a conductor works, the basic conditions are already there.

19

'He's the Bible for me'

Jacek Kasprzyk on Karajan

Barely three months after this interview, an incomparably greater event took place in Vienna. After the major row of the 1960s and his 'definitive farewell', Herbert von Karajan had returned to the Vienna State Opera. The break had lasted thirteen years. Vienna's mayor described his return as 'the Republic's act of submission'. Be that as it may, three performances each were planned of *Il trovatore*, *Le nozze di Figaro* and *La Bohème*. Over 100,000 tickets could have been sold at the box-office and the cheering after each performance is said to have lasted half an hour.

Our present interest is more modest – the consequences of the fifth competition for conductors in Berlin. Held in 1977, it proved a vintage year, with at least two of the prizewinners – Valery Gergiev of the Soviet Union (the silver medallist) and Jacek Kasprzyk of Poland (the bronze medallist) going on to greater things. Ten years after the event I recorded the following brief conversation with Kasprzyk on 26 February 1987. Not only does it allow one of the prizewinners to have his say, it shows that Karajan was entirely serious when he offered to help the young musicians who took part in the competition.

LANG: At the final concert you conducted Strauss's *Don Juan* and in his speech afterwards Herbert von Karajan said, 'If things go badly, come and see me.' Conversely, of course, he could have said: 'If things go well, you don't need to come and see me.' Have you yourself tried to make contact with Herr von Karajan since the competition?

KASPRZYK: Yes, I've seen him three times, twice in Berlin, and he was very, very nice. We talked for two hours, and then came Salzburg. I told him I'd a few problems with my scores, and he said: 'OK, I've no time right now, I've too many concerts on, but come and see me after the Salzburg Festival.' He took three days off, just for me, and he was wonderful.

LANG: How did you work together? You arrived with your scores?

KASPRZYK: Yes, we went through Strauss's *Rosenkavalier*, Verdi's *Otello* and Bruckner's Seventh. It was fantastic what he had to say about them.

LANG: Do you and Karajan listen to records and tapes together, or is it purely a question of working through the score?

KASPRZYK: We've got the music and a piano.

LANG: In other words, he plays the piano?

KASPRZYK: Yes, we both do.

LANG: You play together?

KASPRZYK: Yes. It was a wonderful experience for me.

LANG: Do you listen only to him, or does the great maestro sometimes listen to you?

KASPRZYK: Both. You know, Karajan is a law unto himself. As a conductor, I think he's already a legend in his own lifetime. There are many great conductors, but there's still only one Herbert von Karajan. Of course, I've lots of ideas of my own, but everything he says was the Bible for me. [*Laughs.*]

20

'A diplomat in music'
Wolfgang Stresemann

From an administrative point of view, the Berlin Philharmonic was running perfectly. The only cloud on the horizon was the retirement of the intendant, Wolfgang Stresemann. He was now approaching his seventy-fourth birthday and the decision had been taken to replace him with the thirty-six-year-old Peter Girth. No one could have predicted, of course, that this change of intendant would drag on from 1980 to 1984 and develop into little short of a catastrophe.

Stresemann agreed to give me an interview on 27 April 1978, when it soon became clear from his admirable stamina and vitality that he was far from ready to be pensioned off. He showed no signs, even after two hours, of tiredness or failing concentration. We spoke in his office, and discussed his work not only with the orchestra but with audiences and with his chief conductor. But he also reminisced about old Berlin and the city's fascinating musical life and here, too, he revealed himself an observant witness of his age.

LANG: Herbert von Karajan has been chief conductor of the Berlin Philharmonic since 1955. Did you ever hear him conduct in Berlin before the war?

STRESEMANN: Oh yes.

LANG: He first conducted here in 1938.

STRESEMANN: Yes, I've even told Karajan that at the time he was enjoying his first sensational successes here, I often used to attend his opera performances. I heard him conduct concerts and on one occasion I even secretly attended one of his rehearsals when he was conducting the Brahms Requiem for the radio. We had to spend the whole rehearsal cowering out of sight, since it was forbidden to sit in on these rehearsals. But I went with friends, since I found him so extraordinarily interesting. At that time he conducted completely differently from the way he conducts now. It was a completely different Karajan.

LANG: In what way was he different?

STRESEMANN: Like every young conductor he had different gestures. His musical interpretations reminded me rather of Klemperer in those days. In other words, there was not the deep inwardness that he now possesses to such a marked degree. Even then Karajan was a magician. He radiated an incredible aura. And then he conducted more on the basis of temperament, of the work's structure, whereas – but one must be careful not to stereotype people too much – Furtwängler and Bruno Walter approached each work from a more emotional standpoint. Of course, the approach isn't important. The main thing is that the person concerned reaches a high interpretative level, and that applies to everyone.

LANG: Weren't the differences in interpretation fundamentally much greater at that time than they are now, and if so, to what do you attribute those differences?

STRESEMANN: Oh, I don't know whether these interpretations were really so very different . . .

LANG: But if we compare Toscanini and Furtwängler, for example?

STRESEMANN: Of course. The impression which Toscanini made at that time was of a radical upheaval. Here was someone who came along, conducted the notes just as they were and – although I wouldn't go so far as to claim that it was for the first time – he laid very special emphasis on complete technical perfection. But don't forget Toscanini's tremendous charisma. As soon as he stood there, everyone was in such awe of his personality that he could have conducted however or whatever he wanted. Stefan Zweig once said that, in his greatest moments, Toscanini was so overwhelming that you forgot the composer completely. Conversely, he used to say of Bruno Walter that when *he* stood on the podium and was giving all he had, you thought only of the composer.

LANG: Do you think it possible that a conductor might still come along today with an entirely subjective view of a piece, someone who varies the tempi as he likes, in other words, someone who brings out more of the background of the music, in a way that Furtwängler did, for example?

STRESEMANN: Oh, there'll always be conductors like that. It doesn't mean that Toscanini or Furtwängler would have given rise to a school of conducting. *Quod licet Jovi, non licet bovi.* Furtwängler was a unique figure, and so was Toscanini. Herbert von Karajan, too, is an altogether unique figure, and I hope he'll remain so for many years to come. You simply can't imitate these conductors, and anyone who tries to do so is a fool. But to come back to your earlier question. There's no doubt that in those days interpretations were more subjective. Every conductor and every interpreter would ask himself: 'What shall I do in this bar, what shall I do in the next one?' There was less emphasis then on virtuosity – even the word had an unfortunate ring to it. More important was an interpretation which came from within. And, of course, there were variants. Toscanini, as I say, was a kind of breakthrough. But before him – we mustn't forget – came Otto Klemperer. Klemperer, too, was a sensation, since he was one of the first conductors to eschew all *espressivo* and all *rubato*; his only concern was the structure. It was a kind of black-and-white painting in musical interpretation, though he went to the most hideously exaggerated lengths. I heard him do an 'Unfinished' which was absolutely awful. He, too, changed later. Young people, young artists are often somewhat radical, and they've every right to be so. It was often said in reviews of the time that if any of the great German conductors could be compared with Toscanini, it was Otto Klemperer.

LANG: You said a moment ago that Herbert von Karajan changed his interpretations considerably in the course of the years. Is the same true of Karl Böhm?

STRESEMANN: A person who doesn't change is not a human being. Everyone becomes more mature, everyone has to grow up, woe betide him if he stands still. But growing is often a highly unconscious process. Every great interpreter will keep coming back to a work and will never cease to discover new aspects to it – sometimes simply by virtue of the fact that he performs the piece. People have now gone to great lengths – and this I find very interesting – to compare Karajan's old Beethoven recording with his new one. He himself was certainly surprised at the comparison, and rightly so. One can't simply say that he's decided to take the whole thing at a slower speed or else to speed the whole thing up. It's the inevitable outcome of a conductor's lasting involvement with a score. In Japan Karajan was asked, 'You must have changed in the course of the years?' To which he gave a rather nice reply: 'Of course, just look at me, my hair's gone grey, almost white.' That's how people change as interpreters. Life would be terrible otherwise and would lead all interpreters of any stature to commit suicide. Imagine that, by the age of twenty-five or thirty-five, they'd reached a certain interpretative level and acquired certain views, and that they spent the next fifty years conducting in exactly the same way. It doesn't bear thinking about.

LANG: There's no doubt that programming concerts is central to your work. That was certainly the case with the Radio Symphony Orchestra and you've been doing the same sort of thing with the Philharmonic for the last nineteen years. Has anything changed in your view of how a concert should be programmed, especially when you think back to the time before the war?

STRESEMANN: Well, first of all – and we've Karajan to thank for this – programmes have got shorter. That in itself is very, very important.

LANG: Is that what audiences want?

STRESEMANN: Today's audiences wouldn't put up with the long programmes that used to be the norm. I remember a performance of Bruckner's Eighth Symphony under Furtwängler, after which Wilhelm Backhaus played Beethoven's Fifth Piano Concerto.

LANG: I think people would still be prepared to buy that today. But we recently noticed something very interesting: people left after the first half of a programme containing a Mendelssohn overture and a Beethoven piano concerto with Claudio Arrau. In other words, they baulked at Bartók's Concerto for Orchestra. Is this likely to affect the way you plan your programmes in future?

STRESEMANN: Certainly not. You musn't forget that, of an audience of some 2200, only about ten or twenty walked out. The others stayed. If the name Bartók still represents something of a threat to some of the older members of our audiences, forcing them to beat a retreat, why deny them their pleasure? It was their loss. But that has never stopped me from doing what I consider right, and it will never stop me from doing so in future. The Bartók goes well at the end of a concert, so that it's not a good idea to transfer such a piece to the first half of the evening.

LANG: You often used to put new works at the beginning of the programmes you organized for the Radio Symphony Orchestra. That's something that's largely been abandoned now.

STRESEMANN: Occasionally we have a new work, after which there's the solo concerto. But they have to go together somehow. In part these are matters of pure intuition. There's no manual telling you how to plan a programme. Either you hit on the right idea or you don't.

LANG: Well, who's responsible for hitting on the right idea and how do programmes develop here at the Philharmonie?

STRESEMANN: Oh, that's not so difficult. First you have to decide whether the conductor – who's already been asked and who has to give his agreement – gets a soloist or not.

LANG: Is it you who decides that or can the conductor himself express a preference?

STRESEMANN: Let me give you an example. When our dear friend Karl Böhm comes, I'll probably ask him to conduct without a soloist. After all, what he brings us is so valuable and so wonderful that one shouldn't use him to accompany a soloist. Unless he himself says it's too much of a strain for him. But that's never happened so far.

LANG: So it's less of a strain to accompany a soloist than to conduct a symphony?

STRESEMANN: Certainly. Don't forget that if there's a soloist, it's he who has to carry the interpretative weight. Of course there are pieces like Brahms's First Piano Concerto where both parties enjoy equal status. Accompanying a soloist can be extremely tiring and difficult, particularly if the soloist doesn't stick to the exact tempi . . .

LANG: That's exactly what I meant.

STRESEMANN: But that's a question of experience. It's obvious, after all, that it's the task of the conductor and orchestra in a piano concerto to accompany in the style of the soloist. And that, of course, is fundamentally more straightforward.

LANG: I'd like to come back to Karl Böhm. Is it also a question of cost if you dispense with a soloist when he's conducting? After all, the maestro on his own is expensive enough.

STRESEMANN: I'd prefer to avoid such questions.

LANG: Why?

STRESEMANN: Because I think that with a man like Böhm you shouldn't talk about the cost. If Böhm were to say, 'I'm now eighty-three' or 'I'll soon be eighty-four, I'd prefer to conduct a Mozart concerto before the symphony, since it's a bit tiring for me now' – of course, that would be done. So far, however, he's regarded it almost as an insult if we've given him a soloist – as if he couldn't impress people here sufficiently.

LANG: Every music-lover must have been surprised to glance through your programme booklet and discover that all the great standard works appear only once. With the thirty or so conductors who perform with the Philharmonic every year, it's clearly not the case that each of them does what he wants.

STRESEMANN: No. That wouldn't work at all. Quite the opposite. These famous standard works I generally keep back to the very end. It often happens that we have a whole season without Brahms's First Symphony or without all the Beethoven symphonies. I like to use these as little as possible, in any case. If someone like Böhm, for example, says that he'd like to conduct Brahms's First, that's what he'll conduct – unless Herr von Karajan needs it for a particular reason. I should add that Karajan is the first person to say that, if Böhm wants something, he himself will be happy to do something else.

LANG: But otherwise Herr von Karajan is of course the first to tell you what he'd like to conduct.

STRESEMANN: I wish it were as simple as that. Sometimes he's rather late with his ideas. But he always gives me a list of three or four of the main works that interest him – indeed, I always ask him for such a list. Otherwise, it's annoying to have to start all over again, changing the programmes.

LANG: But perhaps we ought to look in more detail at the order in which things happen. You begin with the dates: in other words, you presumably know years in advance on which days the orchestra can give concerts in the Philharmonie.

STRESEMANN: Yes, it's like this: I ask Herr von Karajan to give me his dates, if possible in the spring, for the season after next – which he does. Sometimes he changes them and then you have to see how you can work it in. I should add that he doesn't change things out of spite, but because other things have come up in the mean time. So far it's always worked out. That means that the dates are all fixed.

LANG: *His* dates. The others then all grow up around them.

STRESEMANN: A list is drawn up for the whole season. Guest conductors are then invited for the numerous dates that Herr von Karajan has not claimed for himself.

LANG: So they have to fit in with him?

STRESEMANN: Yes, of course, it's often happened that a conductor will say, 'I really can't do 18/19 March, since I'll still be in Milan or Stockholm on the 17th.' Then we try to arrange something for two days later. You have to be very flexible here and not say: 'Accept our terms or simply don't come.'

LANG: When do you in fact engage a conductor or a soloist?

STRESEMANN: Generally during the spring months.

LANG: So soon? But what are the reasons for engaging an artist? The majority of the thirty conductors whom you have here in any one year have already conducted the orchestra on several previous occasions.

STRESEMANN: Yes, I've always laid the greatest emphasis on having the same people back to conduct the Philharmonic. If the orchestra weren't so unbelievably flexible and if the players themselves weren't concerned to maintain the same high standards, the whole system would break down. It's very difficult getting used to a new conductor and producing decent results with him. That's the reason why it tends to be the same guest conductors who come to us year in, year out.

LANG: But is there also a younger generation of conductors that you have to include? Do you look for them in other cities, with the help of records, or are they recommendations of Herr von Karajan?

STRESEMANN: It depends on various things. Karajan has often drawn my attention to particular conductors after he in turn has been told about them. It was he, for example, who drew my attention to Claudio Abbado. Whenever anyone tells me that there's some unusually talented conductor, I like to hear him for myself. Of course, I can't travel all round the world listening to conductors – the Berlin Philharmonic's budget wouldn't run to that. But when you consider that we had Zubin Mehta here at the age, I think, of twenty-six, that Ozawa was thirty-one and that Barenboim and other top candidates were still very young when they first conducted here, you can't deny that things have worked out of their own accord, without the need for overseas travel.

LANG: Yes, of course, there are well-tried conductors, whose development can be traced back many years and where you can be sure that they'll maintain their standards over the next two years. But you've also had novices such as Antonio Ros-Marbà here for the first time. On what basis would you invite such a conductor back? Does audience reaction have any influence, how important are the reviews in the daily papers, and does the orchestra also have a say in the matter?

STRESEMANN: Ros-Marbà was recommended by Karajan himself. With other young conductors who are highly spoken of it's useful to hear them in action. If you take on a conductor too soon you can cause him a very great deal of harm. But even if a concert's not entirely successful here, either because he's still too young or because he's inexperienced, the audience will eventually forget it. He may have been frightened of the orchestra and unable to give his best. But the bad reviews that he receives or – let's say – a certain resistance on the part of the orchestra will dog him for four or five years. It's important to invite conductors to the Berlin Philharmonic only when you've good reason for hoping that they'll come back again. There should be no question of any nine-day wonders.

LANG: We've talked about your work in programming the concerts and how that work begins. Does each conductor specify his own repertory and do you try to co-ordinate what he'd like to conduct with the overall plan?

STRESEMANN: Of course. If a soloist is planned, you first have to know what he or she is going to play, since the conductor's whole programme depends on that. If you have a pianist playing Chopin, you can't have the same programme as you would, say, if he were performing Brahms, Beethoven or Mozart. So we tell the conductor who the soloist is, and what he'd like to play. And then we'll talk to the conductors and find out what they'd like to include in the rest of the programme. Since I know their repertory after all the years I've been working with them, it's often happened that the suggestion has come from me and that they've accepted it without further ado. But there's another point, of course, that has to be borne in mind. Since, whenever possible, I like to include a great deal of contemporary music in the subscription concerts, I always ask the conductors whether they have some new work for which they can vouch. In this context I look at lots of scores, though I'd never like to force them on a conductor. Imagine what would happen if I liked a piece but the conductor was less attracted by it: a good performance is possible only if the conductor is convinced that the piece has merit. Only then can he convince both orchestra and audience. That's why I hate it and why I've never done as some composers have suggested I should: 'Simply tell the conductors they've got to do it, otherwise they won't be engaged.' There's nothing to stop us doing that, since there are very many conductors interested in coming here. It wouldn't take them long to learn the score and they'd conduct it in a mechanical sort of a way, but no good would come of it. I don't think that's the right way to go about it. That's why I've often suggested to conductors that they might like to take a look at a score and even asked them to include it in their programme, but only if they're convinced they want to do it. Next year, for example, Václav Neumann will be conducting Wolfgang Rihm's Second Symphony. I've given him the music, since I know it's a good piece. It's already been performed once, and I think one should take a serious interest in a young composer like Rihm. I've sent his Third Symphony to Michael Gielen and am waiting for a reply to find out whether he can do it and whether he can find a date for it. But if they say: 'No, the work doesn't appeal to me,' I'm not offended or angry. One simply has to try a different approach.

LANG: We spoke about dates, and then about contracts and programmes. There's another point I'd like to discuss with you and that's the question of what you include in the subscription series.

STRESEMANN: I try to ensure that every series includes one or more soloists – pianists, string players, singers or a choir. If possible, Beethoven, Brahms and Mahler should all be represented at least once, though not necessarily Bruckner. Generally, there's a total of three Bruckner and three Mahler symphonies. Yes, and then . . .

LANG: . . . you have to make sure that there's enough Karajan in every series.

STRESEMANN: Yes, Karajan has already declared his willingness – it's stipulated in advance – to do one programme in each series. That goes without saying.

LANG: It used to be different with Series P.

STRESEMANN: That was the Philharmonic Series, when only Karajan conducted, but, with his agreement, I got rid of it. It didn't seem right that thousands of music-lovers and very loyal subscribers attended the concerts and never heard or saw our chief conductor at their particular series.

LANG: Then you also ought to have got rid of the letter P.

STRESEMANN: You're perfectly right. We've got series A, B and C, so we could now go on with D.

LANG: That's something for your successor to do.

STRESEMANN: He can do whatever he wants.

LANG: A series which, I think, has turned out very well with the Philharmonic is 'Music of the Twentieth Century'. How much have attendance figures gone up in recent years?

STRESEMANN: Well, they've gone up a bit, but this series has always been a problem child. So far we've had around 1200 subscribers. How many there'll be next year I can't tell you at the moment. It's helped us a great deal that Karajan has declared his willingness to conduct one of the concerts. There's no doubt that, in the course of the last nineteen years, we've introduced more avant-garde music into our concert programmes in general, though it's this particular series which has seen the greatest increase. I believe very strongly that we must take a genuine interest in the things for which we're ultimately responsible. Of course, we can do this to only a limited extent since every orchestra of this kind has a double function. On the one hand, it has a purely historical role to play. The Philharmonic has to present the repertory of the past in really first-class performances. This is important for the younger generation above all, since music comes alive only when it's performed. Gramophone recordings and radio broadcasts aren't enough. Attending a concert with other people adds to the experience immeasurably and, in my own view, is indispensable in the long term. Ultimately, music is written for hundreds and even thousands of people, who come together for a specific purpose. The other function of such an orchestra is to take an active interest in the music of the present day both in subscription concerts and in this particular series of concerts. At the same time, it's perfectly clear that works written since the breakdown of tonality are not immediately accessible to modern audiences. We're at a great disadvantage here when compared with the visual arts. You can look at a Kandinsky a hundred times and keep on coming back to it. You'll then find some sort of access to the work. In our case you have the opportunity to hear a piece by Stockhausen, Penderecki or Boulez, but every expert – even every professional musician – needs to hear it at least ten times before he can form a definitive opinion or even any opinion at all. And what about the poor audience, which suddenly hears completely alien sounds and finds itself disliking what it hears?

LANG: Are you yourself in favour of these concerts with exclusively new music or would you have preferred it if, during your term of office, these works could have been taken over into the subscription concerts?

STRESEMANN: That's a question I've often asked myself. There are avant-garde pieces that are so radical that they simply wouldn't find the right sort of response on the part of a subscription audience. But if you invite an audience to a concert when it's clear in advance that it's going to be extremely avant-garde, at least you can assume an inner preparedness. Even this doesn't always work out smoothly, but at least no harm has been done. But if you present a subscription audience with a new work by Stockhausen and end the programme, let's say, with Beethoven's 'Eroica', first of all you don't know whether half the audience – or a third – have come only for the 'Eroica'. Some audiences react more slowly than others, and although I wouldn't say that there's a danger of your driving these people away from the concert hall altogether, you run the risk that more and more people will be afraid to come to such a concert or that they'll have reservations about coming. The best policy here, I believe, is to take one step at a time. My own personal view is that genuinely experimental works, in other words, very avant-garde pieces, shouldn't be performed at subscription concerts but should be given only when they've begun to find acceptance. Next year we're performing a piece by Boulez at one of the subscription concerts. We've already performed Lutosławski's Second Symphony and *Livre pour orchestre*, as well as symphonies by Henze, in this series. Penderecki even performed his Magnificat at a subscription concert.

LANG: And the subscribers didn't cancel their subscriptions?

STRESEMANN: No, they even shouted 'Bravo'.

LANG: The mainstay of your work is your collaboration with the Philharmonic and with Herbert von Karajan. How does that work out in practice? Do you have regular meetings with the orchestra's committee of management?

STRESEMANN: No, that's simply not possible. If you think of the large number of orchestral duties and, at the same time, of the orchestra's extensive private commitments such as gramophone recordings, or of the chamber groups, you'll see it's out of the question. A member of the orchestra's committee of management, Professor Zepperitz, leads the Philharmonic Octet, so for that reason alone it's not possible to meet, say, on the second Wednesday in the month or even once a week. We meet whenever there's a need to do so, as is in fact laid down in the constitution. Sometimes we talk by telephone, during the interval or – if there are important questions to discuss – an hour before the afternoon's rehearsal. It all has to be co-ordinated with the orchestra's extraordinarily extensive activities.

LANG: Is it basically the two chairmen you talk to? What about the so-called 'Council of Five'?

STRESEMANN: That's been less prominent of late. We've developed the practice whereby the chairman himself confers with the Council of Five and then comes to see me. These five members of the orchestra are even harder to get together.

LANG: I believe Wilhelm Furtwängler was the first to speak of a 'small orchestral republic', by which he meant that the Berlin Philharmonic Orchestra manages its own affairs. Can it also influence what goes into the programmes and even express a preference as to which conductor it would like to work with?

STRESEMANN: Most certainly. Unless the intendant is completely out of his mind and doesn't know what he's doing, he'll soon notice whether a guest conductor gets on well with the orchestra or whether there are problems on a musical or perhaps even on a personal level – though it's entirely possible, of course, that neither the guest conductor nor the orchestra is in any way responsible. You know that people sometimes hit it off together at once and that sometimes they don't – for reasons that are very difficult to explain rationally. Now and again we've had conductors who haven't got on with the orchestra as well as others. With John Barbirolli, for example, it was love at first sight. It worked wonderfully and I believe many music-lovers still remember these concerts vividly. If things don't work out quite as well as that, it doesn't mean we're dealing with lesser conductors. It just means I don't ask them back; you have to have a feeling for that kind of thing. But if a conductor is a complete failure, it's up to me to apologize, since I should never have invited him in the first place. Thank heavens that's rarely happened.

LANG: I've often heard people complain that Georg Solti and Leonard Bernstein have not come to conduct the Philharmonic. Perhaps the reasons need spelling out more clearly.

STRESEMANN: Solti is coming next year. He has a standing invitation from me. He can come whenever he wants, and the same is true of Pierre Boulez. But both of them have assured me repeatedly that they've simply too much on. A year ago, however, Solti sent word that he's somewhat freer next year and so he's coming then.

LANG: And what about Leonard Bernstein?

STRESEMANN: I've been in contact with Bernstein since 1940. I won't say we're friends, but we've known each other for thirty-eight years, and some form of relationship is bound to develop during that time. Bernstein says he'd like to conduct the orchestra, but on two conditions: first, it would have to be a charity concert for Amnesty International and, second, it has to take place in the Deutschlandhalle. My answer was that one day we would certainly be able to meet these requests, but that we had every right to ask him to conduct a normal concert first in the Philharmonie, as, indeed, is only proper. So far he's not agreed to this. [Bernstein finally conducted his first Philharmonic concert on 4 October 1979. The performance took place in the Philharmonie and was a benefit performance of Mahler's Ninth Symphony with all proceeds going to Amnesty International.]

LANG: He seems to have been very impressed by the concert he gave in the Deutschlandhalle with the New York Philharmonic. Herbert von Karajan, I believe, was not so taken with the acoustics.

STRESEMANN: First let me say that the acoustics have now improved, there's no doubt about that . . .

LANG: . . . but then there was the concert with Karajan and the Philharmonic.

STRESEMANN: They played at the official opening at the express wish of the local Minister of Finance, and the acoustics certainly hadn't been sorted out at that time.

LANG: They were experimenting with electroacoustics.

STRESEMANN: Exactly. But to return to Bernstein's request. Just suppose that Herr von Karajan were to be invited to conduct the New York Philharmonic and that he were to say: 'I'll conduct only if you play for charity in Madison Square Gardens, but I refuse to play in your Avery Fisher Hall.' Everyone would say: 'You're mad.' All I can say is that we've made Bernstein an offer and done so, moreover, with Herbert von Karajan's express approval. So far he's not accepted it, but we're still waiting to see if he does.

LANG: An extremely sore point with the Berlin Philharmonic Orchestra is their former chief conductor, Sergiu Celibidache. You continued to work with the Romanian maestro when you were intendant of the Berlin Radio Symphony Orchestra: I remember him conducting a concert in the Titania Palace in honour of his composition teacher, Heinz Tiessen. Why is it that, ever since Celibidache and the Philharmonic parted company, he's avoided the orchestra?

STRESEMANN: You know, I'm not familiar with the background to all this, since it wasn't until 1955 that I returned to Berlin. Immediately after the war Celibidache did a great deal for the Berlin Philharmonic Orchestra, but I've been told that he expected to be appointed Furtwängler's successor. He was no doubt very disappointed by Karajan's appointment and, although I may be wrong, I think he now feels a kind of love-hate relationship towards the Philharmonic. He's often attacked the orchestra in public, which isn't exactly helpful and which is why I believe concerts with him would immediately be fraught with tension. I think it's much better if he comes to the Philharmonie with other orchestras – as he now does on a regular basis. That he's an exceptional conductor has never been in any doubt.

LANG: There's another conductor who's never been here, although one might have thought that, as a native Berliner, he might have conducted the Philharmonic long ago. I'm thinking of Carlos Kleiber.

STRESEMANN: That's not true. I've invited him myself and even persuaded him to conduct an all-Beethoven programme. It consisted – if my memory serves me right – of the *Egmont* Overture, after which Maurizio Pollini, whom Kleiber knows well, would have played the Fifth Piano Concerto, and the concert would have ended with the Seventh Symphony. (As you know, Carlos Kleiber has a very small repertoire.) We'd reached that point in our discussions and had even started talking about the number of rehearsals. I said to him: 'Listen, there's no point in having more than three rehearsals. You know the score, the orchestra knows the pieces and you have to give your own interpretation; the more you rehearse, the worse it could get.' He saw the point of what I was saying. But then he demanded 15,000 marks per concert – and that was four or five years ago. At that point I had to tell him that, with the best will in the world, I couldn't accept that, though I'd gladly offer him the highest possible fee simply so that he would come. But it had, of course, to be less than Karajan gets. And so I suggested a princely sum, which I'd never offered anyone else. To which he replied that he'd have to ask his wife. Needless to say, I never heard from him again.

LANG: We were talking earlier about your work with the orchestra. There are, are there not, always problems in finding a new generation of players, but the Philharmonic seem to solve these problems for themselves. Do you attend auditions, whenever a post has to be filled, and do you have rights and obligations here?

STRESEMANN: No, I've neither rights nor obligations. No one's allowed to encroach on the Berlin Philharmonic Orchestra's extremely important right of self-determination, since it's as a result of this that the orchestra bears joint responsibility, not to say chief responsibility, for every concert. I should add, of course, that Herr von Karajan has a kind of veto where decisions relating to new members are concerned, though he's never made use of it. Anyone wanting to join the Philharmonic has to audition in the presence of the whole orchestra and be accepted by a majority of its members. Although I'm not a member of the orchestra, I go to the most important auditions. But I never express an opinion. That's the job of the orchestra and also, of course, of the individual sections. Let's say that a horn player is auditioning, then it's the horn section that will express its view. If they're looking for a violinist, it's the leaders who'll have a say, and so on. The most important thing is that one doesn't interfere in these matters, even from a distance. The orchestra's own democratic life is of overriding importance not only for the way musicians are engaged but for their ensemble playing. My job is purely formal here. Following successful auditions, I have to persuade the authorities to draw up the appropriate contracts. Initially, it's a probationary contract for one year. The orchestra has to agree to this by a two-thirds' majority. Then there are the corresponding definitive contracts.

LANG: Throughout your nineteen years in office, you've not managed to get a woman appointed to the Berlin Philharmonic Orchestra. Is that something that saddens you?

STRESEMANN: Women in the orchestra is a topic that keeps on coming up. Of course, any woman can audition for the orchestra, and many have done so. It's simply that, for various reasons, they've not been accepted. Could I remind you in this context of Roswitha Staege, whom Karajan had already told the orchestra would be their new solo flute. He was so enchanted by this woman's great talent that he said in his rather impetuous manner: 'Yes, it'll definitely be she who comes.' And she played superbly. She's an extraordinary musician and interpreter and in both these respects was more than qualified to take up the position. But – and it was a big 'but' – it turned out that her tone was still too small in relation to the solo oboe, Lothar Koch. All right, but they play together most of the time and there has to be some sort of balance between them. Finally Karajan was forced to admit that precisely for that reason we couldn't take Roswitha Staege.

LANG: But she could soon have changed.

STRESEMANN: The position has now been filled, and Staege is making a brilliant career for herself as a soloist. As far as I know, she's still solo flute with the Saarland Radio Orchestra.

LANG: We ought finally to say something about the sort of relationship that you have with Herbert von Karajan. Now that you can look back on nineteen years of collaboration, would you say that your relationship has been purely professional, sometimes personal or even friendly?

STRESEMANN: Well, I wouldn't like to say that it was purely professional.

What monsters we'd have to be! We've been together so long, even if not permanently. In fact I don't see Karajan all that often.

LANG: When do you see him then?

STRESEMANN: Well, I see him when problems arise or when there are questions to be answered. Then I ask for a formal meeting. I'm one of those people – you won't believe me when I say this – who can and must be brief. And so I ask him specific things and ask for specific answers. Sometimes I get them immediately, sometimes I don't. Certain things have to be deferred. But it's definitely not a purely professional relationship. I think I can speak for Karajan too when I say that feelings of friendship are also involved. But Karajan is not necessarily someone who opens up to others. I can think of several remarks of his that are entirely sincere and show that he has complete confidence in me. I should add that he once told his biographer, Ernst Haeusserman, that he has difficulty making contact with people. He always maintains a certain distance. Perhaps he's also afraid that people will violate his inner being, which certainly isn't the case with me, since I, too, like to keep my distance. But I'd regard it as very depressing if, after so many years, I had to say that there was no more than a professional relationship between the Resident Conductor of the Berlin Philharmonic Orchestra – to give him his official title – and his intendant.

LANG: I don't want to descend to the level of anecdote, but there must have been something during your long collaboration with Karajan which would allow you to say: 'Those were particularly wonderful experiences I had with this conductor.'

STRESEMANN: You know, this man has given his listeners – including myself – so many great moments that it's really very difficult to single out any individual one of them.

LANG: But there must have been tours that brought you particularly close together.

STRESEMANN: No, I wouldn't say that. There's just the same degree of contact on tour as there is in Berlin. I remember once – although this really has nothing to do with Karajan and me – something happened that moved me very much. It was in Finland. Karajan has a particular affinity with Sibelius and we travelled to Helsinki with the Philharmonic for the centenary celebrations. Karajan conducted two wonderful concerts there, including Sibelius's Fourth, in a hall that really wasn't very good and where he'd normally have refused point-blank to conduct. They were performances I'll never forget. Since there was something so special about them, I went to see him afterwards to thank him. And he said something I've never heard him say before or since. He said: 'Well, it couldn't have gone more beautifully.' After the concert – and this is something else I found quite delightful – there was a fairly grand dinner, and you know Karajan is never very happy having to attend a formal dinner after having conducted. But he turned up and – even more remarkably – he gave a speech.

LANG: What did he say?

STRESEMANN: He talked about Sibelius, his attitude towards him and what pleasure the reception had given him. He also visited Sibelius's house and laid a wreath on his grave. And he said: 'If you want us to come back, you only need write. We'll come at any time.' I really had the feeling that here was the real Karajan. He behaved in a completely natural way, which is perhaps why I've always remembered this particular incident.

21

'As long as I can still hold a baton'

The fiftieth anniversary of Karajan's conducting début

History may well judge Karajan's competitions for conductors and youth orchestras with an indulgent eye. After all, Karajan had thrown himself into his work in 1969 with such enthusiasm. But with the decline of his physical powers, he noticed increasingly that the reins were slipping from his hand. The competitions were still being run by the irrepressible Herbert Ahlendorf, but the youth orchestras could no longer afford to pay for their own travel arrangements, and so the end of the competitions coincided with Karajan's failing interest in them. Moreover, it was proving impossible by 1978 to create a worthwhile programme of events to go with the competition: the orchestras played their programmes and then spent a few days' holiday in Berlin at the expense of their individual sponsors. And since Karajan had slimmed down the International Youth Orchestra's programme from a long Brahms symphony to a short Verdi overture, it was impossible any longer to speak of any real commitment. Of course, his primary interest lay in the competitions for conductors, which no doubt helps to explain why these survived until 1985.

'A wonder turns seventy', *Stern* headed its birthday tribute in April 1978. Five months afterwards came his mysterious fall from the platform during a rehearsal in Berlin on 21 September 1978. The first to claim that its cause was a stroke was Roger Vaughan in his 'biographical portrait', written eight years later. At the time it was treated as an accident, causing an outcry in Berlin and prompting uncertainty there and elsewhere: 'The world of music is thunderstruck and is holding its breath,' the *Morgenpost* announced. Klaus Geitel went on:

> As so often before, Karajan dropped his baton during the rehearsal. On this occasion, however, it rolled off the platform, which is less than nine inches high. In trying to catch it Karajan lost his balance and, before the musicians' horrified eyes, fell from the platform, where he remained, clearly unable to rise to his feet by his own strength alone, whether as a result of the shock or because of some other injury is not clear. With great presence of mind, Professor Rainer Zepperitz, the orchestra's chairman and double-bass player, leapt to the fallen conductor's assistance, lifted him up and helped him out of the hall, together with the orchestral

attendant, Heinz Bartlog, who has always taken particular care of Karajan in the Philharmonie.

Karajan was taken from the Urban Hospital in Berlin to a private clinic in Munich, from where he travelled to Zurich for a period of rest in a private sanatorium. *Die Welt am Sonntag* put its money on 'labyrinthine dizziness' as the cause of Karajan's fall, while Hans Klaus Jungheinrich, writing in the *Frankfurter Rundschau*, wished the patient a speedy recovery in his own inimitable style:

> It is not the person who, losing the firm support beneath his feet, plunges into the void; no, as he falls, he clearly drags the whole of the world of classical music with him, to say nothing of any banal commercial repercussions. The slightest fall entails the greatest concern, if he who slips is the greatest of men. We hope that all concerned will maintain their confidence, and wish both the maestro and ourselves a speedy recovery.

By 1978 Karajan had fully recovered from his stroke and attendant fall, even if the paralysis in his leg was causing him visible problems. It was almost as an act of defiance, therefore, that he conducted the overture to Verdi's *La forza del destino* on 30 December, repeating the work the following day at the BPO's New Year's Eve televised concert.

And so we come to 27 January 1979. The players had discovered that Karajan had first conducted before a relatively large audience fifty years previously, on 22 January 1929, and used the rehearsal and evening's concert to honour him with an *intrada* and fanfare.

The following speeches were made during the afternoon rehearsal.

RUDOLF WEINSHEIMER: Herr von Karajan, what you have achieved in fifty years as a conductor, what you have built up and the ideas you have promoted – that's something no one in the world can equal. We at least look forward to many further years of joy, harmony and deep friendship. [*Applause.*]

EMIL MAAS: We should like to take this opportunity to offer you not only this small gift but also another present in the form of a quite specific thank-you offering. We recently lost a post, as you know, and I just want to say that it is thanks to your initiative that we shall probably be able to fill it again this coming September. As far as I recall, it has never been said before in the presence of the orchestra how much you have done for the welfare of the Philharmonic, not only recently but in the past, too. [*Applause.*]

KARAJAN: It's curious, but the date had slipped my mind completely. In fact, my conducting début was earlier, since the first time I conducted was in Vienna at an Academy concert. We were, I believe, ten or eleven students. There was a long list and only one of the pieces to be conducted had no soloists. Everybody wanted to do it. I spent five minutes rehearsing just the introduction, with its difficult trumpet entry. Professor Franz Schmidt, the composer, was head of the commission at that time and said: 'If anyone ever gets all four trumpets to play in time, he'll be your man and should be allowed to conduct the piece.' That was really the beginning of my work. Fifty years ago today, by contrast, was my first real concert in Salzburg. I scraped together all my savings and financed it all myself. Since no one engaged me, I told myself: 'I'll stake everything on a single card.' And so I conducted *Don Juan*, Tchaikovsky's Fifth Symphony and so on. I remember my father played the clarinet in the orchestra, hence my predilection for this instrument. When I told him the clarinet was too low, he was terribly put out. He'd rehearse at home for hours on end and not come down for his meals. I did the concert on three rehearsals and with an orchestra which made life really difficult for itself. But that's all a long time ago and a lot has happened since then. It's odd, you start off thinking that everything will somehow fall into your lap. And it takes some time until you're certain that things really will work out as you imagine. And then completely different things become important, things which you hadn't seen at all at the beginning. One started off as a kapellmeister, conducting here, there and everywhere. Then suddenly the human element entered into it and seemed much more important. That's the reason why I don't regret for a moment having spent almost eight years in Vienna. For I find that, at some point, you need to be able to influence a larger group of people. The way in which I learned to take an interest in purely human matters there has really been only to the good. My attitude changed completely as a result of my years in Vienna. I now know not only that things will go on but also *how* they will develop. A great source of satisfaction to me is that for twenty years I have taken care of the younger generation of players. [*Minor dissension among the musicians.*] Of course we know that those who are now new still have to be trained. But I believe that anyone who has been a student here for a sufficient length of time won't like it anywhere else. If we need him, he'll be there. This kind of continuity is particularly important to me, so that founding the orchestral academy proved a sensible idea. The young conductors that we've found in the competitions are important, too. Things have to continue somehow when those of us who are now old are no longer here. That you've helped me so much over the years to turn the orchestra into a family is something for which I'm very grateful. It's that that has made this work so wonderful. Let's keep it that way. [*Applause.*]

During the interval at the evening's concert Karajan made a further speech:

Ladies and gentlemen, Dr Girth has said in the course of his few kind words about me that I have spent half of my fifty years as a conductor with the Philharmonic. I can assure you with all my heart that I had genuinely forgotten this date. Psychiatrists would say that's because I've repressed it: I didn't want to know when it all began. It was a very long time ago. But it's really no accident that it was exactly then – in the mid-fifties – that I was appointed to this orchestra. I once heard the Berlin Philharmonic under Dr Furtwängler. It was during my final year of studies in Salzburg. From that moment onwards I felt something gnawing at my heart, and I said to myself: 'A great deal may happen, but that's something I'd like more than anything else in the world.' There are people who divide up their time before and after Christ or before and after Muhammad. For me, time is divided into the period before and after I came here. Throughout those long and sometimes difficult years I kept saying to myself: 'Be patient and prepare yourself. You're not yet good enough. The day will come when you are.' And I went on working. When I finally *was* ready, I said to myself: 'Now I know I'm up to the job.' That's why I also said that I'd consider it only if it were for life. And I can assure not only my orchestra but all the rest of you here this evening: as long as I can still hold a baton, I'll remain with you here.

22
'A firm of marriage-brokers'
The sixth conducting competition

A summit meeting of a special kind was arranged for April 1979, to mark the opening of the newly built International Congress Centre in Berlin. Those responsible for planning the opening ceremony had omitted to book the city's most famous orchestra, together with its star conductor. Their presence, in any case, would have been problematical since the Minister of Education and the Arts sent the BPO to Salzburg every Easter. That year they were looking forward to playing in Verdi's *Don Carlos* and, together with Karajan, earning a little extra money for themselves, when it was announced that they were needed in Berlin on urgent business. All concerned were highly embarrassed. Since the company which had built the centre, AMK, refused to allow it to be inaugurated without the strains of classical music, it had taken the precautionary measure of signing a preliminary contract with the Vienna Philharmonic, with Karl Böhm as its conductor. The matter was made more difficult by fears that Karajan's fury would know no bounds and that the truth would have to be told not only to the Berliners but also to the world at large. The Berlin Philharmonic – which had long since started rehearsals in Salzburg – was asked, therefore, to undertake another 'business trip' from the Salzach to the Spree and back, and even Karajan loyally agreed to appear at the International Congress Centre concert on 2 April 1979. The city, however, had plenty to boast about, and since it could scarcely expect its 4500 guests of honour to settle for a single banquet, Karl Böhm and the VPO were flown in the following day and a hall placed at their disposal which, from an acoustical point of view, proved less than wholly ideal. Thus Karajan, Böhm and their two respective orchestras found themselves in closer proximity than they would otherwise have wished.

Already, within the ranks of the Berlin Philharmonic, there were those who were ready to question the maestro's policy decisions. The timpanist Werner Thärichen was a local man who had joined the BPO in 1948, while Furtwängler was still conductor. This wise and critical man had long since harboured doubts about the way in which Karajan's conducting competitions were developing. As a member of the 1979 jury he had considerable reservations about the selection process and made no secret of his hardening attitude. Indeed, he was even prepared to speak his mind in the presence of his chief conductor, a man not noted for tolerance of outlook. Certainly, he did not share Karajan's belief that the latter's work with his orchestra was like that of one big family. What I sensed in Thärichen's remarks was the faded dream of a genuine orchestral democracy.

LANG: Professor Thärichen, from your position behind the timpani you have a sovereign overview of the entire orchestra. As a composer, you know every detail of the score, and your colleagues in the Philharmonic, too, are experts who know at least the standard works backwards. Why – a stupid question – do you then need a conductor for the evening concert?

THÄRICHEN: Oh, I wasn't expecting a question like that! I think it's obvious that an orchestra needs a conductor. But perhaps I can say something about the orchestra's relationship with its conductor. As I see it, the orchestra as a whole has its own personality and stands on an equal footing with the conductor, like partners in a successful marriage. They need each other, they stimulate one another, they talk, they play – and somehow they have to fit in with one another. They have to feel a sense of togetherness. That's one of the reasons why my colleagues put me on the jury, so that I could express an opinion from the standpoint of an orchestral musician.

LANG: Why were you in particular put on the jury? In the past it was other members of the Philharmonic.

THÄRICHEN: I'd been on it eight years ago, so I was interested to see how things had developed. My colleagues took it amiss, since not all of them felt that the orchestra has a proper say in the matter. After all, I've only one vote, and there are around fourteen of us on the jury.

LANG: What do your colleagues imagine happens?

THÄRICHEN: If I said a moment ago that it's like a marriage, I'd say that the jury at a competition like this is regarded as something of a firm of marriage-brokers or like parents who decide which partner will make my son or daughter happy. I think it's very important that the partners themselves have a view on the matter. I can perfectly well imagine that there'd be a different result if the competition were held in New York or Tokyo rather than in Berlin. That's why I'd question whether such a jury should be so international. People have different ideas through-

Top: The Berlin Philharmonie, 1967. *Above:* Aerial view of the Berlin Philharmonie, 8 July 1976.

Top: Karajan at a press conference, 1 October 1968. *Above:* Karajan congratulates Dmitri Kitaienko on winning the 1969 conducting competition, 28 September 1969. Left to right: Herbert Ahlendorf, Okko Kamu, François Huybrechts.

Top left: Emil Maas, a member of the BPO's committee of management. *Top right:* Lothar Koch, oboist *Above:* Werner Thärichen, timpanist, October 1981.

Top left: Anne-Sophie Mutter, violinist *Top right:* Karl Leister, clarinettist. *Above left:* Peter Girth, 13 July 1978. *Above right:* Sabine Meyer, clarinettist.

Top: Karajan receives the freedom of the city of Berlin, 23 November 1973.
Above: Karajan and the Berlin Philharmonic Orchestra, 19 April 1975.

Top: Eliette von Karajan and her daughters, Isabel and Arabel, at the Philharmonie, 19 April 1975 *Above:* Werner Eisbrenner welcoming the Minister of the Interior, Werner Maihofer, to the 1975 Berlin Film Festival. Left to right: Margot Hielscher, Brigitte Horney and Horst Buchholz.

The Mayor of West Berlin, Eberhard Diepgen, hands Karajan the Federal Republic's Grosskreuz des Verdienstordens, 27 September 1988.

Karajan at eighty.

out the world, so that you certainly won't find a norm that's fair to everyone; no one will be acclaimed everywhere.

LANG: This raises the question of who can really judge whether a young conductor will become a good conductor or not. The layman would no doubt assume that only conductors should sit on the jury.

THÄRICHEN: Yes, that's really a very difficult one. One could probably draw up certain criteria in terms of musical technique. But since this isn't done, there's nothing I can say on the subject. In other words, I don't know on what basis the individual members of the jury reached their decisions.

LANG: You're saying that the jury votes only on the basis of numbers? Perhaps you could give us a brief description of the way the voting procedure works after each round.

THÄRICHEN: Unfortunately, it's just like a game of ice hockey. You have a number – in our case, from one to twelve – and everyone gives his or her number. The best and worst marks are eliminated, and the remainder are then added together and divided by the number of people on the jury.

LANG: Presumably you think that it's much more important – in spite of the numerical decision, which must, I suppose, have a certain significance – to discuss each individual candidate?

THÄRICHEN: Yes, I do, if only because Herbert von Karajan said in his foreword that each participant should return home with valuable insights. But if the person concerned doesn't know the criteria by which he's been judged or perhaps doesn't even know what suggestions and recommendations he could take away with him, I think something has gone badly wrong.

LANG: Are you alone in your criticism here?

THÄRICHEN: There are lots of different points of view. Certainly, it's perfectly possible for two people to get together and discuss the criteria by which individual judgements are reached. But that sort of thing never comes up for general discussion. So I really can't say anything on the other points, either. I have to do what I see and feel, and form an opinion on that basis.

LANG: On one occasion I noticed that, instead of sitting in the stalls with the other members of the jury, you went and sat in the tier at the side.

THÄRICHEN: I need to see what's going on between the conductor and the orchestra. It's not only a question of the particular conductor communicating what he wants to say, it's also important how he puts his ideas into practice: what's the expression on his face, how does he react to his partner and what does he do to get the orchestra to play? After all, you can't *force* the orchestra to give of its best, just as you can't force a real-life partner to do something. You have to invite them, and they have to do it voluntarily.

LANG: Is it harder to judge a candidate when it's the Berlin Philharmonic Orchestra sitting up there or when it's the Berlin Symphony Orchestra, which is the orchestra that's now used for the competition?

THÄRICHEN: The result will be slightly different, but why not? Why not indeed? The world is a richer place as a result of such variety, even if every orchestra were to choose a different conductor. People say the orchestra chose wrongly, but there's no such thing as a wrong choice. Of course, one can make a mistake, whether it be the orchestra, the jury as a whole or each individual member, but that's something different. But perhaps people should decide once and for all with whom they'd like to live or make music.

LANG: Well, the Symphony Orchestra was able to decide in only an indirect way, since not even its leader, Götz Bernau, was on the jury and had a vote. The orchestra's rating only played a part in the decision to the extent that it was of greater or lesser help to the individual candidate.

THÄRICHEN: I think the situation's far worse than that. After all, they weren't looking for a conductor for the Symphony Orchestra but for the best conductor for any orchestra anywhere in the world. That's an impression that I know many others share with me. But that's also why the results achieved on these occasions are rated so highly – too highly, I believe. How can a result be as valid here as it would be in a completely different country, where people may well have different ideas on what a work should sound like or where they may make music in a totally different way? The world will certainly be a poorer place if we're all given only one guideline. Even intendants – like the rest of us – are sometimes fallible in their judgements. Of course, they're jolly glad to be able to say: 'There's someone who deserves to win first prize.' If you don't know a conductor and still engage him, you must at least be able to assume that there's real quality there. It used to be like that in the past. To that extent there's an immense responsibility in showing young people the way ahead. There's no question that we shouldn't be holding such competitions and helping talented youngsters. What's so difficult is the way they're managed and how they proceed. It may be that the side-effects are such that the whole thing needs to be re-examined.

LANG: Perhaps we should say something more about the final concert, when the decisions are taken. Can a critic or, indeed, any member of the audience who hears only this round form his or her own opinion as to which conductor is best? Or has the jury virtually made up its mind before the concert starts?

THÄRICHEN: Perhaps one could go so far as to include the audience as well. After all, an audience also senses when our orchestra sounds particularly good with a particular conductor.

LANG: I've just come from the final concert at the College of Music and noticed that the first prizewinner, Ronald Braunstein, was much applauded by the audience. I don't know if I was mistaken, but I had the impression that, throughout his performance of Beethoven's Fifth Symphony, Herr von Karajan was shaking his head in disagreement.

THÄRICHEN: It's difficult to say anything to that, since we all have rather different views. All I can say is that, when the vote was taken, he received most votes. That's something one has to accept.

LANG: What vote does Herr von Karajan have? Can he exercise a right of veto once the jury has delivered its decision?

THÄRICHEN: He didn't do so. Whether he can, I don't know. He simply didn't vote. Instead, he left the decision to the jury, who'd been involved with the candidates all week. He told us what he thought, but he wasn't there when the vote was taken.

LANG: I don't suppose you're allowed to say what he thought.

THÄRICHEN: I don't know whether I'm allowed to or not, but I'd rather not tell you.

LANG: At the final concert, the prizewinners perform with the Berlin Philharmonic Orchestra. How many rehearsals are scheduled?

THÄRICHEN: Just the one.

LANG: Do you think that's enough? Shouldn't you assume that such young musicians need lots of time to realize their interpretations?

THÄRICHEN: That's always the problem. We've often found that conductors demanded a large number of rehearsals to communicate their views to the orchestra. And they've still not managed to do so at the actual concert. Conversely, many manage without any rehearsal at all. Well, let's hope these young people are as gifted as that.

LANG: Although you sit on the jury as a representative of the orchestra, you do, of course, have your own personal opinion, so that it may be that the orchestra will reject one of the prizewinners. Do you then have problems with your colleagues?

THÄRICHEN: No, although I know very well that the orchestra has often been very annoyed with me and that in this case, too, many of them will react differently. But that's quite normal.

LANG: There's not only money and a medal for the prizewinner, there's also the promise of a concert with the Berlin Philharmonic Orchestra soon after the competition. Do you think that's a good opportunity for conductors, or do you see a great danger in it? In the past we've noticed that, outstanding though your orchestra is, the rehearsals and concerts have often turned out to be fairly problematical – I'm thinking of three names in particular, Daniel Oren, Dmitri Kitaienko and Okko Kamu.

THÄRICHEN: It's always a problem, coping with sudden fame. For many people it's not at all simple. And I don't know whether they can then relate to the orchestra in a useful way. Some have even said that they applied to take part in the Karajan competition simply to have an opportunity to work with an orchestra. Many have no opportunity to do so. At home they stand by a loudspeaker or in front of a mirror, so that, for many of them, it's already something to be able to work properly for once. But if that's so important for them, they really ought to have more opportunities than simply a final concert. Perhaps they could prepare two or three concerts.

LANG: With the Berlin Philharmonic Orchestra?

THÄRICHEN: It doesn't have to be us. It might be possible to organize concerts as part of the selection process, though the number of applicants would probably then have to be reduced. Only when they're at work can one really see what they're capable of achieving and the sort of ideas they have.

LANG: Have you noticed in the course of your many conversations with the other jury-members that there's been a certain change of direction and a desire to improve the system?

THÄRICHEN: That's something that should have been discussed all round, but nothing's been done. You'd have thought that after ten years it was a matter of some urgency. I can well imagine that new ideas have emerged in the mean time. And even if everything is working well in principle and people have made an effort, there are still lots of things that could be improved.

LANG: What would you suggest?

THÄRICHEN: I think the group of conductors should be somewhat smaller.

As I said a moment ago, there should be three or four concerts, with four applicants at each concert. Each of them would then prepare a piece lasting about half an hour. They could work with the orchestra and perform everything there and then. Then you'd have a good idea of what they could do. Perhaps you could even go a stage further and extend the jury to include those people who always hear our concerts in Berlin and who are in a wonderful position to compare the way the orchestra normally sounds with what it sounds like under these new conductors. And why not also ask the audience? Of course, that's more problematical, but ultimately it's a question of hearing and feeling music. And that's something, after all, that non-experts can do.

Four days after this conversation with Werner Thärichen, on 30 September 1979, Karajan was again engaged in his favourite activity, awarding the prizes for the Sixth International Conducting Competition to Bruno Weil, Christian Ehwald and Ronald Braunstein. In his closing speech he revealed himself once again as a brilliant raconteur. Everyone present could tell that he had a sense of humour and that he sympathized with the artists' entirely practical needs. If his utopian vision included a reference to 'moral resistance' on the part of the Berlin Philharmonic, there can have been few people in the hall who suspected that the first clouds were already appearing on the distant horizon. Certainly, Karajan showed himself to be completely untouched by Werner Thärichen's reforming ideas and, in public at least, he continued to give the impression that total harmony reigned among the distinguished jury-members:

I'd just like to welcome our audience most warmly and thank them for the interest which they've taken in this Foundation. After ten years and six conducting competitions, it is perhaps a good idea to look both backwards and forwards and see what's good and what's not so good. Some of our critics have said that in the past people managed without competitions: Toscanini and Furtwängler were appointed without this sort of publicity. But if we're going to draw comparisons, we should also take account of the conditions that prevailed at that time. There's no doubt that a great deal is different today. I always call it the explosion of music, which has taken on worldwide significance. That sort of thing didn't exist before. Our concern must be how to find the right people to meet this incredible need. But this competition is not, of course, a factory for turning out leading conductors. It could never be that, there's no such thing. A conductor's training is basically very very long. People have always wished it could be otherwise. Perhaps you know the story of Hans von Bülow, the great Wagner conductor, who was in charge of the Meiningen orchestra and one of the leading figures of his age. One day a woman came to see him with her seventeen-year-old son and said: 'Professor von Bülow,

I'd very much like my son to study music. What can he do?' To which Bülow replied: 'Well, get him to learn the violin.' – 'How long does it take?' – 'Well, about seven or eight years.' – 'Oh dear, that's a bit too long.' And so they work down the scale – the clarinet takes five years, percussion even less. Then the woman says: 'I don't think I've expressed myself properly. My husband has died and my son has to support the family.' To which Bülow says: 'Good Lord, then get him to be a conductor, then you'll be well away.' [*Laughter in the audience.*] We really should bear in mind that proper training as a conductor lasts a very very long time. Of course, we now have media such as tape recorders and gramophones which make life a lot easier for students by allowing them to hear what's already been done. We didn't have any of that. We really had to pick out the notes on the piano, and, of course, it sounded completely different with the orchestra. But there's one thing that no one can do without: simply knowing a work is certainly not enough to allow you to interpret it.

There's a nice story about Walter Gieseking. You know he had a fantastic memory. While he was sitting in his train in Hanover, a composer handed him a piano piece lasting about fourteen minutes. At that time there was a direct rail link with Berlin and the journey was relatively quick, about two hours. Gieseking looked through the music several times and as soon as he arrived in Berlin, he drove straight to the concert hall and played the work there for the first time. I once questioned him on this, and he told me: 'You know, learning it by heart was basically very simple. What's difficult is to come face to face with the raw material without any previous rehearsals.' That's the problem with which every artist has to deal, whether he's a conductor with an orchestra or a sculptor who has a block of rough, unhewn marble in front of him and who now has to produce his work of art from it. There's bound to be some resistance. And that resistance is also, of course, in the keys of a piano. With the orchestra, naturally, it's not moral resistance [*turning round to face the orchestral players*]. But a note needs such and such an amount of time, and that's not something you can learn, you have to experience it with all the difficulties caused by your hands and by your whole tense body. That can develop only over a long period of time, and it's a never-ending process. Believe me. I often catch myself saying: 'My God, at the age of seventy-one you've suddenly managed to bring off a passage that you've spent your whole life trying in vain to solve.' It's a wonderful feeling, I can tell you. But there's so much still to do.

But back to our Foundation. We said it mustn't be a factory. What, then, can we offer these young people? The opportunity, of course, to be heard in public, which normally isn't so easy. Some 372 conductors have been tested in the course of our conducting events. It is from these that the prizewinners emerged, and we've had really very good results. Now, of course, we're up against the same sort of danger that any new drug has to contend with. It's intended for beneficial purposes, but if it's wrongly used, it can cause death. That's something we have to avoid. You can imagine that if someone wins a prize here today, managers throw themselves at him. One of them immediately hired two secretaries and I have to say that his career has rather levelled out. He's simply conducted too much. When you're still young, you can't learn all that and then pass it on again so quickly. It's not possible. And I always try to tell my young friends: 'If you've won the prize, be satisfied with what comes of its own accord. That means certain concerts that are directly linked to winning. Stay here, you can sit in on the rehearsals and we can talk things over; and they have a concert once a month. In that way they slowly get into the run of things, it's presumably an organic development. There are many who've done so very successfully. Of course, there's no guarantee that we'll find some outstandingly talented young conductor every year, but in that case persistence also has its rewards. Persistence and patience are two very fine qualities in life. The man who can wait is well served by time. For my own part, I see no reason to do things differently. And we'll see what happens in the next five years. But it certainly confirms us in our approach that such and such a number of conductors have emerged from here and that we can say with pride: 'They took their first steps here with us.' What they do then is their own affair. Art is always a statement by one human being to another. And the human aspect is ultimately what matters. [*Applause.*]

I've now a very personal request to make, but one of which I make no secret. When the long-awaited Philharmonie was built, the plans included a chamber-music room. But, as time has passed, those plans have repeatedly been put off. During the coming days a series of meetings will be taking place to decide whether the hall can be included in the building programme for 1984. To the mayor and all those involved in the project I should like to say that it is my most urgent and sincere wish that they should approve the plans. There is no longer a single concert hall anywhere in the world today that does not have a chamber-music room attached to it, since each is as important as the other. Our Philharmonic players in particular include a number of chamber groups and would be spared a great deal of time and trouble if they could always rehearse here. There are also plans for ten rehearsal rooms, which it would be far more sensible to have here in the immediate vicinity rather than some distance away. At all events – and I'm sure you'll all support me in this – I hope we'll see our wish coming true in the shortest possible time. [*Applause.*]

23
'The future lies before us'
Twenty-five years as chief conductor of the BPO

From now on Karajan's leg showed signs of paralysis, causing him visible difficulties, yet no one knew the explanation. Concert-goers, too, observed the worsening decline: 'The most disturbing aspect of Karajan's recent concert was his fall on the way to the podium,' Klaus Geitel wrote in *Die Welt* on 28 January 1980: 'He stumbled and suddenly fell, provoking a startled cry from the audience . . . Karajan's proneness to fall shows all too clearly that his health, alas, is not of the best.'

Karajan celebrated his seventy-second birthday in Salzburg; the event was marked by a popular concert with the BPO as part of the Salzburg Easter Festival. Anne-Sophie Mutter played the Beethoven Violin Concerto, which was followed by Tchaikovsky's Fourth. It had, of course, been hoped that such birthday celebrations might have taken place in Berlin, since it was twenty-five years to the day, on 5 April 1955, that Karajan had been appointed chief conductor of the BPO.

But Berlin had to wait to honour its conductor and a long wait it turned out to be. Not until 7 December was a concert held in the Philharmonie at which Stravinsky's *Apollon musagète* and Berlioz's *Symphonie fantastique* provided the musical framework to a speech by Berlin's ruling mayor Dietrich Stobbe, who was to lose his post soon afterwards, on 15 January 1981, in the wake of the Garski building scandal. Karajan was certainly right to want his contract extended 'for life', since only in this way would he be protected from constant changes of government.

For the time being, however, his declared friend Stobbe was still in power. In the course of his speech (the authorship of which is still a matter of debate) he managed not only to disparage Furtwängler's achievements (while not actually mentioning the conductor by name) but to paint a picture of Karajan as the great progressive. So plausible did this evolutionary theory seem that it reduced its subject to tears. And yet Stobbe's speech is worth reproducing, containing, as it does, one of the finest tributes ever paid to Karajan:

STOBBE: Herr von Karajan, honoured freeman of our city, members of the

Berlin Philharmonic Orchestra, ladies and gentlemen. We are currently celebrating a jubilee which is a stirring occasion not only for all of Berlin's music-lovers. Herbert von Karajan has been conducting the Berlin Philharmonic Orchestra for twenty-five years. When we discussed the matter in the Senate, we said that, in however small a way, we should honour Herbert von Karajan here in his Philharmonie, in the presence of his orchestra and of his audiences. The continuity of this quarter of a century is perhaps unique in the world, an event which in 1955 – when Otto Suhr was mayor and Professor Tiburtius signed the contract on behalf of the Senate – no one had dared hope would come to pass. Soon after that Herbert von Karajan became perhaps the world's most celebrated conductor, a position he retains today, remaining loyal to our city and to this orchestra throughout the vicissitudes of time and above all – as we must appreciate – throughout all the inner vicissitudes of an artist's life. Every city and orchestra in the world could have been his, but he remained in Berlin with the Philharmonic.

There is in the character of this contradictorily versatile man, this aloof and yet – as I know for myself – warm-hearted human being, this implacably earnest artist, who takes such pleasure in the workings of technology, this logician of music who, like no other, is capable of extracting pure enjoyment from the beauty of sound; there is, I say, in the character of this man one outstanding feature and that, quite simply, is his loyalty. And it is very much because of this that Berlin is grateful to him, as – I believe – is his musical public. [*Applause.*]

Twenty-five years – a sequence of great successes, a time in which conductor and orchestra set new aesthetic, technical and musical standards, a time which has formed and transformed this orchestra. There is scarcely a musician here who has not grown into the ensemble during Karajan's time in Berlin. The conductor's day of celebration is also a red-letter day for the Berlin Philharmonic Orchestra. My dear Herr von Karajan, I believe that in upholding this continuity, in insisting so incessantly on form, you have revealed something that may be called Classicism. As a non-expert I shall not, of course, attempt to do something that even those better qualified have scarcely succeeded in doing, which is to describe the parameters of your art of interpretation. But, to the extent that I am familiar with your concerts, two factors have struck me, two factors which perhaps go together and which I should like to mention here. One is a tendency towards objectivity, a reliance on the formal law of a work and on its logic, a highly artificial quality of interpretation and hence – we must accept – a rejection of the former, very German tradition of subjectivism, of allowing a work to be overwhelmed by the experience of the great interpreter, a rejection, in short, of dramatization and also of exhilaration. I feel that this concentration on objectivity and form – for music *is* form – produces an entirely free and unintimidated beauty of musical sound or, if you like, its *melos*, and this is particularly true of works which in many other hands – if I may be allowed to say so – threaten to fall apart. I have felt this with a work such as the 'Pastoral' Symphony, but also just now with Stravinsky's *Apollon musagète*.

And it is certainly entirely consonant with this, and not in the least contradictory, that you, Herr von Karajan, are a man of the age of technology and that you are not intimidated by controls, amplifiers, microphones and sound mixers, all of them musical instruments of a producer, which, after all, is what you are. 'He can play symphonies, but he can also X-ray them,' one critic wrote about you. And yet, even when the performance is exclusively tailored to one particular medium and is, as it were, absorbed by that medium, there is never any danger of that anonymity which we suspect and, indeed, have good reason to fear when too much technology is involved. Instead, new aspects of the work are revealed, aspects which remain hidden in a conventional or subjectivist interpretation.

There's so much one could say today, as Berlin takes this opportunity of thanking you for your work and for your presence here. One could mention the Orchestral Academy, the Karajan Foundation, the conducting competitions, the tours and guest performances which have made this Berlin orchestra famous and – let us not forget – also raised the city's reputation in the eyes of the world. But I prefer to end now. For you are the lord of the concert hall, and these hours belong to music. And for that I should simply like to thank you – thank you in the name of the city, in the name of the Berlin Senate and, if I may, in the name of your public. I hope it may give you pleasure if, by way of thanks, I present you with a portrait of Richard Strauss painted by Max Liebermann. [*Applause*.]

KARAJAN: My Lord Mayor, ladies and gentlemen. You will, I hope, understand how moved I am if I begin by thanking you for the kind things you have found to say about me. No one, in fact, has offered a better description of the range and character of our work here.

There's a passage in *Der Rosenkavalier* which runs: 'Time is a strange thing.' In many cases it can't be measured, it's something you have to feel. Or it simply doesn't seem to exist. Twenty-five years is a long time, but it's suddenly become compressed in my imagination to a single second. I've never had the ability to look backwards. I was always at the front of the ship. And now that it's all behind us – the countless problems, the work, the pleasure in work, the pleasure in contact with the orchestra and the fact that we've travelled all round the world together – it suddenly shrinks to a single second and all that remains is the awareness that the future lies before us.

We must continue to make just as much effort as before, if not more so. When you go up into the mountains, the air becomes thinner and every step costs more effort, often ten times more. That's how it is with us now: the smallest improvement is immensely laborious, since there's a quality that can be achieved only after many, many years. But I think I can say that this quality is now firmly within our grasp. Which is why it is easier to look into the future and see how things can be made even better.

I am grateful to the mayor of Berlin above all for his constant readiness and the helpful concern that he has evinced for all our problems. I have had to deal with many political leaders in my time but to you I am bound by feelings of genuinely human and warm friendship.

I am grateful to my public. For twenty-five years you have revealed your loyalty time and again. You have given us your trust and we have done what we could to satisfy you. Above all I am grateful to my . . . [*turning to the orchestra, his voice choked by emotion; loud applause from the audience*] . . . I have conducted many orchestras in the world, but it's completely different arriving somewhere, having two or three rehearsals and then giving a concert – something I gave up doing a long time ago. Something has been acquired here, something that can happen only over a period of many, many years with the same constant love – there's no other word for it. We've become a family, not just people performing to the beat of a single baton, but a family that does all it can to bring about as much good music as possible, with willing self-sacrifice, untiring commitment and also, of course, through human contact.

You know, I've now reached the third generation of players, and each time I'm told that a long-serving member of the orchestra is taking his final leave today, I feel as though a part of my own heart were being torn out. [*Emotion; applause.*] But life must go on. That's why we've set up the orchestral academy and I must say that we've made great progress down this particular road. I believe I shall leave my successor an orchestra where, for twenty or twenty-five years, he won't have to worry where a new generation of players will come from. [*Applause; turning to the orchestra*:] My dear friends, may I thank you once again, most warmly, for all that you have done. [*Loud applause.*]

24

'Lifeblood'

Karl Böhm: an attempt at an assessment

Karl Böhm could be said to have been extremely lucky in his artistic career: it is difficult, after all, to think of any other conductor whose worldwide reputation increased so incessantly in direct proportion to his advancing years. And to none was it granted to remain so true to himself in matters of style and interpretation throughout the whole of a lifetime's conducting.

It must be remembered that Böhm was born only eight years after Furtwängler, whose subjective and creative interpretations of Beethoven, Brahms and Mozart were much closer to the spirit of the 1920s and 30s. For the Graz-born Böhm, by contrast, what mattered most was the painstaking picture of the score: what he found there in black and white in the music – including tempo and dynamic markings – was the starting-point for his mission.

Böhm was awarded a doctorate in law in 1919, and there is little doubt that his legalistic outlook coloured his often sober thinking, and yet there were moments of inspiration when he outgrew that sense of sobriety and, as audiences in Berlin and elsewhere often had cause to be grateful, shed his own 'lifeblood' (as he himself called it) in investing the music with glowing warmth and drama.

Early recordings from Böhm's years in Dresden attest to the fact that, even then, he took composers at their word, so that, as time went on, he could justly, and with messianic fervour, proclaim his concept of fidelity to the original. His concern in music was clarity and purity, while Karajan's was beauty. When Böhm conducted a Mozart symphony, you had to hear not only the upbeat but each of the main melodic lines, and the inner voices, too. With Karajan it was more a sense of fluidity, an elegant gliding movement. Where Böhm opted for relative harshness, Karajan would choose a soft-focusing lens. Yet no one will deny that both could convey high drama in their different approaches to Bruckner, for example. Only after Furtwängler's death were they hailed as 'modern' conductors, though both had always harboured a taste for the technological age.

Böhm's appointment, on 14 April 1964, as 'Austrian general music director' must have seemed a considerable snub to Karajan. For, as he never tired of stressing, Böhm had accepted the title simply to stop any other conductor from claiming it for himself. He had made it a condition of his appointment – precisely a month before Karajan's resignation from the Vienna Opera. These two giants tormented one another all their lives and yet, like the public at large, they could not live without each other, be it in Berlin, Vienna or Salzburg.

Both were orchestral virtuosi and both had amorous relationships with the Berlin and Vienna Philharmonics. Böhm, too, had stood on the podium in the Philharmonie and received a standing ovation even before a note of music had sounded. In later years it became the rule that he had to bow twice to the audience before turning round to face the players, who found his rehearsal manner often grim and surly. Like Oistrakh or Barbirolli, he was not in the least a showman, small-scale gestures indicating that it was not the attention of one on high that he was courting but rather the music itself on which attention had to be focused. Unlike his rival, he never stood erect but always slightly stooped. A few small steps towards the strings were all he needed to draw out a torrent of sound. Even at the age of eighty, he would bend at the knees for rhythmical cruxes or sudden changes of tempo, the whole of his body a well-coiled spring.

Total gravity informed his features. Strong glasses shielded his eyes which, unlike Karajan's, remained wide open. Not once did his facial expression relax, even at the sublimest passages. Only at the end of some of Schubert's longer movements would he smile at the players, a smile that was happy, kind and contented as though at a job well done. He never sought the audience's acclaim but always shared it with the orchestra.

When the strength in his legs gave way beneath the effort of so many concerts, he was offered a stool, on which he would sit in an upright posture, ever alert and sharp-eared, conducting, as always, without a score. The tip of his baton barely moved but its fractional vibrations were enough to inspire the players to some of their finest performances. Böhm seemed indestructible.

He died in Salzburg, shortly before his eighty-seventh birthday, on 14 August 1981. Flags in the town were flown at half-mast, and all anger and discord between the country's two foremost conductors was finally buried. The Salzburg Festival was in full swing and Karajan was due to conduct a concert in the main house with the Vienna Philharmonic. Mozart's Masonic Funeral Music was added to the programme: never can it have sounded sadder or more stirring. Before the concert Karajan, clearly moved, had addressed a few words to the audience:

Karl Böhm: an attempt at an assessment

Two days ago Karl Böhm passed from our midst. We are still speechless with grief, unable to grasp the fact that the man who, for forty-three years, gave of his best in the service of art and the Festival will never again appear here. In Brahms's Requiem it says: 'Let them rest from their labour, for their works follow after them.' This is a ray of light in the midst of our grief. He has left us an immeasurable treasury of recordings in the form of records and films of concerts and operas. Those who honoured, knew and loved him will always be able to live with his music as a symbol of an age of music which is now, perhaps, gone for ever. For those who do not yet know him, he will be an example and a challenge to the future.

The Festival has lost an irreplaceable colleague and the staunchest mainstay of these events. I have lost a dear colleague and a loyal friend [*sobbing*]. Let us honour his memory with what was dearer to him than anything else in the world: with music.

25
'Nothing's regular'
Emil Maas on the internal life of the Philharmonic

The Schöneberg Town Hall was the scene of a series of major clear-outs between January and June 1981, as one ruling mayor replaced another. The SPD politician Hans-Jochen Vogel was appointed to replace the compromised Dietrich Stobbe, but no sooner had he been installed than the CSU elected Richard von Weizsäcker as its leader. All the more reason, therefore, to rejoice in Karajan's continuity. But whether the chief conductor was really as happy with his players as he had just assured them is more than open to question. On 27 June 1981 a 'service ruling' was agreed between the intendant, committee of management and staff council, which was presumably instigated by Karajan himself. It could hardly have escaped notice that the orchestra's best players were missing from rehearsals and concerts, an absence attributable not least to the recent emergence of the Berlin Chamber Ensemble. Although a chamber concert was arranged for victims of the Italian earthquake disaster, a ten-concert tour of Japan at the height of the concert season must have had a somewhat greater appeal for the band of deserters. Accepted with a bad grace, the service ruling stipulated that all leave of absence and part-time activities had to be reported to the committee of management and agreed by the intendant.

None of these wranglings, however, reached the outside world. The orchestra was soon to celebrate its centenary, which seemed a good enough reason to do a series of interviews. But I wanted information not only from the Olympian heights of the intendant's office but also from the depths of the orchestra pit. And so, on 16 September 1981, I found myself interviewing Emil Maas, one of the two members of the orchestra's committee of management. This marvellous man and passionately committed member of the BPO had studied in Freiburg and for many years had been leader of the Munich Chamber Orchestra.

LANG: You've been a member of the BPO since 1958. Three years later, in 1961, you were appointed leader of the second violins, a post you still hold today. In other words, you've been working with Herbert von Karajan for over twenty years and, quite apart from any questions of standard, you're characterized by a quite specific style. How 'Karajanesque' is the BPO? And how far are you prepared to depart from this style when someone else is conducting?

MAAS: That's a very interesting question, even when you think back on our four great conductors. Next year we shall be one hundred years old, and during that time we've had four chief conductors, each of whom was the greatest conductor of his day – Hans von Bülow, Arthur Nikisch, Wilhelm Furtwängler and Herbert von Karajan. That's bound to leave its mark on such an ensemble, even if only from the point of view of the quality of the orchestral playing. If you look at these four conductors one by one or if you follow their interpretations on record or in other eye-witness accounts, you're bound to say – given the great differences between them – that no one could wish for a better school than the one we've been through or the one we've been put through. The individuality of this orchestra has developed so organically that one perhaps can't even speak of a Karajan sound or a Furtwängler sound. That's something we feel time and again, whenever orchestral positions have to be filled and the young wind players or string players need quite a time to settle down. I think that's a good thing and that it says something for the individuality of the orchestra.

LANG: If, for example, a young conductor were to come and take a Mozart symphony too quickly, are you likely to say to him at the rehearsal: 'We don't want it like that.' Or, to put it another way, would you first try to do it the way he suggested?

MAAS: I believe we would. But it also depends on how such a rehearsal proceeds. We've often told young conductors what we think – and not only young ones, though it's easier with them. Even with people we know well we wouldn't hesitate to say: 'We're not happy with that tempo.'

LANG: If one takes a closer look at the programme for 1981/2, your centenary year, there are a number of things that strike one. The nineteen prizewinners of the Karajan competition, for example, will be appearing remarkably few times this year. The only one who'll be conducting here is Christian Ehwald from the GDR. All the others who've already been here, people like Gabriel Chmura, Kazuhiro Koizumi and Dmitri Kitaienko, have not returned, while Okko Kamu will shortly be giving a concert with the Symphony Orchestra of Berlin. Is that a capitulation and do the players think that these competitions are not leading in the direction that Herbert von Karajan originally had in mind?

MAAS: No, I certainly wouldn't say that. It's not doing violence to the idea of the conducting competition to hold the view that the competition should run its course, a corresponding award should be made, and the young conductor should then be given a piece to perform with us at the closing concert. These young people should then be left to develop. That's true, for example, even of Okko Kamu, although I can't say at the moment why he's not been back here for so long. It may be only right and proper that people don't reappear straight away but only after they've made a name for themselves elsewhere. Certainly, that's what has happened with Emil Tchakarov from Bulgaria, to judge by the stories I keep on hearing about him. That's why he's occasionally here with us. Christian Ehwald, I believe, is bringing a very special programme . . .

LANG: *Bluebeard's Castle* by Béla Bartók.

MAAS: Yes, he's written something about it, although the intendant didn't know that at the time when the invitation was made. But I find that a wonderful coincidence, and we're all looking forward to it. To sum up, one shouldn't attach too much importance to which of the prize-winners appears and which of them doesn't. It's simply the way it works out.

LANG: I asked the question only because it was Herbert von Karajan himself who touched on the matter of his successor, not you and the orchestra. As long ago as 1969 he said that nothing would give him greater pleasure than to see one of the series of prizewinners become his successor. But that's now more than unlikely.

MAAS: Isn't that understandable? I really can't say any more than that.

LANG: I see that on 3 October you'll be attempting to play without a conductor. Karajan originally intended to take over the concert, since Böhm was ill; but he then withdrew. Now, following Karl Böhm's death, it's been turned into a memorial concert. How did it come about that the orchestra wanted to play without a conductor?

MAAS: We found the idea great. We had a friendly, almost intimate relationship with Böhm, especially during the latter years of our work together. And so we took up the intendant's suggestion entirely spontaneously and are very happy to be doing so.

LANG: This will raise some interesting questions. I believe it's the first time you've played without a conductor with such a large orchestra.

MAAS: Possibly. Certainly it'll be the first time here in the Philharmonie within the framework of an official concert.

LANG: This kind of interpretation is never really discussed. Whenever a gramophone recording comes out, people always say: 'It's great, the way he does it.' Don't you think that rather too much importance is sometimes attached to the role of the conductor? Now you suddenly believe yourselves capable of offering your own interpretation. People will say: 'It's the Philharmonic, yes and who's conducting? No one.'

MAAS: I could easily leave it at that, but I won't. We mustn't forget that, in the case of the Böhm memorial concert, we chose a programme that can be put on with a relatively small orchestra. But we're happy to perform this way for once.

LANG: You'll have to have a lot of rehearsals.

MAAS: Certainly more than usual.

LANG: Working with a conductor is also a question of economy.

MAAS: Yes, but there's another point I'd like to mention. We play a great deal of chamber music. And it comes out at once at such points. I wouldn't like to attach too much importance or exaggerate the number of rehearsals. We'll sit down and come to an immediate understanding. Anyone who has ever really played chamber music knows how to listen. And anyone who knows how to listen can play. So there's no need for the audience to come along wondering whether we can get it together. I've no worries on that score.

LANG: The programme that's emerged is made up of Mozart's little G minor Symphony and Clarinet Concerto, with Schubert's Fifth Symphony after the interval. Did you discuss it with the whole orchestra, and how did you choose your colleague, Karl Leister, as soloist? I can well imagine Lothar Koch saying: 'I'll do the oboe concerto'; Norbert Hauptmann would pounce on one of the horn concertos, and Thomas Brandis would naturally want to play one of the violin concertos.

MAAS: That's perfectly true. But Thomas Brandis said right away that he wouldn't push himself forward as soloist, and we were happy that he was able to lead the orchestra on this occasion. The decision – it's a ticklish question, but I want to answer it as frankly as possible – came rather suddenly. Ideally, we'd have liked to inform the whole orchestra, but to some extent we were presented with a *fait accompli.* Thomas Brandis told me he'd initially discussed the matter only with the intendant. But ultimately the Clarinet Concerto is a wonderful piece, we shouldn't argue over who plays what. Karl Leister is currently one of the most brilliant clarinettists around. And given his qualifications, it can only be all right by our horn player, Gerd Seifert, for example.

LANG: We were talking about playing without a conductor. The Chamber Ensemble was established here about a year ago and, as everyone knows, it's made up predominantly of members of the Philharmonic. How is it fixed in your constitution? Is it a rival enterprise?

MAAS: That's exactly what it's trying not to be. It has absolutely nothing to do with the orchestra. It's a purely private undertaking. But I've already said that we do a great deal of chamber music. To that extent we take an entirely positive view of these activities in terms of the sound that the orchestra produces and the way in which the individual players develop. On the other hand, it may well be that the term 'chamber orchestra' – it's all the same whether it's preceded by the word 'Berlin' or 'Philharmonic' – has led to misconceptions. One could indeed assume, particularly outside Berlin, that it was an offshoot of the Berlin Philharmonic or, rather, the Berlin Philharmonic Orchestra. But that's something that can't be rebutted often enough.

LANG: Is this 'Berlin Chamber Ensemble' identical with the 'Berlin Chamber Academy', since this latter group has now started to make records describing them as 'Members of the Berlin Philharmonic'? Also, another three Mozart concerts are due to be held in the Philharmonie under Thomas Wilbrandt.

MAAS: As far as my own information goes, they've nothing to do with each other. Members of the Philharmonic also play in the 'Berlin Baroque Orchestra' and on many other occasions. Organizers really ought to do everything possible to avoid mentioning our orchestra, especially when it comes to drawing up contracts.

LANG: To what extent is the management committee anxious that things taking place within the orchestra should come to public attention?

MAAS: Not at all.

LANG: Is there not what I'm tempted to call an iron curtain between the audience and the orchestra at your concerts? It's a question that's also of relevance for the future. Is it possible that, by being told certain things, audiences might have a greater feeling that the orchestra was made up of real human beings? Perhaps you'd then have more contact with young people.

MAAS: I'm sorry if I sounded rather curt when I said 'Not at all' a moment ago. It wasn't meant like that. I'd more than welcome it if the 'iron curtain' were to be removed – though I'm not entirely sure I understand what you mean by the term. However, I don't believe that could be achieved by bringing internal matters to public attention.

LANG: In the September issue of the magazine *Das Orchester* I read, for example: 'The Berlin Philharmonic Orchestra is looking for a first solo clarinet (co-ordinated) with immediate effect.' Ulf Rodenhäuser played here until 1980, and I think many concert-goers and especially your subscribers would be interested to know why Rodenhäuser is leaving and who they can expect to see sitting in his place.

MAAS: It's like everywhere. If someone wants to change, in other words, if Herr Rodenhäuser wants to take up teaching, he's every right to do so. Teaching posts are relatively thin on the ground, so that if an opportunity is offered him at the Stuttgart College of Music – well, it's a highly prestigious position. Perhaps he has pronounced pedagogic leanings and would like to face the firing-line in this way. That's the essential reason, there's nothing more one can say.

LANG: Could we talk about something else which also takes place away from the public gaze – auditions for new orchestral players?

MAAS: I think this is an internal process all over the world, including America. Sir Georg Solti, the music director of the Chicago Symphony Orchestra, once said in the course of a panel discussion that he and a small committee drawn from the section in question would decide among themselves who was to be taken on. He had to do it himself, he said, since he had a better overview of the situation. But one can hold a completely different view of the matter. We players have to sit alongside these people afterwards, and I'm not even thinking of the human aspect. If someone spends a probationary year with us – irrespective of whether he's a string or wind player, a percussionist or a harpist – we get to know him in a completely different way. We find out whether he can be integrated in the long term. Sometimes it doesn't work, even though the performer in question may be doing outstanding things right up to the end of the probationary year. That's something that a conductor can't easily tell among the strings, for example.

LANG: None the less, it was interesting to hear Solti say that conductors in America have a position of power that musicians over here simply don't want. But to return to my question about auditions for the

Philharmonic. Can we go back first to the advertisement for a 'solo clarinet'? How many, approximately, will apply?

MAAS: That's very uncertain. Whatever the general public may think, it's not as though people have to scramble for a position with us. In other words, we're not swamped by applications. Particularly with the high strings things are really difficult – though that's virtually a worldwide phenomenon. We recently had an audition for a fiddle player, and fortunately we were able to fill two places. When I spoke with Herr von Karajan afterwards, his first question was: 'What else was there?' Certainly there was no one else worth considering. The location is clearly a disadvantage. And rivalry from the radio orchestras means that the attraction of a highly qualified orchestra is no longer as great as it was. You can earn just as much nowadays in broadcasting. If you also consider the free time, which is so highly valued today, anyone can earn a living making recordings and taking part in broadcasts. Unfortunately, we've not yet been able to persuade the Senate to pay us rates comparable to those of the radio orchestras, rather than according to wage agreements worked out with cultural orchestras. We're still a long way behind the radio orchestras. We've just heard that twenty-three musicians applied for the post of second violin with the Bavarian Radio Symphony Orchestra. That's something we can only dream about.

LANG: Is the radio orchestra the reason for that or is it also a question of people feeling a bit afraid of your standards? After all, you're supposed to be the best orchestra in the world. There, I've said it now!

MAAS: That may play a role. But, damn it all, I can't imagine that a young musician who believes in his own abilities wouldn't come and simply audition for us. But they don't.

LANG: And you wouldn't lure anyone away from the other Berlin orchestras? There's no question of that?

MAAS: We've just 'lured away' a bass clarinettist, if that's what you want to call it, but there was a gentlemen's agreement with the intendant of the Berlin Radio Symphony Orchestra. So we'll get over the immediate problem, at least, by sharing this one player. We're very happy with this solution.

LANG: I know you're not trying to evade the issue, but I think very few people know what happens in practice at an audition. The whole orchestra gets together with its chief conductor.

MAAS: Yes, it's listed in the duty rota. We meet, if possible with Herr von

Karajan. But more often than not, he's not there. Then we simply listen to the applicants and afterwards a free vote's taken.

LANG: By a show of hands?

MAAS: Yes, there's no secret ballot here.

LANG: And if the clarinettist – male or female – has your approval, does there then have to be a solo audition with Herbert von Karajan? Or is it sufficient for them to turn up with the orchestra?

MAAS: We have an arrangement among ourselves, though Herr von Karajan does in fact like to hear the player once again, which is entirely understandable. And so far the system has worked well. As far as the clarinettist is concerned, the auditions have not been very satisfactory so far, and we're actually engaged in discussions with a woman at the moment. She came off best of all and will probably join us on our next tour of Japan. But she's not yet been accepted into the orchestra.

LANG: That's a topic that we naturally need to talk about. The Berlin Philharmonic has been in existence for one hundred years – and in 1982 you'll still be 120 men. Where's the first woman? People are talking. You're always being asked this question. A few days ago I saw with great interest that you and your colleagues were taking a lively interest in the Young German Philharmonia. This orchestra ought to be our great model. It must be at least 30 per cent women.

MAAS: Yes, there's an alarmingly large number of them. But I mean that only in an appreciative sense. I've often spoken on the subject with Thomas Brandis and Wolfgang Boettcher, both of whom give outstanding classes in their respective instruments, and we can see how good the girls are there. We don't want to chalk up some record and say, for example, that in no circumstances will we have a woman in the orchestra until we've celebrated our hundredth anniversary; that would be stupid. But, going back to the clarinet, the woman concerned is Sabine Meyer from Munich. I can well imagine her being the first woman to join the orchestra. I've always said that there's no taboo against accepting women into the orchestra. We can't avoid that sort of development, we're not so simple-minded. If there's a woman, she'll be accepted.

LANG: She'll be accepted, if at all, for only a probationary year in the first instance. Then a secret vote will be held to decide whether she should become a permanent member of the Berlin Philharmonic.

MAAS: Exactly. That's how we proceed in every case. I've told Fräulein Meyer myself – as I keep on telling my colleagues – it really doesn't matter now whether it's a man or a woman. We have to see who performs best, since achievement is all that's relevant with us.

LANG: You often have men and women from your orchestral academy to help out. But, as far as I know, not a single post in your orchestra has been filled from this institute, which is a part of the Karajan Foundation and which has been in existence since 1972.

MAAS: No, that's not true. The bass clarinettist, Manfred Preis, whom we mentioned earlier, came from the academy. There's also a solo trombone working with us at the moment, and I think there's someone else, though his name escapes me at present. But let me say one thing: the academy doesn't provide a free ticket into the orchestra. Not that we're entirely opposed to the idea, it's just that it's simply an academy like any other. We have to lay the greatest emphasis on receiving applications from the whole area that interests us, in other words, from the whole of Germany or, rather, the whole of Central Europe. It's certainly not the case that people no longer need come here to us. Those who've graduated from the academy do not receive privileged treatment. As the statutes indicate, enrolment at the academy allows them only to study with a very good teacher and to play with us in the orchestra at one or two concerts a month. Apart from that, all that matters at the auditions is how well the applicants play.

LANG: Do all your sectional leaders have a duty to work with these students at the academy and are contracts signed there?

MAAS: There's a sort of contract. Not only do they have a duty, they are very happy to perform that duty, I believe. What other teacher has the opportunity to train his students and at the same time to have them sitting next to him in the orchestra? It's a great idea. I'm thinking particularly of the wind, where I've noticed that it meets a real need on their part.

LANG: The Philharmonic involves several organizations, including the committee of management and the Council of Five. There's also something called the 'Group of Comrades'. What's that?

MAAS: It's a stupid expression. I've tried thousands of times to get them to change it and call it something like a Working Party. 'Group of Comrades' suggests something completely different from what it is. We're responsible for everything that promotes human contact. We consider anniversaries, for example, or plan Christmas parties. When we're on tour, we discuss honours and invitations. For our retired members, there used to be something called a pension fund; there's still one in Vienna, incidentally. At least it reflected the name of the group, since it sprang from genuine need, in other words, from a sense of comradeship towards those who had left the orchestra. Looking after the elderly used to be completely different from what it is now – it was something wonderful and extremely important.

LANG: Are there at least regular meetings or – as you said earlier – do they, too, not meet any longer?

MAAS: No, they've stopped meeting, too.

LANG: So it's not too sweeping a statement to say that there's nothing regular any longer at the Philharmonic.

MAAS: Everything's changed a bit, I suppose. And I think that's a very good thing.

LANG: You spoke of honours. Who, for example, can receive the Hans von Bülow Medal and when?

MAAS: The silver medal is usually given to colleagues when they leave. Those who've been with the orchestra for more than thirty years receive the Ring of Honour. As far as I know, the Hans von Bülow Medal has only once been awarded in gold, and that was to our chief conductor. We also give it to conductors with whom we've enjoyed working a lot. Another award is 'Honorary Membership of the Group of Comrades of the Berlin Philharmonic', to give it its full title. It, too, is intended for particularly deserving conductors and soloists.

LANG: It's obvious that, as regards the strength of the orchestra, the number of players is largely conditioned by the score. But why is it that members of the orchestra – and I'm thinking particularly of the strings – will sit at one desk for one concert and at another one for the next concert? Do you have an orchestral manager who sorts it all out or are there also wrangles over who sits where?

MAAS: We're very lucky not to have a manager. It's all arranged for us by our 'organizers'. For example, the first violins have a man who can be consulted on this subject. But he can't say, for instance: 'This player will now sit there.' It's simply that a certain flexibility has got built into the system. Many decisions are already taken simply on the basis of the forces involved. If you begin with a Haydn symphony, then play a Brahms piano concerto and end up with a Mahler symphony – that's an exaggeration, since it never happens like that, but my point is simply that more and more people will arrive from one piece to the next. They'll simply sit behind the others. In the first violins we've always set out from the assumption that the players at every desk must be able to play everything. In that way you remain independent of the part: in other words, of the fingering and bowing written into the music. Of course, the bowing remains the same in principle, but there's a difference depending on whether I always play from the same part or from different parts. It simply allows us more freedom.

LANG: But when reduced forces are required, who doesn't want to play?

MAAS: It's all arranged by the organizers. We discuss a particular grouping with the conductor. For a Mozart concerto, for example, there may be twelve first and ten second violins, eight violas, six cellos and four or five double basses. With those kinds of forces, certain colleagues will be released according to a points system which we've devised. In other words, anyone who has played an 'accompaniment', as we call it, will automatically be let off the next accompaniment. If he has a free point, he doesn't need to play – indeed, he's not allowed to do so.

LANG: Or he can come a bit later.

MAAS: Yes, or go home earlier, as sometimes happens.

LANG: How are the sectional leaders divided up? In the advertisement, it says: 'First solo clarinet' and, in brackets after it, 'co-ordinated'. What does that mean?

MAAS: It simply means they're both of equal status, in other words, they alternate.

LANG: And how do they alternate?

MAAS: As they themselves think fit. All first desks – the two leaders, the solo cellos, first woodwind and so on – simply arrange their duties among themselves, that is, unless Herr von Karajan expresses a particular wish. And, of course, his wishes (which are never in the least bit personal) are respected.

LANG: But it's often the case with Karajan that two leaders sit at the same desk.

MAAS: That's what's called 'doubling', so that the sound is better at certain passages. Then you'll also have a first woodwind sitting in third position.

LANG: But it may happen that Karl Leister is out of town, performing as a soloist, and that the 'co-ordinated' clarinettist – currently unfilled – is ill. Is it not then possible for the third clarinettist to play the solo passages, or does it always have to be a first clarinettist from another orchestra?

MAAS: This problem has been solved in all other orchestras by allowing the third clarinettist to take over from the first one. Our contract doesn't allow us to do that. We've got the so-called 'Berlin model', that was introduced here over ten years ago. It has very great advantages, but also these minor disadvantages. If necessary a first woodwind player who may be giving a concert in London would have to fly back to Berlin. But fortunately that's never happened.

26

'Let's wait and see'

A portrait of Peter Girth

The Philharmonic's new intendant, Peter Girth, took over as Wolfgang Stresemann's successor in 1978, at the age of thirty-six. Everyone recognized and admired Stresemann's sagacious decisions and conciliatory manner, but now they had to come to terms with a novice. To be fair, Girth brought to his new appointment a certain youthful flair and imagination. As early as February 1979 he had already announced a 'Chancellor's Gala', scheduled to take place in the Philharmonie on 6 October. *Bild-Zeitung* headed its article: 'Karajan invites Chancellor Schmidt into his bath.' It was said that the players were planning to let down their hair with a cabaret and 'musical jokes'. Their chief conductor had also agreed to take part and the programme was to include Gershwin's *Rhapsody in Blue*, with Alexis Weissenberg as soloist. It was a dummy run for the 1982 'Philharmonic Revue'.

In the eyes of the orchestra, however, Girth had simply changed sides, moving over from manager of the Association of German Orchestras (which also represented the interests of the BPO) to a position of employer and supervisor. After his initial welcome it was inevitable, therefore, that a sense of distance should open up. Unlike his predecessor, he was quite ready to wield his power, and the fact that he accepted his chief conductor's wishes and demands without demur inspired the orchestra's instant mistrust. The players were growing more and more disillusioned at increasing signs of erratic behaviour on Karajan's part, while the new intendant was beginning to see in him an almost godlike figure of veneration. In Girth's view the orchestra played, at best, the role of a submissive and manipulable body of players, a view that could not have been further from the truth.

It should not be forgotten that, for the most part, the Philharmonic players were no longer the same as those who had helped to found Karajan's international reputation. They were young and, perhaps all too readily, they had come to accept the blessings of video and the CD industry, so that they no longer saw the need to pay their ageing chief conductor the same degree of boundless respect as before. His increasing obduracy only made things worse, at a time when one might have expected and hoped for the wisdom born of old age. The orchestra had little time, therefore, for Girth's reserved and intellectual manner.

Some of Girth's innovations showed him to be dynamic and enterprising. He made up his mind, for example, that coughing among members of the audience had to be suppressed, so he placed witty notices in the programmes and recommended the use of handkerchiefs to muffle the sound of bronchial attacks. With his rimless glasses, he bore a close resemblance to Gustav Mahler, and he immediately set about planning a Mahler cycle within the framework of the Berliner Festwochen. By reducing the number of concerts for existing subscribers he made room for an extra series or two and in that way reduced the waiting-lists. He gave up the 'Music of the Twentieth Century' series and integrated new and unusual pieces into the ordinary subscription concerts. Following the success of the 'Chancellor's Gala' there were plans for a 'Philharmonic Revue', including rock music, to mark the centenary year. Commissions were offered to some of the leading composers of the day, and a competition was even announced for local composers. Books, exhibitions and historical programmes were also announced. It was the start of a whole new era – but built on the wrong foundations. The orchestra not only *should* have been involved, they wanted to be involved, so that Girth's initial concern ought to have been to make them his closest friends. Instead he threw in his lot with Karajan, believing that the latter's fame would cast its undiminished glow over the BPO until the bitter end. None the less, I was able to conduct a relaxed interview with the intendant in his office on 30 September 1981.

LANG: As a twenty-three-year-old student in Berlin you are once said to have exclaimed that you would study law only if, one day, you could become intendant of the Berlin Philharmonic. But this is contradicted by something you said in October 1977, when you compared the offer to become intendant of the Berlin Philharmonic with the story of the Virgin and Child. What did you really say?

GIRTH: There's no contradiction. When I made the remark which you quoted first, I was twenty-three and had been reproached for the fact that, as a trained musician, I was now returning to the classroom, starting my first term of a law degree. At that age – think back to the sixties, when everything was geared to growth – we felt that what mattered most was to earn loads of money, so that my fellow students and friends felt it was an unusual step for me to go back to school of my own accord. It was more or less to justify myself in the face of their remarks that I said, by way of an alibi, that, after studying law, I could become intendant of the Berlin Philharmonic. By 1977 this dream had all but faded, so that the offer came as a great surprise. A friend commented: 'Goodness, there are still people who can make the dreams of their youth come true.'

LANG: You're a cellist by training and studied with Zara Nelsova. When you're presented here as intendant, do the players say: 'Let's see what he can do on the cello', or do they ask what legal qualifications you've got?

GIRTH: As far as my cello playing is concerned, I've done all I can to conceal the fact. On two occasions I failed to do so, and on both occasions I was invited by the Berlin Philharmonic Cellists to take part in two official events, once when President Scheel was given the freedom of Berlin and again when Chancellor Helmut Schmidt received a similar honour. So I can restrict myself to these two occasions and shall certainly not be tempted a third time. I think I was well advised to deny my knowledge of the cello. And since I've stopped playing, I've virtually forgotten all I ever learned.

LANG: It's well known that the orchestra has to give its approval when a new intendant is elected here at the Philharmonie. How does the process work?

GIRTH: It's always said that all three parties involved have to come to a unanimous decision, in other words, the orchestra, the chief conductor and the Senate, since it is the latter that makes the appointment. I wasn't present when the decision to appoint me was taken or when they reached their agreement. So I know what happens only from hearsay: that's what's said to have taken place.

LANG: So you weren't introduced to the orchestra to face a series of questions?

GIRTH: As manager of the Association of German Orchestras I was already known to the orchestra as someone who had represented their interests. There was no need, in my view, for a special introduction.

LANG: For what period were you elected?

GIRTH: The election as such has no limit attached to it. But if you're asking about the length of my contract, it's limited, of course, to seven years.

LANG: And can it then be extended for as long as you like?

GIRTH: Let's wait and see.

LANG: I'd like to know something about your functions, duties and solitary decisions.

GIRTH: The simple answer would be that my functions are described in my contract. I have to see to the orchestra's artistic and financial welfare. The most important thing I have to do is plan the concerts, hire artists, whether they be conductors or soloists, plan tours and organize the budget. It's more than ever desirable that we balance our books, which is a job in itself. At the same time the intendant is expected to superintend operations, working towards new horizons and new ideas. But that's not something that can be forced, though I find that there's a great deal in this position that one can do. The qualities that are offered by the members of the orchestra make everything possible in principle.

LANG: The conducting competition run by the Herbert von Karajan Foundation has been operating since 1969. The chairman of the jury has always been Dr Stresemann. Is this position tied to that of the intendant at the Philharmonie?

GIRTH: When I came to Berlin in 1978, it was a surprise for everyone, including Dr Stresemann. Both he and the others were still reckoning on his contract being extended for another year. There simply wasn't enough time for a new appointment. But I allowed Herbert von Karajan and the orchestra to talk me into saying yes sooner rather than later. I'd have preferred it if Dr Stresemann could have remained here for at least another year. In the circumstances, I asked Dr Stresemann, as soon as I arrived in Berlin, to retain all the other functions involved in the exercise of his office, including chairmanship of the jury for the conducting competition. I think I should say that I can only learn from Dr Stresemann if, for a time, I step back into the lower ranks. At some point the time will come when he says of his own accord: 'I'm now giving up the post.' But I must say that I'm completely relaxed about it all and am happy for him to stay on as long as he wants. If you see him today, he's more ebullient than he ever was during his time as intendant. And I'm always glad to have him here beside me, so kind, cheerful and mentally alert is he.

LANG: There was no conducting competition in 1981 – 'for organizational reasons' is all it said in the press. Of course, one's tempted to suspect that there's some sort of crisis.

GIRTH: No, I can refute that very quickly. The real reason was that Professor Ahlendorf was ill, although he's now better, thank goodness, and is already back in harness. During his absence a letter arrived at the Foundation's offices from the Philharmonia Hungarica, the orchestra appointed to play at the competition, saying that, in spite of the agreement that had been reached, they were no longer prepared to place themselves at our disposal for three hours each morning and afternoon. They wanted to play for two and a half hours at most, as is in fact laid down in the relevant wage agreement for cultural orchestras. And so, since Professor Ahlendorf was ill, I spoke to Herr von Karajan and we decided to short-circuit the process: there was only one thing to be done and that was to cancel the competition. We weren't prepared to get involved in arguments with staffing councils and other institutions only to come up with two hours and forty minutes. We could only cancel the competition, and we were certainly well advised to react as we did. There was also a third thought at the back of our minds, which was that the Philharmonic would be celebrating its centenary in 1982 and that it would be nice to have the conducting competition then, in order, so to speak, to be able to choose a centenarian conductor.

LANG: Are you in fact intendant of the Philharmonie, the Berlin Philharmonic or the Berlin Philharmonic Orchestra?

GIRTH: That's a question that emphasizes the legal distinctions involved. I'm intendant of the Berlin Philharmonic Orchestra, whose home is the Philharmonie. In other words, I'm also financially responsible for the building, for renting it out and for everything else that's done with it. You and our audiences know the Berlin Philharmonic through gramophone recordings. Here the set-up is as follows: the Berlin Philharmonic makes recordings as a private company, a non-registered company, or however you want to define it. According to the contract of employment which the players have signed with the regional government, they're not obliged to make gramophone records or, rather, to go into the studio. In other words, they can make recordings as a sideline and, to the extent that their duties are not affected by it, I'm forced in practice to allow it, which I do gladly. This opportunity the orchestra has of working under a different name is, of course, one of the financial pillars of the entire enterprise. If I compare the economic conditions we can offer players on behalf of the regional government with those under which radio musicians in West Germany work, for example, we get very little more and, in terms of providing for our members in old age, we're considerably worse off. It's very important, therefore, that there should be a second pillar of support. I always take this opportunity to point out that it is thanks to all this extra work that improvements in the financial position of individual members of the orchestra have been so hard won. It certainly isn't handed to them on a plate. Don't forget there are two recording sessions a day: highly concentrated work for two three-hour periods. If you add the travelling time, it's very hard work indeed, which is perhaps why it's suitably remunerated.

LANG: It's said that you're very proud of the orchestra's recording commitments, and no doubt also of the chamber activities of the Berlin Philharmonic Duet, the Berlin Philharmonic Cellists, the Berlin Philharmonic Octet and so on. But I believe you're less happy with an organization which is making more and more of an impact on Berlin's concert life. At the foot of your advertising space is a large poster introducing the 'Berlin Chamber Academy'. The publicity states that this group is made up almost exclusively of members of the Berlin Philharmonic. And we read: 'Under the baton of the young Thomas Wilbrandt, the Berlin Chamber Academy is concentrating on the immense oeuvre of Wolfgang Amadeus Mozart, whose countless masterpieces have – scarcely conceivably – been largely neglected by our three great concert orchestras.' That seems to me a serious attack on your work.

GIRTH: It doesn't strike me like that. Everyone knows – it's objectively verifiable – which of Mozart's works are included in our programmes, and they also know that we put on programmes made up exclusively of Mozart: there are two in the current season alone. Of course, it's nothing new that, given the extent of Mozart's oeuvre, we still do too little. But it's obvious that an orchestra the size of the Berlin Philharmonic can't concentrate on Mozart. It's nonsense what we're reproached for or, rather, what we're said to be reproached for. As far as the conductor of the Chamber Academy is concerned, it makes me very unhappy to see him associated in any way with the Berlin Philharmonic Orchestra. That's not our world. As for the Chamber Academy itself, it certainly isn't made up primarily of members of the Berlin Philharmonic Orchestra, though it wants to include three concerts of works by Mozart here in the Philharmonie in the course of the present season; the concerts are to be given in rotation, with the participation of ten members of the orchestra. I've looked at their programmes and attended their first concert last year to find out what the quality was like, and I've come to the conclusion that I should simply forbid the members of my orchestra to play for this Chamber Academy at the expense of the Philharmonie.

LANG: Is that legally possible?

GIRTH: It's stated in the contracts of employment that the regional government signed with the members of the orchestra that every incidental activity is forbidden if it runs counter to regional interests. In this case I think that regional interests *are* being flouted in several respects. First, they're attempting to give the impression within our own four walls that the Chamber Academy is, so to speak, simply an offshoot of the Berlin Philharmonic Orchestra, with a conductor cheating his way into the building who is not a member of the orchestra and who, I believe, ought to produce evidence of his qualifications elsewhere before he conducts in the Philharmonie. You really can't begin your career with the Berlin Philharmonic. It's simply not honest, in my view. If it's a question of supporting a conductor on the shoulders of members of the Berlin Philharmonic Orchestra, then all I can say is that I want nothing whatever to do with it.

LANG: And who's to blame for the whole disaster?

GIRTH: I don't know. No one discussed it with me. I was merely confronted with the problem afterwards and have had to reach my own decisions. But they're not isolated decisions, I can tell you; they've been agreed with the Cultural Senate.

LANG: You see, the impression has arisen that the Berlin Philharmonic can somehow be bought by all and sundry.

GIRTH: You're the only one who's said that, although anyone can buy the services of the Berlin Philharmonic Orchestra. We play at congresses, for example, but the income accrues to the regional government. In much the same way the Berlin Philharmonic can be bought as a recording orchestra, but, as I've just said, there are good reasons for arguing that that sort of money is very hard-earned. The additional formation of a chamber orchestra would naturally dissipate the energies of its members, and I really can't imagine that this tendency to engage in unlimited amounts of solo work or chamber work can be to the good of the orchestra. At some point there's bound to be a decline in quality when people will say: 'They're doing too much.' One sometimes gets the impression even now that individual players have been doing too much and that they ought to do a bit less. But I don't want to institutionalize this shortcoming.

LANG: When the orchestra celebrates its centenary, you yourself will be just forty. Your predecessor, Dr Stresemann, once said that the position of intendant with the Berlin Philharmonic was the unsurpassable high-point in any career. Do you think this appointment can provide you with a lifetime's fulfilment?

GIRTH: The demands of the job and the vitality that it involves here could certainly provide a lifetime's fulfilment. After all, you live alongside different generations, you see others developing and have to adopt the same relationship to them. But, since you mention Dr Stresemann, it's worth adding that, when he became intendant, he was perhaps fifty-four. I really can't imagine that I'll still be here at that age.

27

'I don't see anything at all'

Third interview with Karajan

It was not only its music-loving readers who received a present with the Christmas 1981 number of *Stern* magazine: the title page of its 23 December issue featured a cat, Karajan's favourite animal. The cat, however, had its tongue stuck out, which proved an ill omen for the contents of the article in question, an account of internal goings-on during the Philharmonic's recent major tour of Japan, which had taken place between 24 October and 8 November. What was interesting about the feature – written by Emanuel Eckardt, with photographs by Dieter Blum – was less the tales of artistic success than the very thing that Emil Maas had been anxious to avoid: the players' views of their chief conductor and guest conductors, together with Peter Girth's opinion of the orchestra.

To begin with there were the 'sensational' photographs – Seiji Ozawa kneeling before Karajan, the orchestral players photographed in their underpants while changing for the evening's concert, and an inspired shot of two trumpeters caught with their trousers down in the local sauna. Never before had it been possible to read such damning remarks on the orchestra's regular guest conductors: Eugen Jochum was said to be 'finicky', Zubin Mehta had 'gone downhill of late', Riccardo Muti was 'a tyrant', Klaus Tennstedt a 'hot-air merchant' and Georg Solti 'the most overrated conducter of all'; Leonard Bernstein 'wept buckets at every piece'.

Karajan, too, was not spared: although the players would do anything for him, the only thing that held them together was fear of their chief conductor. When Eckhardt observed that they had not undertaken a tour of Germany for six years, the answer he received was: 'That's because Karajan doesn't get 100,000 marks a concert there.'

It was Peter Girth, however, who really took the biscuit, when he said:

> This orchestra is a terrible collective. Many of them don't know how lucky they are to have Karajan. There's poverty, unemployment and war in the world but this orchestra is completely blind to it all. They're frightful. And remote from life. But they all know how to count.

The author of the *Stern* article, Emanuel Eckardt, saw himself obliged to confirm Girth's remarks in the *Tagesspiegel* of 1 May 1983:

It's true that Dr Girth's remarks were quoted incomplete – but in his own interest. He had already given me a wealth of information during our first interview in Tokyo which, for good reason, I have not published. If I could sum up my impression of the interview, it would only be to say that it is not the representative of an institution who speaks in this way but its victim. Dr Girth did not represent the Berlin Philharmonic Orchestra and its chief conductor, he denounced them.

Since the *Stern* article was widely read, it must be assumed that Karajan's spies had drawn his attention to those who had fouled their own nest. His mood can hardly have been improved by Fred K. Prieberg's revelation, published in *Music in the National Socialist State*, that Karajan had joined the party not just once, but twice.

The orchestra's centenary celebrations were fast approaching, so that it was with a certain sense of relief that the parties involved were able to seize on a distraction in the form of an advance advertisement from Deutsche Grammophon:

Germany's top orchestra plays the hundred most popular masterpieces of great symphonic music in top recordings from Deutsche Grammophon – conducted and personally chosen by Maestro Herbert von Karajan and illustrated with original paintings by Eliette von Karajan.

It was possible to think of pure art once again and to celebrate the higher things of life with a brilliant concert performance of *Tosca*, held in the Philharmonie on 22 February 1982, with Katia Ricciarelli, José Carreras and Ruggero Raimondi in the leading roles. Since the final rehearsal had taken place that morning, Karajan was ready to give a lengthy television interview, which I was able to observe from close quarters.

Everything had been prepared in his dressing-room for a ten o'clock start. The spotlights were trained on the sofa, one camera was set up to film the maestro from the front, the other from his right-hand side. It was winter and the temperature outside was around 5°C. Karajan appeared at ten past ten, wearing a long black coat resplendently lined with grey fleece. Beside him was the American impresario, Peter Gelb. They all shook hands in a friendly manner. Karajan took control of the scene at once. The television producer was told to go and sit on the sofa to test the composition of the shot. Karajan went to the middle camera, looked through the viewfinder and declared himself well satisfied. He then went to the side camera, glanced swiftly through the lens and immediately gave instructions for the camera to be moved from the right-hand side to the left-hand side of the sofa. They had forgotten to take account of Karajan's best side. The interviewer, Klaus Geitel, said by way of a joke: 'Don't tell Axel Springer that you only like being photographed from the left.'

It took at least fifteen minutes to reposition the camera. Meanwhile, Karajan slipped outside to discuss something with Maximilian Schell. He then returned and sat on the sofa himself. He was wearing a roll-neck pullover to which the clip-on microphone refused to be attached: 'Whatever you do, don't cut a hole in my pullover.' He had brought a change of clothing with him and, anxious to help, disappeared behind a curtain, asking what colour he should wear, before reappearing in black. Sitting there, he suddenly looked quite young. The interview began and lasted an hour, during which time he barely paused for breath.

During all this, I had ample time to consider whether I could catch him afterwards for a radio interview. My ploy worked: he was ready to help but, in keeping with his life's motto, 'I hate everything that's unexpected', he asked me to discuss the questions with him beforehand. Acoustics? 'OK.' The way the Philharmonic sound has changed? 'Too complicated, I'd need three hours for that.' Family? 'OK.' Berlin Chamber Academy? 'I don't know anything about this orchestra or its conductor.' Sabine Meyer? 'It's not a good idea for me to say anything on the subject, there's been so much trouble.' The *Stern* article? 'I can't say anything about that because I haven't read it.' Really?

LANG: Your biographer Ernst Haeusserman includes a chapter on the Berlin Philharmonic which begins with the sentence: 'Benjamin Bilse founded the Berlin Philharmonic Orchestra in 1882 and gave concerts in a rebuilt ice-skating rink in Köthener Strasse.' I don't want to be petty, but there are three inaccuracies in this sentence. Benjamin Bilse didn't found the orchestra: it was formed when members of the Bilse'sche Kapelle split off from the parent orchestra. The rink was used for roller-skating, not ice-skating, and it was situated in Bernburger Strasse. The next sentence, however, is interesting: 'Since it was famous for its perfect acoustic, it was later called the Philharmonie.' Herr von Karajan, it was on 8 April 1938 that you first conducted the Berlin Philharmonic Orchestra in the Alte Philharmonie. Were the acoustics there really of the kind that people still dream about today?

KARAJAN: Most definitely. They struck me as very similar to the acoustics in the Musikvereinssaal in Vienna, which is, of course, world-famous for its acoustics. There are a few halls that were built or rebuilt at more or less the same time, and in every case it seems that the architects went back to a fairly precisely calculated design of floor plan and cubic capacity. Also, they built less in concrete in those days and used a lot of wood, of course. That almost certainly produced good results. At the Vienna State Opera the floor to which the stalls seating is fixed can be lowered when they have balls, in other words, an opening appears and the seating disappears inside it. The whole space is then like a sounding-board, which naturally helps the acoustics enormously. The same was true of the Philharmonie, and I know how appalled we all were when it was destroyed.

LANG: So the sound was really outstanding?

KARAJAN: Without a doubt.

LANG: I know – as you've just shown – that you're very interested in problems of acoustics. The conductor, after all, stands on a podium and has a completely different position from the audience. How can you tell that what you're doing in terms of the balance of sound is also the best from the audience's point of view?

KARAJAN: It's a question of experience. If you've known a hall for a relatively long time and not only conducted in it but also listened to concerts from various seats, you'll be able to produce the sound you want on the basis of experience. You know such and such is correct. Of course, you can never say what it will sound like from every individual seat, that would be impossible. But one thing you mustn't forget: in the Alte Philharmonie the conductor was basically in a different position from here. He was relatively far away, towards one end of the hall, where the orchestra was. Everything else was the auditorium. In Scharoun's Philharmonie the conductor is almost in the middle of the hall. And everything around him is built on what has been called the 'vineyard principle' ever since the Stuttgart Liederhalle was opened: the seating in every terrace is arranged in such a way that it catches the sound at the best angle. In other words, the sound actually strikes all the individual segments of the hall directly. And together they form a virtual circle. Here in the Philharmonie the ratio is 45:55. But the centre is the place where the conductor stands. A critic once said, quite correctly, that in this particular hall you never know where the orchestra stops and the audience starts. It's this that makes music-making such a concentrated affair. I must say that, from my own personal point of view, it's my favourite hall today.

LANG: You sometimes walk around the hall, listening to the orchestra playing on its own.

KARAJAN: Yes, at concerts with other conductors.

LANG: But I've also seen the orchestra playing without you – for example, when Professor Keilholz made alterations to the Deutschlandhalle. You walked round the hall in order to hear what it sounded like. Are you often very disappointed or even appalled by what you hear?

KARAJAN: Of course, it can't always be equally perfect. We knew there'd be only *one* concert in the Deutschlandhalle. If a lot of concerts were to be planned for this hall, there'd have to be a proper study of the acoustics. I was very lucky with Professor Keilholz. Together we built or adapted a vast number of halls, and it was a source of great sadness to me when he died last year. His last project appears to have been the Palace of Culture in Sofia, which I've seen and where we shall be giving a concert. It's a very large hall, with 5000 seats, though it can be made smaller. It incorporates the experiences of a lifetime. One of his finest achievements is certainly the Salzburg Festspielhaus, which has the same good acoustics in every category – concerts, choral concerts and operas. There's really nothing like it any longer in the world, for all the well-known theatres that have very good acoustics – think of La Scala, Milan, for example – are far inferior when used for concerts.

LANG: Can we go back to 1938? The first programme you conducted with the Philharmonic was Mozart's Symphony K319, Ravel's Second Suite from *Daphnis et Chloé* and Brahms's Fourth Symphony. That's a programme you'd never conduct today.

KARAJAN: True.

LANG: Why not?

KARAJAN: I can explain it by repeating an answer I once gave in London. I was at a press conference and someone asked me why concerts which, in the past, used to last three hours now lasted only one and a quarter. I said: 'Look, go outside into Piccadilly Circus and count how many horse-drawn carriages you can see.' That's the answer.

LANG: I've the feeling that you now do programmes that are made up either of a single part – a great Mahler symphony – or of two parts – Stravinsky's *Apollon musagète* and Strauss's *Alpine Symphony*, for example. Is it more of a breathing in and breathing out?

KARAJAN: It's not so easy to say. Programmes are not really designed in that way, they force themselves on me as though of their own accord. You've not conducted a piece for a long time and suddenly you feel a desperate need to do it. That's what's so wonderful about it, that you can then follow it up and see what you can do to integrate it into the other parts of the programme. For example, I've just conducted the *Alpine Symphony* for the first time in my life. I've simply never got round to it before. With the relatively small orchestras that exist in other towns and cities, it's very difficult to assemble such huge forces with all the extra players that you need. I know it was Strauss's favourite work, and it became clear to me during the rehearsals and while I was studying it why he must have liked this piece above all others. Quite apart from the description of nature in 'On the Summit', the final section is of such immense beauty and depth that it bowls me over every time.

LANG: Your interpretation was an enormous success, there's no denying that. Had you expected audiences to take to the work?

KARAJAN: To be honest, I hadn't thought about it. If I'm convinced of something, I can't imagine anyone else saying it leaves him indifferent.

LANG: Could we talk about the Philharmonic? After all, it's their centenary. You keep talking about a family, but the roles must be divided up, which would make you the father and the players the children. Is that more or less the picture you have of this family?

KARAJAN: Absolutely. Of course, it's turned out like that only because we've lived together for so long, which means that on tour, for example, one's really together the whole time and sympathizes with other people's problems and incidents. And that's developed in a wonderful way. For instance, the individual string players often buy very expensive instruments. I was delighted to hear that and have advised them on matters of finance. Of course, it helps the orchestra's tonal picture enormously, so that the whole thing grows even better. All these things can be discussed, including, for example, the way that a job can be made easier or divided up in a better way. You then trust each other, which certainly doesn't happen overnight but takes a long time to develop. I really can't remember how it all began, it all seems so long ago now. But when I see the road we've travelled together, it's still quite a short section of my life, albeit the most important one. Everything has become so compressed that I no longer have any concept of time. And it's things like this that have brought home to me just how relative time is. On the one hand, these events have unfolded over what's almost been a historic age, while, on the other, they're the experience of a single day. One hears of people who've had accidents while mountaineering and who, while falling, have seen their whole lives flash past them. It seems to be the same with me.

People ask me whether I keep rethinking things, or they ask: 'How did it strike you then?' 'What's become of the tonal picture of this orchestra?' It's not the same as with an architect, who draws up plans to build a house. No, you hear something inside you and reconcile it with what you actually hear. Suddenly you feel deep down inside you that you've found what you were hoping for. But there have even been many cases where what you've got out of the orchestra has surpassed your expectations. Those are the happiest moments you can have.

Of course, I began with orchestras that were far less perfect, so that there was an enormous gap between the two. I had to concentrate as hard as I could in order to hear what I thought it should sound like. And then, with this orchestra, the time came when imagination and reality drew closer and closer together. It inspires one with a great sense of gratitude. It's fabulous how an independent personality suddenly emerges from the corporate actions of a group of 120 people, all doing and wanting the very same thing. It's the secret of how birds fly, something I never tire of watching. You simply can't ask how it happens. There's a mass soul, or whatever you want to call it, that functions according to completely different laws. Birds always get it right, and exactly the same is true of the orchestra. Suddenly everything works of its own accord. These are secrets which, if you can experience them for yourself, are always a blessing. But it's almost impossible to explain them to anyone.

When Buddhists meditate, for example, concentrating on the Zen produces a sensation not only in the individual; they share the experience with others who are concentrating on the same thing. In music, too, the communal experience is much stronger than when you concentrate on the individual aspect or simply read the score. I can form a good impression of what a symphony will sound like. But this purely emotional experience, which is felt when everything really comes together, can't be produced on its own.

LANG: And – this is a very intimate question – when you stand there now, with your eyes closed, what can you see?

KARAJAN: Nothing. Nothing at all.

LANG: Don't you see tonal elements moving around? Certainly, you won't see the notes on the printed page any longer.

KARAJAN: Certainly not, never. It's something I really can't explain. You simply stop seeing and enter a totally different world.

LANG: But you still must have an objective awareness of the audience and its reactions.

KARAJAN: No, no, no. Absolutely not.

LANG: A long time ago there was a man sitting in the third row. He was hard of hearing and his hearing aid was suffering from feedback, making it squeak terribly. He himself didn't notice.

KARAJAN: All right . . .

LANG: I asked you later whether it had disturbed you and you said: 'It went in one ear and out of the other.' But you'd been aware of it . . .

KARAJAN: Yes.

LANG: . . . and not felt it.

KARAJAN: No, not at all. I know I once lost a kidney stone during a concert without noticing it. My doctor told me afterwards what had happened. Normally you'd fall off the platform in pain.

LANG: But I assume you put more into a concert than into a gramophone recording, where you record the work bit by bit.

KARAJAN: How do you mean, 'bit by bit'?

LANG: The audience must inspire you to give of your best.

KARAJAN: Just a moment. You said, 'bit by bit'. Even in the studio the whole piece is played right through.

LANG: You now record works movement by movement, right through to the end?

KARAJAN: Certainly.

LANG: But you then have corrections which can be added later.

KARAJAN: Yes, all right. But they're so insignificant that they're not worth mentioning.

LANG: So you'd say that the result is just the same as at a concert?

KARAJAN: It's exactly the same.

LANG: So there's no need to have an audience with you. There are other conductors – Furtwängler, for instance – for whom an audience . . .

KARAJAN: . . . but why should they be dispensable? Why should you stop people – assuming you've the means of shutting them out – from having what, I hope, is an uplifting experience? It's only at rehearsals that I don't like it, there's no need to have anyone present then. But why shouldn't one allow them to attend concerts? Your question's not legitimate.

LANG: Well, you've a very fortunate gift, not to need an audience but to be able to come up with the goods at any time, including gramophone records.

KARAJAN: You can't say I don't need an audience, since we've known since time immemorial that there are people present at a concert. It's like asking a child today: 'What would you do if there were no cars on the roads?' A child knows that there's always a car in front of it and behind it and that there are thousands driving around the streets. It's so obvious, people no longer think about it.

LANG: And later on they may find the cars are terrible and would be happy to be rid of them.

KARAJAN: I don't know.

LANG: But you're happy to have your audiences?

KARAJAN: Certainly. If you know that you can make a person happy and if the person tells you so, it's a wonderful feeling. Why should one get involved in elaborate arguments on the subject?

LANG: Let me break off at this point and ask one final question: what do you wish the Berlin Philharmonic Orchestra on its hundredth birthday?

KARAJAN: That we remain together as long as possible.

28

'That's my final word on the subject'

The Berlin Philharmonic's hundredth anniversary

Contradictions are inherently interesting and have always been among Herbert von Karajan's principal characteristics. Does the audience really have only a walk-on role for him? Are they there only because of a historical accident? 'Why shouldn't they be admitted?' His words are arrogant and offensive, even contemptuous. But is it true what he says? Why did he say, shortly beforehand, that making music in the Philharmonie was such a concentrated affair precisely because, in this particular hall, 'you never know where the orchestra stops and the audience starts'? Or think of what he said on the occasion of his twenty-fifth anniversary as chief conductor of the BPO: 'I am grateful to my public. For twenty-five years you have revealed your loyalty time and again.' Are those the words one addresses to a tiresome companion?

In the run-up to the orchestra's hundredth birthday celebrations on 1 May 1982, the seventy-four-year-old conductor found himself battling with a protracted bout of influenza. The press suspected malaria. The news cast a shadow over the event, but it was the orchestra, after all, which stood at the forefront of the celebrations. With a truly Prussian sense of duty he managed to get through the two concerts on 30 April and 1 May (both began with Mozart's 'Jupiter' Symphony and ended, respectively, with Beethoven's 'Eroica' and Mahler's Ninth). He then flew to Vienna with his orchestra for two performances of Beethoven's Ninth, which he conducted in a state of high fever, after which he cancelled all his other commitments, including a planned recording of *Der Rosenkavalier*.

It was scarcely likely that Karajan would be fully recovered from such an illness within a month, and yet he was not the man to let slip an opportunity, especially one as sensational as the chance to present the world's first compact disc to the international press at a conference called in Hamburg in June 1982. He had, of course, been deeply interested in the development from the very outset, and launched the novel format with a technologically stunning recording of Strauss's *Alpine Symphony.* The Berlin Philharmonic, playing with all the technical mastery at their command, thus opened the doors on a new and triumphant era in media technology. On the front of the booklet that came with the disc was the Matterhorn's shimmering outline, a peak in the maestro's career.

The infamous article in *Stern* magazine of 23 December 1981, which had poisoned the atmosphere between Karajan, the orchestra and Peter Girth, proved to be only a prelude, since it now encouraged the players to avail themselves of the press to vent internal grievances. The children had all grown up and were starting to question their father's tyrannical sway, leaving the process of disintegration that takes place in every family to run its organic course.

The next thunderbolt struck on the very day that the celebrations were due to be held. On 1 May 1982 the gramophone magazine *HIFI-Stereophonie* published an unsigned article headed 'Berlin Philharmonic: Notes from an Insider'. The players themselves can have been in no doubt who the author was, but outsiders had to wait until 1987 to have their suspicions confirmed. It was in 1987 that the solo timpanist, Werner Thärichen, published his memoirs under the title, *Drumrolls: Furtwängler or Karajan*. It breathed an identical spirit, as the following 'Notes from an Insider' make abundantly clear. Karajan had founded his academy 'with the aim of training a new generation of orchestral players, but so far without any appreciable success. Apart from his valuable name, there was nothing he needed invest.' As for Karajan's interpretative skills, 'A great tonal and dynamic range was achieved, but the differences in volume, from the virtual inaudibility of many string passages to the ear-splitting din of the full orchestra, sometimes assumed absurd proportions.' And – drawing an odious comparison with Furtwängler:

> In general he attempts, as far as possible, to dispense with *rubati* and changes of tempo. In the case of their additional recording work, the Philharmonic players have bowed completely to the will of the individual. The majority abandon all sense of solidarity with their colleagues when threatened with a suspension of recording work, and unpopular people are put out of harm's way.

Harsh words from an insider – presumably Werner Thärichen. What detracts from this picture of Karajan are his questionable characteristics. In his memoirs Thärichen revealed that Karajan had systematically destroyed him and then driven him from the orchestra. Having been humiliated in this way, he took over from Herbert Ahlendorf as artistic co-ordinator of the Karajan conducting competitions. Did Karajan realize that he had appointed his severest critic to this influential position?

In October 1982, on the occasion of the seventh conducting competition,

Karajan gave his last major speech in Berlin. The physically decrepit founder, the semi-paralysed Herbert Ahlendorf and the increasingly ancient jury made it all too plain to everyone present what agonies lay behind these competitions for young conductors. It proved the penultimate one of its kind. A packed house heard Karajan enunciate Werner Thärichen's reform proposals:

Ladies and gentlemen. We are now going to award the prizes. You know that we have not awarded a first prize and that the second prize is divided between Nikolai Alexeev and Igor Golovchin. The third prize goes to Oleg Caetani.

I'd like to say one last word on the subject. Anyone who has followed all seven competitions over the last fourteen years will perhaps notice that their structure has changed substantially: in other words, we've been forced on two or three occasions to divide one of the prizes and sometimes not to award the first prize at all.

What has happened? It is quite simply that the difference between 'very good', 'good' and 'mediocre' has shifted in the course of time and become less and less clear-cut, so that the quality that has emerged has been almost all of the same high standard. This makes me wonder whether, in the long term, we should try to reorganize the competition. I have the feeling that until now it has been a question of taking note of various talented conductors and sending them out into the world, where many of them have certainly made their own way. But we need to give something more than this. It's my opinion that we should perhaps divide the competition over two years, so that in the first year we simply decide which of the candidates – say, three or four of them – should be specially singled out. In the second year they would then work on certain pieces with an orchestra which would be at their complete disposal. It would have to be a first-class orchestra, with everything under my overall control, at least as long as I can manage it. You mustn't forget that the prizewinners really have only a single rehearsal with the Philharmonic. Basically, they ought to be together very much longer with one and the same orchestra and then play in the final concert together. Don't misunderstand me. This isn't a vote of no-confidence in my friends here [*turning round to the BPO*]. But it's clear that these young conductors have had too little time so far. They were able to break off only three times perhaps but were otherwise forced to improvise. I'd like them to be able to go away from here and to know for themselves, from a stylistic point of view, too, what it means to bring an orchestra to the point where it really plays what they want it to play.

We shall have to think the matter over. As always, of course, it's a question of money, but that, too, will be found, so that when these young people leave here, they have a year to think things over and reflect on what they've achieved. And then they should really work on something under guidance, which, ultimately, is essential for their whole careers. That's my opinion, and we'll see whether we can find a suitable solution.

I don't think one should stand still, simply because something has proved its worth in the past. No, one must always look for ways of making it better. That's my final word on the subject, and it remains only for me to thank you for your attention and, above all, to thank my friends here [*turning to the orchestra; applause*]. In particular I'd like to thank the members of our jury, who are no longer here. Believe me, it's a very difficult job, sitting there for ten days and deciding who's best. As always, they've performed with great self-sacrifice. And now that they are once again scattered across the world, my especial thanks go to all those who have worked with us here so enthusiastically. [*Applause.*]

29
'All that remains is a monologue'
Sabine Meyer

It was in Onolzheim, of all places, that a clarinettist was born, on 30 March 1959, who came close to driving a wedge between the Berlin Philharmonic Orchestra, now celebrating its hundredth anniversary, and Herbert von Karajan. The young lady herself was hardly to blame. She had trained in Stuttgart and Hanover and, a diligent and talented student, had been awarded a teaching certificate in music, as well as picking up qualifications as a concert performer. Prizes in Bonn and Wiesbaden were followed by radio and television recordings. By 1981, when she was still only twenty-two, she was deputy solo clarinet in the Bavarian Radio Symphony Orchestra. It was a fabulous career, which lacked only the final touch.

Accordingly Sabine Meyer turned to the 'Situations Vacant' column and saw that Ulf Rodenhäuser's post had still not been filled in Berlin. In January 1981 she auditioned for the BPO and was the best of all the applicants. Karajan, too, shared this view, so that Meyer could now be flown in from Munich at any time to stand in for ailing colleagues. There were artistic reservations, however, and the orchestra refused to accept a one-year probationary contract, although this did not prevent the clarinettist from travelling with the BPO to Salzburg, Lucerne and America and playing under Karajan.

What were their objections to her? The orchestra conceded that she had outstanding abilities as a soloist, as her subsequent international career was to demonstrate. What was problematical, in their opinion, was her playing as leader of her section: in ensemble passages she still had difficulties.

The *Berliner Morgenpost* later asked four solo wind players from the BPO to spell out the criteria behind their decision. The predominant view, in Lothar Koch's words, was that what mattered most was a 'romantically mellow, warm, sonorous and substantial tone'. Karl Leister, the solo clarinet, added that 'sound is a constant dialogue with the person sitting at the same desk, so that the individual player not only gives but, to a far greater extent, takes. If two musicians insist on different ideas of sound, no dialogue can emerge. All that remains is a monologue.' He was referring, of course, to Sabine Meyer. What was so paradoxical about the whole banal affair was that Karajan had wanted three women as sectional leaders – Roswitha Staege, Sabine Meyer and Maria Graf – whereas the orchestra found that in one case the player's tone was too 'weak' and in another 'too soloistic'. Was it possible that, as an acoustician, Karajan had got it wrong on all three counts? Had he, of all people, fewer scruples when it came to bringing new blood into the orchestra?

At the beginning of the 1982/3 season the orchestra made a highly astute move. The fires kindled by the non-appointment of Sabine Meyer were still smouldering in the background, when the possibility presented itself of appointing a female violinist, one of fourteen applicants for an orchestral vacancy. The applicant in question was the Swiss violinist, Madeleine Carruzzo, who had emerged victorious from the auditions and who was appointed for a probationary year, starting on 1 September 1982. Her qualifications were undisputed. More important, it could no longer be claimed that the orchestra would rebel against women members. And, as everyone recognized, the Meyer case could now be dealt with on a purely objective basis.

The general public had little understanding for the whole affair, preferring to hear good music. And that was something that the orchestra, with its literal love of beautiful sounds, was determined to provide. The result was a vicious circle in which the intendant, Peter Girth, also became involved. But, having already forfeited the good will of this 'terrible collective', he proceeded to make the biggest mistake of all. He threw in his hand with Karajan, leaving the orchestra – which continued to insist on its right of self-determination – to shiver outside in the cold.

The orchestra met on 16 November 1982 and decided once and for all that Sabine Meyer would not be accepted for a probationary year. Nor were the players prepared to discuss an extension of Peter Girth's contract, which was due to run out on 31 August 1985. Karajan was bound to feel snubbed on both fronts and – to take up the much-abused simile – resolved to punish his children. This time he hit where it hurt and made it clear, in public too, that in the course of their lengthy relationship the players had grown too independent. On 3 December he sent them his best wishes from Vienna, observing, at the same time, that he had come to the conclusion that Sabine Meyer had met 'all the conditions for this position' and that, in judging artistic standards, he found himself 'in diametrical opposition' to the views of his orchestra. As a result, he was adjourning *sine die* (he used the legal term) all further tours with them and postponing all recordings and video work. That this was no empty threat became all too clear on New Year's Eve, when the live television transmission of the Johann Strauss concert, which ought to have been recorded for Karajan's company, Telemondial, was called off, causing the players a loss of income of around 100,000 marks. The orchestra refused to be blackmailed and on 4 January 1983 called another full meeting, when they once again voted against taking on Sabine Meyer for a probationary year.

The warring factions became more entrenched when Girth demanded permission from the Senate to sign a one-year contract with the clarinettist. The name of the former intendant, Wolfgang Stresemann, was suggested as a mediator. Events took an unexpected turn on 16 January when Girth chose to go it alone and drew up a contract with Meyer, offering her a probationary year. Legally, he may have been within his rights, but the result was undisguised horror on the part of the Philharmonic players: 'The orchestra notes that there is no longer any basis of trust which would allow it to continue working with its intendant, Dr Girth, and demands his immediate dismissal.'

What made the situation doubly difficult for the players was that, from now on, reports in the local papers were split right down the middle. Whereas the *Volksblatt* and *Tagesspiegel* tried to be fair and objective, Klaus Geitel in the *Morgenpost* saw it as his duty to stand up for Karajan right to the bitter end. In Geitel's view the chief conductor's reputation was far greater than his contestable qualities as a human being; Girth, too, should be left at his side for the rest of his days on earth. 'It appears incredible', Geitel wrote on 20 January, 'that the orchestra should make a stand against an artist to whom it owes its pre-eminent position by virtue of that artist's life's work.'

It was increasingly difficult, therefore, for the battered and deeply depressed musicians to find any sense of justice, still less could they vent their grievances in public. The debate concerning the qualities of Meyer's tone had long since become a burning political issue. The mayor of West Berlin, Richard von Weizsäcker, was asked to intervene, while Wilhelm Kewenig, the CDU minister with responsibility for the arts, was accused by the SPD of adopting a 'zigzag course'. 'The senator's actions in this case have been altogether unfortunate.'

Following Meyer's appointment for a probationary year, Karajan's loving-kindness certainly knew no bounds. He ratified Girth's decision and on 27 January announced that his punitive measures were over. 'Let's make great music together,' were his first words at the rehearsal. And they played as though nothing had happened – Beethoven's Fourth Piano Concerto, with Ashkenazy as soloist, and Saint-Saëns's 'Organ' Symphony.

Of course, nothing had been resolved, and Girth was perfectly right to remark that there were people in the orchestra 'who want to break with Herbert von Karajan'. He, however, was of the opinion that now was the time for the players 'to give thanks to a great man for his life's work'.

Once before, on 10 January 1972, the Lessing University in Berlin had persuaded Karajan to take part in a public discussion. Now, in the midst of this major crisis, the parties came together again, this time at the International Congress Centre, where the topic for discussion was 'Thoughts on Performing Music in the Future'. The subject was badly handled by Karajan – let that be said at the outset – for not only had he come unprepared, his inspiration failed him. Infuriatingly, he squandered his endless abilities on half-completed sentences, hackneyed phrases and anecdotes. Fortunately, the media had been excluded. A woman sitting next to me began to knit. When two people walked out, Karajan watched them go, then commented: 'I suppose they were expecting something different.' No doubt they were. His uncompromising faith in progress and condemnation of gas lighting – and this from someone who lived in the depths of the countryside – were already sufficiently known. 'I've looked increasingly into the future.' Perhaps, but what of the future performance of music? No one dared ask, though for two whole hours everyone present had hoped to hear the words 'Sabine Meyer' and 'Peter Girth' on Karajan's lips. Their hopes were in vain. With the words, 'I hope to come back again soon', he was gone. Few of those present shared that wish.

Scarcely was this 'public discussion' over when Karajan suffered a further series of setbacks. Thomas Brandis, his favourite leader, announced his resignation after twenty-one years in the post. His departure had nothing to do with the crisis, he assured anyone who would listen: it was merely that he wanted to devote more time to his students and his quartet. The second slap in the face came when Senator Kewenig finally succeeded in preventing Peter Girth's contract from being renewed. Karajan would therefore have to reckon on having a new intendant from 1985, an appointment which, according to the orchestra's constitution, would be made not 'by mutual agreement' but 'after consultation with' Karajan. All the maestro could do would be to nod his approval.

Anxious as ever to stir things up, Klaus Geitel shifted the blame from Karajan to the orchestra, revealing ostensible shortcomings at the latter's recording sessions. Riccardo Muti ('a favourite to succeed Karajan') had

had to interrupt his recording of Strauss's *Aus Italien*, for example, 'because the first clarinet, who had been brought in from outside as a stand-in, had proved artistically inadequate'.

Trouble was already brewing, therefore, when Peter Girth invited the press to the annual conference on 15 March and announced the programme for the forthcoming season. He began by reading out a telex from Karajan in Sofia, which ended with the words: 'You have my continuing trust.' At that point Hans Heinz Stuckenschmidt, now eighty-one years old and the doyen of the city's music critics, rose to his feet and said: 'Herr Girth, you have destroyed the sense of unity between Karajan and the Philharmonic Orchestra.' The meeting ended on an even more depressing note with an unworthy exchange of insults between the orchestra's managing director and the critic, Klaus Geitel.

30

'May harmony reign'

The Chamber-Music Room

At 11 o'clock on 28 December 1982 the Berlin Philharmonic was pleased to invite its friends to attend a reception in the Philharmonie's south foyer. Dr Wilfried Haslauer, head of the regional government in Salzburg, had come with a bronze plaque weighing some twenty-seven kilograms in order to congratulate the players not only on their hundredth anniversary but also, and more particularly, on twenty-five years of active involvement in the Salzburg Festival. Included in this vote of thanks was their longstanding contribution to Salzburg's Easter and Whitsun Festivals. Haslauer ended his speech with the hope that the Berliners and their chief conductor, Herbert von Karajan, would continue to work together for many years, creating that 'harmony, sense of perfection and euphony that are altogether without equal'. But these were the very qualities which were now in short supply. None of the players struck a note throughout the whole of the ceremony, the drinks tasted flat and Karajan himself was reduced to playing the unfamiliar role of onlooker. He maintained a steady silence, as the look of indifference in his eyes slowly began to harden. On his nose – to everyone's surprise – was perched a pair of glasses. The bronze had now been installed above him, its inscription having already been the subject of speculation. The text was said to have been discovered in the course of excavations at a Roman villa in the old part of Salzburg and was therefore being dedicated to the Berlin Philharmonic Orchestra. Karajan left the oppressive gathering without a word of greeting but, before he did so, the tablet was unveiled. As the cloth that was covering it fell away, the assembled company read the words: 'Good fortune dwells within these walls: may evil never enter here.'

On 31 January 1983 Karajan conducted Beethoven's Fourth and Seventh Symphonies at a concert designed to raise funds for the chamber-music room that was still to be built. It was noticed that a change had been made to the railings surrounding the podium. A barely noticeable small black velvet cushion allowed the conductor to lean against it during the concert, making the audience think he could still remain standing throughout the whole of a symphony, though no one would have held it against him if he had sat on a chair.

Shortly before his seventy-fifth birthday, he was interviewed for *Stern* by Felix Schmidt. 'Even you must step down one day,' Schmidt suggested. 'But I expect that you'll die conducting.' – 'A beautiful way to go,' was Karajan's answer. His mind was as active as ever and his artistic activities undiminished. But, increasingly, physical decline made every step a form of torture, causing audiences to catch their breath as he fought his way to the podium. Nowhere did the gap between appearance and reality find clearer expression than in a book of photographs issued in a de-luxe edition by Deutsche Grammophon to celebrate the maestro's birthday. One such photograph showed him surrounded by smartly dressed young men, at the helm of his ocean-going yacht: 'I was always at the front of the ship.' The maestro's inescapable glance was shaded only by the blue of his 'Goodyear' cap. The man would never admit he was mortal. Even his 'contract for life' with the BPO refused to accept such a possibility. But should one not have felt pity for him for still wanting to be an autocrat at a time when the world no longer needed autocrats? For the argument over Sabine Meyer threatened the orchestra's very future with its chief conductor for life. The players had turned down Karajan's chosen candidate, for which they were thoroughly reprimanded with patriarchal rigour: in March 1983, for example, he cancelled a tour of Bulgaria with them and instead invited their Viennese rivals to open Sofia's new Palace of Culture. But that was merely a prelude.

At the same time, the workload that Karajan placed on his players in Salzburg alone roused universal wonder. The 1983 Easter Festival included three performances of *Der fliegende Holländer*, with its Helmsman's Song, 'Through tempest and storm, from distant seas' – a piece well suited to Karajan's life on the ocean waves. It was also the sesquicentenary of Brahms's birth, making him twice as old as Karajan – a welcome excuse to perform all four symphonies and the *German Requiem.* Away from home, it seemed as though the conductor could breathe a little more freely.

In Berlin, meanwhile, changes were taking place in the Senate. Wilhelm Kewenig, the senator with special responsibility for science and the arts, could no longer be trusted to deal with the complexities surrounding Karajan, Meyer, Girth and the Philharmonic and was replaced by the former minister of the environment, Volker Hassemer, who was given the job of cleansing Berlin's Augean stables. But devious schemes were being plotted, as is clear from a conspiratorial letter of 15 April 1983, which was not published until 18 July 1984. The letter in question was written by Peter Girth and addressed to 'my most esteemed and dear Herr von Karajan'. In it Girth put forward the suggestion for a 'complete reorganization' and promised Karajan that in future he need conduct only subscription-free concerts in Berlin. Subscribers who ultimately bore the costs of the Philharmonic concerts were to be spared the maestro, since they brought him too little acclaim. Girth then went on to advocate the appointment of a 'Principal Guest Conductor as an outflanking manoeuvre, so to speak'. 'As for the appointment of an orchestral inspector, that is something on which I do not need to comment, given the shortcomings which have come to light.'

We come now to Karajan's second serious back operation. Predictions that it would have to take place were first voiced on 5 May 1983, when Karajan, in spite of considerable pain, was conducting an extraordinarily successful Brahms cycle at that year's Vienna Festival to mark the composer's sesquicentenary. Immediately after the *German Requiem* he was admitted to Hanover's Nordstadt Hospital and treated by Dr Madjid Samii. Karajan insisted that he still intended to conduct the première of *Der Rosenkavalier* at the opening of the Salzburg Festival on 25 July. The operation, which took place on 7 June and lasted three and a half hours, proved a success, and Karajan was able to walk again without the contorting pain he had suffered during the previous period. He was able to resume lessons for his helicopter-pilot's licence only a few weeks later, and to stage and conduct his sixth *Der Rosenkavalier* at the 1983 Salzburg Festival.

Back in Berlin, the two-pronged Amazonian attack on the BPO had finally paid off in the face of half-hearted opposition from the rank and file. On the very day that the violinist Madeleine Carruzzo signed a permanent contract with the BPO, Sabine Meyer began her probationary year. Her new male colleagues, it must be said, went out of their way to treat her fairly, knowing well enough that, if she had been accepted into their ranks, it was through no fault of her own.

Whether Karajan himself could expect fair treatment was a rather different question. At all events, he must have thought he was dreaming when, back in Salzburg, he received a leaflet for the town's forthcoming Mozart Week, which was to include an all-Mozart concert by the 'Berlin Chamber Music Ensemble' mentioned above, at which the soloists would be the woodwind players Andreas Blau and Hansjörg Schellenberger. The concert, moreover, was scheduled to take place at the town's Mozarteum on 21 January 1984. An all-Mozart programme in the Mozarteum in the town where Mozart was born – Karajan must have felt that his pitch had been queered good and proper, and duly wrote a letter of protest to the new Minister for Science and the Arts in the Berlin Senate. The Senate's staffing council was hastily convened and on 20 December 1983 was able to assure the conductor that, in future, any involvement by the Philharmonic in chamber music ensembles must be limited to thirteen players. The Salzburg concert was abruptly taken over by the 'Salzburg Camerata Academica', its programme virtually unchanged, with the BPO's two solo wind players conducted by Sándor Végh. Was it an act of rapprochement on the part of certain orchestral players – or was it, rather, an indispensable provocation in the run-up to open warfare?

Scarcely had this hurdle been cleared when a fuse blew in the intendant's office. Berliners read to their great astonishment that Peter Girth had allegedly hit his press officer, Ulrike Springer, on 22 February 1984 and that, for good measure, he had thrown a programme booklet at her on 21 March. It was hardly surprising, therefore, that at the foundation-stone-laying ceremony for the new chamber-music room on 2 May Karajan was conspicuous by his absence. There was an oppressive atmosphere as Peter Girth and Wolfgang Stresemann delivered their three traditional hammer blows and invoked the empyrean vault.

GIRTH: In honour of the Berlin Philharmonic Orchestra and its members, to the delight of the countless friends of the orchestra and lovers of chamber music everywhere, and in memory of that man of genius, Hans Scharoun.

STRESEMANN: May the Chamber-Music Room, the Small Philharmonie, enhance Berlin's reputation as a city of music. May great chamber music of all centuries be played in this new hall. May harmony reign in both of Scharoun's buildings for the good and well-being of the Berlin Philharmonic Orchestra, its chamber groups and its highly esteemed chief conductor, who cannot, alas, be with us here today.

31
'Interminable tensions'
Karajan abandons Sabine Meyer

Stresemann's fine-sounding words had scarcely died away when the *Morgenpost* published a front-page article headed: 'Karajan's favourite Sabine Meyer to leave.' On 12 May 1984 she wrote to inform the chief conductor, intendant and committee of management that she did not want the secret ballot to go ahead on 23 May: 'What is decisive for me is the realization that there is a danger that the arguments over whether I remain in the orchestra could lead to interminable tensions between it and its artistic director.' The committee accepted her wise decision, which it 'respected and appreciated'. The question now was how would Karajan react? He was beside himself. In a telegram dated 24 May and first published in the *Tagesspiegel* of 18 July Girth revealed himself as something less than a peacemaker.

Herr von Karajan confirmed yesterday by telephone that he has no wish any longer to speak in person to Herr Hassemer, nor, at present, to the ruling mayor, which I understand perfectly. [. . .] In view of the fact that Senator Hassemer has promised to do nothing against the wishes of the orchestra – which I regard as a prime political error – it must be asked whether any of the parties concerned (with the exception of the orchestra) can consider talking to him at all.

Karajan certainly had no wish to talk to the orchestra but sent them a memorandum which made his cancellation of the previous New Year's Eve concert in Berlin seem positively innocuous. Three concerts with the BPO were scheduled for that year's Salzburg Whitsun Festival, two of which would be conducted by Lorin Maazel and Seiji Ozawa, while the third and final one, on 11 June, would be under Karajan himself. Karajan now cancelled the invitation to the BPO for 11 June and invited the Vienna Philharmonic instead. As Hassemer later had to concede, there had never been any formal contracts. Still less had Karajan given any reason for his catastrophic announcement. No doubt he had been told that a poster had appeared in New York, advertising the Berlin Philharmonic Chamber Orchestra and mentioning '34 Soloists and Members'. Although the American organizer confirmed that contracts had been signed, the cellist Klaus Häussler denied this in an interview with the *Frankfurter Allgemeine*

Zeitung on 9 June 1984: 'As far as I am aware, no request has been made for permission to give the planned concert in New York.'

Calls for a mediator in the person of Wolfgang Stresemann grew increasingly strident. But if Stresemann called Karajan's onslaught a 'public insult to the orchestra', a different line was adopted by Klaus Geitel, who, writing in the *Morgenpost* on 31 May, agreed with Karajan on every point, accused the Ministry for the Arts of failing the conductor all along the line and raised the spectre of Karajan's successor: 'Every candidate will draw his own conclusions from this disagreement.' Moreover, damages – which would 'run into millions' – would have to be paid if the players did not go to Salzburg for the two remaining concerts. He ended by recommending that 'the hatchet be buried between Girth and the orchestra'.

Bruited abroad in this way, such remarks were less than helpful. In any case, the orchestra had reacted rather differently to its chief conductor's disinvitation: 'We note that your attitude in this affair, as in other matters affecting our orchestra, is no longer reconcilable with the duties of artistic director.' And so they suggested a separation, but one which, under the terms of his contract, only Karajan himself could implement.

A solution to the problem was made additionally difficult by a further change of mayor in the Schöneberg Town Hall. Richard von Weizsäcker had been elected Federal President, to be replaced by Eberhard Diepgen, who could scarcely be said to have been a regular patron at Philharmonic concerts in the past. None the less, he was quick to see that the music drama currently unfolding in Berlin had become a matter of worldwide concern and, as such, a threat to his own position. Diepgen and Karajan were soon in contact for, within twenty-four hours of receiving the orchestra's letter of protest of 4 June, Karajan was already asking Diepgen:

> Could I ask you personally to ascertain and specify the artistic director's rights and duties, and let me know to what extent the observation of these rights and duties could have been reconciled with the orchestra's conduct during the last two years.

On 6 June Diepgen was interviewed by Gerd Kolbe in Bonn:

KOLBE: Do you think that politicians can mediate in the row between the Berlin Philharmonic Orchestra and Herbert von Karajan?

DIEPGEN: I don't know if 'mediate' is the right word here. It's true that the Berlin Philharmonic Orchestra plays an essential part in upholding the cultural quality of our city, and that's due simply to the orchestra's artistic achievements under Herbert von Karajan. But in a discussion of the kind that is currently being conducted, with provocations on both sides, I believe that a politician's concern must be to preserve the orchestra in its totality, in other words, chief conductor *and* players, and ensure that in future they work together harmoniously for the greater good of the city. I must do what I can to bring this about. But let me make this clear: I've used the term already – there is too much provocation. As I see it, we must try to approach the matter more calmly, not argue in public and examine things with more *adagio* and less *fortissimo*.

KOLBE: Does that also mean that you, the Berlin Senate and the city would like to retain Herbert von Karajan as chief conductor, if it can be achieved in any way?

DIEPGEN: There's a contract with Herbert von Karajan and no reason for the Berlin Senate to terminate that contract. That's simply not on the agenda. All that matters is that the Berlin Philharmonic Orchestra should continue, if possible, to work together with its chief conductor in a way that has helped it achieve its international reputation; that problems are put to one side; but, above all, that the orchestra should be artistically active in the city in future.

KOLBE: Have you already arranged to meet the maestro in Salzburg?

DIEPGEN [*smiling*]: Well, I shall be going to Salzburg in order to hear the orchestra's concerts. It's there for two concerts, the rest will follow on from that.

32

'The orchestra's self-respect'

The end of Karajan's autocracy

Eberhard Diepgen did indeed have a meeting with Karajan, which went on for several hours. The two men met at the conductor's Anif home on 9 June 1984, when emphasis was laid on the 'very matter-of-fact atmosphere' and on the need for both sides to stick to the terms of the Berlin contract. But each time that Karajan insisted on the continued appointment of his intendant, Peter Girth, he found he was banging his head against the Senate walls. As early as 5 June the Minister for the Arts, Volker Hassemer, had given a press conference at which he had leaked the information that Girth might soon be sent away on leave of absence.

The three Whitsun concerts, though overshadowed by wider events, passed off successfully, with the Berlin Philharmonic being acclaimed and the Viennese players receiving a standing ovation. Audiences wanted them all – the orchestras, Maazel, Ozawa and, above all, Karajan himself. And according to Joachim Kaiser, writing in the *Süddeutsche Zeitung*, Karajan gave the impression of being 'happy'. That did not mean, of course, that he *was* happy, especially now that the Senate's decisions were being published in Berlin's daily papers. Girth was described as someone who 'made existing problems worse': he should give up his job voluntarily or, if necessary, be sent away by the Senate on enforced leave of absence. The former intendant, Wolfgang Stresemann, could keep things ticking over until the job was advertised and a suitable successor found. But any successor would have to be appointed with Karajan's 'agreement': the first word still belonged to him.

Of course, the seventy-six-year-old conductor, having suffered setbacks over both Girth and Meyer, was less than happy with these arrangements. Although the players spoke of a 'pile of broken pieces', they were now on course to deprive their chief conductor of his old despotic hold on them. In December 1983 he had 'adjourned' the video recording of that year's New Year's Eve concert and in June 1984 he threw out the Berlin Philharmonic from a Vivaldi recording, using the same Vienna players as those who had gallantly come to the rescue for the third of his Whitsun concerts in

Salzburg. The fact that there was not even a sound reason for doing so proved to be the final straw.

No one, however, realized then that, in the last analysis, Karajan's sole concern was with his own reputation: the orchestras merely provided the pedestal on which to raise the hero's statue. Among the conductor's estate were discovered forty-five music films intended not for the common television screen but for video discs, with their far superior quality. In almost every case it was the Berlin Philharmonic that Karajan had invited, at his own expense, to take part in seventeen live concerts and twenty-eight studio-based recordings. All these recordings were covered by a contract signed by the players and accepted by Karajan's Monaco-based company, Telemondial. And yet it was perfectly clear what Karajan meant by the term 'exclusive contract': in signing such a deal with the BPO in the early part of 1982, he still felt able to call on their Viennese rivals whenever a crisis occurred.

Vivaldi's *Four Seasons* provided a chance to show the Berliners that their conductor meant business. The recording was due to be issued by EMI and, as always, Telemondial put up the costs of the video recording. It should be mentioned here that, under the terms of their television contract, the Berliners were paid a flat fee of 200,000 marks for every recording made, irrespective of the number of players involved. Since, apart from the violinist Anne-Sophie Mutter, only twenty-four strings were needed for the Vivaldi, Karajan's film company wanted to break the agreement and reduce the price they were willing to pay. The Berlin Philharmonic refused to bow to such dictatorial pressure. And so, in time-honoured fashion, Karajan asked the Viennese to step into the breach and, after a secret vote, the VPO agreed. The result was the famous recording, whose sleeve tells the tale of the bright red pullover.

On 13 June 1984 the Berlin Philharmonic voted to terminate their recording contract with their chief conductor with immediate effect: 'The orchestra's self-respect must take priority over any financial disadvantages.' They had touched a raw nerve of Karajan's, since the foregoing season had been set aside for video recordings of all the Beethoven symphonies, a project which was still in a state of fragmentary incompleteness. Damages to the tune of several million marks threatened Telemondial, since, on this occasion at least, the conductor could not go behind his Berliners' backs and call on the VPO. Even his official protest, lodged with the Berlin district court, was unsuccessful, since, according to *Der Spiegel* of 17 September, the firm of Telemondial and the Berlin Philharmonic were bound by ties of 'permanent indebtedness'. The orchestra, which had hitherto merely reacted to events, now took a rather more active line, plainly determined not to comply with at least one of the four demands which Karajan had formulated on 17 June, whereby their intendant had the right to appoint new players for a probationary year even without their express approval. The viola player Dietrich Gerhardt vented his feelings in the *Spandauer Volksblatt* on 24 June: 'That's simply out of the question. We're not prepared even to discuss the matter, since it would mean that the Sabine Meyer case would become the general rule.' But even Karajan's other wishes met with a certain reserve on the part of the players. If a new intendant could be appointed 'by mutual agreement', there was the danger, they feared, that the decision would be taken by Karajan and the Senate alone. The question of how much leave of absence they were entitled to take for additional work was already regulated, while the requirement that they desist from making 'public statements' was tantamount to an act of self-censorship. 'We hope', Gerhardt concluded, 'that Karajan will renew contact with us. He must make the first move. It's really up to him now.'

The players met on 20 June, resolved to take official action. Peter Girth was dismissed by the Senate and Wolfgang Stresemann returned to the scene of his former successes, appealed to the orchestra's right of self-determination and received a huge bouquet of flowers.

The mood, however, was not one of unadulterated joy, since no one knew, when the season came to an end on 30 June with the first open-air concert in the orchestra's history, whether the concerts planned to take place in Salzburg and Lucerne would go ahead with Karajan. The open-air concert – a cold and wet affair – had been conducted by Reinhard Peters. Eberhard Diepgen, the ruling mayor, was heckled, since the audience had not come for political speeches, and Werner Thärichen took his leave of the orchestra after thirty-six years as timpanist. An audience of some 20,000 cheered the players at the end.

That same day Karajan sent off a telegram to Hassemer, in which he stressed that it now depended on Hassemer's good will and on that of the orchestra to 'rebuild the foundations on which the work of twenty-eight years had proceeded so happily and splendidly and to which the whole world has been witness'. Hassemer's reaction was wholly at one with the feelings of the players when he replied by saying that he did not think that this was the gesture they had all been hoping for on the part of their chief conductor.

33

'A damned sense of duty and obligation'

Wolfgang Stresemann reappointed intendant

A telex dated 2 July from the Mayor of West Berlin to Karajan remained unanswered, so that the players left for their annual leave with the situation still unresolved. Only Wolfgang Stresemann stayed behind in the Philharmonie to keep watch over the building. Just nine days before his eightieth birthday I visited him in his office and found him relaxed and in the best possible state of mental and physical health.

LANG: It's curious, isn't it, that we last spoke here six years ago, in April 1978, and discussed your nineteen years as intendant of the Philharmonic. You were seventy-four and a little aggrieved that you weren't to be allowed to remain in office until you were seventy-five. And now – completely unexpectedly – here we are again. You've been wrenched out of your well-earned retirement and, in your eightieth year, reappointed intendant of the Berlin Philharmonic Orchestra. How do you feel about it all and who was it who reappointed you?

STRESEMANN: I was appointed, of course, by the Minister for Cultural Affairs, evidently in agreement with the Berlin Philharmonic Orchestra. You know, it's no great matter. When difficulties unfortunately arose with my – how shall I put it? – successor and predecessor [*amused*], a solution had to be found quickly. Everyone knew I was still living in Berlin and attending the orchestra's concerts – as a very happy concert-goer, I may add, since I no longer needed to take responsibility for what was happening. And so there were already certain contacts, and it was fairly self-evident that I should be asked to make myself available for a *short* time – and it's not allowed to be too long. When one knows that a crisis has arisen and one's sense of duty is appealed to, it's impossible not to answer the call. For ultimately – and I'm bound to feel an infinite sense of gratitude and would even be prepared to pay for it – nature has granted me a certain stability in my advancing years, and in that sense I certainly don't yet feel that it's all a bit too much. Then there's a damned sense of duty and obligation, assuming that body and mind hold together – as I hope they will, though I'm certainly open to protests – so that one feels one has to do *something*. That's why I said: 'Good, I'm prepared to take it on for a short time.'

LANG: The most interesting question, of course, is whether the great maestro agreed to your reappointment. I've a letter of August 1978 which contains the words: 'My thanks to the outgoing intendant, Dr Wolfgang Stresemann', followed by an altogether prophetic phrase: 'Remain devoted to us in later years and show us the same warmth and interest as before.'

STRESEMANN [*amused*]: I don't suppose he'll be pleased to be reminded of that. He threw his whole weight behind Dr Girth and said that it was indispensable that they continued to work together in future. In other words, he wouldn't tolerate anyone other than Dr Girth as intendant of the Berlin Philharmonic Orchestra, so that – to put it mildly – he can't be very happy at the moment that I'm back here once again. But that's understandable. After all, he spoke out so forcefully in public in Dr Girth's defence that he needs to be allowed a certain amount of time to accept the fact – which I hope he will – that old Stresemann is back. He needs to be given time.

LANG: So the answer's clear: although you're back in office, you've not yet had any contact with Karajan?

STRESEMANN: No, I've tried, since I heard from his office that he's twice enquired whether I'd rung. I immediately called back, of course, but he'd already left and was on his way to the Salzburg Festspielhaus. I've no reason to doubt this information. He went straight from the entrance to the stage, since he wanted to avoid any unnecessary stairs. So in the end I didn't reach him, indeed I'm not even certain whether it was the right thing to do. His whole sense of disappointment, not to say anger, could rise to the surface now that his favourite, Dr Girth, is no longer here. So I ought to let a little time pass. I can understand that. It was certainly a setback for him. So great and wonderful a man, so brilliant a conductor – after all he's second to none in terms of his international importance – should be left a little time to think about this and other setbacks – I'm thinking of Sabine Meyer and various other things. He needs to sort himself out and come to terms with the facts as they now exist. It's the first time things haven't gone the way he wanted.

LANG: And you think it's conceivable in theory that he'll apologize to the orchestra and that the Salzburg concerts will take place after all?

STRESEMANN: He certainly won't apologize. Why should he do that? You know, 'sorry' is always an unfortunate word. All right, insults have been traded, and one certainly can't say: 'You've insulted me and I've insulted you, so that we're now quits, let's make wonderful music together again.' That's scarcely conceivable from a psychological point of view. On the other hand, the orchestra – as far as I know – isn't expecting him to go down on bended knee or to eat humble pie. But they're certainly expecting some conciliatory gesture on Herr von Karajan's part. My God, Karajan and the Philharmonic represent perhaps one of the greatest periods in the whole history of the orchestra: they've now been working together for twenty-eight years, and many of their concerts – especially recent ones, at least those I've heard here in Berlin – have been pure gold. Even allowing for all the difficulties that still exist and all the mistakes that both sides have made, I still think that, ultimately, they should approach each other and at least attempt to reach a settlement. If things still don't work out, at least they'll have done their best. There's one insult, however, which was delivered by Herr von Karajan and which has been commented on internationally and in public; it has far wider repercussions than any insult by the Senate or orchestra, which is why Herr von Karajan really ought to realize that you can't simply trade insults in this way.

LANG: In 1981 you published an extremely interesting book, *. . . und abends in die Philharmonie*, in which you painted a picture of Karajan's character such as had never been done before. If you'd suspected then that you'd return one day as intendant of the Berlin Philharmonic Orchestra, would you have written the book in the way you did?

STRESEMANN: Certainly, most certainly. In any case, who could have said that I'd be reappointed? I gave Herr von Karajan a copy of the book, with a particularly warm dedication, so that he shouldn't think I was trying to hide anything. I told him: 'You won't approve of everything you find there, but you'll see that the chapters about you were written on the basis of my deep admiration of you' – an admiration I feel just as strongly now as I did then.

LANG: Do you think he's read the book?

STRESEMANN: I've no idea.

LANG: So there's no indication either way, except that he's not telephoned? If the friendship of which he spoke when you retired was genuine, he ought to have got in touch with you.

STRESEMANN: No, I wouldn't expect that at all. But I'd have been glad if he'd allowed me to give him my side of events. You see, I've nothing to win or lose any longer. I'm old enough to be beyond good and evil. I only want to help. That's my only wish, to the extent that it's possible to help. We'll have to see whether the many broken pieces that we've unfortunately got can still be put back together again. Whether we succeed or not is in God's hands or at least it depends on whether we're lucky or not. At all events, I'd like to be able to say to myself that I've done everything to help. If it doesn't work, I'll leave this office here without feeling that I've suffered a serious defeat. Just as – in the event that, contrary to expectations, I succeed – I won't go out and say: 'I've achieved marvellous results and scored a magnificent victory.' You know, these questions of success are so unimportant. If people are gifted, they should pursue great goals during their youth. Otherwise you're at a disadvantage if you don't start climbing the ladder. The main thing to avoid is treading on other people's heads. But when you enter your ninth decade, things look totally different. Success and failure then become completely unimportant. All that matters then is that you apply all your energies to achieving a state of harmony and finding a positive solution to a conflict which has been simmering for years, or at least contributing to its solution. No one person is in a position to restore a sense of order to this whole affair. It needs the co-operation of all the parties concerned. But if you can get things moving and provide a little help, well that, I'm sure, would be very nice.

34

'Et in terra pax'

Reconciliation through Bach's Mass in B minor

'One is really only alive when one rejoices in the well-being of others.' With this saying of Goethe's, Wolfgang Stresemann thanked his countless well-wishers on the occasion of his eightieth birthday on 20 July 1984. He would have preferred to spend the day in Italy, as he generally did, but who would then have taken all the decisions that needed to be taken in Berlin? Joy was certainly in the air at this time, for a telex from Karajan arrived at the Philharmonie on 25 July, stating simply: 'Looking forward to our concerts together in Salzburg and to welcoming the orchestra here.' To which the interim intendant replied even more succinctly: 'Orchestra not looking forward to them at all.' The previous day Volker Hassemer had risked a further trip to Salzburg but was forced to conclude from his conversation with Karajan that the latter 'clearly underestimated the drama of the situation and the psychological state of the orchestra, which is characterized by sadness and despair'. It was with the full backing of the Senate, therefore, that Stresemann wrote to Karajan to say that, 'in view of the extremely tense situation with the orchestra', it seemed advisable 'to call off the Salzburg concerts on 27 and 28 August. In the present circumstances it might lead to an open breach, which, given your forthcoming concerts in Berlin and elsewhere, must be avoided at all costs.' In order that Karajan should be fully aware of the seriousness of the situation into which he had manoeuvred himself, Stresemann wrote again a few days later, calling off the concerts in Lucerne on 31 August and 1 September.

Karajan appealed to the VPO to help him in his hour of greatest need, which plunged them into a sudden dilemma. On the one hand, they were fully booked, while, on the other, they were reluctant to ignore the entreaties of the concert organizers and leave a disappointed Festival audience in the lurch. That they were once again stabbing their Berlin colleagues in the back played no more than a secondary role. They failed, of course, to notice that they themselves had now become a pawn in the maestro's game, encouraging him in his arbitrary and despotic acts. At least they should have shown solidarity with their counterparts in Berlin and left the tyrant beating time to empty desks. As so often, it was the third party which, uninvolved in the argument, came out best of all. The rescue operation proved a great success, thanks, not least, to a more than generous offer of help from Karajan's protégé, Anne-Sophie Mutter. The Berliners opened their local paper to read an agency report that must have been hard to swallow – and not only along the banks of the Spree:

> The German violinist Anne-Sophie Mutter has declined to accept a fee for performing at the International Music Festival in Lucerne. A spokesman for the organizers explained yesterday that her action was designed to help offset the additional expenses incurred when the Berlin Philharmonic refused to appear in Lucerne under its conductor Herbert von Karajan.

Karajan was simply unable to understand why 'his' orchestra refused to show any brotherly love, and it took him another month to come to terms with events surrounding Sabine Meyer and Peter Girth. But finally even he came to see that his autocrat's wings had been clipped. If his obduracy continued, he ran the risk of being left sitting on nine incomplete Beethoven symphonies. This and this alone was the reason why, on 24 August, he forced himself, with manifestly bad grace, to write the following highly emotive lines to the BPO:

> The international world of music and our audiences expect us to play together in Bach's B minor Mass at this year's Berliner Festwochen. Here is a work that is deeply imbued with a sense of humanity and Christian spirit, and it ought, therefore, to make it easier for us to forget what has happened and, in a spirit of reconciliation, renew our earlier work together.

The players had no wish to reject this olive branch and replied in a similar vein: 'Herbert von Karajan's Christian and humane desire that the performances of Bach's B minor Mass should go ahead within the framework of the Berliner Festwochen is one that the Berlin Philharmonic Orchestra ought not to reject', although the players would have preferred it if 'the talks proposed by Herr von Karajan to which the orchestra attaches such great importance could have taken place before the Festwochen concerts'.

Bach's 'In terra pax' – Peace on Earth – had brought the combatants together again, and the orchestral rehearsal in the Philharmonie began with the maestro's inimitable words: 'Right, let's get on with it.' The parties involved in the altercation had met during the afternoon of 29 September 1984 and vowed to make 'a fresh start on the basis of their artistic partnership'. In future, any problems that arose would be resolved in good time by means of discussions between Karajan and the orchestra's elected representatives: existing rules and wage agreements would form the basis for such discussions. These official pronouncements might almost suggest that the whole affair was now a matter of some indifference to Karajan, and that from now on it was the players who would call the tune. But is such a supposition consonant with the chief conductor's underlying character?

Be that as it may, the performance of the B minor Mass was an act of musical reconciliation. A few tentative boos greeted the conductor as he came out on to the platform, but the overriding reaction was one of jubilation, while the thunderous applause at the end of the work knew no bounds. Included in the acclaim were the soloists and the Vienna Singverein. Karajan put his arms round the leader, Leon Spierer – something he had never done before in public – and even offered his hand to the sub-leader, Toru Yasunaga, whom he had demoted from leader two days previously in spite of opposition from the orchestra.

On 11 December Karajan confounded everyone's expectations and turned up at the orchestra's Christmas party. According to the *Morgenpost* of 13 December, 'He smiled as he spoke of a "Peace of Westphalia", bringing an end to a war that had lasted only twelve months out of thirty happy years.' These thirty years of collaboration naturally had to be celebrated, and so, at a concert on 12 December comprising Honegger's *Symphonie liturgique* and Brahms's First Symphony, Wolfgang Stresemann took the opportunity to refer to the anniversary, in a speech which stressed the orchestra's right of self-determination:

We have an important, historic event to celebrate today. It is exactly thirty years since the Berlin Philharmonic Orchestra voted to appoint Herbert von Karajan as successor to the late Wilhelm Furtwängler. And, thanks to the orchestra's right of artistic self-government, the great decision was taken as to who would follow Furtwängler.

I should like to congratulate you most warmly, Herr von Karajan, on this anniversary and, at the same time, thank you for so many great moments in music at the head of your Berlin Philharmonic Orchestra. [*Applause.*] And I should also like to thank the Berlin Philharmonic Orchestra. [*Applause.*] Of those players who voted on that occasion, twenty-four are still active in the orchestra, yet it has remained the same great Philharmonic Orchestra, the same miracle as before. How grateful we must be for this Philharmonic spirit and for the inspiration which has come from you, Herr von Karajan. May I close by expressing the wish that many more years of mutual music-making with you and the Berlin Philharmonic still remain before us.

35
'The right solutions have always been found'
Wolfgang Stresemann's final farewell

Karajan's health was not of the best in the early months of 1985. There was repeated talk of impaired balance and, in conversation, he mentioned the names of Semyon Bychkov and Carlo Maria Giulini as his potential successors, although the Italian maestro graciously turned the idea down on the grounds of age. Karajan's own performances, however, were still as spectacular as ever, and included a performance of Mozart's Coronation Mass with the VPO in Rome, in the presence of the pope.

Less than twelve months after the reconciliatory performance of Bach's B minor Mass, he prefaced the same work with the following words to his audience in Salzburg: 'Ladies and gentlemen, may I crave your indulgence if I conduct my forthcoming concerts seated? The reason is quite simple: I am no longer able to stand.' The audience burst into frenzied applause. From then on Karajan sat – not on a stool (as Karl Böhm, for example, had done at the end of his life) but on a special saddle which he devised for himself, a saddle which, not unlike a bicycle seat, was attached to the podium railings in Salzburg and Berlin. During his final years he would drag himself into position, swing his right leg over the edge of the saddle and stand, half-seated, while specially manufactured orthopaedic shoes gave some support to his wasted legs. Stresemann's only comment was: 'Thank God, he's beating proper time again.' Through standing, his beat had become very weak. In September 1984, in an interview in *Stereoplay*, he had explained the reason for his refusal to conduct from a sitting position: 'It doesn't suit me. I find that if you don't have legs any longer, you should give up driving a car.'

In 1984 – unknown to the general public – the Herbert von Karajan Foundation had held its eighth conducting competition. The jury included the former intendant, Peter Girth, and the conductor Kurt Masur, later associated with the revolution in the East. Eight candidates got through to the final round and three of these were invited back in 1985, when they would prepare the prizewinners' concert with the Symphony Orchestra of Berlin in the concert hall of the city's College of Art. What had once begun so spectacularly was now reduced to a very low-key event. The BPO was no longer involved – no doubt to its own relief – and even the cash prizes had been abolished. Karajan, however, continued to give his active support. On 21 September 1985 the Foundation, reckoning on 'considerable interest', sent out invitations to a conducting course but, in spite of the fact that Karajan had never offered such a course in public in Berlin, the concert hall was only thinly attended. Karajan entered, without support, and sat down immediately in front of the conductors, in the middle of the orchestra. For the next three hours the real Karajan reasserted himself – paternal, good-humoured, resolute, almost relaxed, a brilliant teacher dispensing practical tips. Once, during the opening movement of Tchaikovsky's 'Pathétique', the solo clarinet came in a bar too early, causing him to turn round in astonishment. Was he thinking of his father or of the orchestras in Ulm and Aachen? Certainly, he had never heard anything like it from the BPO. During the interval I found him alone in the conductor's dressing-room, sitting on the sofa. He was as mentally alert as ever, his blue eyes wide open, but the brilliance had gone out of them. His glance was friendly, but at the same time cold and distrustful, as though I had a hidden camera with me. 'You know, young conductors need a lot of time before anything emerges. You have to show them how little they need to do with an orchestra. My pilot once said to me: "Don't do anything, the machine can fly by itself."'

The final concert on 26 September was marred for him, perhaps, by the lack of public response to the earlier concert. Although the hall was sold out and everyone present expected him to speak, it was Werner Thärichen who stood up to apologize on his behalf: the maestro was too busy rehearsing the *Missa solemnis*. 'Those of you who know this piece will also know the demands it places on the conductor.' At the New Year's Eve concert, by contrast, he managed to address at least a few words to the audience: 'My dear music-lovers, I wish you every happiness and prosperity in the New Year. Happy New Year, bonne année [*his voice choked by emotion*] to Eliette and the children, too.'

But all was not yet over. On 22 February 1986 a new intendant took over at the Philharmonie in the person of Hans Georg Schäfer. Although Volker Hassemer described him as 'the best-qualified of all the candidates', it soon transpired – as mentioned earlier – that this was not the case. Indeed, it was becoming increasingly clear that Wolfgang Stresemann was a nonpareil among intendants and the fact that his second retirement was even more splendid than his first merely reflected the overwhelming gratitude and appreciation that were his rightful due. The players presented him with a weighty tome containing congratulations on his life's work from such eminent musicians as Rudolf Serkin, Wolfgang Sawallisch, Yehudi Menuhin, Carlo Maria Giulini, Dietrich Fischer-Dieskau, Daniel Barenboim and Claudio Abbado. Karajan himself wrote: 'I know that all your abilities converge on a single centre – your immense attachment to music, as a result of which you have always found the right solutions both artistically and organizationally.'

Karajan's words were there in black and white for all to read who saw the book in question. But the events that took place that evening at the Philharmonie left a different impression. The house was sold out. The programme began with Haydn's Symphony No. 104 and, after the applause had died away, Karajan went to sit on a chair in the orchestra to listen to the various speeches. When Wolfgang Stresemann came out on to the platform, the cheering which broke out caused the chief conductor's face to turn to stone. Everyone, including the orchestra, rose to their feet amid the storm of applause to listen to Stresemann's farewell speech.

> Senator, ladies and gentlemen, I am deeply moved. Please accept my thanks. For me, this second term has been the finest and happiest thing to have happened to me in my life. Although relatively advanced in years, I've again been able to do something for music and for our beloved Berlin Philharmonic.
>
> I've already said goodbye once, and it's not my style to repeat myself. There's only one thing I'd like to say. I'm happy and pleased that you, dear Herr von Karajan, are with us here on this occasion, since you weren't able to be here last time. [*Applause.*] To you, to your and our Berlin Philharmonic I give my very best wishes and, at the same time, I wish you, dear Herr Schäfer, all the very best in your new job. I hope that things will continue to work out harmoniously here, for harmony is the most important thing in music, if only we know how to interpret it correctly. I'm most sincerely grateful to you all. [*Applause.*]

Even before the applause marking Stresemann's definitive departure had fully died away, Karajan had risen from his chair, where he had remained sitting with arms folded and legs crossed. It was the moment everyone had been waiting for. Nothing would have been more obvious than for Karajan to wish his Philharmonic companion of so many years' standing a long and well-earned retirement. Instead, he moved towards the microphone, took it in his hand and waited till there was total silence. And then the greatest conductor in the world spoke the three most pitiful words of his entire life: '*Jetzt ist Pause!*' – 'Now's the interval!'

36

'I may be struck down tomorrow'

Settling old scores

Old age brought Karajan little comfort. Although his abilities as a conductor remained unimpaired to the end and allowed him to give some outstanding performances, the news from Berlin was medical rather than musical. A report in the *Morgenpost* of 11 April 1986 caused renewed alarm:

> The chief conductor of the Berlin Philharmonic Orchestra, Herbert von Karajan, has been admitted to the University Clinic in Essen for tests or a possible operation. According to a report in the *Neue Ruhr-Zeitung* Karajan is being treated by the head of the urological clinic, Professor Rudolf Hartung.

The prostate operation took place a few days later and on 16 April the conductor was allowed to return to his Salzburg home, where security was as tight as ever: a press agency report, filed on the day of his arrival, announced that the Karajans' guard dog had 'shown itself in a very poor light. The dog, which guards the property of the star conductor Herbert von Karajan, chose the knee of the chauffeur of Cardinal Franz König as a suitable target into which to sink his powerful teeth.'

In Berlin there were always people who were numbered among Karajan's 'court correspondents', while others, admiring his artistic achievements, none the less maintained a critical distance. Among the former group was Klaus Geitel, while Stresemann belonged to the second. It was a situation which remained unchanged to the very end, as the following brief account will show.

On 30 April 1986 Geitel presented himself once again as Karajan's mouthpiece, putting a series of questions to the maestro whose answers every reader could have worked out for himself. Even at the end Karajan was still at pains to make the dullest-witted reader believe that he still controlled all the strings and that, as far as his concerts in Berlin were concerned, his only wish was to 'reduce his over-commitment somewhat'. One read with some astonishment, therefore, that the itinerary for the forthcoming tour of America and Japan had been dictated not by Karajan but by the orchestra: 'I simply can't let them get away with claiming in public that they have to take me into consideration by including free days, because I'm old and tired. I don't feel in the least bit old and tired.'

Geitel also asked the conductor about his reduced appearances in Berlin and tackled him on the subject of his successor. Interestingly, the maestro mentioned Riccardo Muti and Claudio Abbado, showing a sense of vision that none of his players shared at that time. As he admitted,

> I'm seventy-eight, I might be struck down tomorrow or something else might happen, and it'll be impossible to stop someone else from being pressed into the job for totally obscure reasons, someone who's ultimately not up to it. As for myself, I'll go on doing my job in Berlin as long and as well as I can.

It also emerged from this interview that Karajan was still anxious to settle old scores with his former intendant, against whom he levelled outrageous reproaches:

> Stresemann and the orchestra entered into negotiations with Daniel Barenboim behind my back in an attempt to bring off that televised concert from the Royal Albert Hall. It was an outright breach of contract from the word go. In a word, I found it quite shameless.

Stresemann, of course, could prove the falseness of these accusations and, at the same time, show that Karajan himself had been in constant breach of contract in Berlin.

For all his devotion to Karajan's cause, Geitel's commitment was always less credible than Stresemann's honesty of approach. It was Stresemann, after all, not Geitel, who was given the honour of making a speech in memory of Karajan at a Philharmonic concert on 10 September 1989. And he did so without lapsing into fulsome hyperbole, preferring instead to paint a picture of the conductor in all his contradictory aspects. Geitel responded by describing the speech in *Die Welt* as full of 'trivia and carping criticisms'. When I congratulated Stresemann on his brave words and sought to defend him from attack, he wrote:

> I haven't even read G.'s critique, though I know he's very excitable. He once hailed me as 'Lord' on my birthday and then swept me under the carpet. But I can't get worked up about that sort of thing, and v. K. was far too great for people to have to deliver graveside speeches in his memory.

Stresemann's own greatness was to be revealed yet again, much later, on the occasion of the memorial concert for Karajan held in the Philharmonie on 6 May 1990. The organizers were the 'Society of Friends of the Berlin Philharmonie' under their chairman, Wolfgang Stresemann. And whom had Stresemann – now almost eighty-six years old – invited as a second speaker? None other than Klaus Geitel. Here, too, there were scenes of reconciliation, not least in the music that framed the speeches, when the Nomos Quartet was joined by the clarinettist, Sabine Meyer.

But let us return to the final years of Karajan's life. At the 1986 Berliner Festwochen he conducted Beethoven's Ninth (including a video recording for his own company, Telemondial), but was forced by a viral infection to cancel the following day's repeat performance, while the orchestra's tour of America and Japan was taken over at very short notice by James Levine and Seiji Ozawa.

The musical world had to wait until 1 January 1987 before seeing Karajan restored to health and back on the conductor's podium. The occasion was the famous New Year's Day concert by the Vienna Philharmonic, a concert which Karajan had expressed a desire to conduct for the first time in his life and which was watched by more than 700 million television viewers round the world. Karajan's absence from Berlin lasted much longer and it was not until 1 March 1987, after four months away, that he returned to the Philharmonie. The notes I made at the time make deeply depressing reading: 'Mozart, A major symphony K201, tired pursuit of tonal beauty, sheer boredom, it's clear that his time has audibly run out. If a young conductor had offered an interpretation like this, he'd be finished for good.'

Those who grow implacable with old age will find their own failings are rarely forgiven. The Philharmonic players found themselves faced with this dilemma, though they would have happily borne their chief conductor aloft in triumph, had he been more humane.

Following the opening concert of the city's 750th anniversary celebrations, the new intendant, Hans Georg Schäfer, announced the programme for the 1987/8 season, from which it emerged that Karajan's appearances during the coming months were to be limited to only seven concerts comprising five different programmes. The *Volksblatt* wondered whether this almost 50 per cent reduction in the conductor's contractual obligations was 'Karajan's belated revenge'. Meanwhile he was conducting two Brahms concerts in Berlin and London which, according to the *Morgenpost* of 14 March, were calculated 'to become addictive all over again'.

It was only to be expected that a commercial event would engage the conductor's attentions rather more than his staging of *Don Giovanni* at the

1987 Salzburg Festival. Anyone who picked up a copy of the *Salzburger Nachrichten* of 30 July would have discovered, to his endless surprise, that no fewer than ten of its pages were given over to the official opening of a Sony factory at Anif, outside Salzburg, where, for years, Karajan had been using his home as an editing-room for his video films. The maestro began by quoting Goethe ('We are gathered here for praiseworthy deeds') and was then photographed beaming, as he handed over the keys to the factory, with his wife and daughter at his side and his mop of silver hair glinting through the hole in the compact disc. The caption read: 'Karajan as Salzburg's economic attaché'. What had persuaded him to dance attendance on the Japanese media giant? His artistic testament stood at the forefront of his thoughts, seventeen live recordings and twenty-eight video programmes, which he planned to commit to video disc, Sony Classical's optimal medium in terms of both picture and sound.

Back in Berlin, the Festwochen programme included a single performance of Brahms's *German Requiem*, which Karajan conducted in a sleekly seamless, mellifluous reading. Never for a moment did it touch the heart, still less did it stir the soul. Among the delighted audience were Volker Hassemer, Karajan's wife Eliette, and the economics experts Dr Uli Märkle and Peter Gelb.

Karajan's next appearance was on 28 October 1987, when he had declared his readiness to inaugurate the Philharmonie's Chamber-Music Room, which had finally been completed. Anne-Sophie Mutter wore an off-the-shoulder dress for her virtuoso rendition of Vivaldi's perennial *Seasons*. The interpretation as a whole was an unexpected surprise, an account of the piece embellished with Brueghelesque touches but also unsurpassed in its delicacy of sound. The morning's rehearsal was a 'thank-you' concert for all those involved in building the hall. Here, too, Karajan conducted from the harpsichord, standing out from the black suits and white waistcoats of the players by dint of his silver-striped trainers and bright blue jogging suit.

Immediately after the opening, Karajan set off on a tour of Germany with the BPO. Although in considerable physical pain, he conducted with his customary brilliance in Hamburg, Hanover and Düsseldorf. In Frankfurt, where the orchestra arrived on 6 November, he asked for an announcement to be made over the Alte Oper's public-address system: he intended to conduct, although he had suffered an attack of 'food poisoning' the previous evening. The concert in the Stuttgart Liederhalle on 7 November was cancelled, however: 'acute food poisoning' was said to be the cause. No one in the audiences knew the background and none of Karajan's aides revealed the reason: his brother Wolfgang had died in Salzburg on 4 November. He had been born in Salzburg on the 150th anniversary of Mozart's birth. (Karajan himself was born at eleven o'clock on the evening of Sunday, 5 April 1908, a day of no particular significance and which he himself described as 'pitiful'.) The young Heribert – to accord him the name his parents gave him – looked up to his brother, who, two years older than he, was equally gifted in music and engineering. This fact, and the seeming symbolism of his birth, inspired the younger brother with that sense of ambition and motivation which may, perhaps, have left its mark on the whole of his later career. During their early years they seem to have got on well together under their father's strict supervision and mother's more indulgent eye. 'My brother and I did not play with soldiers, we played, instead, in a physics lab,' Karajan told a *Stern* reporter in 1983. Wolfgang began to study the violin when he was only four, the same age at which his younger brother turned to the piano. Later on they entered the Salzburg Mozarteum together. When Wolfgang began his studies at the Technical University in Vienna, Karajan saw that the time had come to distance himself from his brother by taking up conducting. Wolfgang's professional interests remained in the sphere of technology, and he opened a small factory for medical instruments in the Austrian town of Dornbirn. It seems likely that the rift between the brothers dates from the time when Wolfgang von Karajan started to tour with his own small music ensemble.

Before examining that particular episode, we may usefully stop to consider the differences between them, differences best summed up, perhaps, in the words of the brothers themselves. Herbert: 'Earlier in my career I travelled round the world in thirty-eight days, giving thirty-two concerts. It was sheer madness.' Or: 'I won't allow anyone to interfere in my affairs where artistic questions are concerned; those are questions I decide for myself. I wasn't born to be ordered around by others.' Or – and this is perhaps surprising: 'Privately, I'm a very timid person. The fear of being rejected is something I feel very strongly.'

And what about Wolfgang and his wife Hedy? 'We don't like to be hounded, we're not really public people at all.' And on his relationship with his brother: 'We went our separate ways. In our early youth we even played football. I played in defence,' Wolfgang told the *Morgenpost* in 1962. Photographs of the time show an informal black moustache and hair combed severely backwards. By 1981, when he gave an interview to *Die*

Welt am Sonntag, his hair had long since turned grey: 'Herbert, of course, kept goal. There he was his own boss.' In 1955 Wolfgang moved back to his parents' home in Salzburg: 'I go to concerts to learn – but there, at the Festival, I learned very little.' When asked to provide a key to the 'Karajan wonder', he replied: 'It lies not so much in the artistic sphere as in the power of suggestion over the musicians – hence his burning ambition. He had the good fortune enjoyed by all who are competent and, at a certain point in time, was washed ashore by the Almighty.'

In 1983, when his famous brother was seventy-five, Wolfgang was interviewed in the *Berliner Zeitung*. By now he was wholly resigned:

> In normal families it's usual to get together from time to time, especially when you live in the same town. But it's not like that with him. If I want to meet him, I first have to make an appointment with his secretary. As a result I gave up trying to see him in private some time ago. I certainly wouldn't want to change places with Herbert. I doubt there's anything more we could say to each other.

The source of their estrangement should perhaps be sought in Berlin in November 1955. Karajan's dreams had come true: appointed to succeed Wilhelm Furtwängler, he was currently giving a series of concerts with his own Philharmonic players and some of the world's greatest soloists, including such names as Walter Gieseking, Wilhelm Kempff and Pierre Fournier. Posters, meanwhile, were appearing in Berlin, announcing a concert at the College of Music at which Bach's *Art of Fugue* would be performed on three positive organs. The surname of one of the soloists had a familiar ring to it: it was Wolfgang von Karajan. He was soon being touted as Herbert's 'twin brother', a connection which no doubt ensured that the concert played to a sold-out house. Was it a challenge or simply naïveté? To an outsider, the 'rivalry' seemed very touching. It must, however, have been a thorn in the famous conductor's flesh. His name seemed somehow besmirched and he cannot have drawn any comfort from the devastating reviews which greeted his brother's début: 'A frivolous waste of time and effort', *Der Abend* reported on 10 November, while *Die Welt* described the concert as 'unmusical and altogether amateurish'. According to *Der Tag*, 'it was not the great event that the world had been waiting for'.

When, many years later, Wolfgang was asked his opinion of his brother's Bach interpretations, his only comment was: 'He understands nothing of the *Art of Fugue*', while Hedy had only one word for her brother-in-law's recording of the Brandenburg Concertos: 'Bad.'

37

'Little more than a spanner in the works'

Retirement and death

As Karajan's eightieth birthday approached, the gifts that came pouring in revealed a wide range of affection. To mark the fiftieth anniversary of his first recording with them, Deutsche Grammophon reissued its 'Hundred Masterpieces' on compact disc, illustrated as before with paintings by Eliette von Karajan. In its issue of 28 March 1988 *Der Spiegel* devised a rather more subtle tribute: under the title 'The Financial Wizard', an ashen Karajan was seen not only wielding his baton but drawing dollar signs in the air. The article itself was concerned with those media mafiosi engaged in unscrupulous dealings with Karajan's video films.

Peter Gelb, vice-president of the American video company, CAMI, had got into dangerous waters attempting to use a tour of the Far East, planned by the Berlin Senate, to line his own pockets. The BPO was due to give a series of concerts in Tokyo in April, followed by its first excursion to Taiwan, where they were invited to perform at the country's new International Arts Centre. Gelb, however, demanded a fee of 600,000 marks and, at the same time, insisted that the Taiwanese should 'take ten existing television programmes about Herbert von Karajan and the Berlin and Vienna Philharmonic Orchestras, each costing 35,000 dollars, in other words, for a total cost of 350,000 dollars'.

Politely but firmly, the Taiwanese rejected the offer. When the first violinist, Hellmut Stern, enquired into the reasons behind the abortive deal, he received a copy of Peter Gelb's telex of 7 October 1987 and lost no time in exposing the scandal. Not only the Senate and BPO were incensed, even in Vienna Karajan was described in unflattering terms as the 'master of the penny-pinching Philharmonic'.

By Easter 1988 Karajan was back in Salzburg rehearsing his new production of *Tosca*, but the results could scarcely be said to augur well for his eightieth birthday celebrations: both casting and conducting caused much shaking of heads and one of Germany's leading critics, Joachim Kaiser of the *Süddeutsche Zeitung*, even went so far as to call the performance 'deadly boring'. When the great day finally dawned, on 5 April, the tributes were somewhat muted. Although Axel Springer's publications maintained their predictable loyalty ('The man who always knows what he wants', *Hör Zu*; 'He taught the world to see music with his eyes', *Die Welt*), other papers were far more critical: 'A traditionalist and technocrat' (*Süddeutsche Zeitung*), 'Autocrat, media star and – musician' (*Neue Zürcher Zeitung*), 'The market leader' (*Frankfurter Rundschau*) and 'The Almighty' (*Frankfurter Allgemeine Zeitung*).

Karajan himself seemed unconcerned by it all. On Easter Monday he deigned to receive the homage of an international audience from the cinemascope stage of Salzburg's Grosses Festspielhaus: sitting, with his wife and daughter, on Louis XIV chairs in the midst of the set for his unsuccessful staging of *Tosca*, he thanked the assembled votaries with a few well-chosen words: 'That was very nice; it gave us such great pleasure.'

The Germans have a word to describe a breakfast of pickled herring and gherkins designed to cure a hangover. They call it a *Katerfrühstück*. Berlin – the cultural capital of Europe in 1988 – must have thought that it was being asked to pick up the bill for Karajan's *Katerfrühstück* when, having agreed to launch the festival with a concert with the BPO and, at a ceremony after the concert, to receive an award from the Federal President, Karajan cancelled at short notice, pleading 'gastric 'flu'. Within days, however, he was boarding a plane for Japan for the orchestra's far-eastern tour. According to Alexander Wedow, a member of the orchestra's committee of management, the tour found Karajan 'in excellent artistic form'.

The fact that the BPO's autumn tour of America was called off by Schäfer and the Berlin Senate was only indirectly Karajan's doing. Even after the Taiwan affair, Peter Gelb and his American CAMI agency were not prepared to disclose if any contracts for further tours had been signed. Volker Hassemer demanded a clear ruling and, as was only to be expected, incurred Karajan's wrath: 'For thirty-three years I have fulfilled, and even exceeded, all my commitments and done so, moreover, with the greatest solidarity and loyalty,' he telexed from Japan. 'I lay particular emphasis on the fact that I have a contract for life and that any discussion of a successor during my lifetime is pure fantasy.' This particular sideswipe was aimed at Schäfer, who had told the *Morgenpost* on 14 May: 'Ever since his serious back illness, Karajan has had to struggle and force himself to carry out every commitment. It's now almost the exception when he can still manage to do anything.' Karajan's reaction was: 'This man must finally be made to realize that he'll have to change his tactless attitude towards me, otherwise I'll institute proceedings against him.' The threatening tone was unmistakable. He went on to list 'the points which need to be changed in my present contract: the rights and duties of the artistic director must be laid down, at least insofar as they affect the number of my appearances, the resultant handling of auditions and the whole complex issue surrounding the intendant, Hans Georg Schäfer'.

Thus spake the eighty-year-old conductor, while failing to notice that there was no longer anyone left in Berlin prepared to dance to his tune. They were preparing inwardly for the future, from which point of view the conductor was little more than a spanner in the works. In Salzburg, too, his time was running out. His resignation from the board of directors on 25 August was preceded by a flurry of cancellations caused by illness, although, according to a German press agency report of 30 August, his reason for resigning was his 'annoyance that far too many measures had been taken behind his back'.

A handful of concerts followed in Berlin – a consummate performance of Brahms's First, the Verdi *Requiem* with an implacably bombastic 'Dies irae' and Beethoven's Fifth, the latter a performance well suited to the age of technology, with its hammerblows of fate distinctly muted. Karajan's final appearance with the BPO was the New Year's Eve concert from the Philharmonie, broadcast live on German television, with a programme comprising Prokofiev's *Symphonie classique* and Tchaikovsky's B flat minor Piano Concerto with the young Russian pianist, Evgeni Kissin.

No one suspected, of course, that, after forty years, this would be Karajan's final farewell to Berlin, and the wranglings over his contract pursued their faintly comical course. It was not until 10 January 1989 that Karajan wrote to Hassemer to say that he would be giving only six concerts in Berlin in the course of the coming season:

> I assume you know that, during the past ten years, I have suffered greatly from the most varied illnesses, including a stroke whose consequences are still plaguing me, three operations on my spinal column and serious circulatory disorders. During the last twelve months I have also suffered from gastric 'flu, which I have not yet got over completely. It was only with the greatest difficulty that I was able to conduct my most recent concerts, including the New Year's Eve concert. This persuaded me, following my return to Germany, to undergo a thorough examination with three doctors. The result is that all three have declared that, unless I reduce my activities drastically, they will refuse to offer any further treatment.

There followed a list of the six concerts which he was prepared to conduct in Berlin. His activities in Salzburg and Lucerne, together with twelve concerts on tour in Europe and overseas, remained unaffected.

Until now it had been far from clear in Berlin whether Karajan was capable of fulfilling the terms of his 'contract for life' or not. Not only his various comments, his actions, too, left several possibilities open. Only his spiritual presence remained undiminished.

On 10 February I received a letter from Karajan's secretary, Lore Salzburger, in reply to my submission of a draft copy of the present book.

We are grateful to you for sending it to us. Herr von Karajan has glanced through it and, unfortunately, has noted a series of errors – but they are really not so earth-shaking, not least because the whole affair has already run its course. We would suggest that, next time, you draw the typescript to Karajan's attention before sending it to him.

So the conductor was still active. Even more surprising was to find a letter of his among the readers' letters published in *Der Spiegel* on 27 February and praising Rudolf Augstein's series about the French Revolution. At the time when the letter appeared, Karajan was in New York, conducting three concerts in New York's Carnegie Hall – with the Vienna Philharmonic.

For the 1989 Salzburg Easter Festival, the BPO was invited back to Salzburg – for the last time, as it turned out. The programme comprised Puccini's *Tosca*, with a substantially different cast, two orchestral concerts with the Prokofiev/Tchaikovsky programme heard the previous New Year's Eve, and, to end the Festival on 27 March, the Verdi Requiem. Karajan's final appearance of all was with the Vienna Philharmonic on 23 April, when he conducted Bruckner's Seventh in the city's Musikvereinssaal.

Berlin, meanwhile, had seen a further change of government. The Senate was now dominated by a coalition made up of Communists and Greens, with the result that Volker Hassemer had been replaced as Minister of the Arts by Dr Anke Martiny. She duly set out for Anif on 24 April in order to 'get to know' the situation and 'to talk about all the things that had been discussed in the past'. It was a journey which, with hindsight, she could in fact have spared herself since, apart from kissing her hand and handing her a letter, Karajan offered her nothing. The letter announced his resignation from his contract for life and ended with an exclamation mark typical of the conductor:

May I ask you to note that, with effect from today's date, I am terminating my work as artistic director and resident conductor of the Berlin Philharmonic Orchestra.

The results of medical examinations which have now gone on for several weeks make it impossible for me to meet the obligations which, as I see it, it is incumbent upon me to carry out.

I must also point out that, for many years, I have been asking your predecessors in the Senate to undertake a thorough review of my obligations *and* rights. Although this has repeatedly been agreed, nothing has been done to date. Last week I asked you yourself to provide written clarification *before* our meeting in Salzburg, since these important definitions are not contained in my contract.

Once again I have not received a reply!

Yours sincerely,
Herbert von Karajan.

The BPO reacted with 'dismay and surprise', but Karajan refused to see even the orchestra's most venerable representatives when they travelled to Salzburg to meet him. Instead, he kept them waiting outside the Festspielhaus on 27 April, for all the world like two of the horse-drawn cabs that ply the streets of the town. According to the cellist Klaus Häussler: 'Herbert von Karajan was in his office all the time but, because he was very busy, it was unfortunately not possible for him to meet our two colleagues in person.'

Further problems beset the conductor, this time of a domestic nature. At the ripe old age of eighty-one, the happy father of two grown-up daughters was taken to court by Ute Gisela de Doncker, who, now forty-five years old, had been claiming since 1987 to be the conductor's illegitimate daughter. Her mother, she said, had been working in a Berlin munitions factory in 1943 and the then conductor of the local Staatskapelle had booked a room in a Berlin hotel for their mutual benefit. Of course, the tabloids published pictures of both the miscreants, pictures which indeed showed a certain superficial similarity between the parties in question. The paternity suit dragged on and on, not least because Karajan was understandably hesitant to undergo a blood test. According to Austrian law, however, a man who refuses such a test may none the less be declared the father. Karajan therefore complied with the law and, on 23 June 1989, a press report from Salzburg announced to the world: 'The test has proved to be negative: that Karajan was the father can therefore be dismissed with absolute assurance.'

On Sunday 16 July 1989 teleprinters carried the message all round the world: 'The conductor Herbert von Karajan died of heart failure at his home in Anif at 13.30. He was 81.' Rehearsals for his production of *Un ballo in maschera* at Salzburg's Grosses Festspielhaus had only just begun. On the very day of his death, in his quest for immortality, he received a visit from Norio Ohga, Sony's Japanese president: his greatest, final concern was the optimal technical marketing of his video films on video disc. He then closed his eyes, for ever.

He wanted to bear himself erect, and that is how he left us – in spite of a thousand torments. He seemed to have planned his own last rites, without flowers, singing or sympathy, waiting for darkness to come, for the grave to be opened and the coffin slowly lowered. A simple wooden cross upon a mound of earth. No one except his next of kin was to know.

The man who was the world's most successful conductor wanted a pauper's grave, a grave which would draw attention to the wealth of his musical legacy.

Select bibliography

Bachmann, Robert C., *Karajan: Anmerkungen zu einer Karriere*, Düsseldorf and Vienna 1983, tr. Shaun Whiteside, London, 1990

Csobádi, Peter (ed.), *Karajan – oder die kontrollierte Ekstase*, Vienna, 1988

Gavoty, Bernard, *Herbert von Karajan: Die großen Interpreten*, with photographs by Roger Hauert, Geneva, 1956

Haeusserman, Ernst, *Herbert von Karajan*, Vienna, Munich, Zurich and Innsbruck, 1978

Löbl, Karl, *Das Wunder Karajan*, Bayreuth, 1965

Osborne, Richard, *Conversations with Karajan*, Oxford, 1989

Prieberg, Fred K., *Kraftprobe: Wilhelm Furtwängler im Dritten Reich*, Wiesbaden, 1986; Eng. tr., London, 1991

Stresemann, Wolfgang, *Philharmonie und Philharmoniker*, Berlin, 1977

Stresemann, Wolfgang, *. . . und abends in die Philharmonie*, Munich, 1981

Thärichen, Werner, *Paukenschläge: Furtwängler oder Karajan*, Zurich and Berlin, 1987

Vaughan, Roger, *Herbert von Karajan: A biographical portrait*, London, 1986

Index

Index

Index